PENGUIN BOOKS

The Gathering Dark

James Oswald is the author of the Inspector McLean series of crime novels. The first seven, *Natural Causes*, *The Book of Souls*, *The Hangman's Song*, *Dead Men's Bones*, *Prayer for the Dead*, *The Damage Done* and *Written in Bones* are available as Penguin paperbacks and ebooks. He has also written an epic fantasy series, The Ballad of Sir Benfro, which is published by Penguin, as well as comic scripts and short stories.

In his spare time he runs a 350-acre livestock farm in north-east Fife, where he raises pedigree Highland cattle and New Zealand Romney sheep.

To all the team at Michael Joseph. Thirteen books
in five years! What were we thinking?

The Gathering Dark

JAMES OSWALD

PENGUIN BOOKS

PENGUIN BOOKS

UK | USA | Canada | Ireland | Australia
India | New Zealand | South Africa

Penguin Books is part of the Penguin Random House group of companies
whose addresses can be found at global.penguinrandomhouse.com.

First published by Michael Joseph 2018
Published in Penguin Books 2018
001

Set in 12.42/14.8 pt Garamond MT Std
Typeset by Jouve (UK), Milton Keynes
Printed in Great Britain by Clays Ltd, St Ives plc

A CIP catalogue record for this book is available from the British Library

ISBN: 978-1-405-92531-0

www.greenpenguin.co.uk

MIX
Paper from
responsible sources
FSC® C018179

Penguin Random House is committed to a
sustainable future for our business, our readers
and our planet. This book is made from Forest
Stewardship Council® certified paper.

I

Christ, but he hates having to use another driver's rig. The cab stinks for one thing, and there's something not right about the engine. The brakes aren't much better than stamping on a block of wood; they make more noise than actually do anything. How it passed its last inspection is anyone's guess. Bloody typical.

He belches, thumps his fist against his chest as the acid burns. Should have taken more time over breakfast, but then if he'd had more time he wouldn't have been driving this heap of shit. Hauling slurry from the sewage works over to some helpful farmer to spread over his fields. If people knew what went into their food.

At least there's satnav, even if it's an old set with half the screen darkened and scratched. Boss said something about it being a special delivery. Just let them empty the tanks themselves and not ask any questions. Aye, like he ever would. Thirty years driving trucks for the old man and his son, he's seen it all before. Do the job, get paid, go home. Be better if he didn't have to drive this piece of shit, though. Dodgy goods are one thing, being expected to drive a crap rig is something else entirely.

Shouldn't be a long trip, mind. He can give Bill in maintenance a piece of his mind when he gets back. Knock off early after that. Last time he does the boss a favour.

Another belch and flames leap up his throat. Christ

what was in that bun? Not like Sheena to serve him a dodgy burger. And the smell's not helping either. Making his eyes water, so it is. He's sweating, too. No bloody aircon in this thing. Fucking marvellous. Satnav wants to take him through the town as well. Must know about a balls-up on the city bypass he doesn't. He'd check the radio for traffic news only that's one other thing that doesn't work.

It's just a job. Be done soon enough and then home. Maybe even get in before Mary's back. Surprise her for a change. Mind you, the way his luck's been panning out lately he'd probably find her shagging the postman.

Traffic's buggered all the way up the Gogar road, buses overtaking each other then pulling into the next stop, holding everyone else up as if there was no rush. Christ, but his chest hurts, and struggling with this ancient truck isn't making things any easier. Maybe he'll stop somewhere on the east side and have a kip. Just got to make it through the city centre.

Through the lights and on to the Western Approach Road. Thank fuck the traffic's easing up. If he can coax this asthmatic engine up above 2,000 revs, maybe he'll even get to the farm on time. Might even get some air through the cab and clear the foul smell.

Finally picking up speed now. Under the bridge, green all the way. The traffic on Lothian Road is surprisingly light, but even so he'll have to slow a bit for the corner. Heavy foot on the brake pedal and this time it sinks all the way to the floor. The fuck?

Everything freezes. He can see the cars, delivery vans. Pedestrians just beginning to register something is wrong. Directly ahead, the other side of the junction, a bus stop packed with people. He mashes his foot down on the pedal again and the truck speeds up. Something in his chest bursts as he tries to turn the wheel, stop what he knows is unstoppable.

And now the people are beginning to panic, eyes wide, mouths open in unheard screams. There is only silence as the horror unfolds. No explosion, no rending of metal, no smashing of glass and cracking of bone. He can hear nothing.

Not even the beating of his heart.

2

Even as he turned the corner, Detective Inspector Tony McLean knew that there was something wrong. He couldn't have said how he knew, but the movement of the traffic on Lothian Road and the junction with the Western Approach Road grabbed his attention. Another warm summer morning and the pavements were packed with tourists, workers hurrying to their offices, people of all sorts. Cars and buses filled the road, almost blocking the view. A horn blared loud, shouts of surprise. A truck travelling far too fast shot out of the turning, its engine screaming like a tortured soul. A hundred yards away, all McLean could do was watch as it swerved across the main road, its long tanker trailer jackknifing as it tried to turn. Failed.

A wave of panic swept through the crowd, but it was too late. McLean could only watch in horror as the cab began to tilt, tyres lifted off the road on one side. That was when he saw the bus stop, the people. Knew that they were doomed.

It happened so quickly he could scarcely make sense of it. The cab tipped completely, smashing into the bus stop and scattering people like straw on the wind. Then the trailer rolled over, split open, thousands of litres of something liquid gushing out over the fallen, splashing against the walls of nearby buildings like a tsunami. The noise was oddly muted, a distant smashing of glass and rending of metal that nevertheless brought back horrible memories of the winter as his beloved Alfa Romeo was ripped apart by something unseen and feral. For a moment it was as if the whole world held its breath in silence, unable to believe what had just happened. Then something clicked and the full horror came crashing down.

The truck's engine was still running, a rear wheel spinning as if it were trying to right itself. Safety railings had ripped open the rusty steel tanker and something noxious was dripping out on to the pavement like poisoned blood. A stench of industrial chemicals hung in the air, hazing it with blue smoke that threatened to explode at any moment. McLean fought back the horror, suppressed the urge to join those fleeing the scene. He pushed against the tide, struggling to get closer, to try and help. In only a few short steps he was through the crowd and into a widening area that cleared around the crash.

Bodies lay like rag dolls on the road, the pavement. The shop window directly behind the bus stop had shattered and a still form lay half in, half out of the display. Glass shards caught the morning sun, some glittering white, others ruby red.

'Control? There's a major accident. Corner of Lothian Road and the Western Approach Road.' McLean approached more slowly now, phone clamped to the side of his face, eyes everywhere as he tried to take it all in. Most of the people had run away, as if they expected something worse to happen. A few still stood close by the upturned truck staring, as if waiting for it. Some even had their smartphones out, and he had no doubt the whole scene would be plastered over the internet soon. If it wasn't already.

'Multiple calls coming in on that one, sir. Ambulance and fire services are on their way.' The young woman at the control centre, miles away beyond the far side of the city, sounded calm and collected. She couldn't see what he could see.

'Tell the fire crews they'll need hazardous-chemical gear.' McLean coughed before he could get the rest of the sentence out, the pale smoke tickling the back of his throat, a chemical reek that was already giving him a head-ache. 'We're going to need a lot of bodies to clear the area, too. Shut off the Lothian Road from Princes Street to Tollcross.'

'I take it you're at the scene, sir.' Behind the voice, McLean could hear the clattering of keys as the Control operative hammered at her keyboard. A distant siren began to wail, followed by another and another.

'I am.' He made an effort to move the gawkers back, concerned the truck might explode at any moment. There were far too many people for his liking, but none dressed in the uniform of Police Scotland officers. 'Looks like I'm probably first on scene, too. Ah, no. Here we go.'

A fire engine appeared at the end of Princes Street and wound a slow way through the halted traffic, siren giving off the occasional slow 'whoop' as if that might somehow magically clear the gridlock. A pair of uniform constables, one talking rapidly into her Airwave set, hurried towards the scene of the accident. McLean ended the call, slipped the phone into his pocket and went to meet them.

'Jesus Christ. What happened here?'

McLean recognized Constable Carter, formerly Detective

Inspector Carter. The female PC, still talking on her Airwave set, was new to him.

'I'd have thought that would be obvious, Constable. Now, why don't you see if you can't get some of these people back, clear some space for the ambulance and fire crews? No idea what's in that truck, but it might explode at any moment.'

Carter stared at him for perhaps a moment longer than was necessary, but it wasn't the normal sneer of ill-concealed hostility. The look on the constable's face was something different, a mixture of barely controlled panic and something else that might have been awe.

'Constable . . . ?' McLean turned his attention to the other officer as she clipped the handset for her Airwave back on to its shoulder strap. Behind her he could see the fire engine pulling to a halt beside the overturned truck, the fire crew leaping out and setting to work.

'Gregor, sir.'

'Right then, Constable Gregor. You're in charge of cordoning off the scene. Get these people back as far from the crash as possible. I'll coordinate with the senior fire officer and any other uniforms who get here before the rapid response unit shows up.'

McLean coughed, tears pricking the corners of his eyes. The smell from the truck almost overpowered him, a mixture of exhaust fumes, sewage and something harsher still. He covered his mouth and nose with one hand as he picked a way through the carnage. Too many bodies lying still, but some were beginning to stir. Where the hell were the ambulances and paramedics?

The truck's engine coughed once and died. A stillness

fell over the scene, not quite utter silence as the city carried on its usual roar, oblivious to the terrible violence that had been meted out on its streets. Then the moaning filtered into his hearing, the quiet whimpers of pain, the sobs of terror and sudden, terrible shrieks of pain.

Closing himself off to the horror as best he could, McLean approached the first body. A young man lay sprawled half on the pavement, half on the road. At first it looked like he was just sleeping, but then McLean saw the pool of dark blood leaching from the back of his head. He pulled on a pair of latex gloves, more normally used for keeping his prints off crime scenes, but just as useful here. The young man's eyes stared sightlessly at the sky, and he had no pulse when McLean felt at his neck. Gently, he eased the eyelids closed and moved on to the next body.

A young woman sat upright and stared wide-eyed at nothing. One arm hung awkwardly at her side, clearly broken, and as she turned to look at him McLean could see the skin on her face streaked with blood and what looked like burn marks. She opened her mouth to speak, but no words came out.

'It's OK,' he said as he crouched down beside her. 'I'm a police officer. You're in shock, looks like your arm's broken, but you're going to be OK.'

The stench from the ruptured tanker made it hard to breathe, a dull headache squatting in the back of his brain. Still, McLean worked his way methodically through the crash scene, keeping away from the truck itself but tending to the injured and the fortunate but dazed. Every so often he would pause to see whether any ambulances had turned up, but mostly it was just police and fire crews, a couple of motorcycle paramedics tending to the more seriously injured. Someone had found blankets and begun covering the dead, too. There were far too many.

A young man sat with his back to a railing just a few paces from where the bus stop had once been. Head in hands, he rocked gently backwards and forwards. McLean picked a path through the carnage until he was standing directly in front of him, but the young man didn't seem to see him.

'You OK?' He reached out and touched the man on the shoulder, felt a jolt almost like static. For a moment the sky darkened, a cloud passing overhead. The young man seemed not to notice.

'Hey. Look at me. You OK?'

Finally the young man looked up, saw him. He still said nothing, and there was something about his face that spoke of unimaginable loss. More even than the shocked reaction to this terrible event. What was his story? Why had he been here? Had he lost someone in all the melee? Slowly, something like understanding softened the fear in the young man's eyes. He nodded once, indicating that he wasn't injured. Or at least that was what McLean thought he must mean. Looking at him, he appeared unscathed, at least physically.

'Stay there. I'll send one of the paramedics to check you over.'

As he took his hand from the young man's shoulders, the clouds moved away from the sun and light burst out across the street. McLean stumbled, light-headed for a moment as he searched for someone else to help. Then a woman nearby started screaming for her baby. No one rushed to her aid.

9

They were all too busy dealing with the wounded, the dead, keeping the camera-phone-toting ghouls at bay. Distant sirens played counterpoint to the wailing of the injured, but there were still too few medics there, too few fire crews. Bitter smoke drifted across a scene like a battlefield, and for a moment all he wanted to do was run, flee from the horror unfolding around him. Instead he took as deep a breath as he dared, then set off once more into the fray.

3

Jesus Christ. What the fuck just happened? My head's splitting like the worst of hangovers, mouth feels like something's crawled in there and died. I'm home, I know that much, but as to how I got here? No idea. Must have been walking on autopilot, dead to the world.

All I can remember is noise, panic, screaming. There was heat, too, like I'd been on the beach all day on the one day of summer we get in this country. Glass breaking, people running in all directions, a man's face in the windscreen of a truck.

Oh God. No.

I sit too heavily in the rickety old armchair, springs threatening to end any thoughts of being a father I might have had. Some chance, like I'd want to bring a child into this shit-stain of a world. Lifting hands up to my face, I notice for the first time that I've got a red scarf draped loosely over my shoulders. Cashmere by the feel of it, ripped at one end. There's a dampness about it, spots of darker red where something has wetted it. I rub one between finger and thumb, stare at them stupidly when they come up with a thin smear of blood on my skin. Whose scarf is this? It's not mine. Not my blood either. Whoever it belongs to, it stinks to high heaven of something corrosive, chemical.

My head spins as I stand, walk on unsteady legs to the tiny kitchen. I meant to throw the scarf away, but as I cross the hall so more memories come back. By the time I get to the bin, lid flipped open by a well-placed foot, I've pieced enough together that I might even throw myself in there, too.

The lid makes a dull metal clang as I let it fall down, wrap the scarf around my shoulders again and go through the automatic ritual of making myself a mug of coffee. I don't want to believe what's just happened, but the pieces are dropping into place now. A crowded bus stop, a truck speeding out of control, tipping in slow motion onto people too slow, too wrapped up in their earphone cocoons, too unlucky to even notice. And I'm reaching my arms out to embrace a stranger, a young woman with long blonde hair and a face I last saw as a child. She has a scarf around her neck, red cashmere despite the summer warmth, and she has a name.

Maddy.

Oh Christ. Maddy.

4

'You all right, sir?'

McLean startled at the words. He had been staring into the middle distance, seeing the slow motion of traffic at the end of Princes Street as it was diverted away from the junction on to Lothian Road. The recovery operation was running smoothly now, the clean-up process well underway as the professionals got on with the jobs they had been trained for. He probably should have left them to it long since, but the fact he'd been first on the scene meant all the uniforms had come to him for instructions. There had been a task to complete and he had thrown himself into it utterly. Now it was done, he was left with a feeling of disconnection, as if he'd been away from the world awhile and was only just returning.

'Sorry?' He turned to see Constable Gregor standing close by. Her gaze suggested she was trying to work out what he'd been staring at, and he wondered just how long he'd been lost in his thoughts.

'It's just. Well, you looked a bit zoned out there, sir. Can't say I blame you, what with all this.' She shook her head gently from side to side as if not wanting to see the carnage. 'Reckon I'll have nightmares for months, and I've just been working the cordon.'

As she spoke, so McLean felt the weariness wash over him, pricked around the edges with a headache that might have been dehydration or might have been the noxious fumes that had burned off the overturned tanker truck until the fire crews had arrived with their foam. The smell was still there, rasping the back of his throat.

'It's . . . I don't really know.' Talking hurt, a soreness that reminded McLean of the early stages of the flu, and he had a raging thirst. He tried to scan the area for the mobile incident truck that always turned up at things like this, then stopped as his vision dimmed. 'Anyone got a brew on, do you know?'

Gregor had been reaching out to give him a steadying hand, but she turned on one heel and pointed to a café a short way up the road. A gaggle of uniforms clustered around its doorway; no other customers this side of the cordon.

'Luigi's been keeping us all fed and watered. Don't think he's taking any money off anyone either. There's not many'd be so generous.'

McLean nodded. Tragedy brought out the best in some people. He set off towards the café, then stopped, remembering something.

'The young lad over there by the railings. He get checked out by the paramedics?' As he spoke, so he turned to look for the man. He'd seen him, hadn't he? It had the quality of a dream, but he was fairly sure of it. White-faced and wide-eyed with shock, sitting with his back to the low wall and railings, curled in on himself but unhurt. How he'd survived unscathed in the middle of such carnage, McLean couldn't know. Must have had the luck of the gods with him.

'Young lad?' Gregor looked around the pavement. Only the dead remained, covered with blankets to protect what dignity they had left from the prying eyes of the press.

Helicopters had been circling overhead like vultures within minutes of the crash. 'Don't recall anyone, but the walking wounded were all shipped off as soon as possible.'

McLean shook his head, then wished he hadn't as a wave of pain broke over him. Too much of that smoke fogging his thoughts. Christ, he really needed that tea. A shower, too, probably. The chance of that happening any time soon was minimal.

'You're right. He's not here, so he's either gone to the hospital or home. Either way I'm sure he'll be fine.'

'Where the bloody hell have you been, McLean? Don't you ever answer your phone?'

Not exactly how he'd been hoping to be greeted, but McLean wasn't entirely surprised. Cadging a lift across town from the crash scene in a squad car had meant he'd been able to check his phone, the endless messages and texts from his new boss. Chief Superintendent Tom Forrester wasn't a bad officer, really. A far cry from Brooks and a breath of fresh air compared to Duguid, but his Glaswegian accent sounded alien in this most Edinburgh of stations. That he was uniform rather than Specialist Crime Division had changed the dynamic in the team even more. Then again, the fallout from the Chalmers case was always going to be messy, and McLean couldn't blame the Chief Constable for bringing in someone he knew and trusted to steady the ship.

'Major incident over at Tollcross, sir. Didn't Control notify you?'

Forrester pinched the bridge of his nose between thumb and forefinger as if trying to staunch a heavy nosebleed.

McLean was growing accustomed to the gesture now, knew that it meant the man was trying to suppress his natural tendency to the sarcastic.

'Are we so short-staffed that uniform have to go stealing inspectors from plain clothes now?'

'Sorry, sir. It's just that I was first on the scene. Accident over the other side of town tied up most of the ambulances and paramedics, so I stayed to help with triage until they got there.' McLean hadn't really processed the incident until he said the words. He'd been so busy he'd been blissfully forgetful of the horrible noise of the crash, the screams of the injured and dying. 'Actually, I was there when it happened.'

Something in Forrester's features softened. He still looked like a rat in a black uniform, but a kindly rat who might only chew at your dead fingers rather than gnaw out your sightless eyeballs.

'Fuck are you doing back here, then? You should be at home, man. Look like you could do with a shower and a change of clothes if nothing else.'

McLean shrugged. He'd thought about knocking off early, but there was the small matter of an investigation into counterfeit goods he was meant to be co-ordinating with Trading Standards and HMRC that was going nowhere precisely because it was split between three different organizations. That was a meeting that would have to be rescheduled. If they'd even noticed he'd not turned up.

'Control's already handed over the preliminary investigation to me. Thought I'd get things in motion before the anti-terrorism squad get here. Set up a meeting with the senior officers and take it from there.'

'Anti . . .' Forrester had been standing in the doorway that led through from the front of the station to the ground floor admin offices and the nicer interview rooms. Now he stepped into the reception area, letting the security door click closed behind him. His face was a picture of thoughts cascading into place like a landslide. 'You think this is a terrorist attack?'

'My gut says no, but we can't ignore the possibility. Tanker truck took the corner from the Western Approach Road on to the Lothian Road too fast. Could have been deliberate, could have been an accident. Driver's dead, along with at least fifteen others.'

All the blood had drained out of Forrester's face. His mouth hung slightly open, eyes staring into the distance as the implications began to mount up. 'Fifteen?'

'At least. I'd be very surprised if that figure didn't go up by the end of the day. It was carnage sir, and that's another problem.'

'Another?'

'Press were there in minutes. There's been a helicopter hovering over the scene all morning. And you know what people are like. Everyone with a phone was taking pictures, filming the whole thing. We did our best to contain it, but there's going to be footage all over the internet already.'

Forrester leaned against the wall beside the security door, drumming his fingers against the fake wood, thinking fast. 'The scene's secure now, though?'

'Fire crews are still dealing with the truck, paramedics have done what they can. We've at least a hundred uniform officers keeping the public away. More being drafted

17

in from the regions. Surprised no one told you already, sir.' McLean glanced at the clock above the unmanned reception booth. 'It's been three hours since it happened.'

Forrester pushed himself away from the wall, turned and tapped out the code to unlock the security door. 'I've been in strategy meetings all day. They told me there'd been an incident, but it was under control. Think I might have to have words. Come.'

McLean followed the chief superintendent as he strode past the admin offices and up the stairs. The station felt empty, almost like school at the end of term. Hardly surprising given how many constables and sergeants had been drafted in to deal with the crash. He'd assumed that Forrester was leading him up to his office on the third floor, but instead the chief superintendent headed for the CID room. It wasn't much busier than the corridor outside.

'At ease, Constable.' Forrester waved down Detective Constable Harrison before she could stand. Looming over her like a giant, Detective Constable Blane was the only other person in the room. 'Where is everybody?'

Harrison tapped twice at her keyboard, blanking out the screen before answering. 'DCI McIntyre's over at Fettes today, sir. She's got DC Stringer and DS Laird with her. DI Ritchie's up in Perthshire on Operation Fenton. Not sure what the other teams are up to but there was a big briefing this morning and then everyone left. Oh, and there was a traffic accident over Lothian Road way. All the uniforms . . .' She trailed off, eyes widening as she saw McLean standing behind the chief superintendent.

Forrester let out a weary sigh. He'd only been in charge a few months, but McLean could guess the pressure he was under. Dropped in from on high to clear up the mess left by his predecessor, dealing with the twin demands of uniform and plain clothes in a station that was seriously undermanned and with a budget under constant review. It couldn't have been much fun.

'OK. Get in touch with everyone you can. I want them back here as soon as possible. Senior officers' meeting at four. Press conference at half five.' He turned to McLean. 'Tony, I'll need a full briefing for everyone, then. As much detail as possible.'

McLean suppressed his own weary sigh, instead just nodded his understanding. What he wanted to do was go home and stand under the shower for the rest of the day. No chance of that happening any time soon.

5

Police have cordoned off the area and are keeping the public well away. Reports of toxic fumes suggest this may be the first terrorist attack on Scottish soil since the Glasgow Airport bomb in 2007. As this footage from a member of the public shows, fire crews in full hazmat gear –

McLean clicked off the television that hung from the wall in the corner of his office, dropped the remote onto his desk. He wasn't sure he liked this new room, two floors up and at the front of the building rather than the pokey-wee broom cupboard he'd used for so many years. It was on the way to too many other places for one thing, the major-incident rooms and the chief superintendent's office among them. People dropped in all the time, which was both distracting and disconcerting.

On the other hand it was a big room with a large window, the view marginally better than the stone wall he had become so used to. His new desk was at least twice the size of his old one, which meant it had taken twice as long to disappear under the mountains of paperwork that followed him wherever he went. Over by the far wall, under the television, a small conference table was strewn with reports, printouts and other collected information as Detective Constables Harrison, Stringer and Blane did their best to make sense of the morning's accident and distil it down into a useful briefing paper. Only half an hour to go until the senior officers' meeting, and they were still waiting on a call from forensics.

'Sometimes wonder why we bother with press conferences these days. It's all over the internet the moment anything happens.' McLean picked up his phone, thumbed at the screen until it lit up. He'd been expecting a call all afternoon but it hadn't come. Soon enough he was going to have to make it himself.

'Aye, but that can be helpful, sir. Some of our best intelligence comes from Twitter.'

McLean couldn't really tell whether DC Harrison was being sarcastic or not. She had a dry wit far too well developed for one so young.

'Your flatmate use it?' he asked. 'Only I could really do with something from forensics before I have to speak to the top brass.'

Harrison pulled her laptop towards her, tapped at some keys and stared at the screen. It was DC Stringer who spoke next, though.

'Email just pinged through now, sir. You want me to send it to the printer?'

'Executive summary'll do.' McLean hauled himself out of his chair and walked over. The space between desk and table was about twice the size of his old office, bare carpet tiles with no stains on them at all.

'No obvious evidence the crash was deliberate. Looks like the driver lost control. Maybe heart attack? He's one of the dead, anyway.'

'What about the fire? The smoke?' McLean could still feel it in the back of his throat, the burning sensation and a metallic taste that made everything unpalatable. His head had cleared a bit, but the dull ache still lurked there, squat and evil behind his eyes.

'Truck was carrying some kind of industrial solvent waste, apparently. They're still waiting on analysis to find out exactly what.'

'They don't know? Surely it was carrying a manifest? There should have been hazardous-chemicals notice panels on the bowser.'

'Aye, there was. We've been in touch with the hauliers, too, and they don't know what's happened. Should have been transporting digestate from an anaerobic digester, whatever that is. Nothing toxic at all.'

McLean thought of the chemical reek, the acid burns on the skin of the victims, the melting tarmac. Rotted down green waste it certainly wasn't. 'So we've got an illegal transportation of hazardous chemicals through a built-up area, a truck that's not carrying the correct plates for its cargo. Anyone been on to Health and Safety?'

'They're in the email trail, sir.' Stringer tapped away at the keyboard on his laptop as he spoke, two industrious fingers doing the work of ten. 'SEPA are involved, too. Pretty much all the agencies, actually.'

'OK. Make sure they're all copied in on the initial report.' McLean leaned forward, rubbing at his face to try and ease his exhaustion. He'd washed as best he could manage without going home and changing, but his skin felt taut and dry with whatever foul chemical had spilled from the tanker. That it wasn't sewage effluent was scant consolation. A mislabelled cargo meant corruption at best. Could this actually be a terrorist attack? It didn't feel right, but then nothing about the whole incident felt right.

Twenty dead at the latest count and dozens injured, how could it? He glanced at his watch, time to go. Pushed himself to his feet and breathed in deeply.

'Right then. Let's get this over and done with.'

'Gentlemen. Lady. I don't really need to tell you just how serious this situation is. We've a dozen and more innocent people dead, the press going nuts over a possible terrorist attack. I've had the First Minister breathing down my neck all day, and while some people might enjoy that kind of thing, she's really not my type.'

McLean couldn't remember the last time he'd seen this office so full of top brass. It might have been Chief Superintendent Forrester's room, but he had wisely ceded authority to the chief constable. The ACCs from all the regions had gathered together like some ancient cabal, accompanied by their personal entourages. There wasn't an officer lower in rank than superintendent there apart from DCI McIntyre – also the only woman present – and himself. As a lowly detective inspector, he should have felt overawed; instead he was reeling at the thought of just how young some of them were.

'McLean. You were first on scene, I'm told. Co-ordinated with fire and paramedics. Got everything under control. That's good work, man. Top work.'

'Right time, right place, I guess, sir. Or wrong time, wrong place. Depends on your point of view.'

'You witnessed the crash, is that true?'

McLean didn't know the chief constable at all. He'd met the previous one a few times but had largely kept out of the way of the machinery that ran Police Scotland. Looking around the room, he only really knew Jayne McIntyre and Deputy Chief Constable Stevie Robinson, once known as Call-Me-Stevie, but now more universally Teflon Steve after he'd come out of the last embarrassment seemingly squeaky clean. The rest of them were from the west. Strathclyde boys. Foreign.

'I was there, sir. I saw . . . something. I know it's a cliché, but it all happened so fast. I was just turning the corner, maybe a hundred yards away. The first thing I was really aware of was the explosion.'

'Explosion you say? So it was a bomb?' The dark-suited man in the far corner was from the anti-terrorism task force. McLean didn't envy him his job, even if Scotland had never been high on the target list for most terrorist organizations. Even so, there was something unnerving about the look in his eyes. An eagerness bordering on excitement.

'Perhaps explosion is the wrong word. Have you ever seen a car crash? Heard the screech of twisted metal and the sound of breaking glass?' McLean didn't wait for an answer. 'Well, imagine that magnified tenfold. The truck was going too fast, only just started to turn before it rolled and hit the bus stop.' As he spoke, so the image unfurled in his mind as if it were being played on a cinema screen. Things he didn't remember seeing began to slot into place. Little details like the group of Asian tourists with their matching bright-yellow backpacks and calf-length boots. An unusually tall man in a loose-fitting grey pinstripe suit, iPhone clamped to the side of his head with a giant's hand. A Morningside lady in tweed and pearls, being dragged towards the Usher Hall by two tiny dachshunds on extendable leads. A young man –

'So what you're saying is you didn't actually see anything.' Chief Superintendent Forrester broke through McLean's flashback before the truck could complete its roll into the bus stop.

'I'm sorry?'

'You were there but you weren't observing the scene. Just a passer-by. Is that correct?'

'Of course I wasn't observing the scene. Nobody was observing the scene. It was an accident. Happened in an instant.'

'An accident? You're sure of that?' the chief constable asked. McLean felt the heat of a dozen pairs of eyes bearing down on him, the prickling of skin as the blush crept up his neck.

'If you're asking do I think this was a terrorist attack, sir, my instinct is to say no, I don't think it was. I'm not up on what the current threat level is for the city, or whether we've been following any particular groups.'

'Robert? You care to add anything at this point?' The chief constable nodded towards the officer from the anti-terrorism task force, who leaned forward, resting his arms on the table and pausing a while before he spoke.

'We've nothing on our radar beyond the general threat level, and that's always been more focused on London and the south.' He shook his head slowly. 'We can't rule it out yet, and I've no doubt the press will be running with it until we can, but I'm inclined to agree with McLean here. It looks like a tragic accident. We need reports from the fire crews and forensics, full background and post-mortem on the driver at the very least before we can be sure. I don't think this was a deliberate act, though. Not that it's going to make the families of the dead feel any better.'

'What about the victims?' DCI McIntyre asked. 'Have we been able to identify all of them yet?'

'Not all, no.' McLean shuffled his copy of the report he and the detective constables had put together for the meeting. There were a few preliminary photographs from the scene at the back of it that didn't make for comfortable viewing. 'Some of the bodies were quite badly disfigured. Chemical burns, crushing and dismemberment mostly. City mortuary are pulling in extra help to work through them all, but I reckon some will need DNA for identification.'

'That bad?' The chief constable leafed through his own copy of the report, his face paling as he reached the end. 'Oh. I see.'

'I'd like to make a start on speaking to the survivors as soon as possible. We've contact details for most of the uninjured nearby as well, but it wouldn't hurt to put out a media call for witnesses. Lots of people with camera phones there, so a trawl of the usual internet sites should help fill in the blanks, too.' McLean paused, aware that all eyes were on him again. 'That is, if you want me to lead the investigation.'

'Looks to me like you already are, McLean.' The chief constable checked his watch, pushed his chair from the table and stood up, leaving his copy of the report behind. 'Now I suppose we'd better go and speak to our friends in the press.'

'There's one more thing, sir. That you should know, I think.'

'Yes?'

'The tanker. It was supposed to be carrying harmless sewage. That's what the cargo manifest said, and the hazard-warning panel on the side of the bowser. You'll have seen from the photographs that it wasn't. We're still not exactly sure what it was carrying, but some nasty industrial solvent would be my best guess. Something that can melt skin and bones.'

'Oh Christ. The press are just going to love that.' The superintendent from the anti-terrorism task force had kept his copy of the report and was peering closely at one of the photographs. He put it down on the desk and pulled out his phone, started to place a call. 'This changes things. If someone's using improvised chemical weapons then we're in deep shit.'

McLean played the scene back in his head again, seeing the truck turn, its trailer jackknife and roll in slow motion on to the crowded bus stop. Could that have been deliberate? He really didn't think so.

'I'm still not sure, sir. Even an empty container truck would have caused just as much damage. This seems like a complication too far. And it would require too much planning, surely? You'd have heard something, wouldn't you?'

The head of the anti-terrorism task force scowled at him, but put his phone down without making his call. 'So what are you suggesting, then? Illegal transport of waste goods? Just happens to crash in the city centre?'

'Something along those lines, aye. We'll know more once we've examined the truck and seen the PM report on the driver, but I honestly think he was doing everything he could to avoid hitting anyone. This is just an unhappy accident.'

'Unhappy.' The chief constable growled the word like a poked bear. 'Aye, that's about the size of it.'

6

'How can you be so sure this isn't a terrorist attack? Shouldn't we be putting the country on alert?'

The smell of the crash still clung to him, a faint but sharp odour that threatened to bring the headache back every time McLean caught a whiff. No one had mentioned it, but he could barely smell anything else. It was in the weave of his jacket, the collar of his shirt, his hair, released whenever he moved. He should have gone straight home from the accident scene, showered and changed before heading in to the station. With any luck the investigation would have been handed to another detective that way. With any luck. He laughed silently, mirthlessly. Sat at the top table in front of the media, the only luck McLean had going his way was that the chief constable and Chief Superintendent Forrester were more senior and more interesting targets for questioning.

'It's Nicky, isn't it?' The chief constable peered over the top of his spectacles into the crowd in the general direction of where the question had come from. He paused a moment, as if expecting an answer, then continued. 'It's true this bears some of the hallmarks of a terrorist attack, and, believe me, the anti-terrorism task force is hard at work already trying to find out who might be responsible. It's also possible that this is no more than a tragic accident. We had no intelligence of an impending attack, and, believe me, we know far more about what's going on than you would suspect.'

'Didn't the truck contain corrosive chemicals though? Surely that just confirms this is terrorism.'

'I rather think you're reading too much into this.' The chief constable shifted uncomfortably in his seat. 'We're not discounting terrorism, of course, but lurid speculation helps no one and scaremongering simply feeds the agenda of the terrorists anyway, doesn't it?'

Nicky the journalist didn't respond to this, which McLean considered a small victory.

'Our first priority is to identify who is responsible for this and prosecute them. We have teams investigating where the truck and its cargo came from, teams identifying the dead and injured. We're reviewing all the CCTV footage we have, and would appeal to the public to come forward with any personal videos they might have. We'll be providing regular updates as things proceed, but rest assured we won't leave any stone unturned until we've got to the bottom of what happened here this morning. Thank you. No more questions.'

No stone unturned. It was a strange expression, and as its oddness rolled across his thoughts, McLean realized he'd zoned out of the press conference, the grating, nasal tone of the chief constable. No one had noticed, of course. All attention was on the top brass in their shiny uniforms; the boss man and the senior officer in charge of the area where everything had happened. Quotes from them would keep the editors happy, and made for far better telly than a bleary-eyed plain-clothes inspector trying not to yawn too much. He covered his mouth with the back of his hand, bringing another headache-inducing chemical onslaught as the senior officers filed out past him. Chief Superintendent Forrester put a hand on his shoulder as he went past, stopping McLean from standing up himself.

'You look like shit, Tony. Get yourself home and an early night. I'll deal with his nibs and the others.' The chief superintendent winked awkwardly, trying to co-ordinate the motion with a nod in the direction of the departing chief constable. 'Reckon this shit-show's still going to be here in the morning.'

McLean tried a smile, but it only made the dry skin on his face ache. 'Think that went well enough.' He wasn't sure if he'd meant it as a statement or a question. Forrester opted for the latter.

'Oh, it's given them something to chew on. For now, at least. But they'll be back. That's the problem with the press. They're never satisfied.'

'Thought you were going home after the press conference, sir.'

McLean could have slipped into his old office at the back of the station unnoticed, but the route to the new one took him past too many other rooms. He'd forgotten, too, that he had pressed it into service as an interim incident room. Detective Constables Stringer and Blane had gone, but DC Janie Harrison was still there, sitting at the conference table, peering at her laptop and scribbling notes down on an A4 pad.

'I was. Well, I will do. Just need to get my thoughts together. Maybe grab some coffee before I try to drive home.' McLean sat down more heavily than he had meant to, the chair tipping backwards and almost dumping him on the floor. Grabbing the edge of the desk toppled stacks of papers and he watched them tumble through puzzled eyes.

'You sure you wouldn't be better getting a taxi home, sir? Or maybe I could ask one of the squad cars to drop you off. You look done in.' Harrison closed down her laptop, stood up and walked over to the far corner of the room. A moment later she returned with a mugful of coffee from the filter machine that was another perk of this office. It had been sitting on the hotplate for too long, but it still smelled better than the dull chemical reek rising from his clothes.

'You know you don't have to wait on me,' McLean said as he took the mug in both hands. It was milkier than he would have liked, and laced with enough sugar to cause a riot at a toddler's party.

Harrison smiled. 'Aye, I know. Doesn't mean I can't if I want to. I'll have a word with the duty sergeant, too. See if there's a patrol headed over to your part of town.'

'I'll be fine.' McLean drank deeply, the coffee only lukewarm. Its sickly sweetness washed away some of the taste of the lorry crash and soon enough the caffeine would get to work on his headache. At least he hoped so.

'You get anywhere with the hauliers?' he asked.

Harrison frowned. 'Jay and Lofty went out to see them but the yard was locked tight. Nobody about. We managed to get on to the boss though. Said he'd called all the other trucks in as soon as he heard about the crash. Going to have his mechanics look over them all before they go out again.'

'Sounds pretty dodgy to me.' McLean reached for his phone, stabbed at the screen to bring it to life. That was another thing about this room; it had a reliable mobile signal.

'Aye, I know. Had a chat with Grumpy Bob about it since you were all in the press conference. He's got a patrol car sat outside the compound gates. Anyone goes inside and we'll hear about it.'

'They've checked there's no other way in, I take it.' McLean put his phone back down on the desk, no longer needing to make the call he'd been intending to. Harrison gave him a look that was far too old-fashioned for one so young.

'Mechanics usually start about seven in the morning. All the drivers have been told to stay home. I've arranged to go and interview the boss first thing. Manda should've had a chance to look at the crashed truck by then, so we'll know whether or not we need to shut the place down.'

McLean leaned back into his chair, slowly this time so that it wouldn't try to kill him. 'Sounds like you and Bob have got everything under control. That's good work, Constable.'

'Thank you, sir. I took the liberty of scheduling a morning briefing for six o'clock. Figured we'd need to be quick off the mark with this, seeing as how the chief constable's involved and everything. Didn't think overtime'd be a problem, at least to start with.'

McLean glanced at the clock above the door, even though he'd only just seen the time on his phone. Almost seven in the evening. Well past shift end for sergeants and constables. An age since he'd headed out of the station to walk across town for a meeting in the West End. He stood up, swaying only slightly. The coffee had woken him enough, though how long it would last was anyone's guess.

'Six, you say? Guess we'd both better get home then. I've a feeling tomorrow's going to be another long day.'

The flash of the indicators and quiet 'plip' of the central lock disarming echoed across the car park as McLean stepped out into the evening warmth. A gentle breeze helped to take the chemical smell away and he stood for a moment just breathing in and out, staring sightlessly at his car.

His new car. The old Alfa Romeo was still sitting in the corner of the forensics service vehicle compound, under a heavy-duty tarpaulin. A mess of ripped steel and broken glass all too reminiscent of the truck crash. Deep down, he knew it wasn't going to be economical to repair. He could buy one the same colour and year that had already been restored, but it wouldn't have been the same. Wouldn't have been his father's old car, owned since new almost fifty years ago. He wasn't sure what he was going to do with it. Amanda Parsons would never forgive him if he scrapped it, though what else he could do with the wreck, McLean wasn't sure. Perhaps it could be carefully dismantled, its organs donated so that another might live a little longer.

It was the forensic scientist who had suggested this new Alfa and DC Harrison's uncle who had sourced it for him. Brand new, impossibly shiny in metallic black, it had the same model name as his old Giulia, but was a different beast altogether. He'd only driven it between his house and the station in the month since it had been delivered, barely taken it over forty miles an hour, but the noise from the V6 engine suggested it would happily go a lot faster than that. More often than not he'd find a group of young uniform constables standing around staring at it with mouths slightly open. It had that sleek, powerful look to it that would be useless for a stakeout. There was no one about this evening, though.

The drive across town took longer than normal, the roads busier than he was used to. Had they managed to remove the truck yet? If not that would explain the traffic. Nothing like closing down one of the main city arteries to bugger up everything else. McLean found himself looking for a place to turn around, go back to the station and find out. The incident room should have been up and running by now, calls coming into the accident hotline, names of the injured and dead collated. Things he needed to know, answers to the thousand and one questions left hanging when he'd walked out of the station. He shook his head to dislodge the stupid idea, winced as the squat chemical headache flared again. It made no difference whether the crash scene had been cleared or not. Other people were looking after that, and other people would be manning the phone lines. He didn't need to micro-manage every-thing. What he needed was a shower, a change of clothes, some food and his bed.

Traffic finally began to ease as he neared home, cruising slowly past the church, slowing down almost to a crawl at the point where his old car had died. McLean still couldn't understand what had happened. An empty road, no other vehicles, and yet somehow the Alfa had been ripped apart, its front smashed in as if it had hit a tree at fifty miles an hour. He'd been drugged at the time, which added to the confusion, but even the forensics experts were baffled.

The kitchen lights were on as he parked alongside Emma's blue and rust Peugeot. McLean found himself gripping the top of the car door as he climbed out, the world swaying slightly. Perhaps Harrison had been right to suggest a taxi or a lift in a squad car, but he was home now. Safe.

Except that there was something strange in the air. Stranger than the way breathing in noxious chemical fumes could account for. He thought he could feel the weight of many eyes upon him, and sure enough when McLean peered deep into the rhododendron bushes that lined the gravel driveway, he caught a glimpse of them. Feline, unblinking. Looking around, he noticed a tabby cat lying on the roof of Emma's car, another on the wall that separated the courtyard from the garden, a third sitting in front of the coach house door, cleaning its ears with a licked front paw.

'Back again, are you?' McLean shrugged, releasing another whiff of chemical headache into the darkening air. 'Well as long as you don't all expect to be fed.'

He pushed open the back door, stepped into the darkened utility room. The kitchen door beyond lay slightly ajar, light spilling around its edge and bringing with it the muted sound of voices in low conversation. Even without being able to understand the words, he knew who the visitor was. Something about the deep yet feminine tones. The cats were a bit of a giveaway, too. Taking a deep breath to steady himself, McLean opened the door and stepped through.

Emma sat on one side of the kitchen table, dressed in

baggy clothes so as to conceal her barely noticeable bump, their child growing inside her. Across from her, massive hands cradling a delicate china cup as if it were as fragile as a tiny bird, Madame Rose, the transvestite medium, turned to greet him with a smile that had more than a hint of worry about it.

'Tony. You're home. I'm so very pleased to see you again.'

7

McLean couldn't quite put his finger on it, but there was something different about the old medium. How long was it since he'd first met Madame Rose? Three years? Four? It had been around the time Donald Anderson had died and all the horror that his killing had unleashed. Jayne McIntyre was the one who'd suggested he speak to her, hadn't she? How had the detective chief inspector come into contact with a transvestite fortune teller and antiquarian book collector in the first place? For some unaccountable reason, he'd never asked.

They sat at the kitchen table, a large pot of tea in between them. Madame Rose was as improbably large as ever, dressed in her finest twinset and pearls. Her hair had gone from grey to white and on into blue rinse, but was still as full as ever and perfectly coiffured. Her flawless makeup, war paint so thick it could hide the ages from her face, spoke of long hours in front of the mirror before ever venturing out into public. She held her cup with a delicacy quite at odds with the size of her hands, and that was when McLean noticed the slight tremor in the extended little finger. The tiniest of things, but as he saw it, so he saw other small signs of ageing. Of frailty. In the years he had known her, Madame Rose had been many things, but frail had never been one of them.

'It's so nice to see Emma back to normal.' Rose placed

her cup down on the table, reached out with a hand that completely engulfed Emma's own. 'You know, my dear? I think travel suits you.'

'Well, I don't think I'm going to be heading off anywhere soon.' Emma patted her stomach with her free hand.

'Indeed no. You must rest, conserve your strength. Take regular exercise but nothing too strenuous. Your child is the future. She brings me much hope.'

'She?' McLean raised a sceptical eyebrow. 'You seem very sure.'

Madame Rose released Emma's hand, lifted her own to her face and tapped at her nose with a fat finger. 'I have my ways, Tony. Same as I knew Emma was back in town even though neither of you thought to tell me.'

'I'm sorry. It's been . . .' McLean was about to say busy, but the first couple of months after Emma's return he had been loafing around at home, suspended while Professional Standards looked into the death of poor Heather Marchmont. The truth of the matter was he'd completely forgotten how Madame Rose had helped Emma recover from her coma and subsequent memory loss. But then he'd forgotten that it was Madame Rose who had sent her off on her worldwide travels, too. Split the two of them apart when they had barely got to know each other.

'It's no matter. I've been busy, too, and making travels of my own.' Rose sat a little more upright than she had been, folded her hands across her lap as if to underline the importance of what she was about to say. 'There is a change in the air. I have felt it, and I'm sure you have felt it, too. Dark forces are gathering on the horizon and we must ward ourselves and our city against them.'

He wanted to scoff, as he so often did when Madame Rose leaned more heavily into her role of fortune teller. It didn't help that he was tired, still smelled strongly of the crashed truck, and was barely managing to suppress the worst memories of the carnage. McLean had wanted nothing more than to come home, stand in the shower until the water ran cold and then wipe out the day with an unhealthily large dram of expensive single malt whisky. And yet he could no more turn Madame Rose away than cut off his own hand; the tradition of hospitality was deeply ingrained in him. He had to admit that he kind of liked her, too, and something about her voice, the mask-like quality of her face and the silence that filled the kitchen after she had spoken made her words all the more serious.

'Dark forces?' Emma asked after a moment that was an age. 'You mean we're in danger? From who?'

'From whom, my dear,' Madame Rose corrected her. 'And well you might ask. Tony knows, I suspect. Although I also suspect he won't allow himself to admit it.'

'How so?' Emma looked at McLean. 'Tony?'

'The cats are back.' He nodded his head to indicate the door and the garden beyond. 'I take it that means someone's out to get me.'

'Exactly so. Remember the last time?'

'How could I forget? It's not an easy thing to overlook, a couple of dozen stray cats taking up residence in your garden.'

'Oh, they're not strays, Tony. The whole city is their home. They are its protectors and its Night Watch. And they will keep you, Emma and your unborn child safe while you are within these walls.'

'Does this mean Mrs Saifre's back in town? Only the last time I saw her, she was busy dying in a helicopter crash.' McLean tried to keep the sarcasm out of his voice, but it wasn't easy when all he wanted to do was sleep.

'Mrs . . .?' Madame Rose cocked her head, flared her large nostrils as if sniffing out evil on the wind. 'No. Not her. Not now. There is something else. I felt it just this morning. Something dark and nameless.'

McLean went to take another drink from his mug, the tea a poor substitute for what he really wanted. At least it had washed the chemical taste from his mouth, which beer and whisky might not have done so effectively. A quick glance up at the clock above the door showed that it was still early by his normal work standards, although he'd been making an effort to come home at a sensible time ever since Emma had announced she was pregnant. Madame Rose noticed, a flicker of a smile ghosting across her face.

'I can see that you're still sceptical, but that is no matter.' She stood up with all the elegance of an arthritic elephant, creaks and groans that might have come from the table, the chair or herself. 'You will see, Tony. Things are starting to happen. Today's events are only the beginning.'

'Today's events?' McLean had stood up on reflex, and now his head spun a little, as if filled with helium. 'What do you know of today's events?'

'Only what I've seen on the news. Which is enough to know that you were at the scene for most of the day. I can smell it on you, too.' Madame Rose sniffed again, then stepped past McLean in the direction of the back door.

'Do you need a lift anywhere?' he asked, unsure whether

he should be driving at all. Madame Rose smiled, and patted him on the shoulder surprisingly gently.

'No, thank you, no. I'm going to drop in on the minister before I head home. I'll get Mary to phone me a taxi when we're done. Besides, you need rest, Tony. You were touched by death today. You must give it the respect it's due.'

He took the wrong turning at the top of the stairs again, heading to the bedroom for a change of clothes. His old bedroom. The room he had slept in all the days of his childhood when he wasn't at that hated boarding school. The transformation was in its early stages, but his bed was gone, the carpet pulled up. Emma had suggested they get the floorboards sanded and sealed, just have some rugs around the cot. Easier to clean the inevitable mess that way. All the furniture had been moved out, the ancient wallpaper stripped away to reveal even more ancient wallpaper beneath it. He stared for a while, taking everything in under the harsh glare of a light bulb stripped of its shade. Change coming, something in the air. Madame Rose's cryptic nonsense mixed in with the mess of images from the crash, his brain addled by too many chemical fumes.

'You OK?'

Emma stood right behind him, so close he should have been able to smell her were it not for the powerful odour rising off his jacket and trousers. She grabbed a handful of fabric and held it up to her nose.

'These really stink, Tony. What the hell have you been doing all day?'

'You saw the news, right? The truck crash?' McLean clicked off the light, struggled out of his jacket as Emma followed him across the landing towards the master bedroom. His gran's old room; it still felt strange sleeping in there.

'I had the day off today, remember? Spent most of it stripping that bloody wallpaper. Heard something about a crash, but I figured if it was important they'd have called me in. Or you'd have called to say you were going to be late. Then Rose turned up and we spent a couple of hours just chatting. He's a strange old bird.'

'She, Em.' McLean stripped off his trousers, holding them up to his nose for a sniff before recoiling from the stench that disturbing the fabric released. 'Think this suit might be better off binned.'

'Reckon you could be right. What the hell is that?' Emma took the trousers and jacket, carried them to the door and dumped them outside on the landing. The improvement in air quality was almost instant, but the smell still lingered in a faint, headache-threatening miasma around McLean's head.

'The truck that crashed was hauling a big tank of something seriously nasty. Still not really sure what it was, but it melted the tarmac and anyone unlucky enough to come into contact with it.'

'You were there?'

The question was so simple, and yet the answer eluded him. For a moment, McLean was back there in the mayhem, doing his best to help those he could.

'What happened, Tony? You've been acting all vague since you got in.'

43

'Sorry. I breathed in a bit too many fumes. Brain's a bit addled.'

'Why did you stay there? Surely the firemen would have dealt with it. They've got breathing apparatus.'

'There were twenty people killed, Em. Probably another fifty injured. The ambulances took for ever to get there, and they couldn't get enough paramedics in, so I helped with the triage. I don't know. Sounds stupid now, but it made sense at the time.' McLean rubbed at his face, his eyes gritty and dry, skin cracked as if he'd been out in the sun for days. He'd been doing a good job of blanking out the memories, but talking about the crash brought them all back. The blood and gore, broken bodies and shattered glass. The moans of the injured and the terrible silence of the dead. Twenty years and change of service had inured him to horror, or at least he had thought so until now. He looked up to see Emma staring at him, mouth slightly open, eyes wide as she processed what he had just told her. How she'd not been called in by the forensics service he had no idea.

'Rose was here for a couple of hours, you say?' he asked after a moment, a weak attempt at changing the subject. It seemed to work, giving Emma something else to focus on.

'Something like that. He must have turned up about five. You didn't get home till after seven.' Emma glanced at her watch. 'Not sure where the evening's gone, really. You want me to order a pizza?'

'Don't think I could eat anything, actually.' McLean slumped down on to the end of the bed, contemplated taking off his socks. The floor was so very far away, and he was all of a sudden so very weary. 'Think I might have a shower, try and wash off this stench and then get an early night. Briefing's at six tomorrow and I've a feeling it's going to be a busy day. I'd really like to face it without a splitting headache.'

'Here, let me.' Emma knelt down and gently eased off his socks, rolling them into a ball and throwing them towards the door. She sat down beside him, expert fingers undoing the buttons on his shirt. McLean still couldn't smell her over the reek of the crash, but her fingers were warm against his skin, her closeness reassuring. She stood up, hauling him to his feet beside her with exaggerated huffing and puffing. He let himself be manhandled, turned in the direction of the bathroom and its promise of soap and shower.

'I'll deal with the dirty laundry. You go. Get yourself clean.' Emma shoved him in the middle of the back. Not hard, but firm enough to propel him towards the door. 'And don't forget to use lots of shampoo. I'm not sleeping with someone who smells like they've fallen into an oil tank.'

McLean snapped awake with such force he was sitting upright before he realized he had moved. Breathing hard, heart hammering, the echoes of his nightmare scream faded into the not-quite-silence of the night-time house. Sweat prickled his back and shoulders, slicked his face and damped the sheets as reality slowly reasserted itself. Beside him, Emma snorted, rolled over and began to snore.

He slid quietly out of bed, padded across to the bathroom, making sure the door was closed before he clicked the light on. No need for both of them to have their sleep disturbed by the nightmare, even if dawn had already begun to light up the bedroom. Peering at himself in the mirror, he half expected to see his skin peeling off, blood oozing from sores, fires burning deep within his eyes, but the same old face stared back at him.

Cold water washed away the last of the dream and the sticky residue of sweat. Turning the light off, he went back to bed only to discover Emma had stolen the duvet. It didn't matter, the room was warm and the alarm told him it would be going off soon anyway. Hardly surprising his brain should deal with the horror of the previous day while he slept. Just a shame it couldn't have waited until it was nearer the time to get up.

8

I've been watching the news almost constantly since it happened. That's the wonderful thing about modern media. And its curse. Rolling twenty-four hours of people talking shite about stuff they don't understand. Anything to fill the void. Half the press is convinced this is a terrorist attack, even though nothing about it really fits. I can still see the old geezer in the cab as it hurtled towards us. He wasn't doing anything more suspicious than having a heart attack. Trying to avoid hitting people, not hit them.

They've named a few of the dead now. Not the driver yet, and not Maddy either. I've still got her scarf on, ends wrapped around my hands. It stinks, and the bits soaked in her blood have gone crusty now, but I'm not letting go. It's my only anchor to reality at the moment, my brain still working through the shock. I can't believe she's gone, right at the moment when I'd just found her again. Fifteen years since I last saw her. Fifteen years since I burned down that house.

It was a big old place, hidden away in rolling parkland surrounded by forest. I'm not supposed to know, but I've pieced enough together to work out that it was in north Essex, not far from a village called Great Hallingbury. It could have been anywhere the sun shined and the rain fell for all I knew at the time. I was never allowed outside, spent most of my time in a tiny room somewhere up in the eaves. I was fed, kept clean, given a few toys to play with and colouring books to scribble in. There were others there, too, mostly boys like me, but a few girls. We weren't allowed to play together, though, barely saw each other except in passing, led by a sour-face nurse along the plain corridors from bathroom to dining room to bedroom. A nod maybe, sometimes a word, though I didn't really speak much back then. Never had the chance to. Mostly it was boring but safe enough.

But every so often the men would come.

I'd know they were coming by the way the nurse fussed over me. Made sure I was bathed and clean. Fresh clothes, no food after lunch and only water to drink. Then some-time in the evening I'd be taken to one of the big bedrooms downstairs. On the good days, the best days, I'd just be asked to undress and stand there while the man did some-thing to himself. Those days were very rare.

I know what it is now that they made me do, and just thinking about it makes me angry. Angry at myself for let-ting it happen, even though I was only six years old so what the fuck else was I supposed to do? It always hurt, some times more than others. I learned early on not to cry if I could help it. Grin and bear it, soon enough it would be over. Usually the nurse would take me away after a while, bathe me, treat any injuries, put me to bed with a mug of hot milk that now I think about it was almost cer-tainly laced with something strong enough to knock me out for a while. Then there'd be a week or so of healing, trying to forget, sitting alone and sobbing. And then the whole thing would start all over again.

After a while they started taking two of us at a time. That's how I met Maddy.

I don't know why they liked us together, Maddy and me. Maybe it was because she looked so innocent, with her hair cropped short like a boy, her clothes ever so slightly ruffled. She had a way of biting her lip that might set a pulse racing if she was a bit older, but at six it wasn't really sexy at all. And yet week after week the men would have us both brought to them.

I didn't understand it then. If I'm being honest, I still don't understand it now. But I was grateful, in that pathetic way of beaten dogs given a scrap of food. Together, the experience was shared and somehow that made it worse but easier to bear, what they did to us, what they had us do to each other. And sometimes, all too seldom, whichever man it was whose lusts we had temporarily sated would fall asleep before the nurse came to fetch us. Before we could be separated and spirited away to our individual attic cells. I came to cherish those short moments, naked and shivering and hurt, when I could just cling to Maddy and she to me. We neither of us had much in the way of language, deprived of conversation in those formative years. But we had our ways, could speak well enough to make up tales of escape, promise that neither of us would ever leave without the other, cry and hug and wonder what we had done wrong to deserve this terrible, enduring punishment.

It was so much more than friendship that was forged in that terrible adversity. More than love, and certainly more than the sickening lusts that drove the men who abused us. Losing her now, after so long apart, feels like someone has cut me in half. Feels like I'm dead, too.

I need to get out of this room. I need to find that someone.

I need to make them pay.

9

'Are we discounting terrorist involvement in this one now, sir? Only the tabloids are all harping on about ISIS cells and everywhere being on heightened alert.'

Morning briefing, and McLean was glad that they had moved operations out of his new office and along the corridor to the major-incident room. It looked like every constable in the city had been drafted in and most of the sergeants, although what they were supposed to all do he wasn't sure. They'd barely started and already the inevitable questions were coming in.

'You should know better than to believe anything you read in the papers these days. Especially the ones with more pictures than words.'

A low ripple of laughter greeted his answer, and McLean allowed himself to relax a little. Morning briefings were never much fun, but at least this investigation had the look of being relatively straightforward. Horrific, yes, but straightforward.

'Forensics are still looking at the truck, but this doesn't bear the hallmarks of a terrorist operation. The truck wasn't stolen, and the driver doesn't fit the profile. His post-mortem's scheduled for later today, and that should shed a bit more light on the matter.' He paused a moment, looking out over a sea of expectant faces. Word had no doubt got out that the chief constable himself had green-lit a full investigation. Nothing like the prospect of unlimited overtime to motivate the workers. That and something a bit out of the ordinary, a change from the day-to-day tasks and repetitive run-ins with the less savoury aspects of Edinburgh society.

'Key tasks are to identify those victims we haven't already been able to name and inform their families. DI Ritchie will be heading up that side of things as soon as she gets here. We've reason to believe the truck was carrying a dangerous cargo without licence, and may have been inadequately maintained. I'll be looking into that myself. DS Laird will be co-ordinating interviews with all the members of the public we took details from at the scene. The hotline number's already out there and generating a lot of calls, but we'll have a team going over CCTV footage and combing social media, too. I want as much information about this crash as we can put together, as quickly as possible. I don't need to tell any of you that we're under public scrutiny with this one. People are worried and the press stirring things up doesn't help much. If you've any more questions, see DC Gregg or DS Laird. Now let's get on with the job, aye?'

McLean watched as the mass of uniforms began to dissolve away, individual officers seeking out the teams and tasks to which they'd been assigned. A few left swiftly, the chancers who'd thought they might get out of regular beat patrols. Or looking for an excuse to be late with their paperwork. Thinking about his own office and the innumerable extra forms this investigation would generate, he could only have sympathy for them.

'Reckon that went well enough. I wouldn't give you

much more than a week before the high heidyins start moaning about the cost, though.'

McLean looked round to see DCI Jayne McIntyre approaching. She must have come in late, as he'd not seen her before the briefing began.

'A week? I should be so lucky. Besides, I can't see this taking that long. Unless you know something I don't.'

'Well, there is one thing. Ritchie won't be back until late tomorrow. Someone else will have to get the ball rolling on those IDs.'

'Tomorrow? Any reason why?'

'If there was, nobody told me. Guess she's not finished whatever it was she was doing up there.'

McLean scratched at his chin, feeling the rasp of stubble where he'd missed a bit in his hurry to shave that morning. Despite his nightmare, he'd fallen asleep again and missed the first alarm completely. 'Doesn't really matter. Kirsty's never been much of a fan of the mortuary, so I'll probably be the one liaising with Angus and the team anyway.'

McIntyre cocked her head to one side like a quizzical sheepdog. 'Like you weren't going to be running the whole thing yourself anyway. Come on, Tony. I know how you operate.'

'Am I that predictable?' It wasn't a question McLean needed an answer to, but it reminded him that the PM on the driver was going to be taking place soon and he'd promised Angus he'd be there. He pulled out his phone, checked the time.

'Somewhere you need to be?' McIntyre asked with a mischievous smile. 'The city mortuary?'

'Aye, well. If Kirsty's still stuck up in the Highlands.'

McLean glanced around the room, happy to see his team under control. 'Guess I'd better go see what made our driver lose control of his truck.'

'OK, but don't be too long about it. You'll need to be back here for eleven.'

'Eleven? Why?' McLean saw the expression on McIntyre's face and had a suspicion he knew. Too much to hope they'd let him deal with the trauma of the truck crash on his own.

'Boss's orders, and by boss I mean the chief constable, not me, not Forrester, not even Teflon Steve. All officers at the scene yesterday have to report for an assessment with the station counsellor.'

McLean opened his mouth to complain, then closed it again. McIntyre was just the messenger for this particular piece of bad news. And a part of him had been expecting it anyway.

'Cheer up, Tony. You'll be fine.' The detective chief inspector slapped him gently on the arm. 'Not like you're having nightmares or anything, right?'

'You really know how to make an old man happy, don't you Tony.'

He should really have been chasing up the investigation into the hauliers and how the truck had come to be carrying illegal waste, but the city mortuary held a curious fascination for McLean. He'd visited it uncountable times in the course of his professional career, true, but it had also been his grandmother's workplace for years before that. Sometimes it felt like a second home, which didn't say much for his choice of friends.

'I mean, we've a busy schedule anyway, what with the staff cuts and everyone doubling up on shifts, but you just had to give us twenty fresh cadavers to examine. Just to keep us on our toes.'

Angus Cadwallader, city pathologist and perhaps the only one of those friends who wouldn't think twice about the amount of time he spent here, struggled into a set of green scrubs in preparation for the post-mortem on the truck driver. Bernard Wilkins lay on his back on the stainless-steel slab in the middle of the examination theatre just a few paces away, covered in a white latex sheet to preserve what was left of his modesty. Unlike some of the other victims of the crash, he hadn't been hard to identify, given that his fleece bore the same logo as that painted on the side of the truck. His wallet and driving licence had been inside the cab, too, even if he hadn't.

'Well, I guess we'd better get on with it. Sooner started, sooner finished.' Cadwallader winked and strode out into the theatre like an actor in search of ham. McLean followed him, somewhat reluctantly. While he was more at ease in this place than most, he still didn't like dwelling too much upon the frailty of the human form and the mortality of others. The mortality of Bernard Wilkins, truck driver, was all too obvious as Cadwallader's assistant, Dr Tracy Sharp, folded back the cover to reveal the battered, naked body.

'Subject is male, Caucasian . . .' A pause while the pathologist read some details off from a clipboard. '165 centimetres. That's, what? About five foot five in old money? Weight eighty-six kilograms, about thirteen and a half stone. Sixty-three years of age. Substantial subcutaneous fat deposits around the arms, legs and torso. I think it's fair to say he was a tad overweight, don't you?' Cadwallader continued his exterior examination, dictating notes to the microphone that hung over the table. McLean didn't need to listen, he could see well enough what had happened to the man. His face was a mess of cuts and abrasions where he had been thrown through the windscreen. As luck would have had it, away from the bus stop. He'd been found a few yards further up the street, the furthest dead body from the crash.

'I'm mostly interested in what killed him, Angus. Was it the impact or something else?'

'All in good time, Tony. All in good time.' Cadwallader leaned close to the dead man's head, peered first into one eye and then the next. McLean stood back, giving his old friend room and preparing himself for the bit when the scalpels and less subtle instruments of torture came out. It was hard to be dispassionate about this post-mortem – intentionally or accidentally, Bernard Wilkins had been responsible for the deaths of nineteen innocent people – but even so McLean had no great desire to see his innermost secrets. Viscera held far less fascination for him than they did the pathologist.

'Ah. Yes. That would explain it,' Cadwallader said after a few minutes of removing, inspecting and weighing organs. 'Poor chap probably had no idea what hit him.'

'Heart attack?' McLean had witnessed enough examinations to know whereabouts the pathologist's attention would be focused by this stage of the proceedings.

'If you insist on such an unscientific description, then yes. Massive and sudden. Bloody bad timing, too, but given the state of him it could have happened anywhere.' Cadwallader held up the dead man's heart for McLean to see, then seemed to remember who he was showing it to and instead passed it to Dr Sharp for weighing.

'So we can rule out terrorist activity, then. This really was nothing but a tragic accident.'

Cadwallader paused a while before answering. With his green scrubs spattered in Bernard Wilkins's blood, arms caked in gore and thinning hair sticking out at odd, unkempt angles, he looked like nothing so much as a latter day Dr Frankenstein.

'Tragic, yes. Accident? Well, I've another nineteen examinations to do, all of which are going to take a lot longer than this fellow. Some of them were brought to the mortuary in buckets, Tony. You tell me if that sounds like an accident.'

10

'Come in, sit down. I won't be a moment.'

Doctor Megan Black, as the plate on her office door had named her, waved McLean in the direction of a pair of empty chairs at the far side of the room. She held a mobile phone to her ear and was sitting behind a desk almost as cluttered as his own. He hadn't met the new station counsellor before, wasn't even sure how long she had been working there. It was a given in the job that you would have to deal with traumatic experiences, some more harrowing than others. He generally managed to compartmentalize the horror quite well, but it made sense to have trained professionals on hand to help those who found sometimes they couldn't cope.

'Sorry about that.' The therapist dropped her phone on to a pile of folders and climbed out from behind the desk. 'You'd be Detective Inspector Tony McLean.' She held out a hand to be shaken. 'Megan Black.'

'Tony,' he said, ever so slightly unsettled by the intensity of her gaze. She was much the same age as him, he guessed, her shoulder-length light-brown hair beginning to show a few streaks of grey, and there was something ever so slightly familiar about her face. 'You didn't study psychology at the university here, did you?'

Doctor Black smiled, crow's feet crinkling around her

eyes. 'Good memory for faces, I see. I was the year above you. Surprised you remember.'

'The name didn't ring any bells.'

'Black's my husband's surname. I was Megan Christie back then.'

McLean tried the name for size, found it still didn't fit. 'Sorry. Still nothing. Just the face. I'd say you haven't changed much, but we all change, aye?'

Something flitted across her eyes for a moment, perhaps a witty retort suppressed. Down to business. 'Why don't we have a seat.' Doctor Black pointed to the two chairs again and McLean took one.

'So, Detect—, . . . Tony. You were at the scene of yesterday's terrible accident.'

'Yes, I was there when it happened. Not the best way to start the day.'

An arched eyebrow, but no other comment. 'I imagine it must have been very traumatic.'

'At the time I was too busy dealing with it, to be honest. I usually find that's the case.'

'Usually? Have you had many such experiences?'

'I've been a serving police officer for over twenty years. What do you think?'

This time the eyebrow arched a little higher, Doctor Black shuffling herself more upright in her seat. 'And have you had any reaction since? Any unaccountable anxiety? Perhaps bad dreams or difficulty sleeping?'

McLean caught himself before he could check his watch. It was a reflex action, he knew, but not one that a therapist needed to see. 'It's maybe a bit early for that, isn't it? I had a bit of a nightmare last night, but I was kind of expecting to. Probably be more worried if I'd not had one, really.'

'Your subconscious mind processing the trauma while you sleep. Yes, that can be a good form of catharsis. But it can also be a warning sign.'

'I'm fine, really. I doubt very much I'll have any trouble sleeping tonight. Especially if I can get on with finding out how this happened in the first place.'

Doctor Black leaned back in her chair, and that was when McLean noticed that she wasn't taking any notes. Nor did she have a folder full of his darkest secrets to bring up for discussion, or even just as a prop.

'Why did you come to see me if you're so sure you've got it all under control?' she asked after a few silent seconds.

'Because DCI McIntyre and Chief Superintendent Forrester both said I should. It's a box-ticking exercise for them. Just in case I go off the rails later, isn't it?'

Again the arched eyebrow and straightened back. McLean didn't want to wind the therapist up, but there were times when other people looking out for his mental health wore him down. He knew how to deal with the trauma he had witnessed the day before, and it didn't involve sitting in uncomfortable chairs and talking about his feelings.

'And if the box-ticking involves you taking a couple of weeks of medical leave?'

He almost laughed, except that Doctor Black's face suggested she was entirely serious. McLean's initial response was going to be to point out how short-staffed they were, but his brain overtook his mouth, spotting the trap well before he could fall into it.

'I rather think I'd need to be showing more clinical signs of PTSD than one bad dream, don't you?'

The therapist nodded her head once in agreement. 'True enough. And sometimes keeping busy is the best way to help the mind come to terms with what it's experienced. But there's a fine line between busy and overworked, wouldn't you say?'

'And overwork can exacerbate the problem. I know. And I'm fine. Honest.' McLean tried a smile. You never knew, it might work.

'I'll need to see you again. Not more than a week's time. That OK?'

The swiftness of the dismissal took him by surprise. 'I . . . Yes. Of course.' McLean stood up. 'Thank you.'

'My pleasure.' Doctor Black followed him to the door, opened it. 'Just remember I'm here to help, though. Any more bad dreams, come see me, OK?'

'We didn't have anywhere big enough to store this out of the weather. That and the stink was putting everyone off their sarnies.'

McLean stood just outside the entrance to a large lock-up shed in a nondescript industrial estate on the western fringes of the city. Inside, the crashed truck lay on a flatbed trailer surrounded by high-power arc lights. It had been emptied of its noxious cargo, but the smell was still overpowering. Two large extractor fans rumbled away in the background in a vain attempt to make things better.

'Not had time to do a thorough inspection yet. It's fairly

obvious this was an accident rather than a deliberate act, though. Here. Put this on and I'll show you.' Amanda Parsons – Manda, McLean corrected himself – handed him a full-face breathing mask, then pulled one over her head. She took a moment to adjust the straps where they had snagged her hair and he noticed for the first time that she had grown it longer than her normal boyish crop.

'Is this really necessary?' He hefted the mask, wondering who had worn it last.

'Depends on how many brain cells you want to have at the end of the day.' Parsons's voice sounded muffled behind the mask. She had a heavy-duty set of mechanic's overalls on, a logo McLean didn't recognize stitched into the breast pocket. As it was at least two sizes too big for her slim frame, she'd hitched it in with a wide belt and rolled up the trousers like a navvy. Perhaps not the most flattering of looks, but somehow she managed to pull it off.

Still unsure about the mask, McLean followed her into the workshop. The smell grew stronger still, watering his eyes far more than it had back at the crash scene. The headache that had haunted his dreams the night before threatened to come back with a vengeance.

'Told youse.' Parsons's eyes flashed a mischievous grin at him as McLean struggled to fit his own mask. 'Here, let me help you with that.' She stepped up close, dextrous fingers adjusting the straps around the back of his head. The difference was immediate, although he could still feel the prick of fumes around his eyes. With a sigh, he realized that his suit was going to stink by the time they were done.

'You found out what this stuff is yet?' McLean nodded at the side of the tanker when they reached it. A long rip along one side revealed its shiny stainless-steel interior under the harsh arc light.

'It's horrible, that's what it is. Best guess is a mixture of all manner of industrial solvents, acids and toxic waste. The labs are analysing it right now but where it came from is anyone's guess. A lot of different places, I reckon. Lucky it didn't explode.'

'Not digestate from an anaerobic digester, then.'

'No. And not something you'd want to spread on your fields. Well, not unless you didn't want anything growing there for, oh, a hundred years or so. There is some digestate in there, though.'

'There is?'

'Aye.' Parsons pointed to the top of the tanker, where several metal domes lined it like a spine. 'See there's half a dozen compartments, all filled and emptied separately. The ones at each end had the real shit in them, it was only the middle four that were filled with that toxic gunk.'

McLean filed away the information as he walked around to the cab and looked up at the open door. Another masked and overalled forensic technician sat behind the steering wheel, painstakingly swabbing at the dashboard. A third peered in from the other side, using a powerful pen torch to look under the seats.

'Any idea why it crashed?'

'Early days, Tony. We've only just got it in here and siphoned off the last of that gunk it was carrying.' Parsons took a step closer to the cab and pointed towards the accelerator and brake pedals. No clutch, so an automatic. 'If I had to hazard a guess, I'd say the throttle jammed open. Might've been something with the gearbox. There's a lot of stuff online about problems with this model kicking down without warning.'

'Kicking down?'

'Dropping a couple of gears at a time. Usually happens when you floor the throttle to get away at a junction or overtake something. It can be a bit –'

'Got a moment, Manda?' Parsons was interrupted mid-flow by one of the other technicians. A frown furrowed her forehead as she answered.

'What's up?'

'Think this might be what the problem was. Should have seen it before, but with all that stuff out of the tank we must've missed it.' The technician led them both around to the other side of the truck, pointing up to the cables and lines that ran from the back of the cab to the tanker trailer behind. McLean was no expert on these things, but even he could see that they were in a parlous state.

'Worst of this happened in the crash, of course. There's a bit of play in these pipes, but they're not really designed for the truck jack-knifing and the whole thing rolling on to its side.' The technician hauled himself up into the gap, heavy work boots slipping slightly on the gunk that covered everything. McLean stepped back, all too aware that he wasn't really dressed for this.

'There's two air lines here. For the brakes. Main and auxiliary backup just in case. Main's popped out of its junction. Not connected properly when they put the trailer on the cab. Any driver worth his salt should've checked that before setting off.'

'And you're sure that didn't happen in the crash?' Parsons asked.

'Sure as can be. If it had been pulled out by brute force it would have given here.' The technician pointed a heavy-gloved finger at the junction. 'It's popped out here instead.'

McLean couldn't be sure he could see any difference, but he was prepared to defer to the experts. That was what they were here for, after all. 'What about the auxiliary?'

'Still connected.' The technician reached up and jiggled another one of the coiled pipes. 'But there's a wee hole here, so it's about as much use as a chocolate fireguard.'

'So what you're saying is this truck had no brakes and possibly a dodgy gearbox that would make it accelerate out of control.'

'Aye, that's about the size of it.' The technician clambered down carefully to the garage floor. 'Thing's a bloody death trap.'

McLean stared at the truck without really seeing it, his mind going over uncomfortable possibilities. 'Could this have been done deliberately?'

'Tampered with? Why would someone . . . ?' He shook his head, then clambered up to inspect the brake lines a bit more closely. McLean watched him for a moment, then took a few steps back to get closer to the open door and the slightly fresher air blowing in through it. He'd only taken a few welcome gulps before the technician's voice called him back.

'Fuck me sideways till Tuesday. That's a bastard thing to do.'

'What is it, Tom?' Manda Parsons asked. She and McLean both inched closer as the technician held up the disconnected main brake line, running a thumb around the edge.

'Could be bad maintenance, but this looks like it's been tampered with. That's why it didn't connect properly even though it might have looked OK. Secondary line probably worked a while before that hole blew out and took the brakes with it.'

'So it was sabotage, then?' McLean asked, hoping that the answer would be no even as he knew life was rarely that easy.

'Can't be a hundred per cent. Not with all the damage done in the crash. But it sure looks that way.'

11

McLean expected the chief superintendent to be in his office, but instead found him in the major-incident room. To an unskilled observer it might have looked like he was directing operations, but mostly he was getting in the way and pestering junior officers for information. When McLean interrupted him, he was berating a terrified young constable for not having a complete list of the names of all the victims yet. His mood didn't improve when he heard the news about the truck.

'I should have listened to what they told me when I took this job.'

'What was that?' McLean asked, knowing full well the answer.

'That anything you're involved in gets complicated and messy fast.' Forrester pinched the bridge of his nose and squeezed his eyes shut for a moment. 'You really think someone sabotaged that truck? They meant for it to crash into that bus stop?'

'Someone tampered with the brakes, yes. But I don't think it was meant to crash into that bus stop.'

'How no?' Forrester's confusion made him look a bit like a startled ferret.

'If the pressure fails on an air brake system, it locks on, sir. Not off. Whoever tampered with the brakes must have known that. There should have been warning lights flashing all over the dashboard, too.'

'Unless whoever fucked around with the brake lines disconnected the warning lights, too.'

'They still couldn't have known when the brakes would have gone, or where the truck would have been when that happened. And the driver had a massive heart attack. Sure, finding your truck's brakes don't work might set that off, but, again, it's impossible to predict where and when. It's not as if they knew he had a dicky ticker.'

Forrester frowned. 'Hate to admit it, but you've got a point. Bloody thing shouldn't even have been driving through the centre of town.' He gestured in the direction of a large map on the wall, and McLean saw three points clearly marked. He walked over for a closer look.

'Hauliers are based in Broxburn. The stuff that was meant to be in the trailer came from a site near Livingston.' Forrester tapped a thin finger against the paper, the fingernail chewed almost to the quick. 'It was supposed to be going here, near East Fortune.' He ran the finger across the map to the location, even though McLean knew well enough where all three places were.

'Should have gone round the bypass,' he said. 'Unless he was using one of those traffic-monitoring satnav units. Do we know if there were any other accidents on the route yesterday?'

'Big pile-up at the Loanhead junction. That's why it took so long for the emergency services to get to the Lothian Road.'

'So unless whoever's behind this is incredibly devious, we're looking at a series of unrelated incidents adding up to the worst traffic accident since . . .' McLean shook his head, partly because he couldn't think of a worse one, and partly because the coincidences piled too uncomfortably upon each other.

'You need to speak to the hauliers. Someone there knew the cargo was illicit, and someone knew the truck had been tampered with. We need to find out who and charge them.'

Something about the look on Forrester's face, the anger in his tone, struck McLean as odd. It was almost personal, as if the crash was his fault until it could be pinned on someone else.

'Health and Safety are going to audit the haulage yard this afternoon.' He checked his watch, surprised at how much of the day had already gone. 'I'll be interviewing the boss at the same time. We'll keep at them until we've got answers.' McLean stared at the map, not really taking any-thing in. 'Still don't get why someone would tamper with the brakes like that. What were they hoping to achieve?'

Forrester nodded towards the opposite wall, where photographs of the dead were being pinned up in rows, awaiting identification or notification of next of kin. 'Not that, I hope.'

'What do we know about this haulage company? Finlay McGregor? Isn't that it?'

Heading out of the city towards the bypass and then Broxburn beyond, McLean had the first chance since his new car had been delivered to open the throttle a bit. He couldn't help but notice Detective Constable Harrison clutching the door handle every time they went around a corner a little faster than was perhaps sensible. She kept the fear out of her voice, though.

'That's them, aye. Not much to say except that it's an established firm. Third generation of the Finlay family running it now, I'm told. No one remembers McGregor.'

'Maybe there never was one. Wouldn't be the first company to add a name just to make themselves sound more legitimate. Do we know anything about the current boss?'

'Mike Finlay?' DC Harrison pulled out her notebook and flipped the pages. 'Had a chat with my uncle about him first thing this morning. Word is old man Finlay, Mike's dad, was honest as the day, reliable. Paid his bills on time. Died about five years back and the church was packed at his funeral. He was a pillar of the community. Folk liked him.'

'I take it they don't feel the same way about his son, then?'

'Uncle Jim, well. He doesn't like to speak ill of people, sir. You know, if you can't think of something good to say about someone, don't say anything? That's kind of how he's always been. He was very quiet about Mike Finlay.'

McLean said nothing, concentrating on the driving for a while. He knew Harrison's uncle was in the motor trade; the man had delivered the Alfa in person. He operated out of an industrial estate in Broxburn, and Finlay McGregor Hauliers and Logistics, as their somewhat amateur-looking website had put it, were based on the neighbouring estate, so it was hardly surprising the company, and its owner, would be well enough known in the area. The compound had been sealed tight pending an investigation by the Health and Safety Executive. It made sense to co-ordinate with them and interview the boss at the same time, hence the afternoon drive out into the countryside. That and it was an excuse to get out of the station for a while.

As they neared their destination, the massive shale bings rose up out of the flat land to greet them, James Young's most enduring legacy. McLean had seen the great slag heaps of spoil left over from the shale mining and paraffin refining many times from afar, but it was only when you got close that you felt the scale of them and understood the sheer human effort that had gone into their formation. The route took them ever closer, first through the tarmac streets of the town and then into the grimy tracks of a decaying industrial landscape. His car was far too new and shiny, splashing through muddy pot-holes as he drove along the rutted lane towards the compound gates. They stood closed, a heavy chain and padlock denying entry to all. A squad car blocked the entrance just to make sure no one could get in, and as he pulled up to it, the two occupants climbed out.

'Heard you'd got a new car, sir. She's a beauty isn't she.' Sergeant Gatford was a bit far from his usual beat, but a welcome sight anyway. If he'd been in charge of securing the compound then McLean could be confident no one had been in since he'd arrived.

'Just getting used to her, Don. A fair bit more power than the old one.' He looked around the empty lane, peter-ing out a few tens of yards away where it opened on to scrubland and a handful of derelict buildings, the last rem-nants of Young and Company's paraffin works.

'Aye, that'd be why you're here early.' The sergeant glanced at his watch. 'Health and Safety team are on their way. Mike Finlay, too. That might even be him the now.'

McLean looked the way the sergeant pointed, back down the lane, to see a shiny new Range Rover weaving from side to side as if the potholes might swallow it whole. As it came closer he noticed that its number plate sort of spelled out the name M FINLAY, but only by breaking the law on how the numbers and letters were meant to be spaced. A white transit van and a couple more cars following along behind meant that there'd be no getting back out unless the gate to the compound was opened first.

'Mr Finlay?' McLean asked as the tinted side window of the Range Rover purred downwards. The driver was a young man with thinning black hair pasted to his scalp. It could have been some expensive product, but might just as easily have been sweat.

'Aye. You'll be the polis, then.' It wasn't a question. 'Got the Health and Safety boys behind me, ken.' He jerked a thumb over his shoulder to the van. Sergeant Gatford had already gone to speak to the driver, his uniform colleague busy with the padlock and chain on the compound gates.

'Head straight to the office,' McLean said. 'I'll follow you. Let the experts give the place a once over while we have a wee chat.'

Finlay squinted as if thinking was something he had to concentrate on. 'You no' need a warrant for that?'

'I do,' McLean said, then nodded at the team already clambering out of the van and cars behind. 'They don't.' He tucked a hand into his jacket pocket and pulled out the slip of paper he'd been careful to collect before leaving the station. 'But, if it makes you feel better, I've got one anyway.'

Mike Finlay might have dressed like a hedge-fund manager, driven a car that cost six figures and spoken with a clipped, almost Morningside accent, but McLean could see through the disguise easily enough. His voice had an underlying tone that suggested he'd been faking it for a while, and the suit wasn't nearly as impressive up close. He smelled too overpoweringly of scented soap to be taken seriously either, but he had a firm handshake and didn't try to avoid looking you in the eye.

They had followed his Range Rover across the deserted compound to a set of grey portable cabins that made up the company offices. Finlay had let himself in with a key, glanced briefly around the empty room as if the lack of activity pained him, then led McLean and Harrison through into an office at the back of the cluster, taking up an entire cabin. He'd insisted on making coffee from an expensive-looking machine before settling down to business. It had all been quite professional until he dropped into the chair behind his desk with a whoopee cushion noise that was perhaps not the impression he'd been trying to make. McLean could see Harrison trying to hide her smirk behind her mug.

'First off, can I say that I'm as horrified as anyone about what's happened and I'll do whatever's necessary to help you with your investigation, Inspector.'

'I'm glad to hear it, Mr Finlay. You'll understand that this is a very serious matter, though. One of your trucks has been involved in the deaths of twenty people.'

'Now come on, Inspector. This is a tragic accident, horrific even, but it's an accident. You can't think that I have anything to do –'

'That's for the HSE inspectors to decide, at least in the first instance, Mr Finlay. I'm just here to get a picture of how you run things. The chain of events that led up to yesterday.'

Finlay slumped back in his seat. 'Should I have a lawyer present?'

'Up to you.' McLean shrugged. 'You've not been arrested, not been charged with anything. You could refuse to answer any of my questions if you wanted to. Or we could get this cleared up quickly and I can get back to the task of identifying the dead and informing their relatives.'

A long silence stretched between them, and for a moment McLean thought Finlay might actually call his lawyer. He picked up his mobile phone from the desk, looked at it for a while without switching it on. Perhaps it would have been better hauling him into the station and making him sweat in an interview room for a while. Given the circumstances, they would have been well within their rights.

'What do you need to know?' Finlay put the phone back down again, the smile on his face about as sincere as a politician on the campaign trail.

'The truck that crashed,' McLean asked. 'You keep it well maintained?'

'We keep all our trucks maintained to the highest order, Inspector.' Finlay straightened up in his chair, and had his hair not been so stiffly gelled, McLean was sure his hackles would have risen, too.

'What about the driver? His medical certificate up to date? He was quite old to be hauling dangerous goods, wouldn't you say?'

Finlay stiffened a little more, the insult getting under his skin. And then something like relief spread across his face. Had he been a toddler, McLean might have thought he'd just filled his nappy.

'Two things, Inspector.' Finlay leaned forward, elbows on the desk as he counted on his fingers. 'First, the cargo wasn't dangerous. Least, not according to the manifest signed by the company we were hauling it for. Second, I'd always give the more important jobs to my best drivers, and Bernie was one of the best. Used to drive for my dad. Reckon he's been here longer than I have. Getting close to retirement, but he had his medical just a couple of months ago. I've got it all on file.'

'Did he often drive that route? That truck?'

'Well, there's the thing, see. Bernie wasn't meant to be driving that truck at all, Inspector. Wasn't even meant to be working yesterday.'

'He wasn't? So who was?'

'Wee Hamish Tafferty was on that route, but he was meant to be driving another rig. He made the collection. Came from that new power plant over by Livingston. Should have gone straight from there to East Fortune, but he wasn't feeling well so he brought it back here. Idiot managed to break a headlight parking up. We're still waiting on a replacement. Swapped the trailer over to the old truck, but by then it was too late to make the delivery so we left it parked up in the compound. He should have been back yesterday morning to finish the job, but he

75

called in sick. Probably didn't fancy going all the way to East Fortune in that old thing. The old trucks aren't so much fun once you've driven something new.'

'So you got Mr Wilkins to do the job instead.'

'Aye. Bernie's old school. Was old school, I guess.' Finlay shrugged as if the death of one of his employees was an inconvenience more than a tragedy. 'He was fine with the old trucks. Didn't mind the extra work either.'

'Have you spoken to the driver who made the initial pickup?'

'Hamish? Aye, I have. He's still at home with that noro thing. His wife says he's not been ten feet from the cludgie in the past forty-eight hours.'

'I'll need his contact details anyway.'

'Of course.' Finlay picked up his phone again, tapped it on this time and navigated to the relevant page before handing it over to DC Harrison to note down the name and address. McLean waited until she had finished before continuing with the interview. 'The truck. You said it was carrying digestate. That's what all the documentation said, too. Any idea how it came to be transporting something so toxic it could melt through skin and bone, turn the tarmac into a sticky mass?'

Finlay shrugged and bobbed his head apologetically. 'It's like I said, Inspector, the whole thing's a mystery.'

'The truck was parked up all night? Here, in the compound?'

'It was, aye.'

'You have CCTV?'

'Of course. We contract that out, but I can get the tapes pulled for you.'

'You do that. And while you're at it, I'll need the names and addresses of everyone who works for you, everyone who has access to this compound. I'll need the details of the contract to transport the digestate, too. Where it came from, where it was going.'

With each new demand, Finlay's face fell a notch further. No doubt he had thought this was a minor inconvenience that would soon go away, a slight embarrassment to his company that people would soon forget. The stench of burning chemicals and the image of broken people fresh in his mind, McLean wasn't in any mood to comply.

'I'll . . . Of course . . . My secretary. I told her not to come in today. Like everyone else.'

'Well, why don't you get on the phone and call her.' McLean looked past Finlay, out of the window to the yard beyond where Health and Safety inspectors were clambering over trucks and poking their noses into everything. 'Reckon we're going to be here a while.'

12

Hamish Tafferty lived in a grubby little ex-council semi on the edge of Broxburn, surrounded by streets of identical grubby little ex-council semis, each with its own variation on a theme of unkempt front garden. Some had been paved over, cars and bikes in various stages of being dismantled and leaving oil stains on the concrete paving. More cars lined the narrow streets, but none of them looked like they'd been anywhere recently. McLean was all too aware as he pulled to a halt outside that his shiny new Alfa Romeo looked as out of place as a Catholic priest at a gathering of the Wee Frees.

'You want me to go and talk to him while you stay with the car, sir?' Harrison asked. 'Or, you know, I could just sit here and make sure nobody tries to key your paint while you go and talk to him.'

McLean undid his seatbelt, opened the door. The afternoon sun beat down on an empty street, and while nearby curtains might have twitched, he doubted anyone would stir beyond their front rooms.

'Not scared of a little norovirus are you, Constable?' he said.

'I'm guessing you've never had it, sir.' Harrison's expression was deadly serious as she, too, climbed out of the car. 'Believe me. Not knowing whether to sit on the toilet or kneel in front of it isn't a fun way to spend a few days.'

McLean bit back a flippant response, and the two of them walked the short distance to the front door. There was no doorbell, so he knocked hard. A moment's silence and then the ominous sound of a toilet flushing.

'Would it be considered impolite if I put on some gloves, sir?' Harrison pulled a pair out of her pocket, then shoved them back again as the door swung inwards. A young woman glowered at them through narrow eyes.

'Whut youse want, aye?' She looked the two of them up and down with an expression of utter contempt.

'Mrs Tafferty?' McLean asked.

'Fuck no. I'd never marry that wee bastard even if he had the balls to ask.'

'Detective Inspector McLean. Police Scotland.' He held up his warrant card. 'Is Mr Tafferty in?'

The toilet flushed again, louder now the door was open. The young woman grimaced at the sound. 'Aye he's in. No' goin' anywhere soon either. Been shitting and puking like a baby near enough two days now. I'm fair sick of it.'

'Who is it, doll?' A gruff voice echoed down the narrow hall behind the young woman, followed by a shuffling sound as a man approached. Hamish Tafferty was dressed in a tartan dressing gown, someone else's fluffy slippers on his feet. Two days of stubble roughed his thin face and his hair looked like it hadn't seen a brush recently.

'Polis.' The young woman managed to squeeze a lifetime of disdain into the two short syllables.

'Aye? What youse want, then?' Tafferty shuffled to the open door, the young woman shrinking away from him. McLean tried not to wrinkle his nose at the smell.

'You drive a truck for Finlay McGregor. Had a tanker cargo couple of days ago, that right?'

'Aye. Big new power plant over Livingston way. Dunno how it works, but they've tonnes of shit needs carting to and from the site.' Tafferty lifted a hand to his mouth, belched, swallowed hard. 'What of it?'

'You took a tankerload back to the yard. Day before yesterday. That when this started up?' McLean waved a hand towards the truck driver to indicate his illness.

'Last time I do my wee brother a favour, aye. Picked up his kid from school the day before. Those places should come wi' a health warning.' Tafferty belched again, his face turning paler.

'Sorry to hear it. Just one more question, if you can?'

Tafferty nodded, mouth closed tight as he swallowed again.

'The tanker. You signed off the manifest for its contents, right? Did you watch it being filled?'

Tafferty paused a moment before answering, although whether that was because he was thinking or just trying not to be sick, McLean couldn't tell.

'Aye,' he said eventually. 'Well, no' all of it. Takes a whiley to fill up one a' them tankers y'ken. Big rig like the one I was on can take thirty thousand litres if you fill all the compartments. That place they usually do. Saves money in the long run.'

'So you saw them put at least some digestate in?' McLean asked.

'Aye, digestate. That's the word. Shit.' Tafferty's stomach made an ominous noise and he clutched at his dressing gown. 'Shit.'

He turned and hobbled at speed down the narrow corridor, flung open a door at the end and disappeared inside. McLean winced at the sounds that came afterwards. He reached into his pocket and pulled out one of his business cards, handed it to the young woman.

'Give him that when he's a bit better, aye? We'll need to speak to him again soon. Get a formal statement.'

The young woman took the card. 'Formal statement? What the fuck's he done?' She looked back down the corridor to the closed toilet door.

'You heard about the truck crash in town yesterday, I take it?'

'Aye, it was on the news. Horrible. Why the fuck would they take something like that through a built-up area?'

'You tell me.' McLean pointed back into the house. 'All I know is that it was the same tanker Hamish there was meant to be driving the day before.'

'Poor sod's not going anywhere soon. I can see why he didn't want to drive a truck full of shit over to East Lothian, though.'

McLean stared out at the line of slow-moving traffic heading towards the airport and the city bypass. Once more the reality of Edinburgh's roads made mockery of the absurdly overpowered engine in his shiny new car. At least it didn't have a tendency to overheat like his old Alfa, and the air conditioning made the interior a pleasant enough place to be.

'You're right, by the way.' He glanced sideways at DC Harrison sitting in the passenger seat. 'Never had norovirus, and after that little encounter I hope I never do.'

'It's no' much fun, I can tell you that, sir. We still need a full statement from him, though.'

'It can wait a few days, I reckon. I doubt he was in much of a state to lie to us back there, and it didn't sound like he was trying to hide anything. Chances are he really didn't know what was in that tanker, and we know from Manda's team that there was digestate in some of the compartments.'

'What do you think, then? This is clearly some kind of scam, but the driver didn't know?' Harrison shook her head slightly as she spoke. 'If he didn't, then someone at the hauliers did. And what about the brakes being tampered with? I notice you've not mentioned that to anyone yet.'

'I want to see what the Health and Safety team come up with first. Let them have a look at the other trucks. It might be that wasn't the only one.' McLean flicked down a gear, blipped the throttle and felt his head pushed back against the rest as the car surged forward into a gap that had opened up in the traffic. 'To be honest, I'm still trying to get my head around that, but I'm not sure it's the story we need to be following right now.'

'How no?'

'Think about it, Constable. Sure, someone made that truck crash, and we need to find who it was and send them to prison for a very long time. But there's another crime going on here, too.'

'The toxic waste?'

'Exactly so. I'd give good money Finlay knows all about it. I'd bring him in and sweat it out of him but I don't think he's working on his own. And proving anything's going to be hard if we can't find where that solvent came from.'

'That where we're going next?' Harrison nodded in their direction of travel, and McLean noticed he was in the wrong lane approaching the roundabout to go straight over and on into the city. Given the mayhem still ongoing from one half of the Lothian Road being closed, it probably made sense to head south around the bypass and in from the other side anyway. Or they could just avoid Edinburgh, the station and the major-incident room for a while longer.

'Makes sense. You got the address there?'

Harrison pulled out her notebook and flipped through the pages. 'Place called Easter Balgenzie. Just outside Livingston.'

'Thought it was something like that.' McLean swept round the roundabout in an improbable sequence of green traffic lights, then accelerated on to the motorway. Away from the backed-up traffic, he could let the engine sing a little, feel himself pushed back into his seat once more. 'Shove the postcode in the satnav, won't you? Think we might pay them a visit.'

McLean didn't know much about the technology of anaerobic digestion; something to do with taking food waste and other organic rubbish, fermenting it down and extracting the methane gas to generate electricity. All very laudable, and he'd expected to find a ramshackle site manned by yoghurt knitters with expansive beards and too-tight trousers. Extech Energy turned out to be something else entirely.

A ten-foot mesh fence topped with razor wire surrounded the site, security cameras strategically placed to make breaking in unseen all but impossible. The security guard at the gate stared long and hard at his and DC Harrison's warrant cards before calling up the office, and only guided them through to the visitors' parking area after confirmation had been given. McLean drove slowly past a dozen gleaming stainless-steel tanks. Squat and round, they wouldn't have looked out of place in an oil refinery or chemical plant. Neat pipework ran between the tanks, everything surrounded by close-cropped grass or freshly laid tarmac.

'Lot of money gone into setting this up,' Harrison said, ever the master of understatement as they parked in front of a sleek, low building, all glass walls and expensive architectural flourishes.

'Where there's muck there's brass,' McLean added, although judging by the look on the detective constable's face he couldn't be sure she'd understood his unconvincing Yorkshire accent.

A young woman in an elegant trouser suit and tiny frameless spectacles greeted them as they entered the building.

'Detective Inspector, Constable. Claire Ferris. Welcome to Extech Energy.' She held out a hand more to be gently squeezed than shaken, smiling with her lips even though her eyes spoke more of anxiety.

'Thank you for agreeing to see us at such short notice, Ms Ferris.' McLean indicated the minimalist yet expensively furnished reception area. 'Nice place you've got here.'

'Thank you. We only finished this building a couple of months ago. Before that we were in an old shed at the back of the site. It's something of a relief to be somewhere that isn't constantly draughty.' Ms Ferris paused a moment before adding. 'Might I ask what this is all about?'

Another smartly dressed young woman sat behind a reception desk a few paces away. She had glanced at them and smiled as they entered, but otherwise had said nothing. McLean considered asking if there was somewhere private they could speak, then realized it didn't really matter.

'Yesterday's crash in the city centre. You'll have seen the news, I take it?'

Ms Ferris paled, lifted a hand up to her neck instinctively. 'Horrible. Yes. All those poor people.'

'Were you aware that the truck belonged to Finlay McGregor Hauliers? I understand they do work for you.'

'We use a lot of different hauliers, Inspector. If you say Finlay McGregor are one of them, then I have no reason not to believe you. But I heard the tanker involved was transporting some kind of industrial solvent. We produce only inert digestate here. It gets put back on the land to improve the soil. The most toxic waste on site is slurry from the local dairy farms, but that comes on to the site. It doesn't leave like that.'

'That is indeed how I understood it. I'm sure there's nothing irregular going on here, but the manifest on the tanker truck that crashed yesterday said it was carrying digestate from this site.'

'You can't think –'

'I don't know what to think, Ms Ferris. That's why I'm here. I take it you'll have records of all movements on- and offsite? CCTV footage too?'

The anxiety was back in the young woman's eyes, but now it was matched by a worried frown, her lips pursed as she considered the implications of what she had heard.

'Of course, Inspector. Everything is tracked and traced.' She looked past him to the receptionist, who made no attempt to pretend she hadn't been listening in to the conversation the whole time. 'Zoe, can you pull up all the records for the inspector, please? And give Jim in security a call. We'll need to collate all the footage from the cameras at the loading bays.' She turned back to McLean 'Will that be sufficient?'

13

An excited buzz of conversation filled the major-incident room as McLean stepped in through the open door, DC Harrison close behind. Over on the far side, a row of uniform officers sat at workstations, taking notes as the calls from concerned members of the public flooded in. Judging by the chatter, the hotline must have been almost overrun. He'd have to see about getting in some more resources, if DS Gregg hadn't done so already.

He spotted her at the back of the room, reaching up to write in a neat hand on the whiteboards. Walking over, he made out some of the names of the victims, a brief summary of their lives. John Sullivan had been a teacher nearby, Eleanor Danton, a film director. McLean suspected there was more to Riuchi Takamora than simply tourist, but that was all he would be remembered as here. Not much of an epitaph. Rachel Sprake, Andy Spong and Fiona Mclellan didn't even have that, just a tick in red that he assumed meant their next of kin had been given the bad news. Other names had no tick, some had question marks and a few lines remained empty, just a number to indicate a body still unknown. Given that not much more than twenty-four hours had passed since the crash, he was heartened to see that there were fewer blank spaces than filled. Still plenty of work to do, though.

'Ah, Tony. You're back. I was beginning to wonder whether you'd make it for the briefing.'

McLean looked around to see DCI McIntyre, surrounded by a small army of constables and sergeants like a queen bee in the middle of the hive. She pushed through the throng as if it wasn't there, leaving a trail of discarded officers in her wake.

'It's just as well the chief superintendent's new to Specialist Crime. I don't think he quite understands how little respect for procedure you have.' McIntyre looked over his shoulder at DC Harrison. 'Or decorum. Going off into the wilds with the youngest female detective constable you can find. I'd have thought you'd know how the rumour mill works by now.'

McLean turned to Harrison, aware that he was blushing and seeing the red across her cheeks at the same time. It was stupid, of course. She was a good detective, true, but the only reason he'd taken her out that morning was because nobody else had been around.

'Really? Is the station so starved for gossip they have to go making up stuff like that?'

McIntyre gave him a smile, but it was weary enough to tell him she was worried. 'Just be careful, Tony. And you, too, Constable. I know it's bloody ridiculous, but the last thing either of you need is a stupid rumour going around.'

McLean looked at DC Harrison, her eyes wide at the DCI's comment. Yes, she was young and he was two ranks senior to her, perhaps twenty years older, but what of it? They were professionals tasked with a difficult job, for Christ's sake. You used whoever was available and preferably most competent. Should he only ever take male detective constables out when he wanted to interview witnesses or review crime scenes? If he did that then the rumours would suggest he was gay. Perhaps he should start evaluating the attractiveness of the female officers he worked with, but then what were the criteria? Christ, there were times he wanted nothing more than to jack the whole thing in.

'I've enough on my plate without having to worry about what the station's latest rumour is, Jayne.'

McIntyre shook her head from side to side just the once. 'I know, Tony. And it's not you I'm worried about. You don't give a damn what anyone says about you. Janie here's still got to prove herself, though.'

'Well, she can prove herself now by getting all those notes on to the system so we can bring everyone up to speed. Go see if you can't find your chums Stringer and Blane, will you, Constable? I need Lofty's particular skills.'

Harrison nodded once, then scurried off. McLean watched her thread her way through the busy incident room, pausing to talk to some officers, watched with critical eyes by others.

'Are they really talking about her behind her back?' he asked.

'Not yet, but it's only a matter of time. Remember how they treated the last keen young DC you took under your wing, aye? And he wasn't anything like as pretty.'

'You're as bad as the rest of them, Jayne.' McLean shook his head to try and get rid of the frustration at having to work with people no more mature than the children at his old boarding school. 'So, what's been going on here while young Harrison and I have been away on our tryst?'

'You can see for yourself.' McIntyre pointed at the whiteboard as Gregg wrote in another name. 'Mostly we've been identifying the dead, informing next of kin, sorting out formal identification procedures with the city mortuary. I'm hoping Ritchie will be back in time for the evening briefing. She's on her way, apparently. I've not had much to do, actually. The chief superintendent's been running things most of the day. He's a damned good organizer, loath though I am to admit it. Every time we get a new name in, he's right there. Been contacting the next of kin himself, I've heard.'

McLean scanned the room, seeing the smoothness of the operation. He'd put that down to DC Gregg's management skills, but it made more sense if the boss had been whipping everyone into shape.

'I'd heard he ran a tight ship. Didn't expect him to be quite so hands on, though. It makes a change from Brooks and Duguid. Which reminds me. Any news on the detective superintendent job?'

'Why? You fancy your chances?'

'Probably just about as good as anyone else here. But seriously, Jayne. I don't see why they haven't just given it to you. Pissing about trying to get someone from the regions to come in and sort us out. I wouldn't mind, but it's taking so bloody long. Not as if we were overstaffed before . . .' McLean stopped. No point going over old news.

'If it makes things any better, the DCC has said that if they can't get anyone by the end of the month then the job's mine.' McIntyre took a breath, let it out as a long sigh. 'Not sure I want it, if I'm being honest. But there's a few DIs and DCIs have put their names forward already. If they're that keen to move, maybe we can encourage some of them to transfer even if there's no promotion in it. Looks like you've got the new constables under control anyway.'

McLean followed McInytre's gaze to the far side of the room, where a group of plain-clothes officers were huddled around a computer terminal. Most were standing, some leaning forwards. One sat on a low chair directly in front of the screen, and even so his head was on a level with the rest of them. Detective Constable Lofty Blane. McLean checked his watch.

'You'll be at the briefing? Forty minutes?'

McIntyre nodded. 'Aye. And you can expect more senior company, too.'

It made sense, McLean supposed. This was a high-profile investigation with a lot of public interest. No surprise that the top man would need to face the cameras. He just needed to make sure the chief constable had all the facts.

'OK. I'll see you there. Meanwhile I've a complicated task needs doing, and I know just the detective constable for the job.'

'You got a moment, Constable?'

'Sir?' DC Harrison spun around so swiftly she almost knocked over the person next to her. 'Almost got them all typed up now, sir.'

'What? Oh, the briefing notes. Fine. We'll be starting at half five. Hopefully won't take long. It looks like we've got most of the bodies identified now, anyway.'

All eyes turned to the whiteboards, where another name

was being written out in neat script. McLean had worked on too many investigations to count, and almost always the scrawl on the whiteboards tended towards the illegible. And yet, here, each name was spelled out with care. The horror of the incident, perhaps; it was as if collectively the investigation team acknowledged how utterly random and senseless these deaths were. How easily it could have been any one of them, or their friends and family. The scale of it was daunting, too. Twenty lives snuffed out in an instant. Many of these officers would have attended car crashes or house fires, accidents that claimed a couple of victims, perhaps even a whole family. But twenty people dead and another fifty injured. You had to go back a long time to find anything comparable. At least up here in Scotland. Manchester, London, the big cities down in England had seen more than their fair share of tragedy and atrocity in recent times, but up here there'd been nothing comparable since before some of these officers had been born.

'It was Constable Blane I wanted to talk to actually.' McLean pulled his attention back to the case. 'What are you working on right now?'

The tall detective swivelled in his chair enough for McLean to see the screen in front of him. A data entry form designed by some statistics genius to capture the information from phone calls, interviews and any other source and put it into a format that computers could use.

'Just collating the latest from the phone lines, sir. And Janie ... DC Harrison's notes from your interviews. Important to get everything cross-referenced and filed correctly. Wouldn't want to miss an important clue.'

'Good, good. There's something else I need you to do,

though.' McLean indicated the computer terminal with a flick of the hand. 'The admins can keep on top of this.'

Blane looked a little hurt at the suggestion. 'What is it you wanted, sir?'

'I need you to look into the financial status and corporate structure of a couple of companies. Finlay McGregor and Extech Energy. You reckon you can do that?'

The look of concern turned to one of pride on the young constable's face. He'd be hopeless in an interrogation, but he knew finance better than any of them. 'Of course, sir. Do we have a warrant? For getting financials from the banks?'

McLean tapped the breast pocket of his suit jacket. He had a warrant to search the compound where Finlay McGregor locked their trucks up at night. If it had been worded correctly it would stretch to investigating any aspect of their operations. On the other hand, he didn't want to go full forensic accountancy on them. At least, not yet. There were budgets to be considered, after all.

'Let's just see what you can come up with through normal channels first, OK? Companies House and that sort of thing. See what the links are between them, if there's anything suspicious. We'll only bring out the heavy artillery if we have to.'

'Thought you were trying to get home at a reasonable hour these days.'

McLean looked up from his overlarge desk and its tide of paperwork to see a welcome face smiling back at him. Detective Inspector Ritchie leaned against the open doorway, her short-cropped strawberry blonde hair looking like it hadn't seen a brush in days. Her clothes weren't much better, her jeans ripped at both knees and sporting some interesting stains, bum-freezer leather jacket over a tight once-white T-shirt. She looked like someone who'd just got home from a rock festival, not a detective inspector at work.

'And I thought T in the Park wasn't on this year,' he said.

Ritchie stuck her tongue out at him, stepped fully into the room. 'Aye, funny. Guessing it's been a while since you last worked undercover.'

'That you just in, then? You could have taken your time, you know. Had a shower, change of clothes.'

'I know that now. Missed the bloody briefing, didn't I. The traffic's all to buggery back the way to the bridges. It helps that this is all over the news, mind you. Nobody's shifting anything at the moment, so I can skive off a few days.'

'And how is Operation Fenton going? Still camped out in the Perthshire Glens, I presume?'

Ritchie dropped into one of the comfortable chairs over by the window that filled most of one wall of the office. 'I'm beginning to think it's a bust. We had good intel. We know they've been working through there before, but we've not seen anything for a fortnight now.'

'I take it that's unusual.'

'Possibly. Might be a seasonal thing, might be that we've been strung along. Could be they're moving stuff through the next glen, safe in the knowledge we're all tucked up in our wee hidey-hole on the other side of the mountains. Bloody waste of time, if you ask me.' Ritchie sighed, ran a hand through her hair, then stared at her palm as if only just noticing how grubby she was. 'So what's the story with the crash. Heard you were there when it happened. Must've been horrific.'

'Not sure I really want to talk about it.' McLean leaned back in his chair. He wasn't so stupid that he couldn't understand his own motivations. Heading out to the hauliers' compound first thing, speaking to Hamish Tafferty and then swinging past the anaerobic digester site: these were all ways of avoiding the quiet moments when he would be able to think about what he had seen. Time would take the raw edge off that experience, but for now he needed something to keep the horror at bay.

'Understandable.' Ritchie shrugged, the buckles and zippers on her jacket jangling quietly. 'How's the investigation going?'

'Early days. Have you seen Jayne yet?'

Ritchie shook her head. 'In a meeting with the boss man. Quite why they dropped him on us and didn't give the job to her I've no idea.'

'Funny you should say that. We were having the exact same conversation earlier.' McLean leaned back until his head clunked against the wall, a distance much further than he was used to. He only managed to avoid tipping himself over completely by wedging a swift foot under the desk. 'We've currently got two strands to the investigation. First one's working out what happened and why. That's what I've been doing all day and it's already looking murky.'

'Doesn't it always when you get involved, Tony?' Ritchie had the decency to grin as she spoke. 'What's the second strand? I take it that's my job.'

'Aye. Jayne's been dealing with it today, and Sandy Gregg's got most of the legwork done already, but you're in charge of identifying all the victims.' McLean held up his hand before Ritchie could interrupt. 'And I know, yes. It would make more sense for me to do that, given how closely I've worked with Angus and the rest of the staff at the city mortuary before. Chances are there won't be much for you to do anyway. Last I saw there were only six bodies still to identify.'

'There's a helpline number? People coming forward with suggestions?'

'Like I said, Sandy Gregg's got it all under control. And, believe it or not, Forrester's rolled up his sleeves and pitched in, too. It'll only get complicated if we can't identify someone from dental records or DNA or something. Then we'll have to start going through missing persons reports, CCTV and the like.'

'Wait . . . What? Dental records? DNA?' Ritchie ran her hand through her hair again, didn't look at the stains on her palm this time. 'I'd heard the crash was bad, but . . . really?'

'It melted the tarmac, whatever the chemical goo was that spilled from the tanker. Stank so bad I had to throw my suit away. There's a chunk of the Lothian Road still closed, likely to be that way for weeks. That's why the traffic's a nightmare.' McLean pulled himself forward again, leaned his elbows on the desk. 'Look, it's probably not going to take long to identify everyone. Collate all the witness statements, sort out the timeline, put it all in a nice report and deliver it to the Procurator Fiscal. Job done, and then you can get back to your splendid isolation in the

Highlands. Who knows? Might even be in time to catch those gun runners of yours before they bring the next batch in.'

'Aye, I'm sure it'll all be fine and dandy.' Ritchie stood, yawned, rolled her shoulders as if she'd been sitting for hours rather than minutes. 'I'll go see if Jayne's finished her meeting. Head home and get some kip. Early start tomorrow, I'm guessing?'

'Six o'clock briefing, yes. I'd probably better get home myself if I want Emma ever to speak to me again.'

14

The sun hung low in the northern sky as McLean parked his car and headed to the back door of his house. He would have liked to think that meant he wasn't coming home too late, but summer this far north was a time of almost perpetual daylight. Emma would have been home from work for a couple of hours by now; he just hoped she wasn't too upset at him, even if he deserved it.

There was no sign of her or Mrs McCutcheon's cat in the kitchen, although there was plenty of evidence both that Emma had already eaten her supper and that the cat had helped. He didn't find them in the library either, so McLean headed upstairs. The door to his old bedroom stood ajar, light spilling out on to the landing, and as he approached he could hear a strange sound coming from within.

'Em? You in there?' McLean popped his head around the doorframe, taking in the partially redecorated room. Most of the wallpaper was gone now, and a smell of fresh gloss paint filled the air. Before he could register that the room was empty, he heard the toilet flush in the bathroom beyond, and then Emma emerged, wiping her mouth with the back of her hand.

'Oh, Tony. You're home.' Something flickered across her eyes that he would have considered guilt were she a suspect being interviewed.

'Sorry it's so late. It's always a nightmare when you set up a new investigation. Still, you've been busy.' He nodded at the freshly painted window.

'Just thought I'd get a little bit more done. Something pleasant after a hard day at work.'

'Let me guess, the truck crash?'

'The same. Spent half of the day in front of a fume cabinet. No wonder your suit stank when you got home yesterday. That stuff's beyond foul.'

'Should you be working with that sort of thing? You know, in your . . .' McLean nodded in her general direction. Experience had taught him that referring to her pregnancy as a 'condition' rarely went well.

'I'm fine. Just a bit tired.' Emma laid a hand on her belly for a moment.

'You sure, Em? Only you look a bit peaky.'

The furrow that ran across her brow suggested he'd said the wrong thing. He couldn't help himself sometimes, though, especially not after she had so obviously just been throwing up whatever it was she and the cat had been eating earlier.

'You must be hungry,' she said, as if reading his mind. 'I ate already, but there's supper in the oven if you've not had anything yet.'

McLean considered lying and going without. It wouldn't be the first time he'd skipped a meal, but his stomach chose that moment to let out a low grumble. He smiled, shrugged. 'I guess lunch was a while ago.'

'Come on, then.' Emma took him by the hand, her touch ever so slightly warm and clammy as she led him out of the room and back to the stairs. Mrs McCutcheon's cat sat on the top step, staring at them both like a disapproving parent.

'She's been keeping a very watchful eye on me,' Emma said as the cat stood, arched its back and shook its tail at them before striding elegantly down the stairs.

'I'm glad someone is. I feel I'm rather neglecting my duties on that score.'

Emma laughed, her pale skin flushing. 'You don't half sound like a Victorian gentleman sometimes, Tony. I managed to travel right around the world on my own. I can cope with a little neglect. Just don't let it become a habit, aye?'

She dropped his hand, taking a hold of the rail as she followed the cat's route down to the kitchen. McLean watched her from the top of the stairs and wondered whether it hadn't already.

He woke with the ghost of a scream on his lips. Heart pounding, breath ragged, he sat upright in bed and stared across the almost dark bedroom. Outside, the dawn had begun, tinging the sky a fiery red beyond the trees. His whole body was slick with sweat, dampening the sheets and the thin duvet tangled around his legs. Beside him, Emma lay on her back, not so much snoring as breathing noisily. He rubbed at his face with fingers still stiff from sleep, then hugged his knees to his chest and just sat there staring at her as the light slowly rose.

The nightmare wasn't a surprise, although its intensity had been worse than the one from the previous night. If he had the time, he could unpack the imagery, but there were more important things to worry about than his brain getting over the trauma of the crash. Finding out how it had happened, and who was responsible, for a start. They'd seen where the truck had come from already, today would be finding out where it was supposed to go. He couldn't help but think there had to be a better way of pursuing the investigation, though. Co-ordinating with the Health and Safety Executive and the Vehicle and Operator Services Agency was a nightmare, too, not the kind of teamwork he was used to at all.

Emma rolled over with a snort, one arm slapping against him in a grim parody of the nightmare that had woken him up. She grunted, sniffed and then opened her eyes. 'You 'wake?'

'Bad dreams.' McLean leaned back against the headboard, shivering slightly as the sweat evaporated from his skin.

'The crash?' Emma hauled herself up, leaning on one arm as she stared at him. Her tousled hair and eyes still puffy with sleep were deeply alluring.

'It's to be expected. I'd be more worried if I didn't have them, to be honest.'

'But you've spoken to someone about it, right? There's a trauma counsellor at the station these days, isn't there?'

McLean bent down, kissed Emma lightly on the forehead. 'I'm fine, Em. Don't worry about it. You've got the day off today, right?'

'The joys of working part-time, aye.'

'Well, make the most of it.' He swung his legs round, climbed out of bed even though the clock told him it wasn't going to wake him up for another hour yet. 'Won't be long until sleep's a rare luxury, you know.'

15

I've been trying to track a few things down since the crash. Where the truck was coming from, where it was meant to be going. It's not easy, even if that's more or less what I do for a living anyway. My head's not in the game at all, and I keep on seeing that brief flash of recognition on Maddy's face as she turned towards me. The smile lighting up her eyes as she started to say my name. But how could I possibly have taken any of that in? It all happened in an instant.

Then again, details have a way of imprinting themselves in your memory at times like that. It's life afterwards that chunks up into blocks of unpleasantness with big gaps of nothing in between. The story of my life, in undigested, bite-size pieces.

Like the house in Essex. Like Maddy.

Her presence emboldened me, as I think mine emboldened her. So when the opportunity presented itself, I dared take it, rifling through the pockets of the man's discarded trousers while he slept, his sick appetites sated at least for a while. The slim, brass cigarette lighter was a prize beyond reckoning. Did I voice my plan to Maddy as we passed it back and forth? Was it some telepathy we shared? I don't really know. And neither do I know what exactly I was thinking when I flicked open the lighter. How could I have possibly known how it worked? And yet somehow I managed to coax a flame out of it, orange and flickering.

The curtains caught easily, the room lighting up in seconds as the fire ate its way through everything it touched. It seemed alive, vengeful. Almost as if it was my own anger and hatred released. It grew with terrible swiftness, devouring everything it touched.

I remember hugging Maddy tight, kissing her on the forehead as the heat grew ever more unbearable. Soon it would take us, too, and the pain would be over. And yet the flames seemed to skirt around us as they searched the room for yet more things to eat. The man, asleep at first, then slowed by smoke and a lack of air, screamed as he burned. I remember the smell of his hair, the way his skin bubbled and his eyes turned white like the poached eggs we sometimes had for breakfast. His death sent a little thrill through me even as I knew that mine would come soon enough, that Maddy, too, would be eaten up by the fire. And still we knelt in the middle of the room, our tiny bodies hugged together so tightly we might have been one.

And that's how they found us. The only two survivors of a blaze that claimed many lives. I thought that house had taken everything from us, but I was wrong. Up until the fire we at least had each other. Then they cut us apart.

If I thought the house in Essex was bad, the care system really wasn't much better. OK, so I came into it as damaged goods, but really you'd think they might have worked that out from the beginning and made some kind of adjustment for it.

The first foster family were nuts. Ted stayed at home all day while Margaret went to work. I never found out what she did. To be fair, they didn't abuse me, but neither did they exactly lavish me with attention. I'd spent my entire life being fed, washed and occasionally presented to some sick old man as a plaything. I had no idea how to look after myself, and they really didn't know how to deal with that. The regular visits to the doctor must have rung some emergency bells somewhere in social services, as I was moved on fairly swiftly.

Pete and Jemma tried to be nice, but I was just beginning to understand both what had been done to me and that I was free of that life. Sometime round about my eighth birthday I started to go off the rails, and I spent the next four years on heavy medication, making life hell for anyone who tried to care. I lost count of the number of homes I went through, never staying anywhere for long. The only constant was the policeman. Gordon. He'd bring me photographs, men, women, children, always the same question. Had I ever seen them before?

I never had, probably wouldn't remember anyway. At the time, I didn't know what it was all about. Now I can see the ongoing investigation, the search for any clues as to how Maddy and I had ended up in that house. How that house could have existed in the first place in a world that grown-ups tried to pretend was good and fair. At least Gordon cared, even I could see that. Not that it did him any good. He aged a decade in every six-month gap between our meetings. At the last one, he told me he was retiring and I'd be seeing a new policeman after that. I never did. Not for a long time, and my stays with foster parents grew ever shorter.

And then when I was about twelve I ended up with Sheila and Jean.

Odd enough that a lesbian couple could have foster kids, but something about them worked for me. It might have been that I had a new doctor by then, new meds. New country, too, since I ended up here in Scotland. Whatever it was, I started to be a bit more reasonable around then. And Sheila was a wizard with computers. Taught me everything I know. She gave me a direction for the rage, a sense of purpose I'd been lacking.

Or it might just have been that I was growing up, coming to understand the injustice done to me, Maddy and all the other kids who died in that fire I started.

Whatever the reason, though, Sheila gave me the knowledge and the tools to fight back. I'll always be grateful to her for that. And so I'll try to put Maddy's face from my mind, if only for a moment. Concentrate on the job at hand. Track down the bastards responsible for her death and make them pay.

16

Coming off the city bypass on to the A1, heading east, and McLean floored the throttle with perhaps a little too heavy a right foot. Something loud and angry roared under the bonnet, snapping his head backwards as it pinned him into his seat.

'Whoa. I wasn't quite expecting that.' He eased off the fast pedal, let the needle on the speedometer drop back down to the legal limit, surprised at just how quickly it had swung past it and on towards three digits.

'Five hundred and ten horsepower, I read. Not quite sure why anyone needs that many horses, but there you go.' Sitting beside him in the passenger seat, Detective Sergeant Bob Laird took a sip of coffee from his lidless paper cup and stared at the newspaper on his lap. A quick glance down confirmed McLean's suspicion that he'd not spilled a drop. It was uncanny how he managed to stay calm in the most desperate of situations. Especially when there was fine coffee involved. But then Grumpy Bob had always been like that. You couldn't wish for a more level head in a crisis. Just don't expect a finger to be lifted unless it's absolutely necessary.

'I'll agree, it's perhaps a little over the top.' McLean accelerated more smoothly this time, overtaking a couple of trucks. 'Not quite as bad as that Bentley I tried a few years back, but it's more comfortable than the old GTV.'

'True.' Grumpy Bob shuffled in his seat slightly. 'Still not sure why you have this obsession with Alfa Romeos, though. Why not get a Range Rover or a Jaguar like all the other senior detectives?'

'Ha. The last thing I need is people thinking I'm a DCI, or, worse, a superintendent. Then they'd give me even more work to do.' McLean rubbed a thumb lightly over the little badge in the middle of the steering wheel, the red cross and the tiny man being swallowed by a serpent. 'As to the Alfa thing; you'd have to have owned one to understand.'

They sped up the road in silence for a while, Grumpy Bob taking the occasional sip from his cup, scribbling the occasional answer to the crossword puzzle spread over his knees. McLean knew the old sergeant could have done this trip on his own, perhaps even sent a constable or two to do it while he found himself a comfortable empty room for a snooze. The same could be said for the visits to the hauliers and Extech Energy he'd made with Harrison the day before. There was no real need for a detective inspector to attend, other than that he hated sitting in his office waiting for the details to be brought to him. Hated not being at the sharp end of the investigation. After his conversation with DCI McIntyre, he'd thought twice about taking Harrison. Grumpy Bob had been next in line. There were worse people to take a trip out into the countryside with.

'Did you call ahead to let them know we're coming?' McLean asked as the satnav steered him off the main road and into the wilderness around East Fortune. The twin lumps of North Berwick Law and the Bass Rock dominated the horizon, good arable land stretching away towards the coast and the Firth of Forth. Grumpy Bob folded his paper away, shoved his cup in a small circular indentation in the centre console that may or may not have been designed for that purpose, and dug out his notebook from a scruffy jacket pocket.

'Aye.' There was a short pause while the detective sergeant searched for his reading spectacles, found them perched on the top of his balding head. 'LindSea Farm Estates. We're to ask for an Emily Fairweather.'

As if on cue, the satnav pinged for McLean to turn left, through a modern stone-walled gateway. Signs set into the stonework identified LindSea Farm, and beyond it a wide, tarmac drive ran arrow-straight through flat green fields towards a collection of modern farm buildings. As he drove along, he could see that the fences on either side of the drive were new, a modern variation of the old estate fences he remembered from childhood National Trust visits with his grandmother. Expensive, although in the long run they outlasted wooden posts and rylock wire netting.

'Somebody's been spending a bit of cash,' Grumpy Bob said as they arrived in a large courtyard. 'Didn't realize the Single Farm Payment was so generous.'

McLean parked alongside a nearly new Land Rover and a couple of Toyota Pickups of the kind favoured by extremist insurgents and African dictators. Most of the farm buildings looked much as he would have expected, if newer and cleaner than those he had seen before. Steel frames clad in dark-green corrugated metal with large roller doors and smaller personnel entrances, all closed. The only building with windows was the one in front of them, a neatly converted part of a much older stone-built steading. A neat plaque beside the door read 'LindSea Farm Estates'.

'Well, at least we're in the right place.' He reached for the door, but it swung open before he could touch the handle. A tall man, dressed in spotless blood-red overalls and wearing dark glasses stared out at him. His short-cropped blond hair reminded McLean of a prison inmate more than someone who worked the land.

'Who're youse?'

McLean reached for his inside jacket pocket and his warrant card, seeing the man tense involuntarily at the movement. Not the sort of reaction you expected from a farmer.

'Detective Inspector McLean. Specialist Crime Division. This is my colleague Detective Sergeant Laird. We're looking for Emily Fairweather?'

The man in the overalls relaxed a little, but still blocked the entrance. He hadn't removed his shades, but he turned his head slightly and shouted into the office beyond.

'You know anything about the polis coming?'

A voice from beyond, too indistinct to make out any words, but feminine in its tone. McLean wondered what they had to hide here that they were so suspicious. Finally the man turned back to him, pulled off his dark glasses to reveal eyes of piercing grey-blue.

'How'd you get through the gate? Not meant to be people just wandering in like that.'

'Gate was open,' McLean said. 'Now can we come in?'

The blond man opened his mouth to say something, but he was pushed out of the door by someone behind him. That feminine voice, but stiff and angry. 'Stop standing there blocking the entrance, Gregor. Go fix the gates.'

A middle-aged woman stepped into the entranceway as Gregor shoved his dark glasses back on, stalked past McLean and clambered into one of the pickups. Short and round, with greying hair tied up in a neat bun and dressed in sensible tweed, she clearly terrified the man even though he was twice her height.

'Inspector. Sorry about that. The security gate should have been closed. If you'd used the intercom we'd have known you were here. Still, never mind.' She held out a hand. 'Emily Fairweather. Please, do come in.'

'We mostly grow grass, actually. Some for seed, some gets made into forage for the equine market. The big money's in turf, though.'

Emily Fairweather, it turned out, was the CEO of LindSea Farm Estates, or at least that was how she had introduced herself after leading McLean and Grumpy Bob through an open-plan office and into a small meeting room beyond. The window on the far side framed an impressive view of the Bass Rock, climbing out of the choppy waters of the outer Firth of Forth. McLean knew it mostly from a series of engravings of famous Scottish castles that had hung on the wall in his bedroom for most of his childhood. From this distance the castle was impossible to see, nothing left of it but a ruin anyway.

'Turf?' Grumpy Bob asked.

'Aye. You wouldn't believe how much it's worth. Time was, if you wanted a lawn you'd sow some grass seed and wait a while. Now everyone wants it done yesterday. I blame all those programmes on the telly. You know, the ones where they go in and make over someone's perfectly good garden. Stick in some decking, maybe a rockery, and lots and lots of nice green turf. Still, I can't complain. Keeps us right.'

'You could say that.' McLean dragged his gaze away from the view, glancing up at the ceiling. The building they were in might have been old, but it had been done up recently, and well. 'You've spent a fair bit on this place.'

'All part of the business plan. We knocked down most of the old stone steadings just over a year ago, converted this bit into the office block and put up the big shed on the site. Most of the old buildings were falling down anyway. Built in the late eighteenth, early nineteenth century, when this was mixed arable and dairy land. Back when everything was horse-drawn and a place the size of the home farm would've employed fifty men. Their families, too, come tattie-picking time. Sad but true, Inspector. One man and a tractor can do more in a day than all of them could in a month. Soon it'll just be the tractor driving itself, mark my words.'

'Just how big is the operation, then?'

'The home farm – here – is twelve hundred acres. We've three other sites in the area. Total is somewhere around five thousand acres. Two thousand hectares, if you like.'

Grumpy Bob let out a low whistle. 'That's a lot of land. My old granddad farmed a couple hundred acres up near Peebles and we used to think he was as rich as Croesus.'

'It's the modern way of things, Sergeant. The smaller farms aren't economically viable these days. Old farmers retire or more likely die. Their families aren't interested, so the land gets sold off to a neighbour. The fittest survive and get bigger and bigger.'

'And sell turf to all the housing estates popping up around the city,' McLean said.

'Exactly so.' Fairweather smiled. 'But I'm guessing you didn't come all the way out here for a lesson in modern farming methods.'

'Not exactly.' McLean leaned forward in his chair. 'Digestate from anaerobic digesters. You spread it on the land here, I understand.'

The tiniest flicker of something marred the corner of Fairweather's eyes, her smile faltering ever so slightly before she answered. 'It's all above board, Inspector. I know the Food Standards people aren't too keen on it going on to land used for vegetable crops, but all the digestate we use is for bulking up the soils after we've cut turfs. And it's regularly tested for contaminants. We have a very good working relationship with our suppliers.'

'Extech Energy. You get a lot of your stuff from them?'

Again that flicker of uncertainty, swiftly locked down. 'They're our major supplier, yes. We get digestate from other outfits, but Extech are the most reliable. And they produce it in large quantities, too. Perfect for us as we expand.'

'When was the last delivery you had?'

'I'd have to check with Elaine.' Fairweather nodded towards the door. 'The secretary. She deals with the admin, all the permits and waste disposal licences and stuff. You wouldn't believe the amount of paperwork.'

'So you don't know anything about a delivery the day before yesterday. Delayed a day, too, so it would have been meant to arrive three days ago. Finlay McGregor Hauliers.' McLean kept his tone flat, stating the facts rather than asking a question. As he named the truck company, that twitch around Fairweather's eyes came back so strongly she had to blink to get rid of it, looked away from him as if trying to cover it up by pretending she had something in her eye.

'As I said, Elaine deals with all that, Inspector.' She faced him again, features locked into a mirthless smile. She picked up the phone on her desk, but pressed no button to put a call through. 'I'll have her dig up all the relevant documents, but might I ask why you're interested in it?'

The gates were closed as they headed back down the driveway half an hour later, a pickup truck parked in the shade of one of the walls. As they approached, the blond man in the red overalls and dark glasses stood up from where he had been squatting beside a control box. He reached over and pressed a button, causing the gates to swing inwards and open, but instead of driving off, McLean lowered the window and pulled to a halt.

'All fixed now?' He tried a friendly grin, expecting nothing more than a scowl in return and not being disappointed.

'Must be some turf you grow here, that it needs all this security to keep the thieves from stealing it,' McLean continued. 'Of course, you'd know all about that, wouldn't you Gregor?'

'You what?' The man took a step towards the car, arms hanging loose at his side, fists lightly clenched. A fighting stance.

'Took me a while, I have to admit. It wasn't until your boss lady named you that the penny dropped. Gregor Wishaw. You used to run with Bunt McGhee and his gang, didn't you? Spent a wee while in Saughton if memory serves. Armed robbery of a post office.'

'Did my time, Inspector.' Gregor leaned down, took his dark glasses off to reveal those pale grey-blue eyes once more. There was something very disconcerting about that stare, like a sheepdog at work. Fixated. Obsessive.

'I'm sure you did. Same as I'm sure Ms Fairweather knows all about your past.' McLean tried the smile again. 'Like you said, you did your time. No reason why you shouldn't be gainfully employed. Beats running with a gang of second-rate hoodlums. How was it we caught you again? That was it. One of your chums posted a photo of himself on Facebook. Only he forgot he was still wearing the same mask he used in the raid. Bet he was popular with the gang, eh?'

'Was there something you wanted? Only I've got a job to do.'

'Not really. I was just surprised to see you. It's not often faces from old cases come back, even less so and they've turned over a new leaf. Good on you.'

Confusion spread across Gregor's face. McLean pressed the button, raising the window a few inches, then stopped. 'There was one thing, actually.'

'Aye?'

'The tanker trucks that deliver the muck here. They all belong to Finlay McGregor, right? You'll know Mike Finlay?'

It was almost imperceptible, the tiniest tightening of

the eyes that might just have been a reaction to the bright summer sun. Might have been, had it not come exactly as McLean spoke the name.

'Never heard of him,' Gregor said. 'Trucks are in and out of here all the time. Can't say I've paid much attention to who runs them. As long as they've got the paperwork they're no' my problem.'

Gregor put his dark glasses back on. Conversation over as far as he was concerned. McLean smiled a final time, raised the window all the way.

17

The phone buzzed on his desk, and for the first time since he could remember McLean was able to pick up the hand-set without first having to find it under a sea of folders. The lights on the front of the machine told him it was an internal call, but he'd not managed to work out anything more sophisticated than that yet.

'McLean.'

'Ah, Tony. You're in.' The chief superintendent sounded a little too chummy, as if he had rehearsed his lines once too often to sound properly spontaneous.

'Sir. Yes. Just going over the day's reports. Was there something I could help you with?'

A heartbeat's pause. The sort of thing that let you know the suspect you were interviewing was lying. Or at least had something to hide. 'There was, aye. Wondering if you could step into my office for a moment.'

'Of course, sir. I'll be right there.'

'Good, good.' Another telling pause. Something was clearly bothering Forrester, but he didn't want to talk about it on the phone. 'Nothing important. Just don't tell anyone where you're going, right?'

'Fine. OK.' McLean frowned even though there was no one about to see him. The chief superintendent's office was just along the corridor at the far corner of the build-ing. It was unlikely he'd be seen going there, but equally wouldn't draw much in the way of suspicion if he was. He hung up, looked around the room as if it might suddenly have sprouted surveillance cameras and hidden microphones. As if this might be the prelude to an elaborate joke at his expense. But this was the chief superintendent. The man in charge of the whole station. Not some sergeant with a grudge and a childish imagination.

As predicted, the corridor was empty. Forrester's office sat at the far end, beyond a wider space that had held a secretary's desk when Duguid and Brooks had occupied the top seat. Before that there had been no need, as Jayne McIntyre had always left her door open. Now it stood just slightly ajar. Not welcoming all who would come, but letting McLean know that he was expected.

The chief superintendent looked up from his desk as McLean knocked once and pushed the door open. Unlike McLean's own, Forrester's desktop had scarcely anything on it. A phone, a laptop and one brown folder. He felt a moment's intense jealousy that the man could get away with so little paperwork, and then he saw the look on his face.

'You wanted to see me, sir?'

'Yes, Tony. Come in. Shut the door. There's something I need to ask you.'

McLean did as he was told, sitting down when indicated to do so. There were no other officers present, so it was unlikely this was a disciplinary matter. Apart from spending time out interviewing people rather than in the melee of the incident room, he was struggling to think of anything he might have done wrong recently. Nothing since the winter, when he'd gone against a direct order from his superior and broken that particular case open.

'How's the investigation coming along?' Forrester asked after an uncomfortably long pause. 'You've been following up questions about the truck mostly?'

McLean could tell that this was just the warm-up to what the chief superintendent really wanted to talk about. Forrester had spent most of the day in the incident room himself, when he hadn't been updating the media with regular press briefings.

'Yes, sir. We've turned the search of the haulage company's compound over to Health and Safety since technically it's their jurisdiction. I've been trying to pin down where the tanker load came from. Can't do much else until forensics have worked out exactly what it is.'

'And the cause of the crash.' Forrester slipped a pair of thin spectacles on to his nose, reached over for the folder and flicked it open with shaking hands. 'Post-mortem suggests heart attack.'

'Myocardial infarction is the preferred term these days, but essentially yes. He'd been passed fit just a couple of months ago, but these things can hit without warning. Couple that with the tampering to the brakes . . .' McLean left the sentence unfinished, the silence in the room making his point far more eloquently.

'We any further on with that?' Forrester asked.

'Still waiting on the forensic report, and anything Health and Safety find out at Broxburn. I want to bring Mike Finlay in for a more thorough questioning, too. There's something he's not telling us, I'm sure, but I need more background info on the company before I can really put the squeeze on him.'

'Aye, well, sooner we can get someone arrested for this

118

mess the better. Twenty dead? Fifty seriously injured? Christ, you can just imagine the fun the press'll have if it turns out we can't charge anyone.'

'Is that what this is about, sir? The press?'

Forrester stared off into the distance for a while, not answering. McLean was happy to give him the time he needed. Something was clearly bothering him, but it wasn't a lack of results or playing fast and loose with established procedure. Whatever it was had disrupted the chief superintendent's sleep, though. His face was lined and grey, bags under sunken eyes. Even his hair seemed somehow weary, and less kempt than was becoming of a senior uniformed officer.

'The press. Well. They certainly could be a problem. It all depends on how things are handled. How things pan out.' Forrester snapped his gaze back to McLean. 'The identification of the dead bodies. Is that all done now?'

'All but five, sir. Two of those we're fairly certain we know who they are, just waiting on DNA confirmation. The other three may take a while longer if they're not on the database.'

'No one's come looking for missing relatives?'

'Oh, plenty, sir. Something like this brings all sorts out. DC Gregg's heading up a team sifting through the calls as they come in. We have to take everything seriously, of course. But when you start looking into it, a lot of the names we get are for people who've been missing a while. Sometimes years. No real reason why they would be at that bus stop on that day.'

Forrester had fallen silent again, his eyes glazing over as

he either listened to what McLean was saying or worried about whatever it was had called him here in the first place.

'I've not been here long. You know that, Tony. Of course you do. Someone had to come in and pick up the pieces after that mess with Bill Chalmers, and the chief constable, bless him, thought I'd be the man for the job. Twenty-five years in Strathclyde region. Dealing with some of Glasgow's more colourful characters, catching speeding motorists, the tiresome but necessary administration that keeps this great organization just about functional. I haven't a clue how you run things over this side of the country, but you don't turn down an offer of promotion, not when you're as close to retirement as I am.'

Forrester paused for breath, or maybe because he hoped that McLean would say something. He knew better than to interrupt, and soon the chief superintendent started up again.

'I moved the whole family over for this job. We've rented a place not far from here. It's nice. Quiet. Deirdre, my wife, is very happy to be living in Edinburgh. My son . . . less so.'

Something about the way Forrester put all the emphasis on 'son' set the alarm bells ringing in McLean's mind.

'He's always been a bit of a handful, has Eric. Bright lad. Well, he'll be twenty-two next birthday so technically not a lad any more, I guess. Still living at home. Sort of. He comes and goes. Plays in a band and half the time they're out on the road. Not famous, not earning millions. I'd be so lucky.'

Why are you telling me this. McLean wanted to ask, but he kept his mouth shut.

'The thing is, Tony. He's gone missing. Should have been home yesterday and he never turned up. I've spoken to his bandmates, but no one's seen him since the morning of the crash.'

It took a while to find Grumpy Bob, but McLean didn't mind searching. He went from empty room to empty room, marvelling at how few officers there seemed to be in the station these days. And all the while the chief superintendent's words rolled over and over in his mind.

At first he'd been as politely dismissive as he could, not wanting to upset an anxious parent. Or his boss. But with each new nugget of information, so Forrester's anxiety had become infectious. Still, unlikely that Eric was one of the three unidentified bodies, but there was enough circumstantial evidence to make it worthwhile looking into. It had to be done discreetly, though. If word got out to the press then the whole investigation would get complicated and messy. Actually, it had already got complicated and messy, but the press would only make it worse.

So he needed a team he could rely on not to tell tales, which meant only one person. Possibly two, though that wasn't a conversation McLean much relished having.

'If you're after anything on Gregor Wishaw, I'm just waiting on a call back from Benny Thomas over at Leith nick. He was on the team that arrested the whole gang.' Grumpy Bob had long since perfected the art of switching in an instant from feet up on the desk and paper draped over the face snoozing to alert and already having done what you wanted. The detective sergeant stifled a yawn and rubbed unselfconsciously at an armpit before blinking a couple of times and looking around the room. It had once housed the local control centre, before all that side of the job had been hived off to Bilston Glen. A pile of old computers and other electrical gubbins gathered dust in the corner, desks were piled up against the far wall and someone had drawn something rude on the whiteboards. At some point in the indeterminate past a couple of expensive orthopaedic chairs had been wheeled in here and it was one of those that Grumpy Bob had been using as a makeshift bed.

'And this call will come here?' McLean pointed at the desk upon which the detective sergeant had been resting his heels. There was a phone at one end, but the cable looping out the back of it ended in a splay of cut wires on the floor.

'Good mobile signal in here, sir.' Grumpy Bob held up his smartphone by way of explanation.

'Never mind. I've got something else I need you to look into while you're waiting anyway.'

As he repeated the chief superintendent's story, so McLean felt that familiar, creeping sensation of cold in the pit of his stomach. Christ, but he hated it when things got complicated.

'We'll have a DNA sample from the chief super on file, won't we?' Grumpy Bob asked when McLean had finished.

'Should have, aye. But I got a cheek swab anyway.' McLean pulled the sample bottle from his pocket and held it up to the light. 'I'll ask Parsons to run it alongside the three bodies, but it'll take time.'

'Can't you sweet-talk them into rushing it through?

Thought you and the wee lassie were best of pals.' Grumpy Bob had the decency to smile as he spoke.

'Not with the new systems they've got in place now. It's more than anyone's job's worth to do that. You should hear some of Em's stories. Ever since the testing was put out to private tender you can't prioritize anything without a hefty surcharge.'

'Wouldn't have thought that would be a problem. Seeing as you've got the chief super on your side. Sure, he'd sign off anything you asked him to right now.'

McLean shook his head. 'No. It has to be low key. The fewer people who know the better, which is why at the moment it's just you, me and Forrester himself. I'd keep it that way, too, but we need more people to look into this.

'Who'd you have in mind, then? Any of the new DCs? Harrison maybe?'

McLean didn't answer straight away. He was fairly sure he could trust Harrison, even if he didn't know her all that well. She was sharing a flat with Amanda Parsons from forensics anyway, so chances were she'd find out sooner or later. But DCI McIntyre's words rang in his ears. She was young, attractive and eager to please. Last thing she needed was her fellow detectives deciding without evidence that she was shagging the boss to get ahead.

'No, I think we need to keep this high level as much as possible. Which is why I'm going to call in a favour I'd rather not have been owed in the first place.'

Prestonfield Golf Club sat at the southern edge of Arthur's Seat, sandwiched between the university halls of residence and Duddingston Loch. McLean remembered it first from his undergraduate days, not so much as a place he had played golf as a clubhouse he and some friends had been banned from for messing about on the eighteenth green late at night. As was so often the case in his misspent youth, alcohol had been involved.

It wasn't far from the station, but far enough for it to make more sense to drive than walk. He would have liked the time to think, letting the rhythm of his feet on the pavement order his thoughts, but time wasn't his friend today. There was too much to do.

The new Alfa looked far more comfortable among the BMWs, Audis and Mercedes in the club car park than his old GTV ever would have. He even acknowledged an approving 'Nice car' from a complete stranger with questionable fashion sense, clearly heading off for eighteen holes before suppertime. He wasn't here to talk about cars or golf, though.

No one tried to stop him as he walked through the clubhouse to the bar. Perhaps they recognized him, or possibly they just assumed he had as much right to be there as any member. McLean was happy to be left alone. Bad enough that he had to come here at all.

The bar was busier than his last visit, but the high-backed leather armchairs clustered around the unlit fireplace were empty. All except for one. McLean recognized the tweed-suited arm, long-fingered hand clutching an almost empty tumbler of malt whisky. With a sigh, he headed over.

'You must be new. Otherwise you'd know better than to disturb me.' For the uninitiated that voice might strike fear to the very heart, but McLean knew better. He glanced briefly at his watch, surprised that it was only just past five in the afternoon. A touch early to be hitting the hard stuff if you worked for a living, but maybe acceptable in retirement.

'Actually, I'm not even a member. Seems they'll let anyone in here these days.' He settled into the nearest unoccupied chair as ex-Detective Superintendent Charles Duguid stiffened, looked round and stared at him with a curious mixture of loathing and disbelief.

'There goes the neighbourhood.' He threw back the last of his whisky like a desperado in a Western saloon bar. 'What the fuck are you doing here, McLean?'

'And a good afternoon to you, too, sir.'

Duguid shuffled in his seat the better to glower at him. 'It was good until you showed up. What do you want?'

'Would you believe it if I said your help with an investigation?'

Duguid's glower turned into a scowl. 'In case you hadn't noticed, they shut down the cold-case unit when they realized you'd just keep digging up all the wrong skeletons. I'm retired. Leave me alone.'

'How's that going, sir? The retirement? Only, last I heard you were spending most of your time here. Didn't know you were such a keen golfer.'

Duguid looked away from McLean, caught the eye of the bartender and held up his empty glass for a refill. He said nothing more until he'd been brought a replacement and indicated with a jab of one overlong finger that McLean was paying.

'I assume this is something you need looked into off the books. No other reason you wouldn't be bullying one of your constables into doing it. Or just doing it yourself for that matter.'

'Not exactly off the books, but certainly low profile. The chief superintendent's keen the press don't find out.'

'Chief super, eh?' Duguid raised a greying eyebrow, his interest piqued.

'His son's gone missing, and his last known movements would have put him somewhere near the truck crash two days ago. We've three bodies so badly damaged we can't identify them yet and Forrester's terrified one of them might be his boy.'

'Terrified. Interesting choice of word.' Duguid took a sip of his whisky. 'But why the hush hush? I mean, if the lad really is one of your bodies then it's not going to reflect badly on him, is it? Quite the opposite. Gives the police a more personal stake in the tragedy.'

'Funnily enough, the same thought had occurred to me. Sure, Forrester was very convincing but even I could tell there was more to the story than he was letting on. He's trying to do damage limitation.'

'Makes you wonder why the fuck he picked you for the job.'

'Ha. Maybe my reputation never got as far west as the Gorbals. Or maybe it's just that I'm in charge of the case anyway.'

Duguid did a passable job of suppressing his sneer. 'So why would I help you? What's in it for me?'

'You mean apart from gratitude to me for saving your life? I'd have thought it would be obvious.'

'Enlighten me.' Duguid raised his whisky glass again.

'I've had too much of this to think straight, otherwise I'd have had you thrown out already.'

'Forrester's got the ear of the chief constable. One of his Glasgow cronies. He doesn't really understand Edinburgh, and really doesn't want to be in charge of Specialist Crime. If you help him, there's every chance he'll return the favour. Plenty of folk want to see the cold-case unit back up and running. Who knows, you might even get a budget to work with, too.'

Duguid put his unfinished whisky down on the table beside his seat, turned to face McLean. The ex-detective superintendent looked greyer than when last he'd seen him, worn at the edges. He'd survived the fallout from the Bill Chalmers case, but only because he'd already retired. Now there was a light in his eyes McLean hadn't seen in a while. An excitement at the possibilities opening up ahead of him. The thrill of the chase.

'I thought your grandmother had brought you up better than that, but you're a sneaky wee sod, McLean.' Duguid picked up his glass again, drained it.

'I learned from the best, sir.'

18

The city mortuary had always been an oasis of calm in the bustle of the city centre. McLean couldn't remember the first time he'd visited, probably a trip with his grandmother and long before he'd joined the old Lothian and Borders Police Force. It was a handy place to go when he needed to get away from the station and its endless round of bullying and politics. Not so far he couldn't walk; far enough for him to take his time getting back once summoned. It was on the way to his next destination, too. Well, sort of. And he had plenty of time to check in on his old friend Angus.

The pathologist sat in his shared office, just off the main examination theatre, peering myopically at a computer screen and munching biscuits from a packet beside the keyboard. At least he wasn't wearing scrubs this time.

'Tony. How nice of you to drop by.' Cadwallader shoved the latest biscuit back into the packet as he struggled to his feet. 'Just been working through the toxicology results from some of your lorry crash victims. Still no idea what was in that tanker, but by Christ it was nasty stuff.'

'Thought the labs had identified it. Some kind of chemical cleaner used in the microchip industry. Not sure where it came from, though. Not yet.'

'Oh, aye. They identified the key compound. Hydrofluoric Acid. Very nasty, very toxic and highly controlled. Well, usually. Problem is it seems to have been mixed in with a dozen or more other things. Helpful in a way, I guess. Some of them have partly neutralized the acid, otherwise we'd probably have nothing solid to do a post-mortem on for your last three bodies.'

McLean grimaced at the thought. 'About them. Any closer to an identification?'

'I can tell you that one's male and the other two are female. Apart from that it's out of my hands now.' Cadwallader shrugged. 'I've sent samples off for DNA analysis. What was left of the bodies didn't give us much in the way of clues. No tattoos, no easily identifiable surgery.'

'No teeth?'

'Oh plenty of those. Just not still attached to anything resembling a jaw. To be honest, Tony, if I'd not found six feet and six hands, three each left and right, I'd be unsure we were only looking for three people.'

McLean leaned back against one of the desks. 'That bad was it?'

'Worse.' Cadwallader yawned, scrubbed at his face with the heel of one hand, the other presumably too biscuit-crumbed to be safe. 'I've been doing this job a long time. Too long, some might say. Thought I'd seen it all, but that crash . . .' He fell silent.

'So my coming here asking questions is probably not helping, then.'

'Oh, you can ask all you want. It's out of my hands now. Sooner or later the DNA results will come back. You can run them against all the various databases our government seems to think it necessary to keep for our safety. Compare them with people who've called in about missing relatives —'

'About that,' McLean interrupted, pulling the sample bottle out of his pocket. Saliva and cells from the inside of the chief superintendent's mouth. Cadwallader eyed it suspiciously.

'What have you got there?'

'Could be the father of one of those three. I really hope it's not.'

Cadwallader reached out for the sample bottle and McLean handed it over. 'I can do a very basic test here. Should be able to confirm that none of them are related to this. It'll take a while, though.'

McLean nodded. 'Thank you, Angus. I was going to ask Manda Parsons over at forensics, but . . .'

'But even the delightful Miss Parsons can't do you favours any more. I know. We've got the same problem here. They call it cost cutting, but I've never seen any savings come from it. Politicians driving cars they couldn't possibly afford? Yes. Getting lucrative consultancy work once they've been voted out of office? That, too. But no actual money saved. It won't end well. Mark my words.'

McLean looked around the office, then out to the examination theatre beyond. This was where people's most intimate secrets were laid bare, where the story of their lives and deaths was told. Subjecting it to market forces seemed crass at best; he didn't want to think what the worst might be.

'Someone swapped inert digestate for highly toxic waste, Angus. Doesn't take a genius to work out they were going to dispose of it off the books to save a bit of cash. I don't know how and I don't know when, but I'll find out who's behind it one way or another. I think we've known each other long enough for you to trust me on that.'

Cadwallader half smiled, half frowned, holding up the sample bottle. 'And this will help?'

'Not directly, no.' McLean allowed himself a grin even though he didn't feel particularly cheerful. 'But it represents a powerful favour owed. I think that's worth bending a few rules for, don't you?'

Loud music spilled out into the evening gloom as McLean walked down Cockburn Street towards Waverley Bridge and the railway station. Tourist season in full swing, the pavement thronged with people not entirely sure where they were meant to be going, or indeed where they were. Some were clearly intoxicated, while this close to Waverley Station you always ran the risk of being hit by a stray backpack, foreign or domestic. He stepped on to the cobbled street to avoid a couple of oblivious outdoor types equipped for an unsupported attempt on the summit of Everest, only avoiding being clipped by a taxi because its driver knew exactly where the horn was. Twisting around sent a twinge of pain up his thigh, reminding him of the broken bone and damaged hip. Three years since that accident and he'd still not healed properly. Maybe never would. Hot, dry weather normally brought some relief, so there was probably rain on the way.

The club he was looking for hadn't actually opened yet. Still too early in the evening for live music. Loud and formless noise came from inside, so he knew there was someone in. He hammered on the door until someone unlocked it, the noise morphing into something that might have been a band rehearsing. A young woman stared at him from the open doorway, shaved head cocked to one side as if he was something she'd rather not have to deal with.

'Not open till nine, pet. Gig don't start till after ten neither. Not sure you're even in the right place. National Opera's over at the Usher.' She went to close the door, but he shoved a foot in the way, held up his warrant card. Her eyes widened in surprise.

'It's not what you think,' McLean said before she could turn and shout 'It's the fucking pigs' or something similar to her friends making a racket at the back of the building. 'I'm looking for Eric. Just want to see he's OK. Nothing else.'

Something about his voice must have struck a chord. Either that or he was being strung along. The young woman tilted her head the other way, revealing a tattoo on her neck that would have made Eddie Cobbold weep. Unless his old friend the tattoo artist had done it himself, which given the quality was very possible.

'Ent seen him in a couple days. Gary's spitting blood, so he is. Had to get Big Tam to come and play bass. He hates Big Tam, but we've had this gig booked for ages.'

Too much to hope that Eric Forrester was just hanging out with his friends and not talking to his dad, then. 'You remember the last time you saw him?'

The young woman shrugged. 'Couldn't say. Three, four days ago?'

'What about the rest of the band?'

Another shrug. 'Ask 'em yourself. If they'll talk to youse.' She opened the door wide enough for him to enter. The volume rose as he stepped over the threshold, echoing down a narrow, high-ceilinged corridor from an open doorway at the end.

'So Eric plays bass, then,' McLean said as the young woman followed him into the auditorium. It reminded him of nothing so much as a set designer's ideal for a 1920s jazz club, only without the charm or flapper girls. Dimly lit and somehow managing to feel smoky despite there being no actual smoke, a dozen or so small tables were dotted around a space barely big enough for a thin person to squeeze between the chair backs. At the far side of the room, the band were setting up their instruments on a low stage, and there the jazz analogy broke down.

'Who the fuck's this, Margie?'

McLean assumed the man who spoke was Gary. He had more hair than the girl, but not much and all of it in a spiky Mohican over the top of his head that wouldn't have looked out of place on the King's Road in 1976. Behind him, a couple of other badly dressed young men were struggling to adjust a drum kit. Scrawled across the front of the kick drum in spidery black ink, the name of the band – Fuck Youse – was unlikely to get them much in the way of mainstream media coverage. Looking at them, he suspected they didn't care.

'He's polis. Lookin' for Eric. Reckon his old man must've sent him.'

If anything, Gary's scowl hardened.

'Aye, well, he's no' here, is he. The useless Weegie bastard.'

'You any idea where he might be?' McLean stepped up to the stage, small enough for him to reach out and take hold of the bass guitar on a stand. A long flex coiled away from it to an effects pedal of some form, and then on to an amp at the back of the room. He slung the strap over his shoulder, tapped a thumb against the bottom string and got a surprisingly clean tone back from the speakers.

'Fuck you think you're doing, granddad?' Gary took a step forward, as did the stouter of the two men fixing the drum kit. McLean flexed his fingers. How long had it been? Twenty-five years? More? The riff was a bit rusty, but tuneful enough to stop them all in their tracks. No point chancing any more than that, though.

'Nice.' He unclipped the strap and put the guitar carefully back on its stand. 'Not played in a while, but some things you never forget, aye?'

'That supposed to make us best buddies is it?' Gary sneered.

'Not really.' McLean held the young man's angry gaze. 'Look, I'm not trying to make friends, not trying to bust you for anything either. I'm just trying to find Eric. Word is he could've been over on Lothian Road the other day when that truck crashed. We've still not identified all of the dead, and I really don't want to have to tell my boss his son's one of them.'

Gary's sneer disappeared, but the expression that replaced it wasn't what McLean had hoped for.

'When was that? Aye, I remember. Couple days back. Fuck, yeah. Stupid twat would've been down that end of town, right enough.' He paused a bit before adding: 'Happened in the morning though, didn't it? Doubt he'd be up then.'

'He wasn't at home. His dad said he left early.'

'Eric? Fuck off. No way.' Gary made a face that didn't attempt to mask his disbelief. 'Look, I've no idea where he is. Don't much care if he's dead. We've got a bass player now, so if he wasn't smashed up by that truck, tell him from me he can fuck right off back to Glasgow.'

McLean dipped his head in acknowledgment. 'Fair enough. I'll be sure and let him know.' He turned, winding his way through the chairs until he reached the exit on the far side of the auditorium, turned back to see all eyes still on him. 'Oh, and have a good gig. Maybe I'll stop by later and have a listen.'

Gary might have said something in reply, but McLean didn't hear it as he headed for the street door. It wasn't important anyway. Twenty years of interviewing suspects had honed his skill at telling when he was being lied to. He just couldn't be sure whether it was about not knowing where Eric was, or not caring that he might be dead.

19

'Where'd you learn to play bass like that?'

McLean was about to step out into the street when a voice from behind stopped him. He turned to see the shaven-headed young woman, Margie, standing in the darkness.

'What, you mean badly?' He saw the smile flicker briefly over her lips. 'I played in a band when I was your age. Probably not the sort of stuff you're into. We were all New Romantics.'

'Oh aye? What were you called then? Your band?'

McLean paused before answering, remembered a time when he was still in his teens. How different the world had been then, and yet in many ways just the same. There'd been a point in his life where music was the most import-ant thing to him. More important even than hopes of getting off with one of the girls from the college for young ladies at the other side of town from his hated boarding school. He'd bullied his grandma into buying him the bass guitar, scrimped and saved for an amplifier. He'd practised until his fingers bled, then daubed them with rubbing alcohol to build up calluses. Never really felt he was good enough to play in a band, but a couple of the other boys in his house shared the same taste in music, so they'd formed one anyway. Until term ended and the dream faded.

'Sweet Jane. After the Lou Reed song. We weren't very good.'

'Neither are that lot.' Margie hooked a thumb over her shoulder in the direction of the auditorium, where something distantly related to music was clattering away.

'You're supposed to suck, though. When you start out. That's the bit no one told me. We were rubbish and gave up after a couple of months. I've not picked up a bass guitar in twenty years. More, probably.'

'Fuckin' 'ell. Gary weren't even born twenty years ago. Talk about old man!' Margie's face lit up with mirth, then hardened again. 'You mean it about that truck crash? Eric? Could he have been one of the . . . ?' She tailed off, too young to contemplate death so easily.

'It's only circumstantial at the moment, but his dad's worried. That's why he asked me to try and track him down. I'm in charge of investigating the crash, too, and we've still a lot of work to do on that.'

'You can do DNA and stuff, though, can't you? Find out that way, right?'

'We can, and we will. But it takes time. Could be Eric's one of the dead. I hope not, but it's possible. If he's not, though, then he's missing. Been gone three days, and his dad's a senior policeman. That's a security risk right there, so I need to try and find him.'

'Eric hates his dad, you know? Hates everything he stands for. The law. Government oppression. The man.'

'I'm not going to try and argue him round to my way of thinking. You neither.' McLean leaned against the doorjamb, cool evening air on the back of his neck, noise from the rehearsals sounding increasingly like a pair of empty dustbins dropped down a mineshaft.

'He's gone missing before, y'ken? His dad tell you that?'

McLean opened his mouth to answer, but Margie interrupted him.

'Eric's a good bass player, you know. Sings better'n Gary, too, but he's shy. Doesn't like to make a spectacle of himself. Only way he can get through a gig is if he's had something. Booze, maybe, or some hash. Sometimes he'll get into something stronger. Fuck, I shouldn't be telling you this. You're a fucking polis man. How'd you do that?'

'Do what?'

'Get people to trust you, like?'

McLean shrugged, fished around in his pocket until he found a business card. He held it out for Margie to take. 'Look, I said it before and I meant it. I'm not here to close you down or arrest you for anything. I'm just trying to find Eric for his father. You've helped me just by letting me know about the drugs. I'll not ask you to give me any more details than that. But if you think of anything, or even if you just see him in the street, give me a call, OK? It'll go no further than that.'

A large, white BMW soft-roader sat on the drive almost blocking McLean's route to the back door when he finally arrived home later that evening. He inched his Alfa carefully past it, not wanting to scratch the shiny new paintwork on the rhododendron bushes that lined the driveway. The house might have been ridiculously large for two people with a small third one on the way, but it had been built at a time when horse-drawn carriages were the most elegant form of transport. Much narrower than modern machinery. He hadn't appreciated how small his old Alfa had been compared to almost everything else on the road with four wheels. Thinking about it brought a curious pang of regret and nostalgia for the little car. Only a few months since it had been destroyed and he already missed it.

Warm smells of curry wafted past him as he pushed through the back door and on into the kitchen. No sign of any people, but Mrs McCutcheon's cat looked up from her space in front of the Aga. An empty beer bottle stood on the table, but there was no sign of any food. Suspicious, McLean pulled out his phone, checking for any angry texts demanding to know where he was. Nothing, and he'd told Emma that morning he would be working late. He'd thought she was going to be, too, given the sheer amount of forensic work that had come in following the truck crash. But it had been her day off, hadn't it. He remembered now.

Voices spilled from an open door as he stepped through into the hallway, but they didn't come from the library. He hardly ever went into the dining room, yet another reminder of how ridiculously large and ostentatious this house was, but now the lights were on and there was laughter inside. As he gently pushed open the door and peered in, it died away slowly.

'Tony. Finally you're home. Thought you were going to stay out all night.'

Emma heaved herself out of her chair and waddled across the room, enveloping him in a welcoming hug. He hadn't noticed before, but she smelled differently. Not just the curry that she had obviously been eating, there was something else. Her face seemed rounder, too, the angles of her cheekbones smoothed away. He was so transfixed by it that it took him a while to register who else was in the room.

The car outside had been a giveaway, of course. He'd borrowed it from his best friend and professor of biomechanics, Phil Jenkins, just a few months earlier and almost not given it back. Phil's wife Rachel smiled from her seat at the far end of the table, alongside a baby chair in which her son, Tony Junior, burbled happily. McLean hadn't been expecting a third adult, although he recognized her well enough.

'Jenny. Hi. Haven't seen you since . . .' He stopped talking, remembering the night that Heather Marchmont had died. The night he'd not known who he could turn to until he had remembered Rachel's older sister. Only, by the time she had arrived at the house, Emma was there, returned from two years travelling the world. Unexpected, complicated. It had been a strange evening.

'It's been busy.' Jenny stood, came over to the doorway and gave him a hug. 'We sold the shop and the flat. Moved everything to a warehouse out of town. It's all online nowadays, but business is booming.'

'I'm . . . pleased to hear that. It's good to see you. All of you.' McLean turned to Emma. 'Did I know they were coming?'

Phil let out a bark of laughter that shocked a little squeak of surprise from Tony Junior and got him a scowl from Emma. He ignored it, stood up and crossed the room. 'No, we dropped by unannounced. When we heard you were working, we were going to reschedule, but she insisted. Even phoned for a curry. Tuck in.' He pointed to the table. 'I'll go grab you a beer.'

20

Not sure I've ever been to Broxburn before, but it's the kind of place you might be forgiven for forgetting. The only noticeable feature's the great slag heap, the bing that's all that remains of the mining and heavy industry that once defined this place. More modern industrial estates have grown up around it like carrion feeders round a long-dead carcass, and it's a compound in the far corner of one of these I'm staring at now.

This is where the truck came from. The news has been surprisingly short on detail about it, preferring to sensationalize the possibility of a terrorist attack. This wasn't anything of the sort. I know that, and so do the men working in this compound. With any luck the forensics teams swarming all over the place will find out the truth soon enough, too.

I don't know what I thought I was going to achieve by coming here, though. There's too many people. Uniformed police at the gates, Health and Safety inspectors, even a couple of plain-clothes detectives in a fancy new car. Who knew they earned that much? I can see the offices, the Range Rover belonging to the man who owns the place, but I can't get anywhere near. I can sit and watch, though, hidden away from sight. And who knows? I might get lucky. They might all pack up and leave for the day, everyone except the boss. Then I can get him to myself. No idea what I'll do if that happens. He's a big burly man if the photographs I found online are to be believed. I'm neither of those things. I've never been strong, more likely to nurse a grudge than act upon it. I didn't grow up in these parts, don't quite fit in and certainly don't understand the aggressive, macho culture. I learned long ago it's best to make yourself small, unnoticed. Not a threat.

I guess they sent me to Scotland because it was far away from the house and its horrible secrets. The west coast was fine enough, but my accent had been formed in the Thames Estuary. Even without the memories, I was marked as other, different. School was hard – an English boy in a Scotland feeling its way towards self-determination and independence. I didn't have many friends, but that was fine. I preferred my own company, that and the world online.

And there was revenge, of course.

I knew everyone had died in that fire. Not sure how I knew, but I did. Everyone except Maddy and me, anyway. At first that was enough, knowing the men who had hurt me were all dead. But as the years went by I realized that was pretty naive. Sure, everyone who was there when the fire took hold might have died, including any number of other children, but it was very unlikely that everyone who ever indulged themselves there was present when I torched it. And a place like that doesn't exist in a vacuum either.

Where to start, though, when you don't know anything except that it was a house in parkland, surrounded by trees? A house that burned to the ground, killing several people? Back then I didn't even know that it was in Essex, just somewhere in England. It's amazing what you can find out on the internet, though, the dark web and the private forums for people looking to lessen their guilt by sharing it. The world is full of sick fucks unable to control their basest impulses, but if you look long enough, patterns begin to emerge. That's what I'm good at, seeing the patterns, connecting the dots. Sure, there's the sickos who used to abuse me and Maddy and all the other kids. There's thousands of them out there, more than thousands. Hell, there's probably hundreds of houses like the one I burned down, too. But behind all that, feeding the perversion, are fewer names. They make money and gain influence, and they're very, very careful not to be found out.

Everyone makes mistakes, though, once in a while. That old gentleman with the flabby buttocks and sad member forgot to ring for the nurse when he'd done with Maddy and me. Worse, he was stupid enough to have a cigar lighter in his pocket. We know how well that ended for him.

It's been the work of years now, nursing that grudge. Ever since Sheila first introduced me to the world of computers, the internet, hacking. She gave me an external focus for the rage that had made me self-destructive. Introduced me to others who felt the same way. There's a group of us, loosely speaking. We've never met in real life, don't know each other's real names, don't particularly want to. All we know is that we're all after the same thing, exposing the rotten core at the heart of society. Big business, politics, organized crime, they're all the same when you go deep enough.

It came as a surprise when the name came up in my research, but not that much of a surprise. I already knew about this family-run haulage business in an old mining town on the outskirts of Edinburgh. Knew it was connected to something bad. I just never thought it would be something that would turn my life upside down like this. Never thought I'd end up out here, hiding in the bushes and waiting for the authorities to leave. Direct action's never been my thing. Not since that fateful night with the cigar lighter.

Not until now.

21

McLean woke with a gasp, the image of his nightmare fading. He lay still, staring at the ceiling as his heartbeat slowed from a gallop to a more normal rhythm. Sticky sweat made his skin feel clammy. The duvet had wrapped itself around his legs, pinned him in place as beside him Emma quietly snored. Dawn had already begun to light the room, still strange to him after so many years sleeping on the other side of the house. Gently untangling himself from the duvet's embrace, he slid out of bed and padded across to the bathroom.

By the time he was cleaned and dressed, Emma had done no more than roll on to her back, taking up the whole of the king size mattress. Her snoring intensified, little guttural grunts that petered off to silence before suddenly starting up again. He stood in the doorway for long moments wondering whether to wake her or not, but she was so peaceful. She didn't have to start work until ten either; it would have been cruel to disturb her now.

His phone rang as he was walking down the stairs, buzzing in his jacket pocket without making any sound. It wasn't often he remembered to mute it before going to sleep, but last night had been good, relaxing. Even if he had felt awkward with Jenny and Emma in the same room. That the two of them seemed good friends only made his awkwardness greater.

'McLean.' He spoke quietly, though he was far enough away from the closed bedroom door to shout without fear of waking a soul.

'Ah. Sir. Good. Wasn't sure if you'd be up yet.' McLean recognized the voice of DC Harrison, surprised that she was awake herself. As far as he was aware, she wasn't on the night shift.

'Just about to grab a coffee and head in. Reckon we've a busy day ahead of us.'

'You're not wrong. I've just got in myself and the call came in from Control. Nasty incident out at Finlay McGregor Haulage.' Harrison paused a moment and McLean could almost hear the gulp down the wire. 'It's Mike Finlay, sir. He's dead.'

The journey out to Broxburn and the compound took less time than he had expected. Leaving at six put him ahead of the worst of the rush hour traffic, and going in the opposite direction. McLean found himself turning into the tree-lined lane just half an hour after he had fired up the Alfa's sonorous V6 engine. Peering through the windscreen towards the entrance gates, he decided it would be more sensible to park and walk. Half a dozen squad cars, a couple of ambulances and a fire engine blocked the way. Something was going to get a dent in it before the day was out.

The massive mine-waste bing loomed over the scene as he walked up the rutted and potholed track towards the compound. All around were signs of past industry, decaying buildings, odd squares of concrete that might once have been factory floors. This whole area had seen decades, centuries, of boom and bust. What cycle was it in now?

A muddle of uniform officers clustered in the gateway as he approached. McLean pulled out his warrant card, even though it was unlikely he'd need it. Some of the faces were familiar despite this being well off his usual patch.

'Body inside, is it?' He nodded towards the set of portable cabins, the front door wide open, white-suited forensic technicians coming and going. Their vans were parked up close, alongside a familiar British-Racing-Green-and-mud-coloured Jaguar. The pathologist here before him. McLean didn't wait for an answer, but as he headed for the offices he thought he saw movement out of the corner of his eye. As he turned to see, he could have sworn there was a man standing by the gate. A familiar face he couldn't quite place. When he blinked, the man was gone, replaced by a complex mixture of shapes and shadows as the rising sun played on the trees. Shaking his head, he carried on towards the portable cabins. There couldn't have been anyone there or the constables would have seen him. Just one of those weird times the brain leaped to the wrong conclusion. Not enough sleep after his troubled nightmares.

'You'll need to get suited up if you're going in there.' A familiar voice hailed him from the back of the nearest forensics van and McLean turned to see Amanda Parsons pulling on a pair of white rubber boots.

'Messy, is it?'

'Very. And we've enough contamination with the sister messing everything around. Last thing we need is to have to eliminate all of your residues from the scene, too.' Parsons smiled as she spoke, but McLean knew she was only half joking. He took the set of overalls she offered, signed dutifully on the clipboard. No doubt an invoice would be raised and passed on to the major investigation team, the cost of processing it several times more than the overalls themselves. He was halfway through pulling them on when Parsons's words filtered through.

'Sister? What sister?'

'Yon wifey in there.' The forensic scientist pointed at the doorway. 'She's the one who found him, poor thing. Not nice to lose your brother at that age, let alone find him in . . . Well, you'll see soon enough.'

He found DC Harrison in the main office, through the first cabin door. McLean was relieved to see that she, too, was dressed in an ill-fitting white bunny suit, paper booties wrinkling over her trainers where they were two sizes too big. The room wasn't much changed from the last time he had visited it, except that there were rather more people in there than before.

'That was quick, sir. Wasn't expecting you for at least another half-hour.' Harrison smiled the smile of a person at ease with early mornings. McLean only wished he had her energy. He stepped to one side to let a forensic technician squeeze past with a battered aluminium case, and noticed a woman he didn't recognize. She sat quietly at the far end of the room on one of the elderly reception sofas shoved under a whiteboard scrawled with work roster details. She was almost as pale as the board, not helped by the black trouser suit she wore. Someone had given her a mug of tea, probably to help her with the shock. That would work better if she actually drank it, rather than clasped it in between her hands, balanced precariously on one knee. Everyone else was wearing protective overalls, so this had to be the sister. She didn't look up at him, hadn't seemed to notice him enter at all. He doubted she could hear their conversation over the bustle of the forensics crew.

'How long since we got the call?' McLean turned back to Harrison.

'Not long. Couple of hours, I think. Maybe less.'

'I take it that's Mike Finlay's sister?'

'Aye. Katie Finlay. Apparently the first officers on the scene tried to take her out to their squad car. Reckoned she'd be better off out of the way. She kicked up a bit of a fuss, so they decided to leave her to us. Well, you I guess.'

McLean glanced back at the woman, but she was still lost in her shock-addled thoughts. A quick glance at his watch showed him it wasn't quite seven yet, and he wondered what she had been doing coming here at half five in the morning.

'Body's still in there, I take it?' He dipped his head in the direction of the door through to Mike Finlay's office.

Harrison let out a sigh. 'Aye, it is. I'll warn you, though, sir. It's not pretty.'

'Manda said much the same thing. Guess I'd better go have a look.'

The first thing McLean noticed as he stepped into the adjoining cabin was the cold. Still in shadow on this side, a chill breeze blew through the narrow doorway, whistling in from the window opposite, which had been shattered. He followed the marked path to the desk he had sat in front of just a couple of days ago. On that far side, more white-suited technicians surrounded the body of a man, lying face down, his head out of the window. A thin sliver of glass stuck out through the back of his neck, dark blood congealed on its razor sharp edges and stiletto point. More blood matted his short black hair and shined the cheap fabric of his suit jacket.

'Reckon we can try to get him off there now. See if we can't take that glass with him, eh?' Angus Cadwallader stood up from where he had been kneeling beside the body, stretched, turned. The light from the window made his face look unusually sombre.

'Tony. Good timing. We were just about to move this poor unfortunate fellow.'

'Unfortunate?'

'Well, he's dead. I'd say that wasn't how he'd planned his day to start.' Cadwallader inched his way out from behind the desk, followed by his assistant, Doctor Sharp. She nodded briefly at McLean but said nothing. Probably unhappy at being called out early to such a gruesome scene.

'Cause of death?'

Cadwallader's smile widened, crinkling the old skin around his eyes. 'You always ask. I can give you a rough approximation of time, based on his core body temperature. Reckon he probably died between eleven and midnight. As to what killed him? Well, let's get him back to the mortuary first, why don't we?'

McLean stepped back to allow the technicians in, looked around the room as they fussed carefully over the body. He tried to remember what he had seen the last time he'd been in here, but broken window and blood smears aside, he couldn't see much that had changed. The desk was still a clutter of papers, a small laptop computer, bunch of keys with a Range Rover fob and not much else. A few faded pictures hung on one wall, a large year planner opposite, and, squeezed into the corner by the door, a pair of four-drawer filing cabinets were piled high with the kind of detritus an office accumulates over the years. Everything he might have expected, except –

'Anyone check his pockets? I don't see his phone anywhere.'

'Nothing on the desk, sir. Floor's clear, too.' A forensic technician with an expensive digital camera slung around his neck stood to one side of the broken window, waiting to record the area under the dead body once it was removed. Another technician wheeled a trolley in, and McLean realized the office was getting quite crowded. Mike Finlay's sister was still sitting on the sofa outside, too. Best she not be there when her dead brother was wheeled out in a bodybag.

'Well, keep an eye out for it, OK? And someone check his car, too.'

'It was my granda who started it, but Dad was the one built this business up to what it is now.'

Away from the portable cabins and her dead brother, Katie Finlay seemed to shake off the worst of her shock. It had taken a while to persuade her to leave, but McLean's suggestion she show him around the compound had finally worked. They had walked from the cabins over to the line of trucks, silent and waiting. Who knew when they would be driven again?

'Did you have much to do with the running of the company?'

'Me?' Ms Finlay had been staring at the ground as if her head were too heavy with grief to hold high, but she looked up sharply at the question. 'No. I wasn't involved at all. I mean, I've a share in the business. Dad left me that. But this never interested me. Mike runs . . . ran it all, I should say. Christ, I suppose I'm going to have to take it on, aren't I.'

McLean scanned the compound. Apart from the trucks it was mostly forensics vans, squad cars and a sole ambulance. Mike Finlay's Range Rover was parked close to the portable cabins and a shiny new BMW much like Phil's sat alongside it. Katie Finlay dressed better than her brother, too, her clothes expensive but not ostentatious. He reckoned she must be in her early fifties, streaks of grey showing in the roots of her dyed black hair.

'What is it you do for a living?' he asked.

'As little as I can get away with these days.' Ms Finlay's smile didn't reach her eyes and died on her lips almost as soon as it was born. 'My husband died five years ago. Left me more than enough to live on. And this place pays a dividend when it's making money.'

'Is that often?'

'I get something every year. Some years better than others.' Ms Finlay gestured towards the trucks and the large shed where all the maintenance was carried out. 'Last year we agreed to invest more of the profits, so I took less cash out. Still more than enough for my needs.'

'You were here very early this morning. Any particular reason why?'

Ms Finlay paused a moment, dug into her pocket and pulled out her phone. 'I'm usually up by half five anyways.

Always been an early bird. Got a text from Mike yesterday. Here.' She tapped the screen, held it up for McLean to see. A single line:

> Meet me at the office. Half six. Need to talk about future. AL asking questions.

'Who's Al?' McLean asked.

'Not Al. Well, yes, Al, but he meant A-L. Alan Lewis. He's the other major shareholder in the company. Doesn't have much to do with the day-to-day running, but he's the money man.'

Another person they should be interviewing with regards to the crash. McLean made a mental note to get his details. There was so much they still didn't know about Finlay McGregor Hauliers and Logistics. But then he hadn't even known that Mike Finlay had a sister until an hour or so ago. He watched as the ambulance backed carefully out of the car park in front of the portable cabins, its grisly cargo stowed away and en route to the city mortuary. He shouldn't really be questioning Ms Finlay like this; she was a potential suspect in the murder of her brother, after all.

'We'll need to get a full statement from you,' he said after a while.

Ms Finlay dragged her gaze away from the departing ambulance. 'A statement? Of course. You want it now?' She paused a moment before adding, 'Am I a suspect?'

McLean's gut told him she wasn't. Her reaction to his death was too real. She was still the first person to have seen her brother dead, though. Statistically speaking, it was almost always a close friend or relative, but right now they didn't even know if Finlay had been murdered, didn't know if his sister stood to gain anything from his death. Didn't know anything, if he was being honest.

'I'd say we were being remiss if we didn't consider the possibility.' He watched her gaze narrow, brow furrowing into a frown at his words. 'We've not arrested you, though, and I'm not going to unless I feel it's warranted. Right now we need to finish processing everything here, get the initial report from the pathologist. We will need to talk to you, though. Under caution and with a lawyer present if you, want one. Perhaps later this afternoon? Around three?'

Ms Finlay stared at him blankly for a while. McLean wondered whether she was fit to drive home, whether he ought to get a uniform constable to take her there. He wasn't entirely sure where she actually lived. Eventually she let out a long sigh, shook her head slightly.

'I understand. Going to have to head into town and talk to the solicitors anyway. Bank manager, accountant, Christ, the list grows longer every time I think about it. I appreciate not being thrown in a Black Maria and taken to the cells.'

'I'll detail an officer to accompany you. You're going to need a lift, anyway.'

'I am? Why?' She glanced nervously over in the direction of the parking area.

'I'm afraid forensics are going to want to give your car a look over. I'll be sure and ask them not to damage it.'

22

'You always did have a knack for making things more complicated than they need be, Tony.'

McLean stood in one corner of the major-incident room, watching the ebb and flow of officers and admin staff as they ploughed through the mass of useless information generated by the telephone helpline. Behind him on the whiteboard, the same three numbers remained nameless, the list of their potential identities growing both longer and more hopeless by the hour. He wasn't long back from Broxburn and the latest twist in what should have been a fairly straightforward case, and yet somehow DCI McIntyre had appeared only moments after his return. He imagined she must have been watching from her office window, waiting for his shiny black car to arrive.

'News travels fast. I take it this is about Mike Finlay?'

McIntyre grimaced. 'Recommend you avoid anyone above DCI level for the foreseeable. There's quite a bit of panic.'

McLean pulled out his phone, thumbed the screen to life. No new messages. 'Surprised I've not been called to a meeting then. I don't suppose they'd believe me if I told them I thought it was an unlucky accident.'

McIntyre stared at him for just long enough to be uncomfortable. 'You don't really believe that, though, do you, Tony?'

'I don't know. It's very early days, but Angus couldn't find any obvious signs of a struggle. The office didn't look like there'd been a fight either. It was just . . . horrible.'

'Lack of a struggle doesn't mean it was an accident, though. Could just be that he knew his assailant. Wasn't it his sister who found him?'

'Katie Finlay, aye. I spoke to her at the scene.'

'She in the cells now, then?'

McLean shook his head. 'She didn't do it. Oh, I know. She needs to be questioned properly. I've got a constable with her now, and she'll be in here for interview this afternoon. The circumstances don't work for me, though. She had nothing to gain from her brother's death. She called it in. I don't know –'

'The famous McLean gut tells you she's innocent?' McIntyre had the decency to smile while she said it. McLean just shrugged.

'Something like that. But don't worry. I'm not going to let her off easily because her brother's dead. I just don't want to make her my enemy. She knows more about the hauliers than anyone now. More than she realizes. I need her onside if I'm going to crack that. We still don't know where the effluent came from, why someone tampered with the brakes. Christ, we don't really know anything at all.'

'But what if this isn't an accident? What if someone's done this to shut Finlay up?'

'The thought had occurred to me, Jayne. And if I was trying to think of the best way to derail our investigation before it even got started, silencing Finlay would probably be it.' McLean stared at the blank screen of his phone, the dark, fingerprint-smeared reflection of his own worried face. 'It's just a very messy way to go about it. Frankly, I'd be more suspicious if he just disappeared.'

'Keep it in mind as a possibility, though?' McIntyre's inflection made it a question.

'You know me. Always an open mind.' He was about to say more, but the screen lit up, a reminder message he didn't remember putting in the calendar.

'Something come up?' McIntyre asked. 'Only I don't like the look on your face right now.'

'It's just a reminder that Em's got antenatal class this afternoon. I was going to join her, but with all this shit going on.' He waved at the room, running more efficiently than any other major incident he'd been involved with. He could leave it alone for a few hours, but he'd agreed to interview Katie Finlay at three. 'I'll give her a call. She'll understand.'

McIntyre didn't argue the point, just shook her head as he found the entry in the phonebook and pressed the dial icon. 'On your head be it, Tony.'

'We've got the security camera footage in from the haulage company, sir. Thought you might like a wee look-see.'

McLean glanced up from his desk to see DC Harrison standing half in the open doorway. He'd escaped the incident room hoping for a moment to gather his thoughts. His phone call to Emma had gone just about as well as DCI McIntyre had predicted. He'd need to do something to make up to her for it, he just wasn't quite sure what.

'You set up the viewing room?' he asked, pushing himself out of his chair and grabbing his phone off the desk. He half expected it to be hot to the touch.

'Aye. Lofty's down there now going over the stuff we got from Health and Safety.'

'Health and Safety?' McLean stopped in his tracks, halfway from desk to door. 'Surely they were all gone by the time Finlay died. Would anyone have put the tapes back in?'

Harrison tried to suppress a smile but failed badly. 'There's no tapes any more, sir. It's all hard drives and backups to the cloud. Finlay McGregor didn't have the best system in the world, but they'd a lot of expensive kit in that yard. Place was pretty well covered. Night vision and movement sensors, too. And it's all run by a contractor, so it's been on the whole time we've been there.'

Suitably chastened in his ignorance, McLean allowed himself to be led along the corridor and down the stairs. One positive outcome from the ever-shrinking workforce in the station was that a reasonably sized room had been repurposed as a full-time video suite. Which was to say someone had put blackout blinds on the windows and wheeled in a few elderly computers, linking them up to the city's expanding network of CCTV cameras. It wasn't on a par with the major surveillance centres at Bilston and City Chambers, but it was better than the broom cupboard and elderly VHS recorder he remembered from earlier cases.

'Find anything interesting?' he asked as DC Blane twisted around in his chair to see who had entered the room.

'Not yet, sir. Just trying to get my head around all the different cameras. It's mostly footage of the forensics team and Health and Safety going over the maintenance shed and offices so far.'

McLean dragged a chair over to the screens and sat down alongside the tall detective. A grid of small images showed different views of the compound: the entrance gates, the car park in front of the cabin offices, the line of lorries awaiting their next job, the diesel tanks and maintenance sheds. He took a while to build up a picture of the place as the images spooled forwards in stop-motion jumps. Mostly there was nothing happening, but occasionally a yellow-jacketed Health and Safety inspector or white-suited forensic technician would wander across shot. One camera, presumably not noticed at first, helpfully covered an area of scrubby land between the shed and the back fence of the compound. A place old machinery went to die, it was also a good spot to steal a crafty cigarette unseen by the boss, or so it appeared.

'How far back does this go?'

'The system overwrites after a week, so there should be footage of the truck coming and going and the night it sat in the compound. I take it you're more interested in last night's footage, though, aye?'

'For now. We need to see who came and went, and when. Can we concentrate on the car park there?' McLean pointed at the relevant image, and with a couple of clicks, DC Blane enlarged it to the whole screen. The cameras took pictures every few seconds, so the video speeded up spooled through the minutes quickly. At first it was a frenzy of activity, figures jumping around the screen like spiders on acid. After a while the vehicles began to disappear from the car park, until there was only Mike Finlay's Range Rover. A couple of seconds later a familiar-looking BMW appeared.

'That's the sister's car. Slow it down, won't you? Let's see how long she stays.'

Nothing much happened as the minutes clicked forward. Then at around half past eight a slim figure appeared at the door, the BMW backed out of its parking space and drove away. For a while the only change was the colours of the scene muting as evening set in. The timestamp moved forward to half ten, on to quarter to eleven. Blane reached for the mouse, presumably intending to increase the playback speed. And then something flickered on the screen.

'Hold up. Back a bit. What was that?'

McLean pulled his chair closer to the screen as Blane ran the images backwards, then inched them forward again one frame at a time. Nothing changed between each slow click, only the timestamp indicating that another ten seconds had elapsed, until suddenly there was something there.

'Is that a person?' McLean rubbed at his eyes, hoping it might make the image less fuzzy. The time on the screen was ten forty-eight and fifty seconds. Another click, ten forty-nine exactly, and the blur was gone. Blane clicked back a couple of frames. Nothing, blur, nothing. Was it possible to cover that distance in ten seconds?

'Anything showing around that time on any of the other cameras?'

Blane fiddled with the mouse some more, keying up a couple of different views. McLean watched closely as he toggled through a ten-minute window around the appearance on the first camera. There was nothing by the sheds, nothing in the space where everyone had been smoking, but then he switched to the video feed of the entrance gate.

'That's not right.' The lanky detective constable leaned in, peering at the screen so closely he was in danger of leaving greasy smears on it with his nose.

'What's not right?' McLean tried to see for himself, but Blane's head was so large it was difficult to catch a glimpse.

'See here, at ten forty-six? The gate's closed, chains hanging round it. Not locked, but then we know Mr Finlay was inside.' Blane leaned back, clicked the mouse and moved the video forward a couple of minutes. 'And here it is again, only look what's different.'

McLean had to stare for a few moments before he, too, saw it. 'The chain's been moved. It's only hanging from one side of the gates, not both.'

'Someone must have moved it, gone through the gates and closed them behind them. Someone went in there between quarter to and eleven that night.'

'And the pathologist reckons he died between eleven and midnight.' McLean let out a weary sigh. So much for it being an accident. 'Oh bloody hell.'

23

'The strange thing is I still can't see any sign of a struggle.'

Early afternoon and McLean found himself once more in the city mortuary, not really watching as Angus Cadwallader peeled back the secrets of the recently deceased. He should have been tracking down Chief Superintendent Forrester and updating him on developments surrounding Mike Finlay's untimely death, but somehow the thought of standing in a cold examination theatre a half-mile away from the station had been more appealing.

He could justify his reticence by telling himself this was the man's post-mortem, which might reveal vital clues as to how the haulage contractor had died. Better to gather the facts before opening yet another line of investigation. Coming here gave him an opportunity to consider the implications of DC Blane's discovery, too. In the hurly burly of the station it was all but impossible to find peace and quiet in which to think.

'I'm sorry?' Lost in thought, McLean only now realized that his old friend the pathologist had said something. He dragged his attention back to the cadaver, then wished he hadn't. Mike Finlay lay on the stainless steel examination table, his naked body pale from blood loss. Only the staining of the skin around his throat gave any indication as to how he had died, the lethal shard of glass now removed and bagged as potential evidence.

'No sign of a struggle, Tony. Do pay attention.' Cadwallader manipulated the body as he spoke, pointing out things McLean couldn't see without coming closer. 'There's a bruise on the back of his head, very slight cut. I'm guessing he fell backwards against the window and that's what broke it. He'd have been fine if it was safety glass, but those old cabins looked like they'd been around a while. Well, you saw how it shattered.'

'What about the cuts on his arms?' McLean didn't like getting too close to the bodies as they were being examined, especially not once the scalpel came out, but he took a step forward to point at the thin lacerations on Finlay's upper arms and shoulders.

'More of the glass, I'd say. If he fell backwards that would explain the marks here and here.' Cadwallader pointed to livid red lines on the dead man's skin. 'His suit took the brunt of it. Probably would have protected him better if it hadn't been a cheap knock-off.'

'So he fell backwards against the glass. Smashed it. A piece is still in the bottom of the frame sticking upwards. How does he turn around, fall down on it and kill himself, all without any sign of a struggle? He wasn't drunk was he? There was no sign of any booze at the scene.'

'Not got to the stomach contents yet, but he'd have to be pretty steaming drunk to do this, don't you think?' Cadwallader picked up a scalpel, ready to incise. 'These injuries are more consistent with panic and flight. Poor sod looks like he was terrified of something.'

McLean took a step back, readying himself for the unpleasant part of the examination. 'Something, or perhaps someone.'

'If it was someone then they never laid a hand on him. I'd stake my reputation on that. There is something, though.' Cadwallader put the scalpel back down again, walked across to a bench at the side of the examination theatre and picked up a clear plastic evidence bag that appeared to be filled with clothing. 'He'd soiled himself. Urine and faeces both. It's always difficult to know whether that's pre-mortem or a result of the body letting go at the moment of death. I didn't think much of it, but it could be someone quite literally scared the crap out of him.'

McLean remembered the CCTV footage, the mysterious blur that might have been a person visiting the office around the time Finlay had died, the chain across the gates that had been moved. How could someone enter the compound without being seen, get into the portable cabins without leaving any forensic trace and scare a grown man into killing himself without even touching him? 'There's no marks on him other than the cuts from the window? Nothing at all?'

Cadwallader held his scalpel up to the light. 'Not a thing. No bruises, contusions, nothing. Hard to believe he even worked in the haulage industry. Still, let's see what's inside shall we? Might find something there to help solve this mystery.'

'I've just got off the phone with the chief constable, Tony. He's . . . how can I put it? Concerned about the way the investigation is going.'

The summons to the chief superintendent's office had come through as McLean was walking back from the mortuary, the image of Mike Finlay's pale dead body still fresh in his mind. Not Forrester himself, but one of his admin staff had placed the call, so McLean had assumed it wasn't important enough for him to have to run. Or forgo the cup of coffee in the canteen that he'd needed to replace the unpleasant taste in his mouth. There was the small matter of not quite knowing how to mention the possibility Finlay's death might not have been as straightforward as they'd initially thought, but Forrester hadn't given him time to bring that up.

'Is there a problem, sir? We're going as fast as we can. This isn't as straightforward as we'd all like, I know.'

Forrester scowled, his face and neck reddening as if he were embarrassed. 'That's the point, though, isn't it? It's been three days now since the crash and it's just getting more and more complicated. Bad enough we've got to constantly reassure the press this isn't some kind of terrorist attack. Now you've got a suspicious death to throw into the mix. And why are you pestering this energy company?' He pulled a notepad towards him, peered at the scribblings on it. 'Extech? Is that it?'

'They run the biodigester site, sir, where the truck's cargo came from. Well, the cargo it was supposed to be carrying.'

'Exactly. Supposed to be carrying. But it wasn't, was it? The paperwork had been faked.'

McLean hadn't been offered a chair. Now, standing on the wrong side of the chief superintendent's desk it felt like he'd been called up in front of the headmaster to explain himself when as far as he was aware he'd done nothing wrong.

'It's still worth our while speaking to them, sir. Wouldn't

you say? Check they actually loaded a tanker full of their waste, how much of it and when? If they did, then that stuff's got to be somewhere. If they didn't, then they're in on the lie.'

'Yes, of course. But you could have phoned them. Had a constable phone them. You didn't need to go out and pester them yourself. And looking into their financial history?'

The penny dropped. McLean almost wondered why it had taken him so long to figure it out. Extech was modern and shiny and had been financed entirely with private money. No doubt the first thing Ms Ferris had done after he and DC Harrison had left the site was call her boss. He, and McLean was willing to bet good money it was a he, had picked up the phone to his old chum the chief constable. Or spoken to a tame politician who had done it for him. There might have been a few more layers of influence and favour, but the result was the same. Quite how they knew what DCs Stringer and Blane had been up to when neither of them had managed to find any company information on Extech was another matter entirely.

'I asked some of the constables to do a quick background check on the company, sir. Who the directors are, that sort of thing. It's surprising how often the same names crop up. Connections where you wouldn't expect them to be. I'd rather we found that out ourselves before some smart-arse lawyer pointed it out in court.'

Forrester leaned forward over his notepad, elbows on the desktop and hands clasped as if that was the only way he could stop himself from wringing them. McLean didn't know him, couldn't read him the way he had learned to with Brooks and Duguid. Even so, he was fairly certain that the chief superintendent was being put under considerable pressure to steer the investigation away from that direction.

'There was one other thing, sir.' McLean clasped his own hands behind his back to stop himself from fidgeting. 'About Mike Finlay.'

Forrester slumped in his chair as if someone had just pricked his balloon. 'Go on.'

'There's evidence to suggest he wasn't alone when he died.' McLean relayed the information he'd gleaned both from the CCTV footage of the yard and from the post-mortem. As he did so, Forrester's balloon crumpled even further.

'Do you ever just solve a crime neatly and simply?'

McLean opened his mouth to answer, but Forrester waved him down.

'No, don't say anything. I know life's complicated. Christ, I wish it wasn't.' He took a couple of slow breaths and McLean recognized the look of a man silently counting to ten. 'So what do you think's going on, then?'

'I honestly don't know, sir. Finlay's death is awkward and suspicious, but it's also very unusual. If someone wanted to silence him, there are easier ways. And Ang—, . . . the pathologist can't find any signs of a struggle, which given how he died is very surprising.'

'So what do you want to do about it, then?'

The directness of the question brought McLean up short. He was conditioned to having his every move criticized, to being shouted at whenever he suggested something that might make life more complicated. To be asked for an opinion rather put him on the back foot.

'I'd like to go over the CCTV footage more closely, and speak to the forensics people again first. Maybe get them out to have another look at the scene. I'm interviewing Finlay's sister later this afternoon, see if I can't get a bit more out of her.'

'You think she's in on this? Why's she not in a cell already?'

'If I thought she'd had a hand in it, she would be, sir, but she was the one who called it in. Nothing she's told us so far has turned out to be false. She could be very helpful with the truck crash investigation, or she could throw up a wall of lawyers to get in our way. I think keeping her on our side is the best approach, don't you?'

Forrester rubbed at his face, working the tiredness out of his eyes. 'I'm getting too old for this. OK. Play it your way for now. But keep me in the loop.'

McLean nodded, but said nothing. He started to walk towards the door, and then the chief superintendent stopped him. 'Any news on that other matter I asked you to look into?'

'I've put some feelers out. Asked a couple of senior officers I can trust to help. I went and spoke to the band he plays with, too. Nice wee lass called Margie.'

'Margie? Margie Cullen? Christ, what's she doing over here?'

'You know her?'

'She and Eric went to school together. She's the one got him into all this mess in the first place. Bad news.' Forrester shook his head as if the mere thought of the young woman were too much to bear. It didn't take a degree in Psychology to see the displacement going on. So much easier to look for an external reason for the collapse of his family than anything he might have done himself.

'I gave that DNA swab to the pathologist direct, too. Angus won't ask questions, but it'll take a day or two to run comparisons on all three unidentified bodies.'

Forrester nodded once, rubbed at his face with his hands again. McLean couldn't help but notice the shake in his fingers. Was this what being a father meant?

'Keep on it, then.' The chief superintendent picked up his pen and started to jot something down on his notepad. Interview over. McLean headed for the door, waiting for the final remark as he left. He wasn't disappointed.

'And don't push too hard with Extech Energy. They're not the ones at fault here, aye?'

McLean said nothing, closed the door quietly behind him. Forrester hadn't told him to stop investigating Extech entirely, only not to push too hard. Well, he could be subtle if he put his mind to it.

24

'Thank you for coming, Ms Finlay. I realize this is a very difficult time, but from my experience I've found it best to get these things done as quickly as possible. While the memory is still fresh.'

They had put Katie Finlay in interview room two, the nice one with the window that opened and pictures on the walls. A uniform constable had brought them mugs of tea and even managed to find some biscuits, although from where McLean could only guess.

'It's a strange thing, Inspector. I've been discussing the ramifications all morning. Spoken to the company lawyers, the accountant, even our old bank manager, but the reality of it's not sunk in. Mike dead, I mean. I'm sure it will soon, but with the crash first and now this . . .' Katie Finlay's voice cracked as she spoke, and she clasped her hands together as if trying to stop them shaking.

'I understand. It's not easy, especially when you've had no warning. I'll try to be brief, anyway. You already told me most of what I need to know back at the compound. There were just one or two points I want to clarify.' McLean glanced at the dour-faced lawyer who had arrived with Ms Finlay. He'd said nothing since arriving except to decline both coffee and biscuits. 'And to make sure your statement is recorded correctly.'

Ms Finlay nodded, but said nothing.

'You have a share in the company, Finlay McGregor, but you don't have anything to do with running it. Is that right?'

'More or less, yes. I'm really not interested in haulage or trucks. It was always horses for me, eventing, that sort of thing. Oh, I knew about trucks. I needed my HGV licence to drive to shows. Dad taught me that, bought me my first box. The mechanics used to keep it running smoothly. I've not really competed since my husband died, though. Sold the box a couple of years ago. It was just taking up space.'

'Your husband. Did he have anything to do with the business?'

Ms Finlay laughed, a short, desperate bark rather than any true mirth. 'George? Good God, no.' She paused a moment, staring at McLean with an odd expression. 'You don't know, do you? George Cameron. The showjumper and eventer? He won a bronze medal at the London Olympics. Proudest day of my life, and his. Then the stupid oaf fell off his horse and broke his neck out hacking.'

'I'm very sorry.'

'Why? You didn't push him did you? You didn't jump out from behind a hedge and spook old Rameses?' Ms Finlay's stare intensified for a moment before she relented. 'Ach, it was a while back now, and we'd mostly drifted apart before then anyway. He was always more in love with the horses than me.'

'So you didn't have much to do with the company, but you headed over there first thing this morning. Your call was logged at half six, so you must have left home quite early.'

'Like I showed you, Mike texted me last night, asking me to come and meet him first thing. He didn't say what it was about, but it was most likely the crash. Health and Safety have closed us down while they carry out their investigations. You lot are looking into it all, too. I'm not saying you shouldn't, quite the opposite. But it could destroy the company. Hell, maybe it already has. Can't see it carrying on much without Mike.'

'Do you still have that text message, Ms Finlay?' Harrison asked. 'It would be useful to know exactly when it was sent.'

The lawyer perked up, and for a moment McLean thought he was going to say something, but he clearly thought better of it, and slumped back into his seat without a word.

'Sure.' Ms Finlay pulled a slim smartphone from her pocket, tapped the screen, swiped a couple of times and then passed it to the detective constable. 'Half ten last night.'

'And when was the last time you saw him?' McLean took up the questioning again as Harrison swiped the screen, wrote down notes in neat handwriting and then gave the phone back.

'About two hours earlier, I guess. Met him at the office. We were discussing the best way forward for the company, but I had to leave. He was going to make a few calls then go home himself. Least, that's what he said.'

'How did he seem then? Was he agitated? Depressed?'

'I'll stop you right there, Inspector. If you're thinking Mike might have topped himself rather than face up to what happened, then you really don't know what makes us Finlays tick.'

'Just covering all the bases. It's fair to say he was under considerable pressure, though?'

'Aye, I'll give you that. Just made him angry. Not suicidal. He'd far more likely hurt someone else than himself.'

McLean glanced across to Harrison, gave her the slightest of nods to make sure she wrote that down. There was no need; she worked her pen with all the industrious zeal of a first-year undergrad. The whole interview was being taped, too.

'You told me before, your brother had no family. Was he ever married? Children?'

Ms Finlay gave McLean that intense stare again. 'God, you really know nothing about him, do you?'

'That's rather the point of this interview. He has no criminal record, and, contrary to popular belief, we don't keep tabs on people just in case they might do something wrong.'

'OK. I get your point. No, Mike was never married. Far as I knew he never had a girlfriend last more than a couple of dates. Dad used to wonder if he was gay, but that's not something a lad can keep from his big sister, aye?'

'So he lived for his work, then? The haulage company?'

'Guess you could say so. He never had much in the way of hobbies. Liked watching the rugby. The company's got seats at Murrayfield, tickets to all the internationals. It's a good way of buttering up potential clients. That's what Mike spent most of his time doing, now I think about it. Wheeler-dealing, always hustling for the next contract.'

'Was he a heavy drinker? I'd imagine there'd be a fair bit of alcohol at events like that.'

'He liked a drink now and then, aye. But heavy drinker? No. He liked to get others drunk and keep his wits about him.'

McLean waited until Harrison had finished writing that down before continuing. 'One more thing, and it might sound a bit odd, but did your brother scare easily?'

'Scare?'

'You know, sudden loud noises, people appearing out of nowhere. As a boy, was he scared of the dark?'

Ms Finlay paused a moment before answering. 'Now you mention it, yes. As a kid he was terrified of the dark. Used to sleep with the light on, sometimes wake up screaming. But he grew out of that. Least I think he did. Not something you'd expect in a grown man. Why?'

McLean stood up, indicating to Harrison to do the same. 'No particular reason, just something the pathologist mentioned.'

'You think something spooked him and he, what? Tripped up and fell through the window?' Finlay's expression spoke eloquently of how ridiculous she thought that idea.

'We have to consider every possibility, Ms Finlay. If only to eliminate it from our enquiries.'

'You'll be telling me it was a ghost next.' Ms Finlay almost made a joke of it as she and the silent lawyer stood up. 'Have you any idea when I can have my car back?'

'I don't, I'm afraid. But I'll arrange for someone to drop it round as soon as forensics have finished with it. Meantime, if I could ask you don't go anywhere far without letting us know, please. We may have more questions.'

'Inspector, my client has been nothing but cooperative. Is this strictly necessary?' the lawyer finally asked.

'A man is dead and the circumstances of that death are very suspicious. I think we're being remarkably understanding, don't you?' McLean held the lawyer's gaze until he looked away.

'Don't antagonize the man, Eustace. You know as well as I do he could arrest me and put me in a cell if he wanted. Come along now. We've more than enough to be getting on with.' Ms Finlay grabbed the hapless solicitor by the arm and steered him to the door with such speed, McLean barely had time to open it for them. She paused for a moment as if she were going to say something else, then just shook her head and stepped out of the room.

'She seems very calm for someone who's just lost her brother, sir. Let alone someone who just found her brother dead in quite such a grisly manner.'

A uniform constable had escorted Katie Finlay and her lawyer away from the interview room, and now McLean and DC Harrison were enjoying their coffee and the last of the biscuits. A bit stale, perhaps, but not so far past their sell-by date that the chocolate coating had started to bleed white. The sun pouring in through the window and the quiet of being tucked away in a corner of the station far from the major-incident room made it a very pleasant place to be.

'You're right, although I've met people like her before. Faced with that kind of trauma, you'd think most folk would just go to pieces, but some shrug it off, roll up their sleeves and get on with what needs to be done.'

'Like you did at the crash scene, sir? The truck? That must have been horrific.'

McLean suppressed a shudder as the nightmares from the past few nights came back to him. They'd pass in time. He hoped. 'A bit like that, I guess. Except I've had training, which helps. You never really know until it happens how you're going to react, though. Thinking about it is always worse than actually doing it.'

'Rather not have to do either, to be honest.'

'You're in the wrong line of work then.' McLean took a sip of coffee and another bite of biscuit. 'So what did you make of the interview then?'

'Hard to say, sir. She's hiding something, but then everyone is. Don't think she killed her brother. Unless . . .' Harrison stopped talking for a moment, her eyes losing focus as she stared out of the window. 'What if she did kill him, sir? Not on purpose, but by accident? Then she tried to cover it up by calling us and making up that whole story about the text.'

'Go on.' McLean wasn't convinced, but they were going nowhere. There was no harm in thrashing out some theories.

'Well, she's a sleeping partner in the business, right? Is it sleeping or silent? Can never remember. Anyway, she has nothing to do with the running of it, but she gets some income every year. Only the crash is likely to end the company, so no more money. She goes to see her brother, has words, maybe even finds out that they've been cutting corners, forging papers. That chemical muck had to have come from somewhere. Maybe they've got a thing going where they collect small amounts from sites all over the central belt, store it all in that tanker till it's full, then . . . I don't know . . . dump it somewhere?'

'You think she's in on that?'

Harrison frowned as she thought about the question. 'Probably not. But she's a partner in the business, so she's liable in some way. What if her brother called her over to confess and she just loses it with him for fu—, . . . screwing up her life. You heard what she said about him. Far more likely to hurt someone else than himself. Maybe she's the same? Fight gets physical, he ends up through the window. It's an accident, but it freaks her out anyway. Christ knows it'd freak the shit out of me. She texts herself that message, goes home and gets changed. Waits till morning and then heads back. Soon as she arrives, she phones us and it all kicks off.'

McLean might have clapped, except that might have seemed condescending, and he was genuinely impressed with Harrison's deduction. It was just a shame she didn't have all the facts.

'There's one wee problem,' he said.

'There is?'

'Aye, there is. Post-mortem on Mike Finlay shows no sign of a fight. You remember the office, right? How much was it changed from how you remember it when we went there before?'

Harrison stared off into the distance again, only this time her eyes flicked ever so slightly from side to side, as if she were mentally re-creating the scene. 'But what if it was really just an accident? What if they weren't fighting, he just got up and, I don't know, fell awkwardly?'

'Then we'd have got the call between half ten and eleven last night, which is pretty much the time of death Angus came up with. And we've seen the security camera footage. Her car leaves at half eight. No reason to think anyone else was driving it. The only thing we've got is a flicker on one image that might just be an electrical gremlin, and a chain that mysteriously unloops itself from the entrance gate around the time Finlay died.'

'It's not much, when you put it like that.' Harrison shrugged. 'Still suspicious as fu—, . . . heck, though.'

McLean smiled at the detective constable's attempt to stop herself from swearing. It was a mirthless smile though.

'Suspicious as fuck is about right,' he said. 'I just wish I could work out exactly what happened.'

25

A knock at the door interrupted him from an endless cycle of thoughts, trying to make sense of the jumble of events and the disparate strands of evidence he somehow needed to knit together. McLean looked up expecting to see one of the detective constables bearing more bad news, or perhaps Grumpy Bob with the suggestion they nick off for a pint. Someone else entirely blocked the open doorway.

'Nasty habit, leaving your door open so that anyone can walk in whenever they want.' Ex-Detective Superintendent Charles Duguid had ditched the tweed suit in favour of dark trousers and a jacket that might have been stolen from a maths teacher. He stepped into the room, looking around with a slight sneer on his mustachioed face. 'Mike Spence's old office. He always said they'd have to offer him the top job or carry him out in a box before he'd give this up.'

It was a joke in bad taste, given Detective Chief Inspector Spence's recent death, but then Duguid had rarely cared what his fellow officers thought about him. McLean put down the reports as he stood up, indicating the conference table across the room.

'I quite liked my wee hidey-hole at the back of the station, to be honest. The new chief superintendent insisted I move, otherwise I reckon this place would have been left empty a while longer. Mark of respect.'

'Misguided respect.' Duguid pulled out a chair and

dropped into it with a slight grunt of discomfort. 'Still, at least there's somewhere to sit down, and the light's better than that dungeon you had me working cold cases out of.'

'I take it this isn't a social visit.' McLean pulled out another chair and sat down slightly further away from his old boss than was perhaps polite. He looked back to the still open door on the other side of the room. 'Should I shut that?'

'What?' Duguid followed his gaze. 'No. Nothing I've got to tell you's particularly secret. And this place is like a mortuary it's so quiet. Where is everyone?'

'I think they call it streamlining operations. That and the new setup mean half of the detectives based here are working somewhere else at any one time. Or away at the Crime Campus getting above themselves.'

'Aye, well. There's progress, I suppose.' Duguid ran thin, long fingers through his straggly hair. 'Been asking around about your missing young man, Eric Forrester. Not been in these parts long.'

'It's not six months since Brooks left and all that nonsense with Call-me-Stevie.'

Duguid laughed, a strange noise to be coming from the ex-detective superintendent. 'Is that what you call him? Ha. And I used to think Dagwood was lame.'

'Most of the station call him Teflon Steve now. We do our best.'

'Aye, that you do. And now you're saddled with Tom Forrester. Decent enough copper. Better at admin than anything else. And his son, Eric. Heard he's quite the musician, which I suspect he got from his mother. Not sure where he got his taste for hard drugs from though.'

'Hard drugs? A bit more than the odd joint with his bandmates, then.'

'You've spoken to them?' Duguid's bushy, greying eyebrows raised in surprise. 'They spoke to you?'

'I have my ways.'

'Well, if you didn't need my help, why'd you ask for it?' Duguid's protest was half-hearted at best. Not like the old firebrand who suffered fools badly if at all.

'I've no contacts in Glasgow. Well, none who'd talk to me without gossiping about it afterwards.'

'Aye, well.' Duguid shifted in his seat like a man who's forgotten his pile ointment. Something was troubling him. 'Seems young Eric almost got himself banged up a couple of years back. Possession with intent to supply. His dad had to pull in a lot of favours to make that one go away. Probably why he's been handed this posting.'

'Are we that bad?'

'Worse. Believe me.'

'So what was young Eric's drug of choice? Who was he getting it from?'

'What do all the young idiots take these days? Heroin's right back in fashion, it seems. As to who was supplying him, I've no idea. Making the problem go away meant not following that up particularly closely. Eric got shoved off to a private rehab centre for six months, and that was about it.'

'He didn't give up any names? Nobody interviewed him? Even off the record?'

'It's possible.' Duguid shrugged. 'But, if so, no one's telling me.'

*

181

He almost missed the phone, vibrating away in his jacket pocket, slung over the chair on the far side of the room. Duguid wasn't long gone, and McLean was still sitting at the conference table, staring out of the window as he tried to make sense of the information the ex-detective superintendent had dug up for him. He hurried over, grabbing it out and hitting the screen with a hasty thumb just before it switched to voicemail.

'McLean.'

'You never came to the gig.' A female voice, unfamiliar at first, but then he remembered. The venue, the bass guitar, the young woman with the shaven head and the tattoos.

'It's Margie, isn't it?'

'Wow. Didn't think I'd made that much of an impression, Mr Polisman.'

'I'm trained to remember things.' McLean dropped down into the seat, catching himself before it tipped backwards too far and deposited him on the floor. 'And, besides, I've not given my card out to many people recently.'

'Aye, well. You missed a great gig. Music wasn't much, but Gary and Big Tam got into a fight during the encore. Looks like we're needing a new bass player if you're still interested.'

McLean smiled at the thought. The looks on the faces of his colleagues if he told them he was quitting the police to go and join a punk band. Maybe twenty years ago he'd have been tempted. OK, maybe thirty.

'Wouldn't want to show you all up, but thanks for the offer. I take it Eric's still a no-show then.'

'Aye. Nobody's seen him all week. I was wondering if

you'd got those DNA results back. Was it him in that crash?'

Judging by Margie's tone of voice, McLean reckoned there might have been something more than the casual friendship of bandmates between her and Eric Forrester. Then again, they'd known each other from childhood, so it might just have been that.

'Nothing yet. Sorry.'

'Can't believe he'd just walk out like that. No' come back. No' even a call.'

'Aye. We tried tracing his mobile, but it's not switched on. Or the battery's flat.' Or it got melted into a puddle of plastic and solder by the same industrial solvent that dissolved half of your boyfriend's body away.

'You think it's really him then?' Margie sniffed, sounding more like an adolescent than the strong, independent young woman he'd met the evening before. 'You think he's really dead?'

'I think it's possible, yes. But I also think there's another possibility. I think you do too, Margie, or you'd not have called.'

'How d'ye mean? I was calling about the DNA, like.'

'Aye, I know that. But I also know about Eric's drug habit. The stuff he got up to in Glasgow. This isn't the first time he's gone off for a day or two, is it?'

The line fell silent, but McLean was confident the young woman was still on the other end. He gave her the time she needed. Not as if he had anywhere else to go. Finally, with a sniff that would have done a teenager proud, she spoke again.

'He's fine. Most of the time. A bit of weed never did nobody no harm, aye?'

McLean said nothing, not wanting to remind Margie that she was talking to a police officer. Better to be the surrogate parent at this point.

'Only, sometimes that's not enough for Eric. He . . . I dunno. He feels. Like, the weight of the whole world's on his shoulders. See when he plays his bass. When he's feeling like that. It's magic. Swear I could just listen and listen. No need for Gary's guitar or Jakey bashing away on his drums. No' even my singing, really, though that's magic, too, singing along to that.' Margie paused as if remembering the feeling of bliss. McLean had an inkling of what she was on about; the magic of being in a band when everything just gelled.

'But see when he comes out of it. Then he's so down, it's like I don't even know him. And that's when he goes off looking for something to bring him back up again.'

'Something a bit stronger than weed. Maybe something involving needles.'

Another long pause and McLean glanced at his watch. Well past time for the antenatal class. He'd find a way of making it up to Emma somehow.

'There was this bloke he mentioned. Think I might have seen him once at one of our pub gigs. Sam. No, Sammy, that's what they called him. Skinny, long hair and shades. He looked kind of dirty, if you know what I mean. Like he never washed. Think I heard he had a place in the Old Town. One of those tenements down underneath the castle, you know? Off towards the Grassmarket?'

It was a start. The smallest of leads, but something he

could work with. Duguid's Glasgow intel had been useful, but it only went so far.

'I shouldn't be telling you this. If anyone finds out I've been talking to the polis I'll –'

'You have my word, Margie. I won't tell anyone about this call. I'll have a wee chat with the drugs boys, see if they know this Sammy and take it from there. No one will ever know you had any part in it, OK?'

'Just . . . Find him, aye? Just find him.' Margie fell silent again. Then the line clicked, and she was gone.

'Who do we know in the drugs squad these days, Bob?'

McLean had tracked down Grumpy Bob to the canteen, hiding away in the far corner behind his newspaper. The detective sergeant glanced briefly at his watch before answering, but showed no other sign of guilt.

'Local or national? Most of the large-scale stuff's SCDEA now, though Vice come across a fair bit, too.'

'I was thinking more local. Looking for a dealer called Sammy. Thin, long hair, greasy.' McLean was all too aware of how little information he had to work with, but it was unlikely Margie would sit down with a photofit-trained officer and come up with a sketch.

'This got anything to do with our missing lad, Eric?' Grumpy Bob asked. McLean gave the canteen a nervous glance, but there were only a few officers in there, and none of them were paying any attention to him.

'The same. I had a chat with his bandmates and one of them gave me that name. Chances are he's dealing heroin. Doubt that's all he's got though.'

'I'll have a look through the records, see if we've anyone

answering to Samuel on file. Probably quicker doing it myself than asking a favour of anyone in drugs. They get a bit antsy if you start poking your nose into their business.'

'Well, we did ruin six months of surveillance work that one time, remember?'

Grumpy Bob stared at McLean with a blank expression. Then a smile spread across his face. 'Oh, aye. Still, if the buggers ever shared any intel we'd no've had any problem. Ha. I'd forgotten that.'

McLean pulled out a chair, wondered whether it was worth his while grabbing a coffee while he was here, then decided against it, given the late hour, and sat down instead.

'You find out anything about Gregor Wishaw yet?'

'Gregor . . . Oh, aye. Funny story there. He's been out almost three years now. Still on licence, but a fair bit before his parole should have come up. Seems he was a model prisoner, never put a foot wrong. That and he cut a deal and dobbed in all his mates. I know that's not how it's meant to work. We don't do deals like that any more. But someone had a word somewhere and he got bumped up the queue for a hearing. Keeping a clean nose paid off, so he's out and working security. Talk about poacher turned gamekeeper.'

'I imagine the rest of the gang aren't best pleased. Take it they know what happened.'

'Aye, they do. First of them's due out in about six months, so that'll be interesting.'

'His problem, not ours. I'm more interested in how he ended up out at East Fortune. Not exactly his patch, is it.'

'No, he was strictly a city boy. Dalry born and bred.'

Grumpy Bob picked up the edge of his newspaper and began folding it. 'Thing is, the job was waiting for him, apparently. All part of the package.'

'Sounds a bit too cosy for my liking. And he knew Mike Finlay's name, even if he denied it.' McLean picked up the mug in the middle of the table, then remembered it wasn't his and put it back down again. 'Not enough to hang a guy for, though. He's an ex con, so he's always going to be suspicious around the likes of us, I guess.'

'Aye, that's probably it. He's kept his nose clean since getting out of Saughton anyway. It's probably just a coincidence he ended up working there.'

McLean leaned back in his chair, caught the look on Grumpy Bob's face. 'Aye, coincidence.'

26

A smell of fresh baking greeted McLean as he walked into the kitchen. His stomach rumbled in anticipation of food, and he couldn't remember whether the sandwich he'd eaten had been lunch yesterday or today. Given the rush of events it had probably been the day before.

'Someone's been busy,' he said to Mrs McCutcheon's cat. She didn't answer him, just held his gaze with her own imperious stare for a moment, then went back to washing her leg with her tongue. He put his briefcase down on one of the chairs around the kitchen table and went in search of the industrious baker.

A deep, rumbling laugh rolled out through the open door to the library. Not Emma's light voice, but not entirely masculine either. Stepping into the room, McLean wasn't at all surprised to find Madame Rose there, sitting on the sofa as demurely as a woman of her great stature could. She looked up as he entered, face creasing into a broad smile.

'Ah, Tony. You're home. You really should try to work slightly more sociable hours you know.'

Emma had been sitting cross-legged in one of the arm-chairs, but she unfolded herself, came over and gave him a hug.

'Want some tea?' she asked. 'Rose baked a cake.'

McLean glanced at the clock. It was more like time for

a beer, and perhaps a perusal of the takeaway menus on the board by the phone in the kitchen. He had learned over the months since she had come back that Emma wasn't particularly interested in cooking. Not for herself or for anyone else. She'd tried at first, keeping the fridge stocked with worryingly healthy things like salads, but that effort hadn't lasted long. It didn't bother him; she shared his taste in curry and pizza anyway. Mrs McCutcheon's cat was considerably slimmer these days, too. Grumpier but slimmer.

'Maybe a mug of tea would be good. Thanks.'

She gave him a peck on the cheek, then disappeared out the door in the direction of the kitchen.

'Why do I get the feeling you'd rather be helping yourself to something out of that wee hidden cabinet of yours?' Madame Rose tilted her head in the direction of the false bookcase, behind which McLean kept his collection of fine single malt whiskies.

'Even I know it's a bit early for that. Maybe later, though. It's been a long day.'

'Aren't they all. You work too hard, Tony. That'll have to change, you know? When the baby's born.'

McLean slumped into the armchair Emma had just vacated. The low table in front of the sofa was piled high with a selection of old books from the shelves, slips of coloured paper poking out from some.

'Finally come back to do that cataloguing have you?'

'Some rare old books here, you know. Have you ever read any of them?' Madame Rose picked up the top one, opened it with surprising delicacy for her large hands, turned it round and presented it to him.

'*Treasure Island*?' McLean flicked the pages, noted the silent tutting from his companion and turned them more carefully. The paper had turned sepia with age, a few mottled spots here and there. The words were familiar though.

'My father read this to me. It's one of my earliest memories. One of my few memories of him.' McLean closed the book and put it back on the pile. 'I tried to read it again when I was older, but I couldn't. I always heard his voice.'

'Losing a parent at such a young age. It must be a terrible thing.' Madame Rose's voice softened, her eyes staring at something far in the past. Absent-mindedly, she picked the book up again, gently opened it to the title page, her fat fingers caressing the paper. Then she snapped back to the present with a shudder.

'It's as well you couldn't read it. Left on the shelf is the best place for a first edition. And signed, too. I hate to be so crude as to talk money, but this is worth a lot.'

'Gran said it was a gift to her father when he was a wee boy.'

'From Stevenson himself?' Madame Rose clutched the book to her ample bosom. 'Oh that just makes it even more valuable. This house is full of such rare treasures. It's an oasis of calm in the maelstrom.'

'You make it sound like the world outside is terrible.' Comfortable in his armchair, McLean had to admit she had a point.

'Oh, but it is, Tony. The forces of darkness gather all around us. Can you not see them? Can you not feel them?'

'Is this where I'm supposed to scoff and say don't be so silly? Because lately I've found that hard to do. I'm not sure I subscribe to your conspiracy, but there's certainly a lot of shit around. I don't know. People just don't seem to care much any more, everyone's out for themselves and screw everyone else.'

'Exactly. That's how it starts. That's how it always starts. Nothing so easy to see as a monster in our midst, but the core of our society is slowly rotting away. We need to gird ourselves against it.' Madame Rose put the book carefully back down on the table, then hauled her considerable bulk to her feet. 'But I'm intruding on your domestic bliss. I should leave now. I will come back and work on these again tomorrow.'

'Emma's at the lab tomorrow, but I can give you a key if you're happy to work alone. Or would I be right in thinking it's as much about keeping an eye on her as the books?'

Madame Rose gave him a shifty look. 'I sometimes forget that you're a detective. And one Jayne McIntyre speaks highly of. Yes, I'm worried about Emma, and your child. There are things you can't see and there are things you won't see. But I can see both, and I can see the threat they pose.'

'If you know something, Rose, then tell me. I'll –'

'You're not listening, Tony. This isn't something you can scare off with a few constables and a restraining order. You've met these . . . people before. Mrs Saifre, Gavin Spenser, Norman Bale. These are not normal folk. But there's something else out there right now. Something indistinct and ill-formed. I don't know what it is, and that scares me. It seeks vengeance, I can see that much, but I can do nothing about it until I can name it.'

The room had gone very quiet, Madame Rose's voice dropping almost to a low, rumbling whisper. Despite the warmth of the afternoon that had persisted well into evening, a chill settled around the library. McLean opened his mouth to say something in response, but the door swung open, pushed by a well-placed foot as Emma returned. She held a mug of tea in one hand, a plate piled high with the most enormous wedge of cake he had ever seen in the other. Warmth tumbled in around her.

'Oh, Rose. Are you going?'

'Duty calls, my dear. But I will see you again soon. These books won't catalogue themselves.' The medium headed for the door, brushing close by McLean as she went with a whispered 'Be wary.'

And then she was gone.

He snapped awake, sitting bolt upright in the wide bed. Sweat sheened his back and chest, hair damp on his head. His heart hammered away as if he'd run a marathon, or the hundred yards from the Usher Hall to the scene of the crash still playing itself out in his mind as the nightmare faded. He let the cool air dry his skin as he calmed his breathing, staring across the room to the still-dark window that looked out on to the garden. Beside him, Emma snored a gentle rhythmic rumble. She snorted once, then rolled over, dragging the covers with her. A moment's silence, underlined by the ticks and creaks and groans of the old house settling around him. Then the snoring started up again.

Demon-red numbers told him that it was almost half past four in the morning. He'd not been late to bed, but even so that was early for McLean. He wasn't going to get any more sleep, though.

He used one of the guest bathrooms, not wanting to wake Emma from her slumbers. The closer she came to term, the more erratic her sleep patterns. The snoring was something new, too. She looked constantly tired, so the last thing she needed was him disturbing what little sleep she could manage. Was this what the future held? When their child was born? Yawning and stretching, McLean wondered whether he was prepared for that. Whether anything could prepare him for that.

Mrs McCutcheon's cat stared up at him from her place in front of the Aga when he walked into the kitchen and flipped on the light. A flurry of motion at the far side of the room, where the door lay slightly ajar through to the utility room and the catflap to the outside world, suggested that she'd not been alone in her slumbers. Mostly the army of cats that had taken up residence in the gardens kept to the outdoors, but occasionally one might poke a nose inside. He didn't much mind as long as they kept out of the main house.

The dream troubled him as he drank his coffee and munched a bit of cold pizza left over from last night's supper. It wasn't perhaps surprising, given the horror of the accident, that it kept coming back to haunt him. He'd lied about it to the counsellor, which was probably stupid. On the other hand, if he admitted to the bad dreams then she would most likely force him to take time off. That might please Emma, but the last thing McLean wanted was to sit around and dwell on the horror. He'd always found that throwing himself into the investigation was the best way to deal with things. Clear up the case, find some small restitution for the dead and the bereaved. Then the nightmares would end.

Not quite sure why he did it, McLean took his coffee back through to the library. The approach of dawn had begun to chase away the deeper shadows, but he still had to switch on the light to see properly. The pile of books lay on the table, untouched from the evening before. He picked up the top one, opened it again. *Treasure Island* by Robert Louis Stevenson. Cassel and Company, first edition, published in 1883. Amazing that something could survive so long undamaged by the unfolding events all around it.

His memories of his parents were vague now, the experiences of a four-year-old warped by ten times as many years laid on top of them. Still, he could see his old bedroom, the pictures on the wall, the solid wooden furniture and narrow, iron-framed bed. His father would come in of an evening, pull up a chair that was far too small for him, open this very book and begin to read. Was this something he would do for his own child? He hoped so.

Carefully turning the pages from the top corner the way he had been shown by the ancient librarian at his hated boarding school, McLean read the opening paragraphs quietly out loud, and wondered how much his echoing voice sounded like his father's.

27

The chemical stench is beginning to fade from the red scarf now. It's there if I bury my face in it, but then so are the crusty spots of Maddy's blood. I keep it close as a reminder of her, a focus for my rage. It sits on the table, partially covering a mobile phone I don't remember owning. Must have found it lying around and picked it up, just can't remember when. No charge in the thing, and it's password-protected. Maybe I'll find a charger for it, hack my way in and return it to its owner sometime. I've more important things to be getting on with right now.

You'd probably call me a hacker, or maybe a hacktivist if you're prone to that kind of thing. Probably got some romantic idea of a techno-warrior for justice, bringing advanced coding skills to bear in the war against the man. Sometimes I might even agree with you, but mostly it's just long hours staring at blurry screens for very little reward. Still, it gives me something to do, a way of fighting back.

I think it was something Gordon the policeman said that set me off initially, or it might just have been his doggedness, his determination to put someone behind bars for the things that went on in that house in Essex. He never succeeded, and I learned early on that the sort of people who did that kind of thing were very good at covering their tracks.

I just needed to be better than them.

And that's what I do. I sit at my computer like a spider at the centre of its web, feeling the strands as they twist and vibrate. Partly it's carrying on Gordon's work, looking for the people who abused me, but partly it's just me against the man. You'd be surprised how close to a perfect circle that Venn diagram is, mind you. There's way too much shit in this world, and most of it's done by the sort of people who get their kicks in places like that big old house in Essex where I grew up.

I guess it makes a certain kind of sense. If you're amoral enough to hoard cash in secret offshore bank accounts and avoid tax when normal folk can barely scrape enough together to eat, then using children for your own sick pleasure's hardly going to keep you awake at night, is it? And it's not as if these people don't know what they're doing is wrong, either. Otherwise they wouldn't be half so good at hiding it.

Spotting the patterns is what I'm good at. Gathering information and sifting through it until the truth emerges from the fog of lies. That's how I knew about Finlay McGregor long before I went out to that compound near Broxburn. Long before the crash tore Maddy from me just when we'd been reunited. The name had popped up in another search, a different target, a bigger scam that goes a long way towards explaining why that truck was carrying highly toxic waste through the city centre in the first place. It ties into so many other things, links them all together in a way that might not satisfy a judge and jury but is good enough for me.

The problem is, I'm not the only one who's found it.

Someone else has been following the same threads as me, pulling on them so delicately I doubt anyone would notice if they weren't looking. They might be after the same thing I am, but it looks more like they're systematically erasing the connections I've spent months tracing. And not only that, they've been constructing a slightly different narrative, setting up various links that weren't there before. Almost as if they know this operation's been rumbled and they want to throw the suspicion on someone else.

I'm careful, always, but now I'm scared, too. What if they traced things back to me? What if they found out what I was doing, and this is their idea of damage limitation? What if that truck didn't crash by accident? Could this whole thing be my fault?

28

McLean stifled a yawn and reached out for the mug of coffee on his desk, disappointed and surprised to find that it was already empty. Waking early had meant he'd made it into work an hour before the morning briefing; plenty of time to go through the paperwork on his desk and decide what could continue to be ignored. There was surprisingly little to deal with, partly because he was no longer the junior detective inspector in the station, but mostly he suspected because Chief Superintendent Forrester was taking on the bulk of the administration himself.

It was a change, and a welcome one at that. For too long they'd struggled under poor management. First from Duguid, who should never have been promoted beyond DCI, and then from Brooks, who elevated favouritism to an art form. Stuff had been dumped on him because he got it done, McLean realized. All those long hours spent wading through piles of reports and overtime sheets that really should have been someone else's job. Now they had a man in charge who understood the importance of playing to people's strengths. Just a pity there were so few detectives left for him to manage effectively.

A glance at the clock showed there was still a half-hour to go before he'd have to head to the major-incident room. Time enough to top up his coffee from the pot across the room, and have a look through one more report.

The knock on the door startled him, and McLean looked up to see DC Blane standing in the open doorway.

'Sorry to disturb you, sir, only DCI McIntyre wondered if you were coming to the morning briefing?'

'Is it time already?' McLean glanced at his watch, surprised to see he'd been engrossed in the file all that time. 'I was just reading your report into the financial side of Finlay McGregor. It's thorough, I'll give you that.'

Blane nodded his head slightly, although whether that was acknowledgement of the praise or embarrassment, McLean couldn't be sure. He closed up the report, as ready as he would ever be to head into the melee of the morning briefing.

'I'm no expert, but would I be right in thinking that Finlay McGregor was a company rather too much in debt?'

'That's what I thought, sir. They've bought a lot of new trucks recently, and I can't see evidence of any big contracts to justify the cost. If I was their bank manager I'd be nervous of the exposure.'

'So who's lending them all the cash, then?'

'As far as I can tell, it's the same person who's just taken a hefty share of the company. Hedge-fund manager by the name of Alan Lewis. He's minted, sir. I mean, serious money. I'd be surprised if he wasn't a billionaire, the things his company's got interests in.'

'Alan Lewis.' McLean remembered the name now he heard it spoken. 'Aye, that's right. Finlay's sister mentioned him. I was going to set up an interview. You couldn't sort that, could you?'

'Of course, sir. Any particular time?'

'Sooner the better.' McLean glanced back at the folder

on his desk. 'Though I might need to read through that wee report of yours again before I speak to him.'

The major-incident room hummed with a quiet excitement as McLean entered, closely followed by DC Blane. He had to push his way through the throng to get to the front, where DCI McIntyre was glancing anxiously at her watch. Her shoulders slumped in relief as she spotted him.

'About bloody time, Tony. Where've you been?'

'In my office. Sorry. Lost track of time.'

McIntyre shook her head, muttered something along the lines of 'men', then climbed up onto a chair the better to get everyone's attention.

'OK people. Quiet down. Let's get this over and done with so you can all get on with your jobs.'

McLean looked around the room for any other senior officers. DI Ritchie was nowhere to be seen, but then she hardly ever was these days. Grumpy Bob leaned back in a chair off to one side of the crowd, and DCI McIntyre was there, of course. He was surprised not to see the chief superintendent, though; the man had been pretty much running the incident room himself since the investigation had started.

'We've still three bodies to identify. This long after the event I'd want that figure to be zero. We've plenty leads from the helpline. I need team one to get working through them as quickly as possible. Team two you're doing good stuff with the CCTV, but the press are hassling us for results, so step it up a notch, OK?' McIntyre turned away from the crowd, fixing her steely gaze upon McLean. 'You want to bring us up to speed on yesterday's developments, Tony?'

McLean flushed slightly at being the sudden centre of attention. He'd not prepared anything, having spent the past half-hour engrossed in DC Blane's report on the parlous financial state of Finlay McGregor. A sea of expectant faces gazed back at him as he stared out into the crowd, but out of the corner of his eye he could see the mischievous grin on McIntyre's face.

'As you'll all have heard, Mike Finlay was found dead in the offices of Finlay McGregor early yesterday morning. I know what you're all thinking; someone's trying to cover their tracks after the truck crash and Mike Finlay was a loose end that needed tying off. I can't deny it's a very convincing theory, but the post-mortem suggests he wasn't physically attacked. We've some unexplained security camera footage that needs investigation and Forensics are going to have another look over the scene, too, just in case. I –'

'You think he topped himself? Done us all a favour?'

McLean didn't recognize the voice, and neither could he immediately tell where it had come from.

'It's unlikely he committed suicide, given the nature of his death. I'm more concerned this might have been a rather gruesome method of silencing him before he said too much. But, as I said, the post-mortem didn't find any signs of foul play, so we're not jumping to any conclusions either way.'

'And we're not mouthing off to the press either, are we, Constable.'

All eyes turned to the door, where Chief Superintendent Forrester had just appeared. He pushed through the crowd with a great deal more ease than McLean's earlier attempt, followed by a dark-suited man the detective inspector didn't recognize. Judging by the look of him he was either SCDEA or NCA. A spook or a fed, depending on whatever derogatory nickname was making the rounds at the moment.

'Tony, Jane.' Forrester nodded to the two of them. 'Sorry I'm late. Had to bring a few people up to speed.'

'We were more or less finished actually, sir,' McIntyre said. 'Just going to get the sergeants to sort out the assignments. Night shift handover's already done. You want to have a word with the troops before they're dismissed?'

Forrester opened his mouth as if to begin a speech, then closed it again, shaking his head. 'No. I don't think that's necessary. Let's get cracking shall we? Plenty to do, and I need a quick word with the senior officers before I meet with the DCC.'

McLean said nothing, just watched as McIntyre dismissed the crowd. Most already knew what they were meant to be doing, the rest clustering around their sergeants like schoolchildren on a day trip. Soon enough the scrum subsided and the four of them were left alone to one side of the room.

'DI Ritchie not about, then?' Forrester looked around like a man trying to find the toilet in an unfamiliar pub.

'No, sir. Figure she's been called back to Perth.' McIntyre turned her attention to the other man. Like McLean, he'd remained silent, careful eyes taking in the unfolding scene. 'You'd know more about that, though, wouldn't you, Tim?'

'Operation Fenton's not my case, Jayne.'

'So what brings you over to our side of the country,

then? Been kicked out of the Crime Campus for bad behaviour?'

'Chance'd be a fine thing.' The man in the dark suit had an English accent, Home Counties if McLean was any judge. It reminded him of boarding school: well-educated but not plummy. He'd scanned the whole room in the short seconds it had taken to walk from the door to where they all stood, but only now did he seem to acknowledge McLean's presence.

'Detective Inspector McLean, I presume?'

'Have you two not met before?' McIntyre's eyes widened in surprise. 'Sorry, I just assumed you'd know each other. Tony, this is DCI . . .' She paused a moment. 'Featherstonehaugh? Is that how you pronounce it?'

The man rolled his eyes theatrically. 'It's pronounced Fanshaw, Jayne, and well you know it.' He held a hand out for McLean. 'Tim,' he said. 'And you're Tony McLean. I've heard a lot about you, Detective Inspector.'

'All good, I hope?' McLean felt the man's grip, firm but not trying to prove anything. His skin was cool and dry.

'Mostly.' Featherstonehaugh tilted his head slightly. 'The bad stuff's more interesting, though.'

'Tim's with the NCA, Tony.'

'Looking to take over our investigation, are you?' McLean meant it as a joke, but he was surprised to see the National Crime Agency taking an interest.

'More our style to wait until all the hard work's done, then swoop in and take all the credit.' Featherstonehaugh smiled as he flicked his head in Forrester's direction. The chief superintendent had wandered off to deal with a query from one of the uniform sergeants, clearly in his element.

'No, it's just some other business I needed to sort out. Nothing to do with this investigation, fascinating though it is.'

McLean watched him as he spoke, catching that slight flicker in the eye he'd seen so many times before, in so many interview rooms. He knew nothing about Featherstonehaugh, had never met him before today, but it didn't take a genius to know that the man was lying. There was no good reason why the NCA shouldn't be interested in their investigation, so what was he trying to hide?

29

'Come in, come in. Please. So you're the famous Detective Inspector McLean. I've heard a lot about you.'

McLean couldn't help but recall the similar words from the NCA agent, Featherstonehaugh, just an hour or so earlier. Bad enough that his fellow officers talked about him behind his back, but to be gossip among international financiers was much worse. What possible reason could this man have for knowing who he was?

'I'm surprised you've even heard my name, Mr Lewis.' McLean took the seat he had been offered, accepted a porcelain cup of coffee but declined the biscuit.

'Alan, please.' Lewis shuffled around behind the desk and sunk into his own chair. 'And actually we've met before. Couple of years back at poor old Andrew Weatherly's wake. I was going to talk to you, but you were hijacked by that awful Saifre woman.'

McLean recalled the event all too well, but couldn't remember the short, affable man who spoke to him now. The mention of Mrs Saifre's name sent an involuntary shudder down his spine, but he wasn't fooled by the faux-camaraderie implied by Lewis's description of her as awful. He knew it was all an act, but he let it play out anyway. How close the financier tried to make himself would give McLean a good idea of how much he was trying to hide.

'I always knew the Edinburgh financial circle was small. Hadn't appreciated just how small. You'll be telling me you worked with Gavin Spenser next. Or Bill Chalmers.'

Lewis answered with a shrug, a wry smile and by spreading his arms wide, hands palm upwards. 'What can I say? My business is built on contacts.'

'Contacts like Mike Finlay over at Finlay McGregor?'

The shrug disappeared, replaced by a weary sigh. 'Mike. Yes. That's not turned out very well, has it?'

'You financed his recent expansion, I understand. Took a share in the business.'

'It's what I do, Inspector. If I see an opportunity, I grasp it. Logistics is a rapidly growing sector. All those online purchases have to be delivered by someone. And someone else has to move everything from factory to distribution warehouse. Hundreds of thousands of trucks up and down the motorways and A roads every day. Smaller vans going the final mile.'

'Finlay McGregor is strictly heavy goods, though, isn't it? HGVs and artics. The sort of work they do's being squeezed hard by fuel costs. Trucks are only getting more expensive, too. Not much chance to make a profit, I'd have thought.' McLean studied Lewis's face as he spoke, grateful for the crash course in the haulage industry he'd gained from reading Blane's report. The financier's smile froze on his face, stare hardening as he listened.

'You've done your homework, Inspector. Either that or you're entirely wasted on the police force. Have you ever considered a move into the private sector? Ah, but you're independently wealthy, I understand. Don't really need to work for a living.'

'We all need to do something, Mr Lewis. The devil makes work for idle hands.' McLean waited a couple of breaths before speaking again. Just enough for Lewis to start to open his mouth. 'So you had plans for Finlay McGregor beyond what it's doing right now? Perhaps branching out into the courier side of things? Was this something you shared with Mike Finlay at all? How about his sister, Katie? Or were you going to leverage them out first?'

Lewis opened his mouth, hesitated as he waited for McLean to interrupt again. 'Truth is, Inspector, without me, there'd be no Finlay McGregor. OK. Given the recent events I can understand how folk might think that'd be a good thing, but we are where we are. As it happens, I had discussed expansion plans with Mike, and he was very keen. Katie was more of a problem, but she doesn't have that much say in the running of things. It's more that Mike always looks to his big sister before making any decisions.'

'Did you have much to do with the business aside from writing the cheques and planning the future strategy, then?'

Lewis leaned back slowly in his chair. 'Ah, I see where you're going. Am I culpable in any way for that terrible tragedy? I don't think so, Inspector. But if there's any doubt, I have a team of highly experienced corporate lawyers who I'm sure will be able to help you with that.'

McLean took a sip of his coffee. For all the elegance of the cup in which it was served, it smelled like it had been in the pot too long and tasted more like burned tarmac than anything that had come into contact with a bean.

The chemical aftertaste reminded him of the truck crash, that squat headache just lurking at the back of his brain.

'As it happens,' Lewis continued. 'I'm having a meeting with the delightful Ms Finlay this afternoon. It's my intention to wind up Finlay McGregor. The company has no future after what happened. And with Mike gone . . .'

'That's going to put quite a few people out of work. Not the nicest way to treat them.'

'Most of the drivers are on contract anyway. They'll find work elsewhere quickly enough. There's some mechanics and a couple of part-time admin staff. They'll get a decent severance. I'm not a monster, Inspector. As it happens, I've already put a considerable sum of money into a relief fund for the victims of the crash. The company's insurance will see them well compensated for their injuries, too.'

McLean bit back the retort he wanted to make. Alan Lewis's fake bonhomie was beginning to grate. 'You're aware that we're treating Mike Finlay's death as suspicious, I take it?'

Lewis's gaze narrowed. 'Are you trying to suggest I might have had anything to do with that? Should I call for one of my lawyers?'

'That won't be necessary. Not for now, anyway. I'll not waste any more of your time.' McLean put the unfinished coffee down on the desk, stood up. Lewis remained seated as McLean made his own way to the door.

'There was one other thing,' he said as he pulled it open. 'You wouldn't have a financial interest in Extech Energy or LindSea Farm Estates, would you?'

Something flickered across Lewis's face. Not quite a

frown, more a glower of annoyance. The first real emotion McLean had seen since arriving at the offices of AML Holdings.

'They don't ring a bell, but then I have interests in so many different companies, and they in turn have interests in other companies. It's the modern way of finance. I could check, of course. But there's a matter of fiscal confidentiality . . .' He left the sentence hanging.

'It's not important. Just a couple of names that came up recently. I'll see myself out.' McLean turned his back on Lewis, left the door to the office open as he walked slowly down the corridor towards the stairs. The financier didn't have to answer the question; the look on his face had said it all.

McLean didn't recognize the number that flashed up on the screen of his phone. He'd taken it out of his pocket to call the station, see how DC Blane was getting on with the financial analysis and perhaps suggest he look into Alan Lewis's empire more closely, too. For a moment he considered letting it go to voicemail, but in the end curiosity got the better of him. He thumbed the accept-call icon, lifted the phone to his ear.

'McLean.'

'Heard you was lookin' for Pothead Sammy. Any particular reason youse want to speak to him?' Male. Slight Leith accent. The worst of the impenetrable dialect worn from the edges so he could at least be understood. Still McLean had no idea who he was.

'Can I ask who's speaking?'

'Aye, fair enough. Jack Parfitt. Drugs squad or whatever

the fuck they're calling us this week. Grumpy Bob put the word out about Sammy. What's he done now?'

Parfitt. McLean recognized the name, had trouble putting a face to it, though.

'I was told he's supplying heroin these days. You know anything about that?'

'Sammy? Selling smack?' The voice on the phone paused a while. 'Well, I guess it's possible. No' his usual poison, mind. He's called Pothead Sammy for a reason, aye?'

'He got a surname? I'd quite like to have a wee chat about someone he supplied to recently.'

'Aye, it's Saunders. Reginald Samuel Saunders. I can email you his file if you want. Should have a fairly recent address for him. He's a restless soul, though, is old Sammy. Never stays put anywhere long. Used to hang out over Helensburgh way, but I heard he'd made the trip east.'

'Too much to hope you've seen him recently, then.'

'No' in the last few days, and that's not like Sammy. He's usually up the Grassmarket, Bristo Square, that kind of area. He was in a squat in the West End for a while. Not sure if that's still on the go. This time of year he peddles dope to tourists mostly, some of the banking types, too. I guess that crash and all us polis hanging about the area scared him off. He'll resurface soon enough.'

The crash. McLean could almost smell the chemicals in the air, and the pit of his stomach turned cold as he remembered it.

'You think he might have been there when it happened?' he asked. 'Doesn't sound like the kind of bloke who'd be up at that time of the morning.'

'Could be. Depends how desperate he was. Like I said, he supplies some of the bankers who work that end of town. They're early starters.' Parfitt paused again. McLean had been walking back to the station, but realized his feet had taken him down towards the Cowgate for some unaccountable reason. He was about to say something when Parfitt spoke again.

'So who's this lad Sammy's been scoring smack for? Why d'youse need tae talk to him?'

'Lad? I never said anything about a lad.'

'Lass then. Figure of speech. You're working that truck crash, aren't you? Heard you've still got some bodies you can't put names to. That what this is all about? You think Sammy might be one of them?'

'Hadn't considered it until you told me where he hangs out. I was chasing down a potential mis per, and Sammy's name came up as a known associate. You know what it's like with a big investigation. We get tons of calls, most of them rubbish. This one's a possibility, though, and the parents are anxious.'

Parfitt laughed, a sound a bit like cats fighting in a bag. 'Anxious and influential if they've got a DI looking out for them. Ach well. If you see Sammy tell him Jack says hi. I'll email you those records. See where you get with it.'

'Thanks,' McLean said. 'That's very helpful.' But Parfitt had already hung up.

30

A cooling breeze ran along the Cowgate, and the tall buildings gave much welcome shade. Perhaps that was why McLean had walked down the cobbles of Niddry Street rather than heading over South Bridge and on towards Newington as he'd intended. Either that or the unexpected call from Jack Parfitt had planted a thought in his mind that he couldn't easily ignore. He'd been looking for Sammy to gain information about Eric Forrester, but what if it was the drug dealer himself lying in the mortuary chill store? It was a long shot, sure, but no one had seen either man since the day of the crash, and both had some reason to have been in that part of town. He had to admit that the thought of the dead man being a drug dealer was a lot more appealing than him being the chief superintendent's only son, too.

Angus Cadwallader's assistant, Doctor Sharp, looked up from her lonely desk when McLean knocked on the open office doorframe. Her face given an unhealthy pallor by the light of her computer monitor, she pulled her spectacles down so she could peer over the top of them and see him properly.

'Tony. What brings you here today?' Her initial frown turned to a smile of recognition. 'Angus is away getting changed. It's been a busy morning and he's lecturing this afternoon.'

McLean glanced at his watch, not quite sure what had

happened to the day. Except that he'd spent a chunk of it wasting his time talking to Alan Lewis.

'It's not a problem. Wouldn't want to keep him from his students anyway. I had a question about the three bodies we're still trying to identify. You'd probably be able to answer it better than Angus anyway.'

'What's that, young man? Impugning my good name?'

McLean turned in the doorway to see Cadwallader approaching from the other side of the examination theatre. He had changed out of his habitual scrubs and now wore a well-tailored tweed suit, shirt open at the collar where he'd not yet tied his tie. McLean had a suspicion that Doctor Sharp would be doing that in a few moments. Quite why the two of them had kept their relationship secret for as long as they had, he'd never understood. Neither had a significant other to cheat on, and the only thing even of passing note was the disparity in their ages.

'I was just asking Tracy about those three bodies. Wondered if any of them might have been a habitual drug user. Cannabis, most likely, but possibly heroin as well.'

Cadwallader stopped before he reached the door to the office. 'Drugs? Hmmm. Come with me.'

McLean saw Doctor Sharp open her mouth, raise a hand to make some comment. Probably along the lines of 'You're wearing your best suit, Angus', then give up and sit back down at her computer with a shake of her head. He gave her a wry smile, then followed the pathologist across to the banks of chiller cabinets.

'We've got them all here.' Cadwallader pulled some latex gloves out of a box sitting on a shelf nearby. He snapped them on swiftly, then opened three doors, pulled out three trays. All the bodies were in bags, and as he unzipped them, so the chemical reek rose to greet them. McLean felt the headache rising, and the memory of that horrible day hit him like a gut punch. The battered remains had been cleaned up and laid out in a semblance of how they might have looked before forty tons of truck and a bath of corrosive chemicals had done their worst. Even so the mess was shocking, adding to the nausea that the smell had brought on.

'Do we really need to look at them, Angus?'

'What?' Cadwallader had reached in and drawn out an arm, perhaps the least damaged part of this particular cadaver and mercifully still attached to the torso. The hand was a mess of bones and flesh, though, taped up in a bag to stop it all falling apart.

'I was only wondering if one of them could have been a drug addict. Thought you might have noticed something in your first examination. I didn't think you'd need to do . . .' He waved at the bodybag. '. . . all this.'

'Well, if you'd just look, I was going to explain.' Cadwallader beckoned him closer with a wave of his free hand. McLean stepped up reluctantly, both because the damage to the body sickened him and because the chemical smell was making him sick. How the pathologist could bear it, he had no idea.

'What am I looking at then, Angus? Apart from an almost severed arm, that is.'

'Well, it's scrawny for one thing. This cadaver's male, a little under six feet tall. The solvent didn't leave much of his hair or skin. This arm was tucked under his body, though, which is how it survived fairly unscathed.'

'And what does it tell us?'

'Not as simple as "he was a drug addict", I'm afraid, Tony. Blood and tissue analysis haven't come up with any of the usual markers anyway, so he'd not taken anything for a couple of days before he died at least. Maybe longer.' Cadwallader twisted the ruined arm to the light a little. 'There's wee scars here that could be track marks, but there's not enough skin left on him to be certain. Now you've brought it up, I'll have a closer look. Would have been easier if we had his other arm, too, but we never did find that.'

'Any other way of telling?'

'It's all a bit vague, I'm afraid. The lack of muscle definition suggests someone who doesn't exercise much and probably doesn't eat a lot either. So yes, he could be a drug addict. Could just be lazy, except that you'd expect more body fat then.'

'Sammy Saunders.' McLean stared down at the mangled torso, not quite convinced. 'How about DNA? I take it you've not had the results back yet.'

'Oh, right. No. Bloody lab's taking longer and longer these days. Sometimes I think they do it on purpose. Especially if you mark the sample urgent.'

'What about the swab I gave you?'

Cadwallader frowned, then seemed to remember. 'Oh, that. Did I not tell you? Sorry. I had one of my students run the sequence, but until we get the results back from the body we can't actually compare them. Probably should have got the student to do them all, now I think about it. He's much quicker than the labs.'

'But inadmissible in court. Not that it applies here. You'll let me know as soon as the lab results come in?'

'Of course.' The pathologist pushed the drawer back into the chilled store, closing the door with a solid clunk. 'I take it this Sammy fellow wasn't who you were thinking of when you brought me that swab, though.'

'No. His name just came up this morning. He's got quite a record, though, so he'll be on the DNA database. If it's him we'll know soon enough.'

Cadwallader turned his attention to the other two drawers, the body bags still zipped closed. 'Good. If that's one more down, then it's just this pair to go. Two women. One young, one old.' He slid first one, then the other back into their dark, frigid homes, pulled off his latex gloves and deposited them in a nearby bin.

'If it's him. We don't know that yet,' McLean said.

'Have a little faith, Tony.' He smiled at the joke. 'And if it's not him, well, we've had their skulls scanned, all three of them. Friend of mine at the university's going to run them through some facial reconstruction program they developed for forensic archaeology. Should be able to put a face to them in a day or two.'

'You can do that?' McLean asked. 'I thought you needed to glue on little blocks of wood and build up the muscles with clay or something.'

'Ah, Tony, you can be delightfully old-fashioned sometimes.' Cadwallader patted him on the arm as they walked back towards the office. 'Now, where's Tracy gone. I need someone to help me with my tie.'

'I wonder if you could spare a moment, Tony. In my office.'

McLean had only just stepped into the cool of the station, barely had time for his eyes to adjust from the sun's glare outside. Either Chief Superintendent Forrester had been waiting for him or the man was psychic.

'Right now?' he asked, then saw the look on Forrester's face. 'Of course. Is it about –?'

'My office.'

McLean nodded, saying nothing more as he followed the chief superintendent up the stairs and along the corridor. Only once they were both inside the office, the door firmly closed, did he speak again.

'I take it this is about Eric, sir.'

Forrester slumped into his chair. 'You've still no news?'

'If I had, I'd not have kept it from you. I'm just this moment back from the mortuary, but Angus still hasn't got the DNA results for the three remaining bodies. One of them is male, as you know, sir, and we can't be sure it isn't him. But we can't be sure it is. There's another possibility that's come up just this morning.'

'Oh aye?' Forrester's face lightened a little. Strange how a man could cling to the tiniest scrap of hope.

'We know your son was an occasional drug user. I think I've tracked down his supplier here and it's just possible it's his body we've got down in the mortuary, not Eric's.'

'He had a regular supplier? A dealer?'

'Bloke by the name of Sammy Saunders. Pothead Sammy to his friends. He's known to operate in the area around the crash site and nobody's seen him since it happened. I know it's tenuous, but . . .' McLean tailed off, seeing the expression on Forrester's face turn from hope to something else he couldn't quite identify. Anger, perhaps? Fear?

'How long until the DNA results come in?' he asked after a while.

'Not sure, sir. They were prioritized, of course, and your swab's been sequenced off the books so we can make the comparison as soon as the results come in. Angus was going to chase them up. Shouldn't be long now.'

Forrester stared into the distance for a while, emotions playing across his face like an actor hamming in front of a mirror. McLean was happy enough to let him work through whatever it was. Nothing he could say would make things any easier for the man.

'You're still looking for him? Eric?' he asked eventually.

'Of course, sir. The drugs angle was only one line of investigation.' McLean wasn't sure what other lines Duguid was pursuing, but he could be certain the ex-detective superintendent would be thorough.

'Good.' Forrester looked like he was going to say something else, then he stopped himself with the tiniest shake of the head. 'Thank you, Tony. This won't be forgotten.'

McLean knew a dismissal when he saw one. He nodded once, then left, closing the door firmly behind him. Only once he was out in the corridor did he let out the long sigh he'd been keeping inside. It was all too clear that Forrester knew the name Sammy Saunders, equally clear that he wasn't about to tell McLean how or why, even if his own son's life depended on it.

31

'Think I've got a potential name for our final male victim.'

Despite his strange interview with the chief superintendent, McLean found himself still surprisingly upbeat. There was still far too much to do, and too many questions unanswered, but it felt like they were making progress now. Something would doubtless come along and ruin his mood soon, but for now he was going to make the most of it.

'You have?' Detective Inspector Ritchie turned away from the group of uniform constables she had been addressing. The noisy hubbub carried on as officers went about their work, answering calls, tapping actions into computer terminals, ferrying stacks of paper from one end of the room to the other. It was amazing how well-oiled a machine an incident room could be with someone half competent in charge. Not McLean, of course. He'd be the first to acknowledge that wasn't where his skills lay. Detective Constable Gregg was in her element, though.

'Reginald Samuel Saunders.' McLean walked up to the whiteboard, searched around for a marker pen. After an awkward moment a constable handed him one and he wrote down the name on a spare space. 'Pothead Sammy to those who know him, apparently. Low level dealer, mostly in cannabis and ecstasy. There's a chance he's been dabbling in harder stuff recently.'

'What makes you think he's our man?' Ritchie asked.

McLean studied the board. All the identified bodies had been scrubbed off now, only the three unknown victims left. While that meant more space for writing notes, queries and other actions, it also meant there was space for larger photographs of their remains. He couldn't help thinking that it was somewhat macabre and unnecessary, since none of their faces had survived, but it did serve to remind everyone what they were dealing with.

'It's very circumstantial at the moment, but Angus is going to get his DNA profile compared with the database as quickly as possible. The victim has some of the physical hallmarks of an addict. Pothead Sammy was known to frequent the area and hasn't been seen since the crash.'

'That's a bit tenuous, isn't it?' Ritchie took the pen from McLean's grip, leaned forward and scrawled a large question mark at the end of the name. 'How come anyone even noticed? Have you any idea how many drug addicts there are in this city? In the half square-mile surrounding the crash?'

McLean paused before answering, his initial enthusiasm leaking like air from an old balloon. He'd not told Ritchie about Eric Forrester yet. Still couldn't decide whether he was going to. Even if he did, in the middle of the busy major-investigation room wasn't the place.

'His name came up and he can be placed close to the scene around the time of the accident. No one's seen him since then. It's worth checking out at least, don't you think?'

Ritchie gave him an odd expression, made odder by the pale, thin arches of her missing eyebrows. 'Thought I was meant to be in charge of the identifications while you chased down the haulage company angle. Aren't you heading up that suspicious death, too?'

'I was . . . I am. Sorry, Kirsty. I'm not trying to muscle in on your investigation. This just . . . came up.' McLean realized he was only digging himself in deeper. He'd have to tell her sooner or later. Probably should have done as soon as Forrester had come to him. What the hell had he been thinking?

'Look. I'll explain what it's all about, but I need to find Grumpy Bob first. No point going over everything twice.'

'He was in the canteen last I saw him.' Ritchie cocked her head to one side like an inquisitive spaniel. 'What's going on, Tony?'

'My office. Five minutes.' McLean winced at the words, too often heard in an angry tone from Duguid or Brooks. 'And see if someone can't dig up the file on Pothead Sammy in the meantime, eh?'

'So you've known about this for three days and haven't thought to tell me?'

Ritchie paced up and down in front of the large window that dominated one wall of McLean's office. He leaned against the edge of his desk, trying to work out the best way to proceed. Never one to pass up an opportunity, Grumpy Bob had sat down at the conference table and put his feet up on one of the other chairs.

'Two days, I think. And to be fair, you were away when Forrester told me.'

'There are things called phones, Tony. Reception's a bit shit right up the top of the glens, but mostly they work even in Perthshire, you know?'

'I also thought it best to let as few people know as possible. Last thing we need is this getting out. Imagine the fun Jo Dalgliesh would have with it.'

'Imagine how much more fun she'll have when she finds out we covered it up? Or had you not thought of that?' Ritchie made another couple of turns around the carpet before speaking again. 'And what if our dead body's not Pothead Sammy but the chief superintendent's son? You going to go public, then?'

'Once his parents have been informed. Yes.' McLean crossed the room to where Ritchie stood. 'Look, Kirsty. I'm sorry, OK. But Forrester put us all in a difficult situation with this. I put Bob and Duguid on to it because that was the best way to avoid wasting resources.'

'Duguid?' Ritchie's missing eyebrows arched high in surprise. 'What the hell did you get him involved for?'

'Contrary to popular belief, he's actually quite a good detective. Shit at man-management, but then I can kind of sympathize. He was doing good work with the cold-case unit until the DCC shut it down. If he can help Forrester find his son – dead or alive, but hopefully alive – then there's every chance we can get that team back up and running.'

Ritchie continued to stare wide-eyed at him for long moments. 'Why would we care about the cold-case unit? We're stretched that thin as it is, and half of the sergeants are due to retire soon . . . oh.'

'Thought you'd get there eventually, lass.' Grumpy Bob took his feet off the chair, pushed it away from the table for her to sit down. 'They'll pension me off at the end of the year whether I want it or not. Dagwood's no' my favourite idiot to work with, but I'd rather be down in that cellar with him than stuck in my wee flat waiting till it's late enough to go for a pint.'

'We need detectives with experience, Kirsty. There's some promising new blood coming up, but they need mentoring. We've lost too many people recently. Brooks and Spence were only the last of it. At least if we've some of the old guard in a properly funded CCU then we can lean on them when we need their expertise.'

Ritchie pulled the chair further away from the table and sat down, Grumpy Bob shuffling to one side so that McLean could join the two of them at the table.

'OK. So what's the plan, then? We need to find Eric Forrester, and you think Sammy the Pothead is connected to him how?'

'He's Eric's dealer. Least, I think that's the relationship. They're not that far apart in age, both grew up in Helensburgh. I wouldn't be surprised if they knew each other from back then. Likely went to the same school.' As he said it, McLean remembered Forrester's expression when he'd first heard mention of Sammy Saunders. There was certainly a connection there, and it went deeper than addict and fixer.

'So how are we going to ask him where Eric is if he's lying in the mortuary cold store, then?' Ritchie asked. 'And what if it's Eric lying there, not Sammy? What if it's neither of them?'

'DNA samples will be in soon enough. That'll give us some answers. Meantime, Sammy's a known quantity. He's got a record, associates we can talk to, places we can search.'

Ritchie fixed McLean with a look of disbelief mixed with something else. 'You only slapped his name up on the board so we could use the resources from the major-incident team to help track him down? Help track Eric down? I'm impressed, Tony. That's far more devious than I'd have thought you capable of.'

McLean began to protest. That wasn't what he'd intended at all when he'd put Pothead Sammy's name up on the board. No one would believe him, though; the links were far too tenuous otherwise. Instead he just shrugged.

'We need the manpower. And it's not as if the chief superintendent's going to complain.'

32

'You got a moment, sir?'

McLean had been meaning to walk past the entrance to the major-incident room and on towards the stairs, his eventual destination the canteen and a much needed cup of tea. Possibly even some chocolate cake, too, if there was any left. DC Harrison's quiet voice interrupted him mid-stride.

'I guess so. What's up?' He looked past her, standing in the doorway, to the hustle and bustle of the investigation beyond.

'West End Station just sent something across you might be interested in.'

Sighing inwardly, McLean followed the detective constable into the incident room. A table in one corner had been piled high with boxes, each containing meticulously bagged pieces of evidence from the crash scene. Unclaimed wallets, items of clothing, the collar and lead from a dog called 'Tiberius': all of it had been through the forensics labs and was now waiting to be catalogued, returned to grieving families or stored until such time as it was no longer needed. And sitting at the front of the pile, wrapped in a clear plastic sheet, was a bright-yellow rucksack.

'Beat constable found it down on the canalside, past Lochrin basin. Didn't think much of it until they got a whiff of the smell.' Harrison carefully opened the plastic bag and McLean's nose wrinkled at the onslaught. Everything from the crash scene had that same, powerful, chemical odour.

'Reckon it must have belonged to one of the victims. There's heartless bastards out there who'd steal the teether out of a baby's mouth if they thought it was worth something.' Harrison's quiet fury suggested a long-nursed grievance, but she had a point. They'd been so stretched after the truck crash anyone could have helped themselves to a backpack, rifled through it and tossed whatever wasn't valuable to them aside.

'Anyone had a look inside it?' McLean pulled a pair of gloves out of his pocket and snapped them on. The incident room had quietened around him, all eyes turned to see what was going on. Or maybe it was just the smell rendering them speechless.

'There's not much. A couple of notebooks, some pens. I'm guessing anything valuable's long gone. Nothing as helpful as a name and address, I'm afraid.' Harrison had also donned gloves and laid out the contents of the backpack as she spoke. It wasn't much at all.

'What's that?' McLean reached out and picked up a slim rectangle of plastic. Not a credit card as he'd first thought; that would have been taken by whoever had stolen the backpack in the first place. Turning it over, he saw that it was a hotel keycard, the name of the establishment printed across the face.

'Foxton House Hotel? That's over in Sciennes, isn't it?'

Harrison shrugged, but McLean knew the place. It was just around the corner from Grumpy Bob's flat. More of a hostel than a hotel. Cheap, the sort of place favoured by visiting students and backpackers. Did that fit with the younger of the two unidentified dead women?

'Think I'll take a quick walk over there, see if this card's still active.'

'You want me to come along?' Harrison's face was full of hope, but McIntyre's words still rung in McLean's ears. Damned if he was going to let station gossip dictate who he worked with, though.

'Aye. Might as well.'

'Room 301. That'll be wee Jen. No' seen her in a day or two. I was wondering when she'd be back.'

Much as he'd remembered it, the Foxton House Hotel was little more than a backpackers' hostel with pretensions. Once a sizeable old town house, its reception hall would have been spacious had it not been filled with teenagers and twenty-somethings sprawling about on old sofas, their luggage strewn everywhere. McLean wasn't entirely sure what they were all doing, but he'd been the same at their age.

'Does Jen have a surname?' he asked of the young woman at the reception desk. She'd looked down her nose at McLean when he'd presented his warrant card, but seemed happy enough to deal with Harrison. She sniffed once, tapped at the computer keyboard on the counter.

'Jennifer Beasley. Booked in a week ago. Staying a fortnight. What's this all about?'

'We found her backpack,' Harrison said. 'Trying to trace her so we can give it back.'

The young woman looked at McLean again, the disbelief writ large across her face. It was fair enough; you

wouldn't send a detective inspector out just to give someone their backpack back, and they didn't have it with them
either.

'Can we see her room?'

The young woman shrugged. 'You've got her keycard,
right? Stairs at the back, third floor.'

Room 301 wasn't much to look at, tucked up under the
eaves at the back of the house. A small dormer window
looked out on to tenement gardens mostly filled with washing and bicycles, the Pentland Hills off in the distance. A
narrow single bed filled half of the room, too close to a
small dressing table and chair to be able to sit comfortably.
Beyond another door, the tiniest of en suites had no window at all. A small bag of clothes sat open on the end of
the bed, and Harrison bent to the task of delicately looking through it. McLean turned his attention to the dressing
table.

'Looks like she might have been a student or something.' He picked up a spiral-bound notebook similar to
the ones they'd found in the backpack, flipped the cover
over to reveal lines of neat handwriting, too small and
condensed to read in the poor light. The pads were lined,
but Jennifer Beasley had managed to fit two rows of writing in each line, squeezing the words on to the page. He
flicked it over, seeing the same on the back, and the next
page in the pad. And the next, and the next, on and on.
Occasionally words were crossed out, or underlined, but
mostly it was as neat as a school essay.

'Can you read any of this?'

Harrison opened another pad and peered down at
the front page. 'Not sure. I think it's something about

an investigation? There's a name underlined here, Daniel Penston. Got an email address too.' She flipped a few pages. 'Another list of names here. Sound vaguely familiar. Jonathan McLellan, Peter Davenport, George Solomon, Andrew Weatherly, Jane Louise Dee –'

'What?' McLean snatched the notebook away from Harrison, who looked at him with wide eyes. 'Sorry. It's just Andrew Weatherly was the MSP who killed his wife and children and then shot himself a couple of years back. And Jane Louise Dee . . .'

'Is a bad penny that keeps turning up when you least expect it to. Aye.'

A bad penny. Well, that was one way of describing her. McLean put the notebook back down on the desk, not liking the sense of cold dread that was beginning to grow in the pit of his stomach.

'Why are we here, Constable?' he asked.

'Umm . . . To find this woman? Jennifer Beasley?'

'And why are we looking for her?'

'Because we found her rucksack and reckon someone half-inched it from the truck crash scene?'

'And why do we think it was there?'

Harrison said nothing for a moment, running through the various steps of logic in her head.

'We should be looking for something with her DNA on it, since she's not here and nobody's seen her in a wee while. Just in case she's one of our unidentified bodies.'

McLean forced a smile. 'Exactly so. And all this . . .' he waved a hand in the direction of the dressing table and the notebooks. 'All this is irrelevant. At least for now.'

Harrison opened her mouth, then closed it again. He

could see the argument written across her face and he understood it all too well. This was a puzzle that needed to be solved, but it was also a puzzle that would have to wait.

'I'll have a look in the bathroom. See if I can't find a hairbrush or something. Manda's bound to be able to do something with it.'

33

McLean rubbed at the corners of his eyes, dislodging what felt like a mountain of grit. He tried to stifle a yawn, perhaps unconvincingly, as he listened to the chief superintendent speak without actually hearing any of the words he said. A whole day of sun shining on the glass wall of the office had left it sweltering inside, and his comfortable seat at the conference table wasn't helping things. Forrester's office was even bigger than McLean's, which made it easy to use for senior team meetings like the one he'd been called to as soon as he and Harrison had returned from Sciennes. He'd sent her off to take the hairbrush they'd found to the forensics labs, then she was going to read a bit more of Jennifer Beasley's notebooks. He still wasn't quite sure why he'd let her take them from the hotel room in the first place. They should really have left the place as it was, instructing the management not to go in there until the DNA results had confirmed whether or not they'd identified one of the final victims of the truck crash.

'. . . things coming together nicely, wouldn't you say so, Tony?'

He snapped out of his daydream, brain racing to catch up with the words that had been said before his name. Failing.

'Sorry, sir. Zoned out a bit there. It's been a very long day and the heat in here . . .'

Forrester gave him a look disturbingly similar to the one McLean's old housemaster at his hated boarding school had used on all the children under his care who didn't match up to expectations. Which was to say all the children under his care.

'The identification of the bodies. We're almost there, aren't we?'

'Yes, sir. We are. Got a very good lead on the second-last female victim today. We're running DNA samples for confirmation, but we think she might be a Jennifer Beasley.' Awake now, McLean studied the chief superintendent's face for any signs that he had been pushing for information on his son. The question seemed odd coming from him otherwise, and yet there was nothing. Unless everyone else attending the meeting knew, of course. DI Ritchie did, but as far as he was aware DCI McIntyre didn't, and neither did the representatives from Health and Safety and the Procurator Fiscal's office.

'Good work.' Forrester's face was a mask as he turned his attention to the next subject. 'And what about Mr Finlay?'

'It's hard to say, sir. Post-mortem suggests he wasn't forced through that window, but he'd have to be the unluckiest man on the planet to die like that accidentally. Forensics are going over the offices again, and I've got a couple of constables studying the security camera footage. There's a lot of it, so they'll be a while.'

'So you think it might actually be an accident, then? Can we wrap this one up?'

McLean hesitated before answering, aware that all eyes were on him. Had it been Brooks at the head of the table, or even Duguid when he had been in charge, then the simple thing would have been to say yes, whatever his gut was telling him, and then carry on investigating until he found out the truth. He'd not yet got the measure of the chief superintendent.

'What evidence we have points to it being an accident, sir,' he said eventually. 'On the other hand, Finlay's the boss of the company whose truck was carrying that illegal waste. The company that was responsible for the deaths of twenty people and horrific injuries to many more. He stood to lose everything, even if we couldn't pin any actual crime on him. Chances are we'd have charged him with corporate manslaughter soon, at which point he'd probably have started talking about who else was in it with him. His death very conveniently shuts that all down, don't you think? So no, I don't think we're anywhere near ready to wrap it up. Sorry.'

The room had fallen quiet as he spoke, and nobody seemed inclined to break the silence. For a moment there was only the rumble of traffic outside and the ticking of the clock above the door. Then Forrester cleared his throat with a soft cough, glanced at his watch.

'You make a good case, Tony, but how do you propose proving it?'

'We're interviewing the rest of the Finlay McGregor staff and I've spoken to their financial backer, Alan Lewis.'

'Lewis?' Forrester reacted to the name perhaps a little too swiftly.

'You know him?'

'I know of him. Can't say I've ever had the pleasure of his

company, though. Careful how you tread there, McLean. He's very well connected.'

'So I've heard, sir. But I'll keep on digging until I find something. Or someone tells me to stop.'

Forrester looked around the small group of senior officers, as if daring any of them to speak. No one did.

'OK. It's getting late. We can pick this all up tomorrow. Good work, people. Keep it up.'

Everyone got up to leave, filing out of the room in swift silence. McLean caught DCI McIntyre's eye, sure by her expression she wanted to ask him something, but before he could escape Forrester's voice boomed out from behind him.

'One moment, Tony. I'd like a quick word.'

'Sir?' McLean heard the door click closed behind him, turned to face the chief superintendent.

'Do you really think Mike Finlay's death was deliberate?'

Of all the questions Forrester might lead off with, this was the last McLean had expected. Was the man not concerned about his son?

'I don't like coincidences, sir. Not even slight ones. This is too big to ignore.'

'I agree. There's far more to this than meets the eye.' Forrester went back to his desk and sank into the chair. 'I'll warn you now, though, it's making some people very nervous.'

'Let me guess, the chief constable's getting calls from some of his golf club friends.'

Forrester managed a weary smile. 'Something like that. Can't stand the politics myself, and I'm not going to cover up a crime of this magnitude no matter who tells me to. You need to watch your back, though.'

'My back's pretty well covered, sir. It's the young DCs and the soon-to-retire sergeants I'm more worried about.'

'Aye, heard that about you, McLean. The sort of people I'm talking about won't just come for your job, though. Your man Alan Lewis there didn't get as rich as he is playing fair.'

'I know. I've met his kind before.'

'Aye, right. The Weatherly case. I remember. Just be careful.' Forrester leaned forward, rested his elbows on the desktop. 'About that other matter. You had any results back from your pathologist pal yet?'

McLean took out his phone, thumbed the screen into life. There were no messages from the mortuary. 'Angus hoped he'd have the results back this afternoon. You want me to give him a call?'

The look on Forrester's face was enough of an answer. McLean tapped the screen until he found the number. It rang through four times before being picked up by Doctor Sharp. The conversation took less than a minute, but even so Forrester looked like he had aged a decade in that time.

'Well?'

'The good news is that none of the unidentified bodies are related to your DNA sample, sir. Eric didn't die in that crash.'

Forrester slumped into his chair, rubbing at his face in a mixture of relief and anguish.

'The bad news is that means we still don't know where he is, and he's been missing for five days now.'

A kind of silence settled in the room, heavy with unspoken

truths. McLean was happy enough to let it linger as long as the chief superintendent needed.

'Deirdre wants me to retire,' he said eventually. 'Move back to Helensburgh, where her friends are. Her friends, can you believe that? She couldn't wait to get away from that place and those harpies, and now she wants to go back.'

McLean said nothing. There was nothing he could say.

'She thinks if she goes back, then none of this will have happened. Eric will still be her happy little boy. Christ alone knows how many pills she's been taking, but her mind's gone completely.' Forrester looked up and McLean could see a shine in his eyes that hadn't been there before. He sniffed, rubbed his nose with the back of his hand like a teenager. 'I can't be angry with you for not finding him yet. You've only had a couple of days, after all, and plenty more to deal with besides. No point shouting at you, however much I want to.'

McLean waited a few seconds before speaking, unsure what exactly were the right words. Forrester was his boss and had given him a specific task which so far he had failed to complete. But he was also a worried father and husband, scared of the possibilities threatening him.

'There was one other thing, sir. From the call. We've not had any hits on two of the bodies yet, but the third is definitely the drug dealer, Saunders. His record's on the offenders database.'

Something unexpected flickered across Forrester's face. Not puzzlement so much as fear. His gaze flitted from McLean to the door, to the window, and back to McLean. Never resting anywhere for more than an instant. 'You're sure of that. Your dead body's the drug dealer? Saunders? There couldn't have been some mistake with the sample or something?'

'As sure as these things can be, sir. But he fits the physical description, far as we can go. He had reason to be in that part of town at that time. And the DNA match was good enough.' McLean studied the chief superintendent's face for a while before adding: 'Any reason why it shouldn't be?'

Forrester started at the question, his pale skin reddening around his neck. 'No. No reason. That's . . .' For a moment he seemed lost for words. 'That's good work. So just the two bodies left to identify now?'

'Two women, one young, one old. Yes, sir. Like I said before, we've a lead on the younger one, too.'

'Good. Good.' For a moment the chief superintendent stared at nothing, and McLean could only wonder what was going through his mind.

'We will find him, sir. It's just a matter of time. He's not in the mortuary, so he's out there somewhere.'

Forrester looked up, the weakest of smiles on his lips. 'Hope for the best, aye, Tony? Hope for the best?'

'You got a minute, Tony?'

McLean had only just escaped from Forrester's office, heading back to his own for a moment's peace before going home. The voice behind him didn't come as a surprise, though.

'The last time someone asked me that it ended up taking half the day to deal with. What can I do for you, ma'am?'

DCI McIntyre laughed, the crow's feet creasing around her eyes. 'You can stop ma'am-ing me for one thing. I was just wondering how you were feeling. You look done in, and you near enough fell asleep in that meeting there.'

'Ah, you know how it is. Just a long day. Didn't get much sleep last night either.'

McIntyre had been walking down the corridor alongside him, but now she stopped, leaned against the wall, forcing McLean to turn and face her.

'Normally I'd make a rude joke about that. Something bawdy. But I suspect that's not the problem, is it? Still getting the nightmares?'

'You make it sound like I've had them for months.'

'No, just since the day of the crash. Honestly, Tony. It's like dealing with children. You experienced something most people can't even imagine. Horrors worse than any slasher movie. Real people dying right in front of you. And that chemical gloop that spilled everywhere and stank up the whole city for a day. That can't have helped things. You need to give yourself time to recover, not throw yourself into the investigation like it was some strange form of escapism.'

'I'm fine, Jayne. Honestly.' McLean knew he was lying even as he said it. McIntyre did, too.

'At least tell me you've spoken to the trauma therapist like I told you. She's very good you know. Not like your old friend Hilton.'

McLean tried not to rub at his face with his hand, but he might have failed a little. The mere mention of Matt Hilton, criminal profiler and station counsellor, was enough to give him a headache.

'I spoke to her the day before yesterday? Maybe the day before that. She wanted me to take a fortnight's leave. I said I'd think about it.'

McIntyre shook her head. 'You're impossible, Tony. You know that? What kind of a father are you going to be if you can't put the job to one side every so often? What kind of father are you going to be if you have a nervous breakdown and end up jumping out of your skin every time someone shouts? Or cries?'

'I'm OK. Really. Just a little tired is all. And it was very warm in Forrester's office.'

'That may be true, but it's no excuse.' McIntyre drew herself up to her full height, almost as tall as McLean, and poked him in the chest with a sharp finger. 'Go home and get some rest. And tomorrow you're going to see Megan again if I have to drag you to her office myself. Understand?'

McLean nodded, opened his mouth to acquiesce, but McIntyre had already turned on her heel and was stalking away down the corridor.

34

I don't know what's been happening to me these past few days. It must be something to do with that truck crash, but I should be over the shock of that by now. I am over the shock of that; I know I am. How else would I be able to focus on finding out all about the company involved?

And it is only one company, I know that now. It has many names and many sites of operation, but it's all just one big, happy, criminal enterprise, screwing over the little people and syphoning all the money offshore. As if that wasn't enough, it's screwing with the environment, too. I've seen the setup, the twenty-four-hour security and razor wire fences, motion sensors spread around as if it were gold bullion in those stainless steel tanks, not vegetable waste and slurry from dairy farms.

Not industrial solvent being disposed of on the cheap.

Fieldwork's really not my thing, and yet twice this week I've been out of the city, gone to visit places I'd only ever heard of from internet searches. All my life, since I escaped the house in Essex, I've hidden from sight, gone under a false name, moved around the country before I can be tracked down by the people I know are out there, still looking for me. Were they looking for Maddy, too? Did they find her? Was that what this was about, the truck crash a hideous attempt to get rid of the both of us in one go?

Am I just being paranoid? Nobody knew we'd both be at the bus stop at that exact moment. And besides, the truck driver had a heart attack, that's what all the newsfeeds are saying. It was an accident that killed Maddy, nothing else. A stupid, fucking accident.

Except that it wasn't really an accident, was it? There's no such thing.

That truck was never meant to be in the centre of town, but something sent it that way. It was never meant to be working that day, but something delayed the delivery. I knew someone else was watching, someone else knew what was going on. This was all set up so that something would happen to the truck out on the open road. That would've got the Vehicle Inspectorate involved and blown the whole scam open, sent the police down the carefully prepared narrative and away from the truth I'd begun to uncover. But the driver had a heart attack at exactly the worst possible moment. Almost as if someone was watching him, reached into his chest and squeezed it just as he made that turn.

As if that was even possible.

I don't believe in coincidences, though. Never have, never will. Someone caused that accident, even if I don't quite know how or why. That's why I went to see the bloke from Finlay McGregor, not that it did me much good, or him. Same with that place where they picked up that gunk. I just hope the police find the little message I left them there, shut down that place sharpish.

They're still closing in, though, the nameless people behind it all. I can sense their presence just out of view, hovering on the edges of my search, rewriting the story as it unfolds, diverting attention on to the little people, the foot soldiers. I need to follow the trail, see where that truck was meant to be going.

Find them before they find me.

35

'You going straight to the station today?'

McLean looked up from his seat at the kitchen table to where Emma stood beside the Aga. He stifled a yawn, yet another night's sleep disturbed by bad dreams. They were getting less intense, though; he could hardly recall any details this time, just a sense of uneasiness, as if he knew he should be doing something but couldn't remember what.

'Reckon so. Why?'

Emma poured boiling water into the cafetière, releasing a wonderful aroma of fine coffee that would go very nicely indeed with his slightly burned toast and marmalade. She had eaten half a slice of pink melon, which didn't seem enough for someone nurturing a child. It wasn't often they managed to have breakfast together, though, so he kept the observation to himself.

'I need to get to the labs, but my car wouldn't start yesterday.' She sat down and patted her stomach, still not showing a great deal of swell. 'It's a bit uncomfortable behind the wheel, too.'

McLean looked up at the clock on the wall above the door. There would be a morning briefing, but it wouldn't be the end of the world if he missed it. 'I can give you a lift. You might have to get a taxi home, though.'

'Not a problem.' She pressed down the plunger, then

filled two mugs. McLean added a good splash of milk to his, but Emma sipped hers black.

'You think it might be time to trade that old banger of yours in for something a bit more practical, and, you know, something that actually works?' McLean tensed himself for the inevitable retort. Emma had few possessions in the world, and was fiercely protective of her car for reasons he couldn't easily fathom. She'd abandoned it with him when she'd headed off on her mystic tour around the world, after all.

'Might not be a bad idea, actually.'

The answer was so not what he had been expecting, it took him a while to respond.

'You mean that?'

'Aye.' Emma took another sip of her coffee. 'We've a lot of happy memories, me and that car. But at the end of the day it's just a car. And it's no good to anyone if it won't start.'

'OK. You any idea what you might replace it with?'

'Me? God no. I wouldn't have the foggiest. Well, except that it doesn't need to be a monster like that growling black penis-extension you bought to replace your old car.' Emma smiled as she spoke, but McLean could hear the chiding in her voice, too. He might have protested, but it was nice just to be sitting at the kitchen table, talking about something that wasn't work.

'Why don't you have a chat with Rae about it. She'd be able to give you some advice on what's best for carting children around.'

'Children?' Emma's smile turned to a frown. 'Plural?'

'Figure of speech, Em. We know you're not carrying twins.'

'I don't know. Some days it feels like it.'

McLean opened his mouth to respond, but the trilling of his phone in his pocket cut him short. He fished it out, squinting at the screen to see the number. 'Got to take this. Sorry.'

He thumbed the icon, held the phone up to his ear. 'McLean.'

DC Harrison's voice wavered down the line. 'Morning sir. Sorry to bother you before the shift and all.'

'Inspectors don't work shifts, Constable. What's up?'

'Just had a call on a suspicious death. James Barnton. Lives in the Dalry Road. They found him this morning in the cemetery, leaning up against a headstone. Possible drugs, possible heart attack.'

'That's all very interesting, but what's it got to do with us?'

'Not entirely sure, sir. But he worked at Extech Energy. His name came up in the morning dispatches. Recognized it from when we visited there a couple of days ago.'

McLean wondered how Harrison could remember something like that. He didn't recall having spoken to anyone except the security guard who had let them in and the rather severe Ms Ferris in the office.

'He still there? In the cemetery?'

'Yes, sir. I was about to head over and check it out.'

McLean glanced at his watch, even though he had only just looked at the clock.

'I'll meet you there in forty-five minutes.' A slight cough made him look up, see Emma's exasperated face. He gave her an apologetic grin. 'Call it an hour, OK?'

*

'Poor bugger looks like something scared him to death.'

McLean stood in the middle of Dalry Cemetery, shaded from the morning sun by mature trees. A police cordon kept the gawking public a good fifty yards away, but even so the forensics team had erected a white plastic tent over the immediate crime scene. Looking through the open entrance, he could understand why.

The dead man sat with his back against a slightly canted headstone. Whether he'd chosen it specifically or simply at random they couldn't yet tell, as his body obscured the words carved into the coal-blackened stone. He was dressed in loose-fitting jogging bottoms and a stained grey hoodie top. The Converse trainers on his feet looked out of place, new and shiny compared to the rest of his clothing. The cap on his head tilted back at an unnatural angle, perhaps tugged that way as he slumped against the headstone, but the most disturbing thing about him was the look on his face.

His mouth hung open, not with the slack-jawed relaxation of death, but a silent scream of terror. His eyes were wide, the whites turned pink by tiny burst blood vessels, pupils narrowed down to black dots. If it hadn't been for the attendant pathologist and all the police activity, McLean might have believed the body a stolen exhibit from the Edinburgh Dungeon, only this was far more convincing than anything made from wax.

'Who found him?' He turned away from the unsettling sight to where DC Harrison was chatting with a uniform constable of her acquaintance.

'Local jogger. Comes through the cemetery every morning, sir. Thought he was just a drunk sleeping it off.

Apparently that happens quite a lot. Only, when she saw his face . . .'

'This jogger, she still here?'

'Sent her home. We've got contact details and a brief statement already.'

'OK. Good work.' McLean risked a look at the dead man again. Even at this distance that face sent a shiver down his spine. 'And this is James Barnton, you say? Worked at Extech?'

'Aye, he had his wallet on him. Driving licence photo's definitely him. Credit cards are all in his name. He had a security pass for Extech in there as well.' Harrison had been facing McLean as she spoke, but now she risked another quick glance at the dead man. 'And I recognize him from our visit. He was the one checked our warrant cards at the gate. Least, I'm pretty sure it's him.'

'Anyone spoken to his boss? Is he meant to be working today?'

A look as much of annoyance as panic flitted across Harrison's face. She pulled out her Airwave set. 'I'll get right on it. I'm sure Ms Ferris will be delighted to hear from us again so soon.'

'While you're at it, see if you can track down a next of kin, too, aye?' McLean didn't want to look at the dead man, but somehow his eyes were drawn to that horrified expression. 'Don't much fancy having to do it, but someone's going to have to make a formal identification.'

McLean loitered outside the forensic tent as Harrison went off to find a quiet spot for her phone calls. He didn't have to wait long before a slight commotion at the entrance heralded the emergence of a white-boiler-suit-clad pathologist.

'Morning, Angus. You got anything for me?'

Cadwallader turned at the question, and for a moment McLean wished he hadn't asked. His old friend looked unsettled, the lines on his face deeper than ever. Behind him, the normally indomitable Doctor Sharp crept past with barely a nod, departing the scene as quickly as she could in her baggy overalls and heavy overboots.

'Tony. Why does it not surprise me to find you here?' Cadwallader's attempt at a smile was half-hearted at best.

'You know me, Angus. Can't stay away from a good corpse.'

'Aye, well. This isn't one of them. Seems to have had some kind of seizure, by the look of things, but I'll not know for sure until I've got him back to the mortuary.'

'Any signs of foul play?'

'Not that I can see here. Again, it's early days. You're going to ask me for a time of death now, aren't you?'

'Am I that predictable?'

'Yes. And I can't be more accurate than sometime yesterday evening, perhaps very early this morning. Not long at all.'

'So he's what? Out jogging through the cemetery when he feels a bit weird? Sits down against the headstone and then . . .' McLean waved a hand in the direction of the tent, its front now closed over the gruesome scene.

'That's one scenario, yes. Judging by that expression on his face and the damage to his eyes, I'm guessing he must have hallucinated something awful. It'll be interesting to see the state of his brain. Might call one of my neurosurgeon friends for some advice.'

'You think there might be any similarities with the other one, Mike Finlay?'

Cadwallader gave him a puzzled look. 'The glass through the throat? Why would you think that?'

'Only that this chap looks like something scared him to death, and Finlay might have tripped while trying to escape something so terrifying he couldn't even control his feet, let alone his bowels.'

The pathologist tapped at his face with one finger, staring off into the middle distance for a moment before speaking again. 'Psychologically speaking, it is possible to scare someone to death, but you'd know that anyway. Quite what could do that and yet leave no trace behind, I've no idea. Interesting you should compare the two cases. It hadn't really occurred to me.'

'There's another link, though. This man works for the company whose waste Mike Finlay's truck was meant to be transporting. There were already so many coincidences stacking up. This is one too many for my liking.'

'Well, I'll bear it in mind when I examine him back at the mortuary.' Cadwallader hefted his bag. 'I'll let you know once we've scheduled a time for the post-mortem. Try to squeeze him in this afternoon if I can. Might not be till tomorrow, though. He's not in any hurry, at least.'

McLean nodded, watched as the pathologist walked away towards the cordon. Harrison approached him, her gaze flicking towards the tent.

'I've spoken to Ms Ferris, sir. Said we'd probably want to interview her again. Barnton's only next of kin is a brother in Aberdeen, according to Extech's personnel files. They're sending through contact details.'

'Thanks. I think.' McLean stared at the forensic tent's entrance flap, steeling himself for going inside. He'd seen so many dead bodies in his career it was impossible to put a number to them. Some had horrified him, most simply made him feel sad at the loss. This was the first time he could remember feeling afraid.

'Right, then.' He took a deep breath. 'Best get this over with.'

Despite the morning cool, the air inside the forensic tent had a damp, muggy warmth to it. McLean paused in the entrance, feeling the sweat collect in the small of his back and trickle downwards. At least James Barnton didn't smell in death. He hadn't begun to decompose, and neither had his bowels let go, as was all too often the case. Instead, the inside of the tent smelled oddly of loam, damp grass and the distant bite of car exhaust fumes you could never entirely escape from anywhere in the city during the summer.

When first he had seen the body, McLean's attention had been drawn inevitably to its face. That look of pure terror made it hard to see anything else. He studied it for as long as he could bear, trying to imagine what could do that to a man. Then with a surprising effort of will, he dragged his gaze away and to the rest of the body.

Barnton sat with his legs up slightly towards his chest, one foot pulled back, the other pointing forwards. His arms lay on his lap, crossed over, hands tensed as if they were made of stone, not flesh and muscle and bone.

McLean tried to imagine the man's final moments, arms up, fending off some imaginary assailant. Dead, they had dropped down, but something had kept the tension in those fingers.

Stepping carefully around the corpse, McLean saw that his back was slightly arched. The crown of Barnton's head and his shoulders touched the headstone, but a gap large enough to fit a hand in opened up below that. Hunkering down, he could see right through from one side to the other. It seemed odd. Not how he would imagine someone slumped against a headstone would end up.

A noise at the entrance to the tent broke his train of thought. McLean looked up to see a white-suited forensic officer with an expensive digital camera. Her hood and face mask made it almost impossible to identify her, and for a moment he wondered if it was Emma. Then she spoke.

'Hey, Tony. Sorry about that. Duff batteries. Had to go and get some more from the van.' Amanda Parsons might have had a similar build to Emma Baird, but that was where the similarities ended.

'You know, you should really have that hood up if you're going to wear it at all,' she said.

Given that McLean had almost not bothered with the paper overalls, he bit back the jokey quip about messing his hair he had been going to make. 'What do you make of this?' he asked instead.

'Me?' Parsons may have frowned, although it was difficult to tell when all he could see was her eyes. 'Well, he's deid for one thing. Looks like he collapsed against yon headstone there. Only, if that was the case I'd expect him to be more hunched up.'

'That was my thought, too. See here.' McLean pointed at the gap he had noticed before. 'It's really only his head touching stone at all. Can you get some photos of that before they move him?'

'Sure can, boss.' Parsons held the camera up to her eye, started framing and snapping. McLean stood up, his knees protesting and a little twinge of pain firing up his hip. He moved out of Parsons's way as she worked methodically around the body, feet placed with delicate care every time she stepped, like a dancer or an athlete. The longer he spent in the forensic tent, the less horrific the scene became, although he still found it hard to look at the dead man's face for any length of time. He focused instead on the shoes, those shiny new Converse trainers or whatever it was they were called.

'What shoes are you wearing, Manda?' he asked.

Parsons stopped flashing and looked up at him. 'Eh?'

'Your shoes.' He pointed at her feet, wrapped up in paper overboots. 'Can I see?'

'Umm, this is a potential crime scene, Tony? I can't exactly go taking my shoes off an' shaking them around. Christ only knows what Jemima would do to me if she saw.'

'You're right. But tell me this. What's the ground like outside?'

Parsons walked around to where he was standing, try-ing to work out what he had seen, no doubt. 'Outside? There's a path up from the Dalry Road, goes off to Dun-dee Street the other way.'

'And what's it made of, this path?'

Parsons looked down at the ground, a mixture of broken asphalt, dirt and overgrown weeds. She scuffed her overboots on it, then lifted one foot up to peer at the underside. Still on one foot, she turned her gaze back to the dead man, and more specifically his feet.

'Shoes,' she said. 'They're clean. Nothing on them.'

'Should have seen it right away.' McLean crouched down, reached a gloved finger to the nearest foot and gently eased it up so he could see the clean tread pattern on the underside of the shoes. 'There's no way he walked here in those.'

'Have to agree with you there.' Parsons crouched beside him and popped off a quick succession of photographs.

'And if he didn't walk here, it's very unlikely he died here. Someone's dumped him and done a runner.'

36

James Barnton had lived on the top floor of a three-storey tenement on the Dalry Road, not more than a couple of hundred yards from the spot where his dead body had been found. The keys that had been in his hoodie pocket fitted the door nicely, McLean and Harrison stepping into a decent-sized hallway, if a little shabby and in need of airing. Fairly obvious that the dead man was a bachelor and lived alone.

'Christ, it's like going round to my brother's place.' Harrison held the back of her hand to her face. McLean wrinkled his nose, but said nothing. The smell was bad, it was true, but it brought some darkly nostalgic memories of his old tenement flat in Newington. Happy days and sad.

They split up, Harrison heading towards the kitchen. McLean poked his head into the living room, dominated by a massive flatscreen television opposite a sofa that most likely doubled up as a bed more often than not. The gulf between them was filled by a low table, piled high with glossy magazines showing cars a security guard could never hope to own, remote controls for at least half a dozen different devices, an iPad and some empty pizza boxes. A couple of other chairs in the room were at least empty, suggesting maybe Barnton had the occasional visitor.

Through in the flat's one bedroom, the smell of deodorant was even stronger. McLean found the can on top of a chest of drawers, alongside an unwanted Christmas gift collection of aftershaves, talcum powders, body-grooming kits and other things he wasn't sure he wanted to understand. Barnton obviously looked after himself, which made the overpowering perfume in the room puzzling. And then he caught a whiff of something else, something horribly familiar that sparked the beginning of a headache in the base of his brain.

A kingsize bed dominated the room, its sheets crumpled and a duvet with a garish print from some American comic strip on it thrown haphazardly across the mattress. Filling up the wall on the opposite side of the room, a built-in wardrobe reflected McLean's image back at him from mirrored doors. He stepped carefully around the bed and opened up the first to reveal a surprisingly neatly hung row of ironed shirts and jackets. Drawers behind the second door held socks and underpants, a few woolly jumpers and some more hoodies. All were folded and clean, almost obsessively so.

A set of shelves split the cupboard behind the third door. At the top were folded sweatshirts and hoodies. Beneath them, sweatpants very much like the ones Barnton had been found wearing. The shelf below it, and the base of the cupboard, was filled with an impressive collection of shoes. Some were work boots, some tidy patent leather for special occasions. Most were trainers in various states of wear. A dozen or more boxes were neatly piled at the back, unopened except for one which lay on the floor beside the bed. The logo on the side was the same make as the trainers Barnton had been found wearing. The ones he couldn't possibly have walked across this room in, let alone all the way up Dalry Road and halfway through the grubby cemetery.

McLean bent down and picked up the box carefully, taking it by the corners just in case there were fingerprints on the sides. He was about to put it down on the bed when he noticed the way the duvet had crumpled, as if someone had lain down on it after it had been hastily thrown over the sheets.

'Find anything interesting, sir?' Harrison appeared at the doorway, latex-gloved hands held in front of her so she didn't accidentally touch anything.

'Only this.' He held up the box. 'And the bed there. What do you make of that?'

Harrison cocked her head to one side, taking in the scene. 'He was an *X-Men* fan?'

'Apart from that.'

'Well, he's not much good at making his bed, but then a lot of people aren't. Too much of a rush at the start of the day. Maybe running a little late.' Harrison crouched down and looked closer. 'Someone's lain down on here afterwards, though.'

'Or been laid down. Can you smell anything odd in here?'

Harrison sniffed. 'Lynx, mostly. Rather too much of it.' She sniffed again. 'There's something else, too. Like a chemical reek. Almost as if the deodorant's been used to cover it up.' She leaned over the bed carefully, holding back her hair as she sniffed the duvet. 'Aye, it's much stronger there.'

'My thoughts exactly. We already know Barnton was moved to the cemetery after he died. I reckon someone brought him here, laid him on the bed and changed his clothes, then dumped him over the road for us to find.'

'You think he died here?'

'No.' McLean paused a moment, considering it, then shook his head. 'Or if he did, it was from something that happened to him elsewhere. My best guess is there was an accident at work and this was an attempt to cover it up. Not sure why they didn't just shove him in the bed and make us think he died there, though. We'd probably not have found him for days.'

He carefully put the shoebox back down where he had found it, then went over to the laundry basket. There were no clothes in it at all. Not even a stray sock left behind when everything else was bundled up to go in the machine.

'Get on to forensics, will you? I need them to lift any prints they can from that box. Also, find out if there's a communal bin for the tenement, or anywhere close by someone could dispose of clothes. After that, you and I are going to go and pay Extech Energy another visit.'

'Why were you even there, Tony? You're meant to be working the truck crash investigation, not swanning off to any and every new thing that takes your fancy.'

DCI Jayne McIntyre's office wasn't the best room in the building any more: that had gone to Chief Superintendent Forrester. Its door was still always open, though, and McLean had gone straight there as soon as he'd arrived at the station, fresh from a growing crime scene at Dalry Cemetery. He'd left Harrison overseeing a team of uniform constables, searching all the local bins for clothing. He hoped to hell they found some, and soon.

'DC . . .' he began, then decided it wasn't a good idea to drop her in it just because she'd been efficient. 'The dead man, James Barnton, worked at Extech Energy out near Livingston.'

'And?' McIntyre wore reading glasses perched on the end of her nose, and she peered over them like a weary headmistress.

'That's where the truck came from. Or at least that's where its manifest said it came from. I went out there a few days back and talked to the CEO. Barnton was chief of security. I don't think his death was an accident.'

'Why would anyone . . . ? No, first things first. How did you find out who he was?' McIntyre made a show of looking at her watch. 'I mean, it's hardly gone ten in the morning. They only found the body a few hours ago.'

'He had his wallet on him. Driving licence photocard confirmed it was actually him. One of the constables recognized him from Extech.

'One of the constables?' McIntyre raised an eyebrow.

'OK, Jayne. It was Harrison. She called me as soon as she saw the printout. Good thing she did, too. If we'd not been there to see the body, we might not have realized he'd been dumped there.'

'You sure of that, Tony? 'Cause I'm not sure I like the way that line of thinking goes.'

'I don't either, but I can't exactly ignore it. First Finlay, now this man? I mean, one suspicious death's bad enough, but two connected to the crash? We've got to look into it at the very least. You can be sure as hell the press'll make the connection before long.'

McIntyre let out a long sigh, pushed her spectacles back

up her nose as she looked once more at the sheet of paper she'd been holding throughout the conversation. 'You're right, of course. I just wish for once things were simple and straightforward. Well, the Procurator Fiscal's going to want a report. It's a sudden death, and in a public place. They'll need to know the circumstances. Normally I'd give it to a sergeant to deal with, but I know you'll just pester them for results.' She put the page down on top of a pile beside her laptop. 'Go deal with it, Tony. But try not to piss too many people off, OK?'

McLean nodded, unsure whether he could say anything more. He turned to leave, had reached the door before McIntyre spoke again.

'One other thing.'

'Yes?'

'Don't think this gets you off your appointment with the counsellor. I've seen her schedule and you're due there at four this afternoon.'

McLean knew that tone, that look. It wasn't worth his life ignoring McIntyre's direct order even if it would make getting out to Livingston and back tricky. No time to lose, then.

'Yes, ma'am,' he said, then hurried out before the DCI could chide him for his politeness.

37

'Did anyone ever get round to looking at the CCTV footage we got from Extech?'

McLean flipped the lever behind the steering wheel, running up through the gears as his new Alfa accelerated on to the motorway. Eight speeds, switchable automatic and more bells and whistles than you'd see at an English village fair in summertime. He remembered his first ever car, bought just after passing his test a few days before his eighteenth birthday. The gearbox in that had been a four-speed. Three if it was cold and second didn't want to play. It had felt plenty at the time, the freedom of having his own wheels intoxicating. How the world changed.

'Not sure, sir. There was a team going through the stuff from the city cameras, and all the footage sent in by the public. Not sure I even remember the Extech stuff coming in. Might have been electronic files, of course.' Harrison hefted her Airwave set. 'You want me to call Lofty and ask?'

McLean considered it, then shook his head. 'We'll track it down when we get back. And if they simply forgot to send it, we'll just have to find out what it is they're trying to hide.'

'Do you really think they're the source of that toxic waste? Aren't they kind of the exact opposite of that?'

McLean dropped a gear, shot past a tanker truck that

claimed to be transporting the best part of thirty cubic metres of whisky. What a different story it would have been if that had crashed in the city centre.

'Oh, I'm sure a lot of what Extech does is legitimate. There's no doubting they run an anaerobic digester there, and I bet ninety-nine per cent of what comes and goes from the site is harmless organic waste. It's a big place, though, recently built with private money. It's perfectly sited to collect waste from all over the central belt, so why not the toxic stuff as well as the cowshit?'

'You think we should get a team together and search the place?' Harrison lifted her Airwave set again, and McLean almost laughed at the idea of her calling the station, putting together a posse. He gripped the steering wheel tight in frustration; going in heavy-handed was exactly what they should be doing.

'Without any hard evidence, the chances of us getting a warrant are virtually non-existent. Especially given the pressure being exerted on the chief constable. There's too much politics going on, too much wielding of influence. Extech's protected for now, but not so protected we can't go and talk to them about one of their employees who's just turned up dead.'

The security guard waved them through, not even bothering to check their ID when they arrived. McLean drove slowly past the lines of digester tanks towards the administration building, half expecting to see a tanker being filled with toxic chemicals tucked away behind one. There were no trucks visible on site at all, though, and very few people.

'Inspector, Constable.' Claire Ferris greeted them in the reception area with a polite nod. Her face had a drawn, weary quality to it as if she'd not slept well since last they had met. She led them through to a small conference room, instructing the receptionist to bring coffee. As McLean took his seat, he noticed a thin brown folder already lying on the table in front of one of the chairs.

'It's good of you to see us so swiftly,' he said as Ferris sat down.

'I'll admit your call this morning came as something of a shock. But I'm always ready to help the police. We have nothing to hide here.'

McLean studied Ferris's face as she spoke, trying to see if she was lying. She would have been very good at poker, that much was clear. She had no obvious tells, and the weariness left her voice flat. Unless it was all part of an act.

'I'm glad to hear it. Sorry we're here on such sad business.'

'Aye, Jim Barnton.' Ferris pulled the brown folder towards her with one hand, running the other through her short hair in an oddly masculine gesture. 'Worked security here since we opened. Before that, I guess. He was part of the construction team.'

'Security for the site, or actually wielding a spade?'

Ferris stared at McLean as if she didn't understand the question. Then it must have dawned on her. 'Oh, security. There's a lot of expensive kit on a site like this. Particularly during the building work. You've no idea how much stuff gets nicked.'

'I'm a detective, Ms Ferris. I've a pretty good idea.' McLean gave her a reassuring smile, unsurprised when it wasn't returned. 'Was Mr Barnton working here yesterday?'

Ferris consulted the folder again. 'Yes. He was on a normal day shift. Arrived here at half seven for an eight o'clock start. Punched out at half five. Front gate has him leaving at five minutes to six.'

'Half hour at each end of the day? What was he doing?' Harrison asked.

'Getting changed? Grabbing a coffee in the canteen? Having a shower? I've no idea, Constable. It's not unusual for staff to arrive before their shift starts, though. In this or any other job, I'd have assumed.'

For the first time since they had arrived, McLean heard an edge in Ms Ferris's voice. He couldn't be sure if it was the question or the fact it had been asked by Harrison that had annoyed her. For her part, Harrison seemed a little taken aback by the CEO's tone, looking to him for advice or perhaps to take over the questioning. McLean merely smiled, nodded almost imperceptibly for her to carry on.

'I . . . So the staff have changing facilities? Showers?' Harrison stammered a little as she picked up the threads.

'We deal with waste. Animal faeces, vegetable matter, even human sewage sludge sometimes. I'd be a poor employer if I didn't provide somewhere for the workers to clean themselves up now, wouldn't I?'

'And does Mr Barnton have a locker in these facilities? Somewhere he'd store his work clothes?'

'I would imagine so. Why do you ask?'

'Would it be possible for us to see it? The locker?' Harrison chose to ignore Ms Ferris's question.

'I . . . I suppose so. I'll have to get one of the security team to open it. They're called lockers for a reason, you know.'

'That would be very helpful, thank you.' Harrison gave Ferris a smile that was as broad as it was genuine. 'Could you tell me, did Barnton need to have medical checkups as part of his job?'

'All our staff have annual health checks, yes.' Ferris flicked a couple of pages in the folder. 'There were no problems at his last one, a couple of months ago.'

'Do you do them in-house, or send them to a local doctor?'

'We use a facility in Livingston for that sort of thing. Senior management have private health cover with them, too.'

'But not Barnton, I imagine.' Harrison wrote something down in her notebook. 'Might we have a contact there? Someone we can speak to about him?'

'Of course. It's all in here.' Ferris closed the thin brown folder and slid it across the table. 'That's a copy of Jim's personnel file. I'd appreciate it if the information in it wasn't spread further than necessary.'

'Thank you. I'm sure once we've concluded our investigations it will be destroyed.'

Ferris relaxed a little, leaning back in her chair. 'And what exactly is the nature of your investigation?'

'A man has died unexpectedly, and in a public place.' McLean answered the question before Harrison could speak. He was fairly sure she wouldn't say anything out of place, but he wanted to study Ferris's reactions. 'Mr Barnton's death is unexplained, and the circumstances of it are unusual. The Procurator Fiscal requires us to prepare a report into the circumstances leading up to it. There will be a post-mortem examination of his body soon, to determine why he died. It's all standard procedure.'

Ferris didn't look particularly reassured by the explanation. 'And standard procedure requires a detective inspector be involved?' she asked.

'We all have to muck in these days. Austerity and that.' McLean offered her another smile, but he could see there was little point in pursuing matters further here. 'Perhaps if we could have a wee look at Barnton's locker, maybe see the places he worked. Then we can leave you in peace.'

'There you go. Not sure what good it'll do you, mind.'

McLean stepped to one side to let the security guard move back, revealing an open locker in a line of a dozen or more. Much like the rest of the operation, the changing rooms at Extech Energy were well-specified, almost overdone. The large lockers filled one wall, a low bench opposite with hooks above it and boot storage space below. Through a wide opening at the far end a line of shower cubicles were sparkly clean, and a set of shelves beside it held a sizeable pile of clean towels. It looked more like the changing rooms at an expensive spa or gym than anything industrial.

'I'll . . . I'll wait at the door. Don't want anyone coming in while . . .' The security guard was a young lad. His name badge read 'R Dawson', but Ms Ferris had introduced him as Bobby. This was probably his first job out of school if the acne dotting his face and the poor fit of his uniform was any guide. Possibly his first day of his first job. He had hesitated when DC Harrison had followed him and McLean into the men's locker room even though it was empty, and he was still nervous of her presence in this shrine to masculinity.

'You sure?' Harrison asked, with a voice that was all innocence. He merely nodded, then retreated to the door.

'Be nice, Constable.' McLean fished in his pocket for a pair of latex gloves, pulled them on before starting to go through the items in the locker. There wasn't much, despite its large size. A uniform similar to the one the young lad at the door was wearing: dark-blue jacket and trousers, white shirt and clip-on tie. He checked the pockets, but they were empty. Hanging at the back of the locker was a set of overalls bearing the Extech company logo on the chest pocket and emblazoned across the back. They had clearly been worn, mud caked around the legs and a suspicious stain on one arm. It smelled more agricultural than chemical when McLean lifted it to his nose, though.

Barnton had two pairs of boots courtesy of his employers. One pair were almost police-issue, halfway between smart and heavy-duty. They were polished black and the chunky soles had only a small amount of grit on them. A drawing pin had stuck itself in the left heel, shiny from being scuffed against the floor tiles. The other boots were more substantial, heavy enough to be steel-toecapped, and would no doubt have been worn with the overalls for outdoor work. Their soles had been cleaned recently, but not well enough to get rid of all the sticky mud that had worked its way into the deep tread. McLean fished in his pocket until he found a penknife, winkled out some of the dirt on to his hand and sniffed it.

'Get anything?' Harrison asked, bending down to see.

'Not sure. What do you reckon?' He held his hand up for her to smell. She took a whiff, wrinkled her nose and backed off.

'Dog, I think. Eugh.'

McLean brushed the dirt from his palm, pulled off the latex gloves and shoved them back in his pocket. 'Nothing interesting here, but then I never really thought there would be.'

'You didn't?' Harrison asked. 'Then why did you ask to see it?'

'I wanted to know if they'd try to stop me. Give us the runaround.' He called over to the young security guard. 'It's Bobby, isn't it? We're all done here, but I'd love a tour of the facilities, if that's allowed.'

38

The leafy cool of the early-morning cemetery was a distant memory as McLean, Harrison and the young security guard stepped out of the administration block. They had been given plastic hard hats and fluorescent tabards emblazoned with the Extech logo, which Bobby had insisted they wear at all times. McLean was reassessing how long the lad had worked for the company, as he seemed to know a lot more about the operation than anyone else had been prepared to tell him so far.

'These big tanks here are mostly for storing waste until we're ready for it to go into the digesters.' He pointed at the line of stainless-steel vessels that sat either side of the long tarmac driveway from the entrance gate. 'We get a lot of slurry from local dairy farms. Green waste from the council collection sites, that sort of thing. The leafy stuff gets pulped, mixed in with everything else. Then it's sealed up with these wee bugs, aye? Special bacteria. They eat it up and fart oot methane.'

'Fart oot? Is that a scientific term?' Harrison asked.

'Aye, well. You know what I mean, ken?' Bobby the security guard blushed so deeply his acne spots almost disappeared.

'What do you do with the methane?'

'See these big tanks wi' the conical tops? They's the digesters. All the gas gets drawn off down those pipes and into the generator hoose over there.' The security guard pointed to a large steel-frame building, clad in green corrugated-steel sheeting. It put McLean in mind of the new buildings at LindSea Farms out near East Fortune, but then all agricultural and industrial buildings looked like that these days.

'We generate about five megawatts of power and it all goes back into the grid. Well, apart from the stuff we use here ourselves. There's a plan to put up greenhouses on the land oot there to the west. They'll pump the gasses from the generator in to help the tomatoes grow.'

McLean followed the direction of Bobby the security guard's pointed finger to an open expanse of scrubland dominated by rushes. 'Tomatoes? In Scotland? Isn't that a bit ambitious?'

'Aye, well, that's just what they tellt me. I don't know half of how this place works, ken?'

'What's that over there?' DC Harrison pointed to a spot at the far end of the site from the entrance, where a couple of smaller storage tanks stood alongside a low building with roller doors along one side. A wide tarmac area in front of them was surrounded by lines of pipework.

'That? That's the washout area. Once the trucks have pumped out all the shite into the storage tanks, they head over there and get cleaned out. The waste all gets filtered, an' anything that can be eaten by the wee bugs is pumped back into they tanks. Sheds are where we store all the maintenance gear and stuff.'

'Must have cost a bob or two, to build this place.' McLean turned and started walking away from the point where they had stopped, halfway between his car and the washout area. If that was what it really was.

'Twenty-five million pounds. That's what I was told anyways.' Bobby hurried to catch up, and soon they were back at the visitor car park. McLean took off his tabard and hard hat, handing both back to the security guard. Harrison had been dawdling behind, but she caught up as McLean fished his keys out of his pocket and plipped the unlock button.

'Whoa! Alfa Giulia Quadrifoglio. This is yours? Sweet.' Struggling with the hats and tabards now that Harrison had handed him hers as well, Bobby still managed to goggle at McLean's car.

'Thanks. I think.' McLean opened the passenger door and threw the keys to Harrison. She caught them with a reflex that would have done a slip fielder proud. Left hand, too, even though she wrote with her right. That was holding on to the brown folder Ms Ferris had given them, so it was fair enough. She said nothing, but he could tell by the look on her face that she was both surprised and a little worried. The car cost more than twice her salary, so maybe she had a point.

'Thanks for the tour, Bobby,' McLean said as he climbed into the unfamiliar passenger seat. 'Tell Ms Ferris I'll be in touch. Don't expect there'll be anything to report, but if there is I'll be sure to let her know.'

The security guard nodded his understanding, but said nothing. He was too busy staring wide-eyed at the car. It didn't help that Harrison blipped the throttle a little more enthusiastically than was strictly necessary when she fired up the engine. McLean was too busy adjusting the passenger seat back so that there was room for his feet. He'd never noticed quite how short the detective constable was.

Then with a click of the gear change paddles and a 'How does this work? Oh', they were off.

By the time they reached the entrance gate, slowing down to allow the barrier to rise, Harrison seemed to have got the measure of the car. Turning out on to the road that would take them to the motorway, she gave it a little gas, then backed off as the wheels chirped and spun against the tarmac.

'Oh. Right. Yes. I can see what they mean.' Her words were directed at the windscreen, eyes fixed on the road and the controls directly in front of her.

'They?' McLean asked. He wasn't quite sure why he was enjoying her discomfort, but he was. It was counter-productive though. The whole reason for making her drive was so that he would have time to think, to process what he had heard and seen in the past hour.

'Umm . . . Just the other constables, sir.' Harrison didn't turn to look at him, and for that he was grateful.

'They used to say all sorts of stuff about your old car,' she added. 'Some of them used to call you Morse, but it never really stuck. Mostly they just couldn't understand why you drove that and not some soulless old Mondeo or Astra that wouldn't matter if it got broken. There was a sweepstake on what you'd get to replace it, the old GTV.'

'There was?' It didn't surprise McLean that someone had organized one, but it did that he hadn't heard. 'Who won?'

'They're still arguing about it.' Harrison indicated, clicked the downshift paddle behind the steering wheel and accelerated on to the motorway. 'PC Harker had you down for a brand new Giulia, but he didn't specify the model. Closest anyone else got was Sergeant Gatford. Reckoned you'd buy a secondhand Giulietta.'

'What about you, then?'

Harrison risked a sideways glance. She was relaxing into driving the boss's car now, swiftly coming to terms with the way it worked. She'd been through the Police Driver Training course, too, he could tell.

'I thought you'd get the GTV fixed.'

'Believe me, I was tempted. There's not enough left to mend, though. Better if the parts that can be salvaged go to keep a few more on the roads. And you never know, I might just buy myself another one some day.'

Harrison opened her mouth to speak, then closed it again. McLean could easily enough guess what she'd been going to say. Something about his wealth, the ability to afford things like the car they were driving in right now and to so casually suggest buying another that could cost him equally as much. She'd seen where he lived. Wouldn't be the first officer to wonder why he bothered with the job when he was so obviously loaded. He sometimes wondered it himself.

'What did you make of that meeting?' he asked, as much to move the conversation on as anything.

'Ms Ferris, or Bobby the Plook there?'

McLean smiled at the word. Scots could be so harsh sometimes. Accurate, but harsh.

'Both, but let's focus on Ferris first.'

'She was well-rehearsed, I'll give her that.'

'Well-rehearsed?'

'You know what I mean, sir? The folder with all the

information in it? Young Bobby there with no clue as to what's really going on?'

McLean settled into the passenger seat, enjoying the comfort of being driven for a change. 'I thought I was cynical.'

'Aye, but she was. If that'd been one of my employees drop down dead like that, I think I'd show a little more . . . I dunno, sadness? It's almost as if she'd known he was dead long enough for it not to be such a shock any more.'

'Maybe she's not the emotional type. Maybe she's got that many people working for her one dying is more of an inconvenience than anything else.'

'Oh, she's cold all right. But it's more than that. You saw the men's changing room, right? I counted fifteen lockers but only five of them were closed. How many workers did we see on site while wee Bobby was showing us around? How many folk in the main building.'

McLean nodded his understanding. It was pretty much what he'd thought the first time they had visited, backed up by their more recent experience. The site might have cost twenty-five million to build, but it certainly wasn't employing all that many. Losing one of the team, especially one who'd been with the company a while, should have been more of a shock. He retrieved the slim brown personnel file Ms Ferris had given them, flicked it open. The top page was basic details, a photograph of James Barnton that looked more like a mugshot than a passport photo. Apparently he'd been thirty years old, educated to Higher level, but not exactly outstanding grades. He'd worked for Extech for six years, and before that for a company called Omega Security. His work record was good, no sick leave in the past four years. Company health check done two months ago, just as Ferris had said.

'I guess we'll just have to wait and see what the post-mortem comes up with.' He settled back into the comfortable passenger seat, relaxing as they sped back towards the city. 'Knowing my luck this will all have been just an unfortunate coincidence.'

Concentrating on the road, DC Harrison said nothing. Even so McLean could tell she didn't believe it any more than he did.

39

The major-incident room had a slow buzz to it, like a machine that's been oiled well, but maybe not as recently as everyone thinks. McLean had worked enough investigations over the course of his career to recognize the signs of slowing, the loss of that initial surge of enthusiasm.

'Still no luck on the last two?' He glanced up at the whiteboard.

'Aye, mebbe. Your young wifey whose hairbrush DC Harrison brought in and the older woman. Might have a potential for her, too. Alicia Dennis. Tourist from America travelling Europe alone. Family's not heard from her in a week now. The US Consulate are sorting out a sample for DNA cross-referencing.' DC Gregg held a clipboard like the responsible adult at a school outing. The image was compounded in McLean's mind by the list of names printed in a column on the top page.

'That all of them, then?' he asked.

'Aye, sir. All nineteen accounted for, if we're right about the two women. God rest their souls.' Gregg handed over the clipboard. 'Plus the driver, Wilkins.'

'Does his soul not get to rest? We don't know if he was to blame yet.'

'Figure of speech.' Gregg frowned as if she had just been told off for something she hadn't done. McLean ignored her, reading the list of names. They meant very little to him, but the column alongside, with funeral details, caught his eye.

'This your idea?' He pointed at the list.

'DCI McIntyre said we should send a wreath, maybe even a couple of uniforms if we can spare them. Just to show we care.'

Ever the politician. McLean had to admit it was wise. They were getting enough criticism from the press for the accident as it was, even if there was nothing the police could have done to prevent it. They were the visible face of authority, though. Getting it in the neck came with the job.

'It's a good idea.' He made to hand back the clipboard, then noticed the name of one of the churches. Scanning back to the name of the man being buried didn't help, he had no idea who Philip Jacobs was, but he knew the church well enough. It was just across the road from his house after all.

'Maybe I'll represent Police Scotland at this one.' He pointed it out to Gregg. 'If he's from my part of town, there's bound to be someone there who'll recognize me even without the uniform.'

'You'll need to hurry up then, sir. It's on this afternoon.'

'It is?' McLean took back the list, peered at it more closely.

'Next page,' Gregg said, flipping the paper for him. He looked at the time, then at his watch. He could make it, if he hurried.

'OK. You man the fort here. I'll be back in a couple of hours. And if anyone asks, they can find me at the kirk.'

*

276

'It was good of you to come, Tony. I know you and God don't exactly see eye to eye.'

McLean caught the smile in the minister's words and knew that she was teasing him. For all her belief, Mary Currie was the sort of person he had a lot of time for.

'I've never really thought of funerals as being about God. More about letting the bereaved know life can still go on.'

'An interesting point of view. Did you know Philip well?'

McLean glanced around the emptying church and the collection of sombre-dressed people who had come to see the dead man off. 'Actually, I don't think I ever met him, but a high-profile case like this, a tragic death. It's sort of expected that someone from the police turn up. And this being my home parish . . .' He shrugged.

'You drew the short straw? Or you took one for the team?' Crow's feet crinkled around the minister's eyes as she smiled at her own joke. It didn't last, her face turning serious once more. 'He was younger than you. Philip, that is. Such a waste. Maybe not the most regular of worshippers, but his family have had a plot here since the church was built. I think I'm right in saying the first one was the master mason who oversaw the building. There's many a Jacob buried here, but I've a suspicion Philip will be the last.'

'No children?' McLean had noticed there were none at the funeral, but sometimes it was best to keep them away.

The minister shook her head sadly. 'Let me introduce you to his wife.'

Before McLean could make his excuses and run, the minister had grabbed him by the arm and was dragging him through the thinning throng to where a slender young blonde-haired woman in a black dress and pillbox hat was talking to a somewhat more familiar figure. McLean had arrived late to the funeral, tucking into an empty pew at the back of the church where he thought he'd be able to see all the rest of the congregation. Somehow he'd managed to miss Madame Rose, though.

The transvestite medium spotted them both approaching, and her glance in their direction alerted the young woman. McLean had only seen her from the side, but when she turned to face them he was struck by how young she looked. But then sudden death was no great respecter of age. He knew that better than most.

'Mary, that was such a lovely service. Thank you. Philip would have been very pleased.' Her accent was soft, almost as anglicized as his own. A Scot who had spent as much time out of her native country as in it.

'I would far rather not have had to conduct it at all, Lucy. But we do our best.' The minister tilted her head slightly as she spoke, her every mannerism gentle and soothing. 'Have you met Tony McLean? He lives in the big house over the road.'

The young woman looked up at him with a slightly startled expression, pausing a moment before holding out a black-gloved hand. 'You're the policeman, aren't you?'

McLean copied Mary Currie's head tilt as he took the offered hand gently in his own. 'I'm very sorry for your loss' was all he could think of to say.

'Will you catch them? The people who killed my Philip?'

She held his gaze with a steady stare it was hard to break from, still holding on to his hand.

'We're doing our –'

'Not the police. You. Will you catch them?' There was an intensity to the question that took McLean by surprise. He'd seen grief take many forms, but never quite such focused rage before.

'I am in charge of the investigation,' he said. 'And I won't give up until those responsible are brought to justice.'

The widow Lucy Jacob stared directly at him for what felt like years but was probably only a second or two longer than was proper. It was her husband they had just buried in the graveyard outside, though, so he was prepared to forgive the lapse.

'I do believe you will. Thank you.' She finally relinquished his hand, and before the moment could become any more awkward, Madame Rose stepped in, the unlikely hero.

'Lucy, it was lovely talking to you again, but might I possibly steal away the detective inspector? I really wanted to have a word.'

The sun shone high in a cloudless sky as they stepped out into the graveyard. The church itself had been cool, a pleasant haven from the oppressive summer heat, but even in the shadows McLean felt the sweat start to prick on his back.

'Surprised to see you here, Rose. Did you know the Jacobs well?'

'Better, I think, than you did, Tony.' The medium produced an elegant lacquer compact from the depths of her

279

patent-leather handbag and dabbed at her face with a little foundation to hide her own perspiration. 'Philip did my accounts. A very well-mannered gentleman. And his wife, Lucy, is an absolute poppet. I feel devastated for her.'

'She seems, I don't know, very young.'

Madame Rose chuckled. 'Don't let Emma hear you talking like that.'

McLean ignored her. 'She was very earnest, too, insisting I personally catch those responsible. It sounded like the sort of thing you'd say, now I think about it.'

'A compliment?'

'Perhaps. Now's not the time and place to tell her, but we've some promising leads. And I meant it when I said I'd not give up until those responsible were brought to justice.'

'Oh, I know, Tony. You're quite the wee terrier when you get hold of something like that. It's an admirable trait in a detective, although I imagine it drives your superiors to distraction.'

'You've been speaking to my boss now?'

'Jayne and I go way back, but I speak to everyone, Tony. You should know that. Even the dead.'

A chill ran down McLean's spine at Madame Rose's words. They were spoken with such a deadpan, serious voice he knew that she wasn't joking.

'And what do they say?' He had not meant it to sound flippant, but he winced as he spoke all the same.

'They are disturbed. Their deaths were sudden, unexpected, violent. Very few are at rest now, not even Philip here.' Madame Rose gestured across the headstones to where two council workmen were shovelling earth on top of the coffin. No room here for a mini-digger. McLean didn't envy them their task in this heat. 'They want to be named.'

'But we have named them. We've identified almost all of them. Possibly have names for the last two.'

Madame Rose placed a massive hand on McLean's arm. 'Are you sure of that? The spirits tell me something else. Anger walks the streets, vengeance on its mind. It comes from the same place as all these poor souls, but it has no name.'

McLean had taken a step back as Madame Rose moved in close, her voice filled with stage show menace. Now something hard stopped him, and looking round he saw a headstone, darkened by centuries of soot and Edinburgh winters. He knew that the old medium believed everything that she said, and in that moment he almost did, too.

'The dead cannot rest easy unknown, Tony. You must find the soul that is still out there. Find it before it finds you.'

40

'This is getting to be something of a habit, Tony.'

Late afternoon and McLean found himself once more in the air-conditioned cool of the examination theatre at the city mortuary. Laid out on the stainless-steel slab, the late James Barnton was ready to reveal his final secrets. The stiffness in his arms and fingers had eased a little now, but his face was still a mask of horror.

'Should he not have, you know, relaxed a bit by now? Don't muscles usually slacken off after a while?'

'Indeed they do.' Cadwallader bent to his task, working his way slowly around the body, examining it in minute detail. 'Rigor mortis can sometimes leave more permanent effects though, and if he died of a seizure, as I suspect is the case, then that would account for his grimace.'

'What about the other thing. You know? How we think he might have died elsewhere and been moved to the graveyard.'

'Give me time, Tony. I'll get to that.' Cadwallader peered at the cadaver's chest, pressing lightly on the skin with his latex-gloved fingers while he made an odd tutting noise under his breath.

'Tracy, have we got the chest X-rays?'

Doctor Sharp went to the viewing screen set up on the wall at the far side of the examination theatre. With a few well-practised taps of the keyboard, she brought up a large image in contrasting shades of green, the dead man's ribs and palely outlined organs. Cadwallader ambled over, pushing his spectacles up his nose as he approached the screen, looking at it for long moments before returning to the table.

'Thought these might have been bruise marks. See, here and here?'

McLean stepped closer. The harsh light of the examination theatre made Barnton's skin almost translucent, veins wriggling just below the surface like hungry worms. His chest was bare, one nipple slightly misshapen, the other more or less normal. A narrow hand's-breadth below both, the skin had a darker hue to it. Not quite a bruise, but certainly a mark.

'Might he have been shoved?'

Cadwallader shrugged. 'Possible. But it doesn't look right. It's not a bruise, more the sort of marking you get sometimes with powerful electric shocks. Only they tend to be small spots, not larger areas.'

The pathologist went over to the workbench that ran along the far wall beneath the screens, pulled open a drawer and took something out. When he came back to the body, he was holding what looked like a flashlight and two pairs of yellow-tinted safety goggles. He handed one to McLean, awkwardly putting the other set over his glasses with his free hand before switching on the lamp.

'We're not looking for fluids, are we?' McLean asked as Cadwallader directed the light at the darker marks on Barnton's skin.

'Different kind of light and filter. This just helps with the contrast more than anything else. Only really works

283

on dead flesh. Ah, that's interesting.' The pathologist bent low to the point where the left-hand mark showed. McLean leaned in to see what had caught his eye. The light washed out what little colour was left in the dead man's skin, rendering it almost monochrome and bringing the dark mark into higher relief. Now it looked very much like a light handprint, but made by the hand of a tiny child. Cadwallader moved the light to the other side, showing a similar mark. When he clicked off the lamp, it almost completely disappeared.

'Seems like your suggestion could be right. This is exactly what you'd expect from a man getting shoved in the chest by a shorter person. Only that would leave bruises, and these aren't bruises.'

'So what are they, then? What made them?'

'I don't know, Tony. I'll have to take a sample of skin, have a look at it under the microscope, maybe send it off for some tests. Like I said, it looks more like the mark from an electrical discharge than anything. But why the shape, then?'

A mystery, but McLean wasn't sure it was relevant to the ongoing investigation. 'OK. Let me know as soon as you've got an answer. In the meantime, what about him being moved after he died?'

'Ah yes, that.' Cadwallader pulled off his goggles and placed them down on the tray beside the examination table, alongside the sharp instruments of his trade and the more industrial-looking tools. 'The lividity is all right for him having sat awhile after death. Blood's all collected around his lower back, backside and thighs. Tracey, can you help me turn him over?'

Doctor Sharp approached the table and between the two of them they expertly rolled Barnton's corpse on to its front. McLean could see the marks clearly enough, the blotchy mess of congealed blood where it had settled after the man's heart had stopped beating.

'His position at the cemetery was interesting, as you pointed out, I think, Tony.' Cadwallader flexed the fingers of both hands together as if the strain of turning the cadaver had hurt them.

'There was quite a gap between his back and the headstone. I had Manda Parsons photograph it. Almost all his weight was being taken on the back of his head and his shoulders. Didn't look comfortable at all. Mind you, he was dead.'

'Aye, that's how I remember it. Which makes these marks a bit strange, don't you think?' The pathologist scribed the air above Barnton's upper and middle back. Faint, but visible even without weird lights and filters, McLean could make out lines of lividity casting horizontal shadows across the spotty flesh.

'He was much more solidly slumped against something for a while after he died. And whatever it was, it had raised ridges on it that pushed into his skin and stopped some of the blood from draining down to his backside. No idea what it might have been, except that the ridges appear to be about two inches apart.'

'Don't remember seeing anything like that in the cemetery.' McLean pulled out his phone, turned to leave, then hesitated. 'You mind if I skip the rest? Think I need to let the boss know the body was tampered with after he died.'

Cadwallader smiled, picked up a scalpel even though Barnton was still face down. 'Go, Tony. I know you don't like the next bit anyway.'

Darkness wouldn't fully claim the city for a couple of hours yet, but it was still late enough for headlights as McLean parked in the courtyard at the back of his house. With hindsight, it had probably been unwise going back to the station after the post-mortem. Given the hours he'd been working recently, he'd have been justified going home straight after the funeral, but Madame Rose's words had unsettled him, he'd needed to throw himself back into the case. It was just a pity his earlier suspicions about Barnton's death had been confirmed. One more complication he didn't want to have to think about.

It was only as he pushed through the door from the utility room and into the kitchen that he remembered he'd dropped Emma at work that morning because her car wouldn't start. He'd been so wrapped up in the day's events, he'd quite forgotten to phone and ask her if she needed bringing home, or indeed to let her know he was going to be late.

Mrs McCutcheon's cat was nowhere to be seen, and now he thought about it, he couldn't recall having seen any of the other cats that had been lurking around the garden for days now. Perhaps it was a shift change or something. He dumped his briefcase on the kitchen table, a small pile of reports that he hoped he might get away with ignoring until tomorrow but probably wouldn't. For a moment he just stood there, listening to the quiet gurgle of the Aga and the hum of the fridge. It was tempting to pour himself a beer, worry about food and a shower later. Chances were it wouldn't go down well with Emma, though.

He found her in the library, laid out on the sofa with one hand over her head as if to shield her eyes from the glare of the light. Dressed in loose-fitting clothes, the swell of her belly was just beginning to show, or at least he convinced himself that it was. How long now until the baby was due? Not long. Not long enough. He didn't feel remotely ready for this.

A quiet groan, and Emma lifted her free hand to her stomach, rolled over and sat up. She blinked a couple of times, eyes bleary with sleep. 'Tony? What you doing standing there?'

'Just got in. Sorry. I know I should have called earlier. Arranged for someone to come pick you up from work.'

'It's OK. Manda Parsons gave me a lift.' She yawned, stretched wide, arms reaching for the ceiling, back arched. And then suddenly hunched in on herself, wrapping her arms around her stomach. 'Ow!'

'What is it, Em?' McLean rushed over to the sofa, crouched down beside her. He wasn't sure whether an arm around the shoulder would help or hinder as Emma squeezed her eyes tight shut against some considerable pain. Eventually, she let out a long gasp of breath and relaxed a little.

'Keep forgetting the wee tyke doesn't like me stretching like that.' She smiled up at him, but it was a weary smile. 'You eaten yet?'

McLean helped Emma to unsteady feet, supported her until she regained her balance. 'Not yet. I was thinking of skipping straight to beer.'

'Rub it in, why don't you.' She punched him on the shoulder, but with no strength. 'Haven't had a drink in ages. You should have given up in sympathy. This is your child as much as mine.'

He hugged her close, kissed the top of her head even though it smelled of musty old sofa. 'OK. Tea it is.'

'Rose dropped by earlier,' Emma said as they walked to the kitchen. 'She was a bit disappointed to find you weren't here. You'd think she'd know you better than that by now.'

'Madame Rose? I saw her earlier in the day. Funeral for one of the crash victims. She say what she wanted?'

'Oh, you know what she's like. All subtle hints at terrible things about to happen, or already happening, or happened and it's too late to do anything about them now. She said there was something ancient and evil stalking the city and she needed to find it before it got out of hand. She did mention a funeral, right enough. Said she'd spoken to you but you'd not been listening.' Emma put on a reasonable impression of the medium '"We must gird ourselves against the gathering dark", or something like that. Oh, and she went through a load more books. That seemed to calm her down a bit.'

McLean filled the kettle and heaved it on to the hotplate, glancing back at the fridge and its bottles of cold beer with a guilty longing. His gaze was distracted by the clattering of the cat flap and Mrs McCutcheon's cat came padding in.

'Oh, that was the other strange thing,' Emma said. 'We were in the library talking about rare books and stuff and your cat jumped up onto Rose's lap, like she does sometimes.'

'*My* cat?' McLean put all the emphasis on the possessive pronoun as Mrs McCutcheon's cat looked up at him, testing the air to make sure he hadn't contaminated it. 'I'm not sure that's how it works.'

'Aye, well. You know what I mean. She jumped onto Rose's lap anyway, and I could swear it was like they were having a conversation. I don't mean a "who's a lovely kitty" kind of conversation either. This wasn't one-sided at all.'

McLean raised an eyebrow, looked down at Mrs McCutcheon's cat, who was now cleaning her arse with her tongue. 'I wonder what they talked about.'

'I've no idea, but Rose left quite quickly after that. Oh, she was polite and everything, but it was fairly obvious she needed to be somewhere else, and I couldn't shake the idea it was all because the cat had told her something. Stupid really.' Emma smiled, the wrinkles around her eyes making her look far older than her years.

McLean took the now-boiling kettle off the heat, poured water into the teapot and set it down on the kitchen table to stew. A splash slopped out of the spout, so he went to the sink for a cloth to wipe it up. Something moved in the gloaming outside, and as he stared through the window into the darkening shadows, it resolved into the largest tom cat he had ever seen. A great shaggy beast, it looked more like a small lion than something you'd let sit on your lap. It stared at him a moment, eyes glinting in the reflected light from the kitchen window, and then it stalked off in the direction of the drive.

He was about to turn, damp cloth already in hand, when he saw another cat saunter across the grass as if following the first. Then a pair of them hurried after it, followed by yet more.

'Something up?'

McLean started as Emma spoke right beside him. She followed his gaze out of the window, where a line of cats now strode purposefully out of the garden. What seemed like dozens of them, all glanced briefly at the window as they passed. Big, small, young and old alike. Then the last one sauntered into the darkness and they were gone.

41

I think I know where they were taking that stuff now.

Sure, it took a while. Going to take most of the day to get there, too, scope it out, add the details to this little dossier I've been compiling. I'd have handed the whole thing over to the police already, but I've not had the best relationship with them, if I'm being honest. Who knows what would happen? What would disappear? No, I need to see this through to the end, then make sure enough of the right people know that it can't be buried.

It's not like they're all bad, after all. There was Gordon at the start, and he was OK, I guess, if a bit driven. All those people he hoped to arrest on the say of a six-year-old boy who'd been traumatized to the point of murdering dozens of men, women and children in a house fire. That's not how I thought of him at the time, of course, or how I thought of myself. I just saw him as a familiar face, a small rock of constancy in an ever-changing world. He never hurt me, never once let show the frustration he must have been feeling. The only times he ever treated me as anything other than an equal was when I asked about Maddy. Then he'd either change the subject or dismiss me with a half-answer.

Once he was gone, interest in the house fire seemed to dry up. I was too wrapped up in my own problems to really notice, but there'd be interviews, a succession of earnest or bored officers explaining what I'd done wrong or that I'd be moving to a new area or any number of other things I didn't hear at the time. Too busy growing up and lashing out, making life miserable for anyone who tried to get too close.

And then I moved to Scotland, the west coast. A pair of middle-aged ladies living an unconventional lifestyle. Jean worked for the council, which was probably how they passed the test as suitable adopters. Sheila did some consultancy work with the police when she wasn't lecturing at Paisley University. I guess that's how I came to her attention in the first place. Or maybe she knew Gordon or something. It's not important. They kept me from going completely off the rails, and gave me a purpose in life; still do, if I'm being honest, even though I don't see much of them these days.

I've them to thank for bringing the police back into my life, too, I guess. That or the drugs.

I was never an addict. I know how that sounds, the sort of thing only an addict would say, but I've not even thought about drugs in years. It was more the crowd I hung with, what they were into. Going along with it just to be accepted. Having an English accent in a Glasgow school when everyone's high on the thought of independence isn't much fun.

It's more fun than being swept up in a police raid though. Something must have pinged somewhere, because I was hauled off away from the others pretty sharpish. Next thing I knew I was talking to a man who said he knew Gordon, knew all about my background and the true name they'd taken from me. He wasn't a bad copper as they go, a bit like Gordon only much younger, posher, like he'd been well educated. That put my back up at first. All the sad old men who'd fucked me and Maddy had talked like him.

But he let me off with a caution, then asked me if I'd be interested in working with him. With the police and the special task force he was assigned to. First job was to hack into a database and switch some data around, so the swab they'd taken from me when I was arrested wouldn't flag up anywhere. 'Call it a test,' he'd said with a smile. It wasn't even really hacking, given that I used a terminal in the police station to do it. They didn't ask me to, but I doubled up a couple of other records, to make it harder to trace. Stuck in a little back door so I could keep an eye on things if I needed. And then I walked free.

Only, you're never really free when someone's got something over you, and that's how I feel about the police. The National Crime Agency, as they call themselves these days. I hope they're after the same sick fucks I'm after, but I'd be surprised if some of them weren't in on it, doing their best to protect the privileged. So I watch them and they watch me.

Sure, I'm paranoid, but can you blame me?

42

The major-incident room had a buzz about it quite at odds with the previous afternoon. Something was clearly up. Despite the strange departure of all Madame Rose's cats – or maybe because of it – McLean had slept well. Untroubled by the ghoulish dreams of recent nights, he had woken feeling rested for the first time in an age. No one had called during breakfast, no new crisis requiring his immediate attention. Even the drive across town had been relatively easy. He'd dropped Emma off at the forensic labs with a promise to pick her up again at the end of the day, heading to the station with every intention of keeping that promise. A heady sense of optimism in the room made him feel like he might even manage it.

'What's up, Constable?'

DC Gregg emerged from the ebb and flow of officers, clasping a couple of report folders to her ample chest. She had a grin on her face that was quite infectious.

'Just in from the US Consulate, sir. Seems victim number eighteen had one of those health screen DNA tests done a couple of years back. They've matched it with the results we sent them.' Gregg presented the first of the folders to McLean as if it were some kind of school prize.

'RIP Alicia Dennis.' He flicked open the report, scanned a few of the dense lines of text within. They never made sense these things, couched in scientific levels of uncertainty, but it was close enough. He was just beginning to explore the implications of the identification when Gregg interrupted him.

'That's not all, sir. See that sample you and Janie Harrison found?'

'Jennifer Beasley? Aye?'

'Well, they've matched that to the last female victim. Eighty-five per cent certain it's her.' Gregg handed him the other folder.

'Eighty-five. Is that good?'

'Given the nature of the sample, it's as good as you'll get. If it's no' her then it's her mother or sister or someone close like that. Balance of probabilities says it's her.'

'That's good work, Sandy. Thanks.' McLean looked up to the whiteboard, where the two new names had been inked in. Both still had question marks beside them, he noticed.

'Don't thank me. You're the one who found her.'

'Did I?' McLean looked at the folders, unsure what to do with them. He'd had nothing to do with the identification of Alicia Dennis, and credit for finding Jennifer Beasley should have gone to the constable who found a discarded backpack and thought it was important. 'I rather think the whole team did it, don't you?'

Gregg laughed. 'Aye, Kirst—, . . . DI Ritchie reckoned you'd say that.'

'Where is she, by the way?' McLean glanced around the room, not seeing the telltale strawberry blonde hair in among the masses.

'Had to go to Perthshire again. Seems the gun runners

are up to their tricks again. Least, that's what the Crime Campus boys think.'

So they were a detective down. Even that wasn't enough to dampen McLean's mood. 'We got anyone looking into these two?' He held up the reports, one in each hand.

'Not much to do, really. Miss Dennis's family are coming over to claim her remains, but they'll take a day or two to get here. We'll need to track down next of kin on the other one, I guess.'

'OK. I'll put the new DCs on to chasing down Beasley.' McLean let his gaze wander across the room, but there were too many people to see them all clearly. 'They in yet? I was wanting a word with Blane about the financial stuff I asked him to look into.'

'Not seen him yet.' Gregg glanced at her watch. 'It's early, though. Should be here in time for the briefing. You want me to let him know you're looking for him?'

'No. It can wait for now. He'll only worry about it anyway.'

'It's been a week, McLean. I thought you were meant to be some kind of detective.'

The chief superintendent paced up and down the carpet in front of the window in McLean's office in much the same way DI Ritchie had done just a few days earlier. Judging by the scuffed and worn sheen to the carpet tiles there, neither of them was the first to adopt that particular habit either. For himself, McLean was content to sit behind the desk, safe from all but his boss's words.

'I've had Grumpy Bob and Duguid on the case since day one, sir. DI Ritchie did as much as she could, but she's being dragged back to the Crime Campus and up to Perth-shire more often than not. We've put out feelers to all the sources we can without tipping anyone off. There's not a lot more I can do short of knocking on every door in the city and asking politely if I can search the premises.'

Forrester stopped in his tracks, wheeled round to face him. McLean tensed for the onslaught, conditioned by years of working under the likes of Duguid and Brooks, but it didn't come. That wasn't the chief superintendent's style.

'It's been a week,' Forrester said again. 'He's never been out of touch that long. Not even when he was at college. It . . . It doesn't look good, does it.'

'At least we know it wasn't him in the crash, sir.' It was scant consolation, true, but the DNA results were at least clear on that score.

'Aye, but can we be sure of that? These things aren't a hundred per cent, right?'

'We compared the body with the swab you gave us, sir. No way that's Eric down in the mortuary.' McLean almost added, 'Not if he's really your son', but managed to stop himself. The thought had popped out of nowhere, but there was no denying the chief superintendent's anxiety. That might have been because the boy was still missing, or it might have been rooted in something even more com-plicated. There was no easy way to ask, though.

'You say he was taking drugs.' Forrester made the state-ment like he still didn't believe it. 'What if he overdosed in some doss house somewhere? What if we never find him at all?'

McLean found it hard to look past the uniform and the

seniority. He'd never had much respect for authority where he didn't think it deserved, and disliked the bullying management style most of his previous bosses had used with such reckless abandon. The legacy of that was part of the reason they were so short of decent detectives after all. But in the short time he'd known Forrester he'd been impressed by the man's administrative skills. He could motivate a team, and had a knack for coming up with resources when everywhere else budgets were being squeezed. He might not have been a good detective, and for all McLean knew he might never have been much of a beat cop either, but he'd pulled the station out of chaos. Seeing him fall apart at the disappearance of his son was uncomfortable to say the least.

'We'll find him, sir. And we've an excuse to be a bit more public about it now.'

'How so?' Forrester fell on the possibility like a terrier on a rat.

'Pothead Sammy, the dealer who we suspect was supplying drugs to your son. We know he's the last unidentified male victim of the crash now. We'll have to find out where he lived, who his next of kin was, that sort of thing. Should be the perfect excuse to go sniffing around his business, wouldn't you think?'

43

Part of Edinburgh's charm was the way respectable areas of the city could rub up cheek by jowl with places you probably wouldn't want to venture after dark. At least, that was how McLean had always seen it. Take a wrong turning off a genteel street of neat terraced houses with generous front gardens and expensive cars in the residents'-permit-only parking spaces outside, and you might suddenly find yourself confronted by a gang of feral youth, out walking something that looked like a cross between a terrier and a wolf. Or you might walk briskly down a narrow passage between two warring sets of council blocks, only for the land to open up to reveal a Scots Baronial mansion set in its own diminished parkland. It wasn't that far from his own house to a part of the city that had seen better days.

The street he and Grumpy Bob walked down most certainly fell into that category. The houses were large, semi-detached stone buildings that would once have been elegant homes for the city's less wealthy merchants and clerks. Where once they would have housed a true Victorian family each, a half dozen children or more in the hope that some might survive to adulthood, now they were split up into three, four or more apartments. The ground to the front – McLean hesitated to call it a garden – had long since gone over to concrete, tarmac, paving slabs and weeds. Cars that would most likely never turn a wheel again sat under mouldy green covers; broken bicycles were chained against railings, saddles gone, tyres flat; wheelie bins were everywhere, some overflowing with evil-smelling black bags, others on their sides, their contents strewn about the pavement and street; and all around was a sense of decay.

'This used to be quite a nice part of town.' Grumpy Bob kicked out at an empty Coke can, sending it skittering across the paving stones and into the shadows. 'Me and Mrs Bob looked at a place at the end of the road there. Not long after we got together. Kind of glad we chose Colinton instead, even if she got the house in the end.'

'Kind of glad we managed to get a pool car to come out here. I reckon the Alfa would've got keyed.' McLean looked back to where they had parked the anonymous-looking BMW. It was still newer than anything else in the street, and suspiciously clean.

'What are we looking for again?' Grumpy Bob stepped over a smear of dog mess that someone else hadn't noticed before it was too late.

'Number twenty-four. That's the last address we had for Sammy Saunders. The only next of kin on file's his mum, and she died two years ago, apparently.'

'So what are we hoping to find here, then? I mean, if he's dead he's hardly going to answer the door now, is he?'

'Hopefully there'll be someone here who knows him, knows who he's friends with and where they hang out. Who knows? If we get really lucky we might even find Eric bloody Forrester hiding here.'

Grumpy Bob stopped walking as they reached a rusty iron gate in front of yet another semi-detached house.

Unlike most of the buildings in the street, the right-hand half of this one looked almost as if someone who lived there cared. The sash windows could have done with a lick of paint, but they were clean. The sun-browned grass had been cut at least once over the summer, and there were far fewer weeds poking out between the paving slabs than next door. Black stains wept down the wall beside the door from a number 22. Looking across from it, over a rickety garden fence to the other half of the building, the contrast couldn't have been more marked.

The top hinge of the gate on this side had broken, so that it could only open a foot or so. A narrow track led from the pavement through a jungle of weeds and up to a front door that was more cracks than paint. Faded red curtains obscured the view in through the front window on the ground floor.

'Remind me again why we're not going in here with a full squad and armed backup in the van?' Grumpy Bob grumbled as he shuffled through the narrow gate opening and picked a way towards the front door that wouldn't involve having to throw his shoes away later.

'Because Saunders was never a threat. He's a low-level pot dealer not some local crime lord. And, besides, the last thing the chief superintendent wants is a big song and dance about his missing son. That's the only reason we're here, after all. DNA's enough identification given the circumstances. Saunders has no relatives. Nobody's going to miss him.'

Grumpy Bob did a good impression of a man unconvinced, but McLean knew it was more that he didn't want to have to search the place than any great fear of danger.

A moment's pause, a shrug, and then he carried on up the garden path.

A small army of more recent additions surrounded the original doorbell, indicating that what had once been a decent property was now far too many tiny apartments. Some of the buttons had scraps of paper beside them, the names barely readable. None said anything that looked remotely like Saunders.

'Where do we start, then?' Grumpy Bob asked, as McLean reached out and pushed the door. It swung inwards, unlatched and unlocked.

'Ground floor, I guess.'

The main hallway had a scent of unwashed people, damp and the sweet odour of recently smoked weed, but mostly it reeked of uncollected bin bags. A line of them marched along one wall, bulging ominously. McLean counted a half-dozen before giving up. He wondered who owned this house, and whether they knew how badly it had gone to seed. Whether they cared.

Two doors that wouldn't have been on the architect's original plans flanked a narrow staircase towards the rear of the house. Cheap partition walls broke up what would have been a sizeable hall into two downstairs dwellings. McLean tried the first door, found it locked, and knocked hard on the flimsy wooden surface. Someone shouted something incomprehensible, so he knocked again, then waited as a series of grumbling noises came ever closer. Finally the door swung open to reveal a small, elderly gentleman in a string vest, thin braces holding up his dark trousers.

'Fuck youse want?'

'Sammy Saunders. You know him?'

'Wants to know?' The elderly man scratched at an arm-pit, then sniffed his fingers. His face was a maze of deep wrinkles and lines, the face of a man who's spent most of his life outdoors.

'Detective Inspector McLean. Police Scotland.'

'Fucking polis. You got a warrant?'

McLean shook his head. 'No. I don't.'

'Well, you can't fucking come in, then.' The old man squared his shoulders as if McLean couldn't have just pushed him over with a gentle shove.

'Why on earth would I want to come in?' He looked past the man to what must have been a bedsit room, piled high with rubbish that was no doubt of enormous senti-mental value.

'Fuck you here for, then?'

'I already said. I'm looking for Sammy Saunders. Pot-head Sammy, some people call him.'

'Fucking druggie.' The old man hawked, then spat something substantial and green on to the dirty floor at McLean's feet. 'Lives upstairs, don't he. Coming and going all hours. People banging on his door at two in the morn-ing. You should be arresting him, not fucking hassling innocent folk like me.'

'It'd be hard to arrest him. He's dead. When was the last time you saw him?'

'Dead, you say? Hoo-fucking-ray. Maybe I'll get some peace now.' The old man started to close the door, but McLean put his foot against it, grabbed it with his hand high up to emphasize how much taller he was.

'I asked you a question. When was the last time you saw Saunders?'

A look more of anger than fear darkened the old man's face, but after a moment he relented. 'Fuck knows. A week ago, maybe? Still folk coming and going though. I hear them in the night. Clumping up they stairs like a herd a' fucking cattle.'

McLean considered giving the old man one of his cards, but judging by the bedlam behind him, it would just be a waste of time. He shifted his foot, but kept a hold of the door. 'There anyone up there now?'

'Fuck should I know? I'm no' his fucking landlord.'

'Perhaps you could tell me who is, then. Same as yours, is it?'

The old man sniffed again, and for a moment McLean thought he was going to spit on the floor. Instead he swallowed loudly, his Adam's apple threatening to burst through the papery skin of his neck.

'Aye. Donnie Wear. An' there's a fuck youse ought to be arresting, right enough. Takes our money and does he do shite to look after this place? Like fuck he does.'

'Aye, well. Maybe I'll have Sergeant Laird here have a wee chat with him. If you'll just let us know where to find him.'

The old man retreated into his den, rifling around on a table not far from the door until he found a battered black address book. He read out a number, almost too quickly to remember, but Grumpy Bob already had his notebook out and scribbled it down.

'That youse done, aye?' The old man chucked the address

book back onto the table, not seeming to notice or care that it slipped off and disappeared into the mess on the floor.

'Reckon so. Thanks for your help.' McLean barely had the words out before the door slammed shut. Muttering behind it receded as the old man went back to whatever miserable activity had been preoccupying him before they had arrived.

'Charming fellow,' Grumpy Bob observed.

'Think I'd be a bit cantankerous if this was where I lived, too.' McLean set off up the staircase, alarmed at the creaks and groans from the uncarpeted wooden steps. 'Let's see what other delights the house has to offer.'

It was easy enough to work out which of the two flats upstairs belonged to the recently deceased Reginald Samuel Saunders. Only one of the flimsy doors had been kicked in recently, and it opened on to a room directly above the curmudgeonly old man's bedsit below.

The smell of weed was stronger here as McLean stepped into what would have been a well-proportioned master bedroom, but which was rather small for an entire dwelling. If the one room apartment downstairs had seemed a tip as he had glimpsed it through the narrow doorway, then this was something far worse.

A bed in the far corner consisted of a narrow mattress on an old iron frame, a cheap sleeping bag wedged against the wall. Sammy didn't so much have pillows as an odd assortment of clothes, most likely unwashed laundry, piled into a heap at the end of the bed. More clothes were strewn about the floor, mixing freely with empty cardboard food containers, plastic bottles and an impressive but random collection of small electrical goods.

'Nice what he's done to the place.' Grumpy Bob stepped past McLean, crouched down and began sifting through the piles of rubbish heaped on a low table in front of a sofa that probably should have been left in the skip it had surely been taken from. He pulled out several mobile phones, none particularly smart and all missing vital pieces. An old catering size coffee tin in the middle of the table was overflowing with ash and the stubbed-out ends of countless roll-ups. A pair of hand-knitted socks draped rather incongruously across the top of it.

'What are the chances of finding anything of any use in here?' McLean picked a path to the window, treading on as few breakable things as he could. Half-drawn curtains let in enough light to see the devastation wreaked on the room, no need to draw them any further. He was about to turn away when he noticed movement through the grubby glass, a person sliding through the narrow gap left by the broken gate. He looked up at the window, but gave no indication he'd spotted anyone. A thin man with long, greasy hair and sloping shoulders. The demeanour of an addict, or just someone who didn't want to conform to society's norms?

'Hold on, Bob. Looks like someone's coming.' McLean waved in the direction of the back half of the room, behind the door, and the two of them moved as swiftly over there as they could without making too much noise. Through the broken door, he could hear the sound of heavy footsteps in the hall and then up the stairs. A pause, and for a moment McLean expected to hear keys in the other lock. Then tired hinges creaked and the thin fellow walked in. He seemed unconcerned by the mess, and also knew exactly where he was going. Oblivious to the two detectives watching him, he went over to the bed, knelt down and cleared a heap of discarded clothing aside. A moment's scrabbling at the floor revealed a loosened floorboard, and from the cavity beneath, a black bin bag not quite as full as the ones downstairs in the hall.

Dumping it to the side, the thin man took his time replacing the floorboard and covering it over with clothes, only then picking up his swag and turning to leave.

That was when he first noticed McLean and Grumpy Bob, much closer to his only means of escape than he was.

'Whae the fuck?' His accent was west coast, nasal and whiny, but that wasn't what surprised McLean the most. He'd not been able to see the man's face properly until now. What he saw was not what he was expecting at all.

'Pothead Sammy? But you're dead.'

44

'I want a lawyer. I know my rights.'

Reginald Samuel Saunders sat on his own in interview room three, shouting at the one-way glass that would appear to him as a mirror. McLean watched from the observation room on the other side. He'd deliberately left the man alone to stew for a while, but it was clear he was no stranger to interview rooms and police cells.

'He's very vocal, for a dead man.' DCI McIntyre stood beside McLean, staring through the window. She gripped the back of one of the two chairs in the room, leaning on it heavily as if her legs didn't really want to work today. 'But he has a point. We can't interview him without a lawyer present. Not if we've already charged him with possession.'

'Grumpy Bob's trying to get someone sorted. It's a pain. I'm not really interested in the stuff we found him with. We can leave that to the drugs squad, let him sweat in the cells a while over it before they get here. What I want to know is where he's been this past week, and why his DNA record's been tampered with.'

McIntyre consulted her watch. 'It'll have to wait. I can't let you in there until the duty solicitor turns up. You'll have to speak to forensics about the DNA cock-up. We'll get a swab from him for possession anyway, so that'll sort itself out.'

'I'm sure that'll come as great consolation to the team when I go and wipe this wee shite's name off the board up in the incident room. Thought we'd got everyone.'

'You'll find your last dead person soon enough, Tony. He's on the database, after all.'

McLean looked round at McIntyre as if she was mad. 'How'd you figure that?'

'Well, think about it. We got a hit from the sample Angus took off the body. It matches someone, just not Pothead Sammy here.' McIntyre nodded at the figure, now picking his nose and tasting what he found up there. 'All we need to do is find out whose sample got mislabelled and you'll have your name.'

If only it were that easy. There were a hundred and one reasons why a DNA sample might have been corrupted on the database, and only half of them were likely to be down to human or computer error. What if the cover-up of Eric Forrester's drug addiction had included tampering with any DNA sample taken when he was arrested for possession? Sammy was another Helensburgh lad, well known to the police over there, possibly even arrested at the same time as Forrester. Someone with high enough clearance or the right connections might well have been able to mess about with the system. And swapping a file was much less suspicious than simply deleting it.

McLean opened his mouth to say as much, but the door to the observation room clicked open. Grumpy Bob stuck his head through the gap.

'That's the duty solicitor just showed up, sir. I'll give them ten minutes, aye?'

McLean looked back round to the glass, where DC

Harrison was showing a very young man in a dark suit and tie into the interview room. Either he was getting old or solicitors were qualifying early these days.

'Aye, ten minutes'll be fine. Then we can have a nice wee chat.'

'You want to listen in?' Bob nodded at the glass, a conspiratorial twinkle in his eye.

'I'll pretend I didn't hear that, Sergeant.' McIntyre swept past him and out of the door before turning back to see if she was being followed. 'Tony?'

'You're right. It's unethical and not particularly helpful. Ten minutes, alone and unrecorded. Meantime, there's someone else I very much need to talk to.'

'Eric was arrested in Helensburgh. Not just possession, but intent to supply. I'm not wrong, am I?'

McLean had found the chief superintendent in his office, going over some admin with a couple of senior uniform officers. Whether it was the way he knocked and opened the door without waiting to be invited in, or just the look on his face, both of them had made mumbled excuses and left in a hurry.

'What are you going on about?' Forrester's face flushed red, the first time McLean had seen anything resembling anger in the man.

'You need to be straight with me, sir.' McLean stood in the middle of the large room, not quite to attention but certainly formal. 'I know about the incident in Glasgow, the cover-up, the other reason you upped sticks from Helensburgh and came over here.'

'It's not like . . .' Forrester's protest died on his lips.

'To be honest, sir, it's not the worst abuse of power I've ever seen. And I get it. I really do. You were protecting your son, your family. I'd probably do the same if it was me.'

Something deflated in the chief superintendent, like a children's bouncy castle after the air pump's been switched off. He slumped into one of the chairs at the conference table.

'Sit down, McLean. I can't bear it when people stand to attention like that. We're not the fucking army.'

McLean paused a moment before relenting. He pulled out one of the chairs and sat down, grateful to take the weight off his aching hip.

'I'm sorry if I overstepped the line, sir, but you asked me to find your son and it's not easy when I don't know what obstacles have been put in the way already.'

Forrester said nothing for a moment, just staring at him. Then something like understanding spread across his face. 'The DNA.'

'Exactly. Tell me you didn't get someone to swap the samples when your son was brought in for questioning?'

'I wish I could.' Forrester shook his head slowly from side to side. 'Christ, I never thought . . .'

'Reginald Samuel Saunders, AKA Pothead Sammy. Remember him?'

The chief superintendent said nothing, but the look on his face was answer enough.

'So someone did you a favour. Sent Eric's swab under the name of another person. Someone else in the cells at the same time, I'd guess. Maybe a local small-time drug dealer called Pothead Sammy?'

Forrester had his elbows on the table now, buried his head in his hands. When he looked up again, there was a desperation in his eyes that almost scared McLean.

'It's worse than that. Saunders was in on it. He knew all about Eric. Got him into drugs in the first place. Only way we could keep him quiet was to let him go, lose his record like we lost Eric's.'

'Only Sammy was already known, wasn't he? Couldn't delete his record completely, that would be too risky. So they swapped his DNA sample with someone else. Is that how it went?'

'I didn't ask. It was just taken care of, that's all I needed to know. Eric's record disappeared. He and Saunders walked free.'

McLean considered his words before he spoke. The logic wasn't perfect, but it was compelling, and there was no easy way to break the news.

'We've got Saunders down in one of the interview rooms right now, sir. He's not dead.'

Forrester was all too quick on the uptake. 'But the DNA sample . . . From the last crash victim . . .'

'The database says it's Saunders, sir. Clearly it isn't. We know the record's been switched with someone's DNA. The question is whose.'

'You don't think . . . ?'

'No, it's not Eric. We know that from the swab sample you gave me.'

'They told me you had a way of getting to the truth, McLean. That you could make people trust you and tell you their most guarded secrets. I didn't believe them, but by God they were right.' Forrester buried his face in his hands.

'Sir?'

'What if Eric's not actually my son? Christ, I don't want to even think it possible that Deirdre would cheat on me, but . . .'

But twenty-four years ago he would have been a young policeman on the fast track to great things, away from home for days on end. McLean knew nothing about Forrester's wife, but if the chief superintendent had brought up the possibility, he must have thought it before.

'I think that's very unlikely, sir. From the pictures you gave me, he has your looks, your build. He's your son. It's someone else down in the mortuary, but that doesn't mean we don't still have a problem.'

Forrester looked up at him, eyes glistening. 'We do?'

'Think about it, sir. That dead man had his DNA on the database or whoever covered this up for you wouldn't have had anything to swap with. Sooner or later we're going to identify him, and then this whole sorry mess is going to come to light.'

'Oh fuck.'

Oh fuck indeed. McLean pushed his seat back, got to his feet. 'I'm going to question Saunders now. He had a sack load of drugs in his flat, and from what I've gathered so far your son was probably one of his customers. If we're lucky he might know where Eric is hiding out. In the meantime, I suggest you get back in touch with whoever it was did you that favour. You might need to ask them for another.'

*

'You were found in possession of several grams of heroin, Sammy. Along with almost a half-kilo of cannabis resin. Not even I can imagine that's just for your own personal use.'

McLean sat on one side of the table in interview room three, Grumpy Bob beside him. Across from them, Pothead Sammy shuffled in his seat like a little boy needing to be excused but too embarrassed to ask. The duty solicitor, who had introduced himself as Alexander Simmonds, looked almost as nervous as his client. McLean hoped it wasn't an act.

'So, we've got you on possession with intent to supply class A drugs. That's a custodial sentence on its own right there. But it says here on your file that you're still on licence. You're not even going to make bail at this rate.'

'My client has been very co-operative so far, Detective Inspector. I'd be glad if you could refrain from trying to intimidate him into incriminating himself further.' Mr Simmonds appeared to have found his voice, although it was perhaps higher than the one he used with his mates down the pub, and it cracked around the edges like fraying paper.

'I'm not trying to intimidate Mr Saunders, just laying out the facts. I think you and I can both agree that it doesn't look good for him now, does it?'

Simmonds said nothing to that, but he sat a little more upright in his seat all the same.

'What is it youse want?' Saunders asked. He had been leaning forward, head down and hidden by his greasy locks, but now he looked up, peering through hair like a dirty waterfall.

'Want?' McLean pretended to consider the question.

'Aye. What youse want? Tha's how it works, int it? I gie youse some't an' youse cut me a deal.'

McLean drummed his fingers lightly on the table beside the pad and pen he had brought in as a prop. The interview was being recorded, so he had no need to write anything down.

'We don't do deals, Mr Saunders. We can't do deals. It's not allowed. But a record of your co-operation goes against your file. That gets considered when it's time for parole again. It gets taken into consideration for a lot of things while you're inside, too. Access to rehab programmes, that sort of thing. Even which prison you get sent to in the first place.' He paused a moment, letting what he had just said sink in. Then, just before the duty solicitor could open his mouth to object, he continued: 'So what I want from you is quite simple. I want your co-operation. Tell me, Sammy. When was the last time you saw Eric Forrester?'

The confusion that spread across Saunders's face was exactly what McLean wanted. It was a bonus to see it mirrored on that of Alexander Simmonds.

'Whut? Who's that?' Saunders asked.

'A client of yours, I believe. Plays bass in a punk band that goes by the delightful name of Fuck Youse. Heard of them?'

'Oh, aye.' Saunders looked relieved to actually know the answer to something. 'I ken them. Play like pish, mind, but thon singer lassy's braw.'

'And the bass player? Eric? You sold him some heroin a couple of weeks back.'

'You don't have to answer that, Mr Saunders.' Simmonds

cut in, much to McLean's annoyance. He was right though. Luckily, Saunders wasn't much for taking advice.

'Oh, you mean Raz? Never heard a'body call him Eric. Raz 'n' me, we go way back. We was at school together. Din't sell him nuthin'. He gets it fer free.'

'That's very . . . generous of you.'

'Aye, well. Friends dae that fer each other, don't they? Raz helped me oot back in Helensburgh, an he's no' a junkie. Maybe takes a toke now an' then, but only when he's stressed, like. Just likes to get away from it all sometimes.'

'So when did you last see him?' McLean picked up his pen, clicked the end as if he were about to write down what Saunders said next.

'I dunno, man. Few days back. Mebbe a week? All blurs into one, you know.'

Looking at him, McLean could well believe Pothead Sammy would have difficulty distinguishing one day from the next, although he wondered how much of it was an act. He tried to think of something memorable that had happened recently to jog his memory. It wasn't hard.

'Do you remember the crash. The truck on the Lothian Road?'

Confusion ran across Saunders's face again as he tried to make a connection between this new question and his earlier train of thought. 'The chemical spill? Aye. Saw all the lights an' the fire engines and stuff. Man, that stank.'

'Was that before or after you last saw Eric . . . Raz?'

Saunders stared into the distance, his eyes glazing over at the effort of thinking. 'Was round about then, aye. That's why I was doon that part of town. Setting Raz up. Aye, that's right.' He nodded, grinning. 'That's right, aye.'

'What's right, Sammy?' McLean leaned forward, caught a whiff of weed on the man's clothes. 'You set him up before the crash or after?'

'I don't know, man. It was then. The same time. It's all mixed up in my head. But Raz was there, aye.' Saunders leaned forward suddenly, catching McLean off guard. They looked straight at each other, and for the briefest of moments something lucid flashed in the addict's eyes. 'You were there, weren't you, man? When all them people died.'

'Detective Inspector, this is most irregular.' The duty solicitor interrupted at precisely the wrong moment. McLean slumped back into his chair, clicked his pen off again.

'Where would Raz go, once you'd given him . . . whatever?'

'Mr Saunders, you don't have to answer that.'

'Mr Simmonds, we've already established that your client gave drugs to Eric Forrester, also known as Raz, apparently. He's not going to implicate himself any more by telling me where his friend might have gone to take those drugs, now, is he?' McLean tried to keep the exasperation out of his tone, all too aware that others would listen to the tape in due course.

The duty solicitor sat back as if he'd been slapped, but there was no denying that he was the youngest person in the room, possibly by a decade. McLean hoped he didn't bear a grudge.

'Now, Mr Saunders. Sammy. I'll ask you again. Where would Raz go? If he wanted to hide out for a few days?'

Saunders shrugged his sloped shoulders, looked around the room as if only just seeing it for the first time. 'I've no idea. Gave him the gear, din't I? Then he just wandered off into the crowd.'

45

McLean wandered the corridors of the station, trying hard not to think about the godawful mess unravelling all around him. Sooner or later Sammy Saunders's previous history was going to come to light, and it didn't take a genius to work out what would happen to Forrester then. At best he'd be quietly retired, but if the wrong people got hold of the story then there'd be all hell to pay. And McLean wasn't sure if he was the wrong people or not. Keep quiet and be complicit in a serious miscarriage of justice? Or speak out and for ever hold the enmity of his fellow officers? Not an easy decision to make.

It didn't help that they now had a body still unidentified, and one whose DNA had been on record for some reason. That it wasn't Eric Forrester was scant consolation. McLean knew better than to hope the switched record was just a random pick from the database either. Somewhere out there, someone knew who it was, and chances were they didn't want anyone else to find out.

Preoccupied with his thoughts, he almost walked into a uniform constable heading up the corridor towards him. Their impromptu dance as they tried to pass brought a shy, embarrassed smile to her face, which quite broke his dour mood.

'Sorry, sir,' she said.

'No need. I should learn to look where I'm going.' He left her standing there and carried on down the corridor.

Fewer officers milled around the major-incident room when he stepped inside. Afternoon was losing its battle with evening, the day shift looking to clock off soon. There'd been plenty of overtime early on in the investigation, but things were coming to a slow halt now.

'Thought we'd got them all, sir.' DC Gregg came over as soon as she spotted him. McLean looked past her to the whiteboard, where Pothead Sammy's name was still scrawled in his crabbed handwriting, DI Ritchie's question mark alongside it.

'Sorry about that. Maybe I should have just left him be. Would've made our jobs a lot easier.'

'Aye, but no' really.' Gregg shook her head slowly. 'We've still plenty to be getting on with tracking down next of kin for the foreign victims. And Harrison's working on Jennifer Beasley yet.'

'Did she get anything from the notebooks?' McLean looked around the room, hoping to see the young detective constable, but she wasn't there.

'Not that she said. Got a call from her flatmate, though, and headed out to the forensics lab about an hour ago. Should be a message on your phone.'

As if hearing its name used in vain, McLean's mobile buzzed in his pocket. He pulled it out to reveal half a dozen messages, including one from Harrison.

Gone to Forensics. Important info re. Crash. Call me.

He was just thumbing the icon on his screen to place the call when the phone lit up to say Harrison was calling him. He tapped accept and lifted the phone to his ear. 'What have you got for me, Constable?'

'Sir? Oh, sorry. You answered so quickly. I . . . Um. I'm at the forensics labs with Manda and Emma. They've been looking at the satnav that came out of the truck, tracing its journey.'

'We know where it came from and where it was going, don't we?'

'Aye, sir. We do. But it's not exactly . . . Well, it'd be easier to show you. Any chance you could come over?'

McLean glanced up at the clock above the door, then out of the window. Sure, it was shift end, but it wouldn't be dark for several hours yet. One of the great delights of Scotland was the long summer evenings; the utter lack of daylight in winter less so. Of course, it could just have been that Emma needed a ride home and the other two thought they might cadge a lift halfway.

'Give me half an hour,' he said, then remembered the clock. Going-home time. Traffic. 'Maybe forty-five minutes, aye?'

'It's not the most up-to-date equipment, but then neither was the truck.'

McLean stood in one of the smaller rooms in the forensics labs, staring at an inert plastic box with a badly melted and blank screen. It had taken him only thirty-five minutes to drive across town, against all expectations. And he hadn't even been hurrying. Instead of instantly asking for a lift home, Amanda Parsons had led him through to this lab, where Emma and DC Harrison were deep in conversation. Both of them fell suspiciously silent when he entered the room, which only made the tips of his ears burn more fiercely.

'It doesn't seem to be working,' he said.

'I can see why you're the inspector and Janie's just a constable.' Emma gave him a weary smile, then plugged a lead into the back of the box. 'The screen didn't enjoy being bathed in that foul gloop they were transporting. What's the technical term you used, Manda? Fucked, I think it was?'

'Aye, completely fucked.' Parsons leaned over and tapped at a nearby keyboard, lighting up the computer screen above it. 'Protected the circuits inside, though. And this wee program of ours can access the memory. See where the truck's been and where it was going.'

'I have to assume that's not where we thought it was going, otherwise there'd be little point of dragging me over here other than getting a lift home.'

'Well, if you were heading that way.' Parsons grinned. 'Actually, I'm on late shift. Don't knock off until eight. I thought this was important, though.' She clicked again, and the screen showed a map similar to the one that appeared on the satnav in McLean's new car. The clunky graphics looked even worse blown up to a much larger size.

'This is a commercial satnav unit. You can programme routes into it, but it also tracks where you've been. It's connected to the tachograph, too, so drivers can't cheat and skip their breaks. The more modern ones link up to the internet and do all sorts of fancy stuff so you can see where your delivery is in real time, but this is a bit older. It just records everything on to its memory. Lucky, really, otherwise we'd probably not have found this out.'

'Found what out?' McLean asked.

'This.' Parsons clicked the mouse again, and the map redrew itself, showing a route picked out in deep blue, from the compound of Finlay McGregor in Broxburn all the way to the corner of the Western Approach Road and the Lothian Road. There the blue line stopped with a terrible finality.

'What am I looking at?' McLean stared at the map, unsure what the point was.

'Please don't tell me you're colour-blind, Tony.' Parsons did something with the mouse and the image moved away from the crash site. That was when McLean saw it, a paler line overlaid on top of the bypass, out east along the A1. He looked for it heading off to LindSea Farm Estates, but instead it turned south, heading into the Cheviot Hills.

'This is the route programmed in to the machine?'

'That's the route your driver was following, aye. He only headed into town because there was a pile-up on the bypass. That's another thing this clever wee box does. Shouldn't have done, mind. But then he thought he was just transporting a load of manure. No harm in taking that through the city.'

McLean stared at the map again. LindSea Farm Estates was marked, but the programmed route missed it by several miles. 'So where the hell's he going?'

'Get on to Control will you, Constable? I want a couple of squad cars and some uniform to meet us at the junction before that turning.'

McLean concentrated on driving, wishing for once that he was in a squad car so he could go the full blues and twos. Evening and morning were always bad times to be trying to negotiate the city bypass, but there was no other way to get from the forensics labs to the A1 and on towards East Fortune without fighting with the traffic in town.

Beside him in the passenger seat, DC Harrison took out her Airwave and began to make the call. 'Do we want to go in all guns blazing, sir? I mean, if it's a proper raid, shouldn't we scope the place first, find out what's there and then work out what kind of force we need?'

McLean eased the car forward another twenty feet before everything ground to a halt again. He hated to admit it, but Harrison was right. Going in unprepared was at best foolish, at worst dangerous. The chemicals in the truck had melted flesh, bone and tarmac. What else might they find, and who might be making sure it wasn't stumbled upon? On the other hand, what if the evidence was being spirited away while they sat in the major-incident room debating the best way to proceed?

'We need to go there, see it. Or at least get as close as we can without raising suspicion.' He paused a moment while the traffic inched forward another twenty feet. 'Can you get DCI McIntyre on that thing?'

Harrison nodded. 'Aye, sir. Or I've my mobile if you don't want to go through the Airwave network.'

McLean looked sideways at the detective constable, raised an eyebrow in surprise at her guile. 'No, Airwave's fine. I'm not trying to be a hero. Just want to get out there and see where that truck was meant to be going.'

Harrison tapped away at the clunky handset, clicking to speakerphone once she had reached the detective chief inspector and explained where they were.

'You're sure you know what you're doing, Tony? We

could have a squad together for first light tomorrow morning. Go in a bit more heavy-handed.'

'And find out we've just blown the department budget on raiding some old farmyard? No. It's better if we do a bit of reconnaissance beforehand. Work out what we're dealing with. I reckon we need to have a closer look at Extech, though. Possibly see if we can't get a warrant to search the premises.'

'You really think they're the source? I thought they checked out. I mean, the sort of thing they do's the exact opposite of spreading toxic waste about the place.'

'Aye, exactly. What better way to hide your real game? And the amount of money that's been sunk into that place doesn't add up. Even if they are planning on growing tomatoes there soon.'

'Tomatoes?' Even over the airwaves, McLean could hear the disbelief in Jayne McIntyre's voice.

'Long story, but as soon as I asked DC Blane to look into the financial side of things the high heidyins started to get anxious. You know how I feel about strings being pulled like that. Especially when it's the constables getting leaned on.'

Silence saw them cover a few more yards, and up ahead it looked like the blockage might have begun to ease.

'I'll see what I can do, Tony. No promises, though. We need justifiable cause for a warrant, not just suspicion and the fact their boss plays golf with our boss.'

'Aye, I know. It would help if I even knew who their boss was, mind. Their chief operations officer was very reticent on the matter, and the paper trail's not exactly straightforward either. The whole thing's got dodgy written all over it.'

46

The sun still hung low in the northern sky as they pulled off the A1 half an hour later and drove into the hills. Much of the journey had passed in silence, which suited McLean just fine. He never had been one for idle chit-chat except when it happened in a bar and with the lubrication of much ale. Harrison had been content to click away at her phone, texting the major-incident room and waiting impatiently for updates.

'Where was that squad car meant to meet us?' McLean asked as they approached a wide layby. Dry potholes threatened to destroy the underside of the car, their depths hidden by shadows.

'Should be here, sir.' Harrison held up her phone with its own satnav map showing the meeting point. Their final destination was only a mile up the road.

McLean checked his watch. 'They're late.'

'Aye, well. Always possible something else's come up. Maybe someone's had a crash on the A1, or there's been a break-in. Want me to call them?'

'No. They know where we're going. They can catch up.' McLean checked his mirror, indicated and pulled back on to the empty road. Trees lined either side, dark plantation conifers that marched up the hillside in uniform monotony. The entrance to their destination looked more like a forestry track than anything, and was in even worse condition than the layby. McLean drove on a hundred yards to a point where the road was straight, the verge wide enough for him to park.

'You got your walking boots on?' he asked. Harrison lifted her feet in the footwell to show off some reasonably heavy duty shoes. 'Near enough, as long as it's dry.'

'OK, then. Let's go have a wee nosey.'

A quiet stillness had settled over the evening, no wind to ruffle the treetops and only the distant roar of the dual carriageway to remind them that life existed elsewhere. McLean took the lead, keeping to the edge of the track and the shadows as they followed it down a shallow, curving slope towards a clearing in the middle of the forest. The light was poorer here, but still plenty to make out old derelict buildings in the trees. The track levelled out in the middle of a collection of old stone sheds, before running off into a deep cutting in the side of the hill. He stopped, looking first at the ground and the tyre tracks, then back the way they had come.

'I think this is an old railway.' Harrison didn't quite whisper the words, but she was very quiet. Something about the stillness of the place discouraged noise.

'How do you figure that?' McLean asked.

'See how the track's made. It goes back that way through the trees, too.' Harrison pointed into the forest, and as McLean followed the direction of her finger, he saw what she meant. The line was almost completely overgrown, but the trees were different from the rows of identical firs that spread all around them. Shorter and scrubbier. 'There's the remains of a platform there. And this looks like a turning area, judging by the way the ground's been churned up. All the traffic's gone that way, though.' Harrison took a couple of steps along the abandoned railway line in the direction of the cutting and the hill beyond. It curved away sharply, making it impossible to see anything more than fifty feet away.

'This whole area's criss-crossed with old railway lines.' McLean started to walk towards the hill, slowly, as if expecting to hear a train coming, even though the iron rails had long since gone. 'They built them for the mines originally. Then passenger railways became a thing and every big landowner wanted his own. Most of them never made any money, but it's amazing the amount of effort, the engineering skill that went into building them.'

'Aye, we did a project in school. Went out to see the viaduct at Dalkeith. Didn't realize there was more this far out, though. The main line keeps closer to the coast, doesn't it?'

'You can thank Doctor Beeching for that, although I suspect this line closed long before he was even born.' McLean peered ahead, the gloom descending as the cutting grew ever deeper. He was fairly sure now what lay around the bend, and a kernel of an idea as to exactly what was going on had begun to sprout in the depths of his mind.

'Bloody hell. I wasn't expecting that.' DC Harrison stopped and stared. McLean followed her gaze to an ornate, stone-built arch that marked the entrance to a tunnel. The keystone high above them was carved with some ancient family crest, and beneath it the entrance had been blocked up. A large, modern metal roller door, big enough for a container truck, was pulled down to the ground, blocking further progress.

'You see any sign of cameras?' McLean studied the deep cutting, the stonework and the surrounding trees for any indication that they were being observed.

'Can't see anything, no.' Harrison moved a little closer to him. McLean couldn't blame her; the place had turned creepy all of a sudden and he couldn't immediately say why.

'Let's just have a wee closer look then, aye? Then we can go back to the station. Find out who owns this place and get a warrant sorted to search it properly.'

McLean approached the roller door with caution. Something in the air of the place had him on edge. It was cooler for one thing, his breath almost misting despite it being the height of summer. As he came nearer, he saw that the roller door had a smaller personnel door set into it on one side. A heavy padlock dangled from a hasp by the latch, but when he looked closer he saw that it wasn't actually locked. Was there someone inside at the moment? Had the last person here forgotten to close everything up properly?

He turned back to speak to Harrison, found her standing right behind him. Her face was that of a young woman both terrified and determined not to show it.

'You got a phone signal?' he asked. Harrison almost jumped at the noise, but she pulled out her phone, checked the screen.

'Aye, sir. Not a good one, mind.'

'Well find out where that squad car is, won't you? I'm going to have a look inside.'

He knew the moment he reached for the door handle

that something was wrong. It wasn't that it was cold to the touch, far colder than being in the shade should have made it. Nor was it the little jolt of static that leapt from metal to flesh as he grasped it, although that was unsettling, too. More it was a deep sensation of dread, much like he had felt just a few days ago when he had heard the blaring of horns, seen the truck jump the lights, turn oh so slowly and smash into a bus stop filled with people. He almost snatched his hand away, but the moment passed and instead he turned the handle.

The latch clicked and the door swung open on to darkness. There was the briefest moment of nothing, and then the stench hit him. Worse than the truck crash, this was almost as if he had been doused in whatever foul chemical soup had spilled out over all those people. He staggered back, coughing. Eyes stinging from the onslaught, he barely registered the shout of alarm from DC Harrison. He felt her grab his hand and he blinked away the tears as she tried to drag him off the old railway track. It was impossible to hide, though, the sides of the cutting too steep to climb. Behind him the unbreathable stench from the tunnel, and in front a familiar-looking pickup truck, engine revving as it threatened to run them both down.

47

The pickup blocked off their escape completely. Steep sides of the cutting hemmed them in on either side, and behind them there was just the tunnel. McLean wasn't prepared to bet his life that there was a way out the other end. Far more likely it had collapsed many years before.

'What now?' Harrison asked, her voice only faltering a little. From where they stood, the windscreen of the truck obscured the face of the driver. McLean had seen that truck before, though, most recently parked at the end of the drive leading to LindSea Farm Estates.

'Get behind me.' He pulled Harrison towards him, then placed himself between her and the truck.

'I don't need protecting, sir!'

'Not protecting you, Constable. Shielding you. Get on that phone of yours and find out where that squad car is. We need backup now.'

Harrison made a small sound that might have been 'oh', then made a good impression of a frightened young woman hiding behind her braver male champion while she tapped away at her phone. McLean put his arms out wide, like a man trying to ward off a charging bull, all the while hoping that it would distract the driver of the truck long enough for Harrison to get through.

And then his skin tingled, the hairs on the back of his neck stood up. The temperature dropped, and it felt like thunder in the air even though there wasn't a cloud in the sky. A strange sensation, almost vertigo, spun his head as something rushed past him, through him. He turned, expecting to see Harrison doing something foolish and heroic, but she was just standing there, eyes wide with fear, frozen to the spot.

'Wha—?' Her question was cut off by a scream. McLean whirled back around to face the pickup truck. For a moment he couldn't make sense of what he was seeing. It was as if a man was standing half in the bonnet, one arm outstretched towards the windscreen. For a split second that made no sense at all, the man turned his head, looked back.

McLean blinked, and he was gone. The scream turned into the wail of the engine revved harder than it was ever meant to go. The back end of the pickup truck fishtailed as it sped towards them, kicking up twin plumes of dirt from the track behind it. As the steep banking shaded the wind-screen from the glare of the sun, he could just about make out the face of the man driving. Gregor Wishaw had never been a killer, if his file was to be believed, but he had been no stranger to violence. Now he seemed possessed with a rage that distorted his features, eyes popping like he was on ketamine, mouth drawn into a spittle-flecked snarl.

'The tunnel. Quick.'

McLean pulled Harrison away from the steep banking and back to the open personnel door. Closer in, he began to have second thoughts about his decision as the chemical stench washed over the two of them. The pickup was closer now, still speeding up, and there was something about those mad, staring eyes that suggested having a reasoned discussion wasn't on Wishaw's mind.

'Jesus. What's in here?' Harrison coughed on the choking air as she stepped into the tunnel. McLean ducked in behind her, moving as swiftly as the darkness would allow to get both of them clear of the roller door. He was vaguely aware of barrels lined up on the tunnel floor, stretching away into the black. Then the truck hit.

The noise set his ears ringing, a screech of twisted metal and broken glass all too horribly reminiscent of the truck crash. The heavy iron roller door buckled under the impact, bending inwards and folding over. They scurried back further into the tunnel, bumping off metal barrels stacked in long lines. McLean felt dampness under his feet, the caustic material eating away at the soles of his shoes. And still the truck, wrapped in rolled door, kept on coming. If it hit these barrels, split them open . . .

'Keep moving. Get as far back as possible.' He coughed out the words as much as shouted, urging Harrison deeper into the tunnel. They squeezed through the narrow gaps, ten, fifteen feet in. McLean risked a glance back, convinced the whole door was going to come crashing down, bring the stone ceiling with it and bury them for ever in this acid grave.

And then finally the truck stalled.

The sound echoed for a while, amplified by the tunnel before dying down to a soft sigh of wind. The roller door creaked ominously, still hanging in its guide runners, but bent and twisted out of shape. Light spilled in around it, illuminating row upon row of rusty metal barrels, piled to the stone arched roof above them. McLean could see drips oozing from most of them, streaks of decay running down the bubbling paint, puddling on the hard packed soil of the floor. The overpowering stench made it almost impossible to breathe in here. He could feel the squat headache bunching at the top of his spine, ready to grab his brain and squeeze it until his eyeballs popped out. Beside him, Harrison swayed, put a hand out to steady herself on one of the barrels.

'Don't.' He grabbed her, almost falling over as her legs buckled and she slumped into his arms. She was lighter than he had been expecting, but still weighty enough.

'Come on, Janie. Get yourself together.' He heaved one of her arms over his shoulder and around his neck, struggling back the way they had come. It was worse now, more difficult to manoeuvre the two of them, and he could see better the seeping effluent that neither of them really wanted to touch. It was a miracle they'd not been burned already, but he was fairly sure he'd just condemned yet another suit to the trash.

It took all his effort to carry DC Harrison outside and away from the mess of the truck. Air had never tasted sweeter, and he took deep lungfuls of it after propping her up against the side of the cutting. She stirred woozily, like a Saturday night reveller once the ambulance has arrived.

'Take it easy. We're out of there now. Safe.'

Harrison either nodded her understanding or was having difficulty controlling her neck muscles. Either way, McLean left her to recover and returned, reluctantly, to the truck. With it half wedged into the steel shutter, there was no way he was going to be able to open the driver's door, but he could clamber in through the back. The airbag had gone off, and now its deflated white balloon splayed across Gregor Wishaw's face, as he slumped over the steering wheel. McLean reached forward, felt a pulse behind the man's ear. Alive. Good. He had a lot of questions to answer.

Stumbling slightly as he climbed back out of the pickup truck, McLean caught movement in the corner of his eye, turned to see a car approaching slowly along the disused track. For a moment he thought it was someone else come to run them down, then the familiar blue lights on the roof began to flash, the car stopped and a uniform officer climbed out of the passenger side. He wandered up slowly, staring at the tunnel mouth, the twisted metal door, the crashed pickup and then at DC Harrison, still slumped against the steep rock side of the cutting. Finally he stopped, not more than a yard away, spoke in the slow, measured drawl of an East Lothian native.

'Detective Inspector McLean, I presume.'

48

'You have a rare talent for upsetting people, you know that?'

Once again he found himself standing in Chief Superintendent Forrester's office, wishing he was anywhere else. A cup of tea would have been nice, even a chance to get changed. Or a chair, he wasn't fussy. His suit didn't smell as bad as the last time, but McLean was still reminded of the stench of the tunnel every time he moved. Some of the chemical waste had got on to one of the arms, and now the fabric was fraying around a large hole. The shirt underneath was probably going to have to be thrown away, too.

'I would say it comes with practice, sir, but that might be taken the wrong way.'

Forrester rubbed at his face with tired hands. He'd aged a year in the past week, his hair showing far more grey now than McLean remembered.

'It's good work. There's no denying that. If what we suspect is true, then you've uncovered an organized network for disposing of highly hazardous waste illegally and very dangerously, but I've just had a call from the chief constable, who's just had it in the ear from one of the country's leading pain-in-the-arse politicians berating him for the cost of the clean-up operation.'

Forrester smiled wearily at that, and McLean relaxed a little.

'They do so like to shoot the messenger, sir. I'm sorry about that.'

'It's not your fault. Not mine or the CC's either, dammit. Doesn't stop everyone moaning about it, though. So how's this going to play out, then?'

With me going home to a shower, a dram and my bed? McLean tried not to let his shoulders slump too obviously. 'I asked DCI McIntyre to get a warrant to search Extech Energy, sir. Reckon that's where the stuff is collected first, before being shipped out under the disguise of inert digestate. Still not sure where they're getting it from, but the number of trucks going back and forth from that place makes it an ideal distribution hub. All those big stainless-steel tanks, too. Could be storing stuff until there's enough to make it worth a trip.'

'Extech?' Forrester's brow wrinkled as he struggled to remember something. 'You had one of the constables looking into their financials, didn't you?'

'Until you told him to stop, yes.' McLean kept the accusation out of his voice, but only just.

'Oh, that lot. Aye.' Forrester rubbed at his face again, his unease evident in every motion. 'I probably shouldn't have interfered, and the senior officer who called me about it probably shouldn't have either. I'm afraid we've all of us got buttons that can be pressed.'

'If it's any consolation, sir. I don't think this will come back to haunt you. Could even be a feather in your cap. If my theories as to what's going on are correct.'

'You really think so?' Forrester's glum demeanour brightened a little, then fell again. 'It's no matter. I'll not be here for much longer. It's a week now since Eric went

337

missing, and you and I both know the can of worms that's opened. My own fault. I should have known it would come back to haunt me.'

'So the warrant?' McLean tried to steer the meeting back on topic. 'Do you think there'll be any trouble getting it?'

'Given what you've just uncovered out in the wilds? I wouldn't have thought so. You'll be wanting to go in at first light tomorrow, I suppose?'

'Aye. Better in daylight, and it gives us time to put a decent team together. We can get Health and Safety on board, too.' As he said it, so McLean could see that shower, that dram and his bed receding ever further into the distance. He'd already called Emma to let her know he was running late, but it would be nice to see her awake so he could thank her for the work she and Parsons had done on the satnav.

'And Eric?' The chief superintendent finally came to the point.

'Duguid's helping Grumpy Bob follow up on all Pothead Sammy's known associates, where they hang out, that sort of thing. If he's holed up somewhere, we'll find him. Going to put a lot of noses out of joint at the drugs squad, but omelettes and eggs, eh?'

Forrester's expression was one of bewilderment for a while, then understanding dawned. 'Well, like I said, it's not like I'm going to be around for much longer. And I don't think Charles ever cared much what anyone thought of him. Bob will have to tread carefully, though.'

'He's a master of deflecting blame. You've no need to worry about him.' McLean paused a moment, unsure whether the audience was over.

'We'll find him, sir,' he said after a while. 'It's just a matter of time.'

'I wish I had your optimism, Tony. I really do.' Forrester went back to rubbing at his ashen face, eyes focused on the past. Then he stopped and sat back up straight, reaching for the phone on his desk. 'Go home, aye? You're all done in and you smell like shit. I'll have Jayne sort the team out for tomorrow morning. Sure she'll jump at the chance to get out of the office for once.'

McLean opened his mouth to argue, then realized that he was being told to do exactly the thing he wanted to do.

'Aye, sir. Thank you.' He left as swiftly as decorum would allow, not wanting the chief superintendent to change his mind.

Forrester might have ordered him to go home, but there were still a few things McLean had to do before he could leave. It was long past knocking-off time for the day shift, so the major-incident room was quiet when he stepped in through the door. The helplines had more or less gone quiet now, just a few crazies phoning about loved ones who had been missing for years and how they were certain they must have perished in the terrible accident.

There was only one body left to identify anyway. Not-Pothead Sammy. Misfiled on the database, but there nonetheless. McLean was relieved that the swab he'd taken from Forrester and given to Cadwallader had proved it wasn't Eric, but that still meant it could be anyone else. Whoever's body it was lying in cold storage at the city mortuary, they had come into contact with the forces of law and order before, otherwise their DNA wouldn't have been on the database, mislabelled or not. It was a small clue, but it was something they could work with.

'Any news on DC Harrison?' McLean asked of the duty sergeant manning the main desk in the centre of the incident room. She looked up at him with a start.

'Oh, sorry, sir. Thought you'd gone home. Yes. Had a call about half an hour ago. She's fine, just breathed in too many fumes. Sure she's done worse on a Saturday night oot wi' the girls, aye?'

McLean didn't feel qualified to make a comment. 'She having tomorrow off then?'

'Doubt it. Not if there's going to be a big raid. Heard the DCI was after a warrant for that place out Livingston way. I reckon half the station would like to be in on that one.'

'Well, tell them all to keep a lid on it, OK? Last thing we need is them finding out we're coming.'

'Aye, I'll do that, sir. There's a fair buzz about it, but this lot know better than to go mouthing off outside of work.'

McLean didn't hold great hopes. They'd carted Gregor Wishaw off to hospital under police guard and a squad car was keeping an eye on the tunnel to make sure no one found out that the secret had been uncovered. But, even so, it was a week since the truck crash and he'd visited Extech twice. If they hadn't already started dismantling whatever illicit operations were going on, then quite frankly they deserved to be caught. Just as long as they hadn't finished. Raiding a site that had been opened by the Environment Minister and touted as the great white hope of the modern Scottish economy was hardly going to go down well if it turned out there was nothing in those big tanks but shit.

He left the incident room in search of DCI McIntyre, even though he knew the first thing she would do would be to tell him to go home. Halfway to the canteen, he met ex-Detective Superintendent Duguid hauling his wiry frame up the stairs towards him.

'Didn't think you'd have gone home yet.' Duguid's greeting wasn't exactly hostile, but it wasn't exactly friendly either.

'On my way. I'm surprised you're still here.'

'Waiting on a call from an old friend.' The way Duguid pronounced 'friend' made it abundantly clear whoever he was referring to wouldn't be getting an invitation to the golf club any time soon.

'Any joy?' McLean asked.

'Yes, as it happens. Which is why I was looking for you. Your drug dealer, Saunders. I had a wee chat with him earlier. Almost a complete waste of time.'

'Almost?' McLean hoped that Grumpy Bob had been present at the interview. Until the cold-case unit was back up and running, Duguid's clearance for things like interviewing suspects wasn't exactly on firm ground.

'He's a shifty wee bugger, so he is. But he let slip a wee nugget about a squat in the West End. Reckon if your boy Eric's anywhere, then it'll be there.'

'You got an address?'

'That's why I was waiting for the phone call.' Duguid held up a slip of paper torn from a notepad. 'How's that fancy new car of yours working out?'

49

McLean glanced at the glowing screen on the dashboard of his new Alfa as he drove through darkening streets towards the West End. Somewhere in the maze of menus was a hands-free option for his mobile phone, but he had no more idea how to make it work than half the other functions in this overly complicated car. Perhaps it was a failing, but he'd always been one to learn just enough about a new piece of equipment to get it to do what he wanted. Until now, that hadn't included making hands-free calls, but a little voice in the back of his head was telling him that phoning Emma to let her know what he was up to might be a good idea.

He could have asked his passenger to make the call for him. Glowering in the passenger seat as he stared out at the slow-moving traffic, ex-Detective Superintendent Charles Duguid would probably have just growled at him. McLean wasn't sure he wanted Duguid to listen in on any conversation he might have with Emma anyway, so he left the call unmade. He'd find a way to apologize; he always did.

'You'd be quicker cutting up Broughton Street and then into the Colonies.' Duguid pointed to a turning a hundred feet up the road. Traffic was always bad in the city centre, and the ongoing demolition of the St James Centre didn't help. Neither did the trams or the ever-changing one-way systems. It was almost as if the council didn't want cars in their city, despite the millions in parking fees they brought in every year.

'Six of one,' he said as he indicated, then waited for the crowd of pedestrians to get out of the road. Edinburgh's population pretty much doubled in the summer, and sometimes it felt like all of those people were getting deliberately in his way.

'At least we're moving.' Duguid settled into his seat as they accelerated over cobbles, the suspension coping with the uneven surface far better than McLean's old car ever had.

The address the ex-detective superintendent had been given was a terraced town house overlooking Dean Gardens and the Water of Leith. Edinburgh's rise as an international banking hub had brought wealth to many locals, but it had also seen properties snapped up by offshore companies and other shady financial concerns more interested in sinking cash into stone and slate than actually living in the Athens of the North. From the outside it was often impossible to tell which of the grand old Georgian buildings were inhabited, which were offices still, and which were just empty shells waiting to be used in the next round of money laundering. Somehow the city's underclass knew, and squatters popped up with the frequency of molehills after a rainstorm.

'Fifty-three, fifty-five, fifty-seven. Ah yes. Here we are.' Duguid counted off the numbers as they drove slowly down the street. Lights shone from less than a third of the windows, some of the houses completely dark, but number fifty-nine shone bright into the evening gloom.

McLean pulled the car into a resident's parking space and killed the engine.

'How do you want to do this?' he asked, but Duguid already had his seatbelt off and the passenger door open, and was climbing out. McLean followed as quickly as he could, plipping the remote lock as he half ran across the road to catch up. The ex-detective superintendent pulled on a pair of thin leather driving gloves as he trotted up the stone steps to the front door, pausing only to make sure McLean was still with him before turning the handle and pushing it open.

That the door was unlocked was confirmation they were in the right place, but the sweet smell of cannabis smoke and the haze in the air of the large hallway beyond was another clue. McLean had always thought of squatters as scruffy ne'er-do-wells, who left the houses they occupied in such a state they often had to be gutted before they could be used again. Not so the people in this place. A pile of coats had been dumped on a wide Chesterfield sofa in the hallway, but other than that it looked fairly tidy.

A well-furnished room on the left lay empty, the only sign of occupation a couple of sleeping bags draped over armchairs near a large fireplace. Back across the hall, the other front room had been converted into some kind of dormitory, the chairs moved to the walls and a series of mattresses laid out on the floor.

'Where is everyone?' McLean crouched down to inspect one of yet more sleeping bags. The house was deathly quiet, even the distant roar of the city outside muted by heavy secondary glazing to the tall sash windows.

'Upstairs? Kitchen? Who knows?' Duguid set off across

the hall once more, towards the back of the house this time. The haze of smoke and smell of weed intensified as they entered a large kitchen, and it was here that they found the first signs of life.

'Who're you?' A young woman in a skimpy T-shirt and tie-dyed skirt stood at the sink, washing up a pile of bowls. Her arms were like sticks, skin so pale it was almost white. She looked them up and down with a slightly unfocused gaze, not quite in the same room as them.

'Just passing through,' McLean said. 'Looking for a friend's son. Eric Forrester. Sometimes known as Raz. You seen him?'

The young woman's eyes widened, pupils big black circles. 'Raz? Aye. Think I saw him here a couple days ago.'

'He still here?'

'Search me.' The young woman pulled her hands out of the soapy water and held them out as if inviting the attention. 'Don't know where everyone's gone. Place is kinda quiet right now.'

'I guess we carry on looking, then.' McLean left the kitchen, Duguid lingering behind, strangely fascinated by the stoned young woman. Unless the heavy smoke in the house was getting to him, of course. McLean's head still ached with the chemical stench of the tunnel.

The higher up the house he went, the more like the kind of squat he was expecting it became. The lack of people was still peculiar, but the damage to the rooms was more extensive. Bathrooms in particular didn't seem to fare well when a bunch of self-declared anarchists used them. It was a shame to see such a fine house trashed, but he couldn't help thinking that it would be equally a shame for it to sit empty, mouldering away as just one more asset on some oligarch's spreadsheet.

'In here.' The voice surprised him; he hadn't heard Duguid come up the stairs. McLean left what once must have been the master suite and followed the noises to the back of the house and a child's nursery. Duguid crouched beside a mattress that had been shoved into the corner opposite a narrow window. Rolls of bedding and clothes strewn about the floor made this look more like Pothead Sammy's digs on the other side of town. As did the stench of night soil and something else more rotten still. McLean trod carefully through the detritus until he could see what Duguid had found, even though he knew what it was going to be.

Eric Forrester lay in a mound of rubbish almost as if he'd been thrown into this little room and forgotten about. His eyes were closed, one arm splayed out and a loosened tourniquet still hanging from his bicep.

'Dead?' McLean almost didn't want to ask as Duguid reached a finger in under the young man's jaw, feeling for a pulse. The ex-detective superintendent prised open one of his eyes, yellowing and bloodshot, when he moved his hand away, the eye stayed open.

'Judging by the smell, he's been gone a day or two.' He pulled out a phone and started tapping out the number, then stopped himself. 'Probably best if you make the call. I really shouldn't be here. Going to need an ambulance, and someone's going to have to tell his father.'

Darkness had long since fallen by the time McLean parked his car and trudged wearily to the back door. He didn't want to think how late it was, or how tired and hungry he felt. The thought of a five o'clock start in the morning wasn't exactly inspiring either, but there was no way he was going to miss the raid on Extech. That was his call, and he'd be the one to take the flak if it went tits up.

It hadn't taken long for the ambulance to arrive and whisk Eric Forrester away to the mortuary. What had taken longer was the clean-up afterwards. He'd sent Duguid off as soon as the first uniforms arrived on the scene, easier to gloss over the fact that the ex-detective superintendent had been there at all. The squad cars parked outside the house meant that none of the squatters had made a re-appearance, only the young woman they had found in the kitchen had needed to be dealt with. McLean almost felt sorry for her, so clearly out of her depth as a team of police officers swept through the house and found more incriminating evidence than was necessary for a conviction. She was currently sleeping off the effects of whatever she'd been smoking in a cell in the station. Something for another team to deal with in the morning.

At least the chief superintendent hadn't turned up. Bad enough to have the news of your son's death delivered over the phone. Bad enough to have it delivered at all. No one should outlive their children; that wasn't how life was supposed to work.

If there was one small mercy it was that the press didn't seem to have found out about it yet. If they were lucky, then the story would stay out of the papers, since very few officers had seen the dead man being taken away, and McLean hadn't told any of them who he was. Hopefully it would just be reported as a random drugs bust, maybe something about squatters taking over the city's empty houses. Another senseless death due to overdose. Another young life tragically cut short. Better yet if it was not reported at all. News lost in the bigger story that would break when the discovery out in East Lothian hit the morning editions.

The kitchen light was still on, Mrs McCutcheon's cat staring up at him from the middle of the table. McLean ignored her and went to the fridge for a beer. Cold and refreshing, it went down far too easily, the alcohol fuzzing his already numb brain. He poked around for something to eat, even though it was late enough for bed.

'Thought I heard a noise. You home, then?'

Emma stood at the kitchen door, her hair tousled where she'd most likely been sleeping on the sofa. Still in her work clothes, he could see the swell of her belly more clearly now. How much longer to go?

'We found the chief superintendent's son, Eric.' He didn't remember taking it out of the fridge, but McLean found himself pouring a second bottle of beer into his empty glass. 'He must have overdosed a couple of days ago.'

Emma said nothing, just walked across the room and gave him a hug. He put down the bottle and glass, held her tightly to him for long moments. She smelled of warmth and mothballs, of this house he had grown up in.

'Eww, you reek of chemicals.' She pushed him away, wrinkling her nose against the stench. He'd been so preoccupied with his beer he'd momentarily blanked out the smell, but now it came back more powerful than before.

'Sorry. I'll get changed. Have a shower. It's probably time I went to bed anyway. Got a very early start tomorrow.'

McLean started to walk towards the door that led through to the main house, but Emma stopped him with a firm hand to the chest.

'Not in those clothes. Not after the headache I had last time.' She pointed at the far door to the utility room and laundry. 'Out there. Strip. Anything you think's salvageable can go in the machine. Everything else in the bin.'

50

McLean woke with a start, rolling over and drawing his feet up to his chest in a reflex, defensive action as the nightmare released its slow hold on him. He stared into the semi-darkness trying to remember the details as if they were somehow important this time. There had been something, a face perhaps. A young man?

The room was oppressively hot, sweat covering his body and soaking the sheets so it felt like he'd wet the bed. For a moment he was back at his hated boarding school, bewildered, lonely, frightened. Soon the bell would ring, waking them all for breakfast and another day of just barely surviving. Matron would find out, chastise him in front of everyone. Ridicule him. Shame him. None of the other boys wet the bed still. Not now they were seven. But he was still only six. And none of the other boys had lost both their parents to a plane crash. None of the other boys had left a home 500 miles away to be here.

Slowly reality reasserted itself, seeping back into his consciousness as he moved from the nightmare to properly awake. He wasn't the baby, not six years old any more. You could add another forty to that, more or less. He wasn't a small child, and he hadn't wet the bed. That was just anxiety playing on his mind, fuelled by the stinking chemical waste and the fact he'd not had a day off in over a week. He rolled around, slid his feet to the floor and sat upright, casting the thin duvet aside. The bedside clock told him it was ten to five and would soon be shouting at him to get up. He rubbed at his face with aching fingers, felt the damp of sweat on his skin. Hadn't the nightmares gone? But then he'd breathed deep of that foul air again in the tunnel, ruined another suit. No wonder his brain was working overtime to deal with the damage.

But there was that man, that face. What the hell was that about? He knew him, but from where? He'd seen him at the tunnel, only that was impossible. There'd been nobody but him, Harrison and Wishaw. And the man had been standing in the truck, his body coming out of the bonnet. That made no sense. Must have been the fumes. Some trick of the evening light.

McLean sat for a while, trying to piece together the images from his dream as Emma snored and snorted in the bed beside him. He'd showered the night before, washing away the horror and sweat of the day, but he was so sticky now he needed to wash again. He took himself off to his old bathroom, through the room he had grown up in and which was being prepared for another generation now. Hot water and soap pummelled away the sweat and the last vestiges of chemical taint, but he still couldn't rid himself of the nightmare, that strange face staring back at him, familiar and yet utterly unrecognizable.

Two suits down in a week, he pulled out one of the tailor-made three-pieces and started to dress. There had been a time when his fellow officers had thought it funny to play pranks on him, jealous of his inherited wealth. Someone with more wit than brains had phoned a local tailor, highly respected in his trade, pretending to be

McLean and asking if he might be measured up for a new suit at work. Unaware of the cruelty of police officers, the tailor had turned up as requested. As was ever the way with these things, the officer behind the prank had only thought of the embarrassment McLean might feel, and given no consideration to the time and effort of the tailor. McLean's response had been to act as if it had been his idea all along, and two very fine dark-tweed suits had been the result. They fitted perfectly, even allowing for the inevitable expansion of his waistline, but they were far too good for police work. And yet two encounters with corrosive waste, two cheap suits in the bin, and he was left with little choice.

'Job interview?'

He looked around, seeing Emma awake and staring at him through the growing dawn light. She sat up in their bed, naked and unashamed, the swell of her pregnancy more evident than before. That was their child growing inside her. The future, and a life change he still couldn't come to terms with no matter what the shrink might tell him.

'Run out of options.' He smiled, then stood up, crossed the bedroom and sat down beside her. 'It's early. You should get some sleep. Both of you.'

Emma punched him lightly on the arm. 'I'm not an invalid, you know?'

'Aye, I know. But you've a day off you lucky so and so. Make the most of it. Sleep in late, slob around in your jammies. I've a feeling it's going to be a long one again.'

Emma's smile turned to a frown and he felt her stiffen beside him. 'You work too hard, Tony. That's going to change when the baby's born, isn't it?'

He couldn't be sure if it was a statement or a question, didn't know how to answer it either way. He hugged her to him, breathed in her scent and felt her warmth through the prickly wool of his suit. A second kiss on the top of her head was all the assurance he had to offer.

51

'We're all in place. I've got two teams of uniform officers and a half a dozen Health and Safety inspectors ready to go.'

'That many?'

'Aye, well, it's a big site. Wouldn't want anyone sloping off while we weren't looking.'

McLean sat in the front of a white Transit van beside DCI Jayne McIntyre. They were parked in a layby a quarter of a mile from the front gates to the Extech Energy biodigester site, and squinting through the trees he could just about make out the tops of the stainless-steel storage tanks. Almost six in the morning and the sun was already poking up over the top of the hills to the south of them, casting long shadows on the road.

'No point hanging about then. Let's get this done.'

McLean climbed out of the Transit and went back to his Alfa. As predicted, DC Harrison had shown up for work bright and cheery, and now she sat in the driver's seat. 'We off then, sir?' she asked.

'Aye. Take it slow, mind you. Don't want to cause too much alarm.'

Harrison did as she was told, driving the car slowly up the road and stopping at the closed barrier. A security guard looked up in surprise from the glass-fronted hut beside the entrance. Then his face widened into a smile of recognition. He put on his peaked cap, straightened his hi-vis jacket and stepped out of the booth, leaning down as Harrison dropped the window to greet him.

'Morning, Bobby. How you doing?'

'Detectives. Good morning.' Bobby the security guard grinned at them, his face a mess of red spots still sore from where he'd shaved. Something he probably only had to do once a week. 'This is a wee bit unexpected. I've nothing on the schedule about a visit.'

'This is a somewhat unusual visit, Bobby.' Harrison picked up the warrant that was sitting folded in the space between the two front seats. 'You ever been served with a warrant before?'

Bobby's face could hardly have reddened any more than it already was, but his earlobes went a dark purple colour. 'W-Warrant? Like, as in search warrant?' His eyes strayed from the piece of paper in Harrison's hand to the line of white Transit vans now waiting patiently behind the Alfa.

'Very much like search warrant, Bobby. Signed by a judge and everything.'

'I . . . I don't know. What should I do? I have to call the office.' Bobby the security guard turned away, but Harrison leaned out, grabbed his arm.

'No, Bobby. You have to take this.' She slapped the warrant into his hand. 'You have to read it, and then you have to open the barrier so we don't have to break it. Or Sergeant Gatford can open the barrier instead.'

Bobby had been staring at his arm and the folded piece of paper in his hand, now he looked around again to his little glass-fronted booth. Police Sergeant Don Gatford gave him a smile and a little wave, then pressed the button to open the gates.

'Thanks, Bobby.' Harrison took back the warrant and slid the window back up again, gently eased the accelerator pedal and drove forward into the compound, leaving the open-mouthed security guard behind.

'This is really quite intolerable.'

McLean sat with DCI McIntyre and DC Harrison in the small conference room to the rear of Extech Energy's admin building, drinking the fine coffee that had been brought to them by a worried receptionist. Claire Ferris had turned up at the office twenty minutes after they had raided the place, and now she was pacing back and forth in front of the window.

'You don't need to be here, Ms Ferris. I think we've explained that already?' McIntyre sat at the head of the table, the warrant spread out in front of her. Unlike Bobby the easily duped security guard, Ferris had actually studied the document, made a few calls and then grudgingly admitted that it was in order.

'What is it that you hope to find?' she asked after another couple of circuits in front of the window. 'We're an environmental-waste-management company, a renewable-energy generator. We're the good guys. The environment minister himself opened this site not a year ago.'

'And yet a bulk liquid container filled on these premises spilled ten thousand litres of highly toxic and acidic waste on to a crowded bus stop in the city centre. Twenty people died.' McIntyre spoke the facts calmly, in sharp contrast to Ms Ferris's agitated movements.

'That wasn't . . . We didn't . . . We can't be held respon-sible for that truck crashing.'

'No. Not the crash, that's true. But the liquid? I think you know more about that than you're letting on.'

Ferris finally gave up her pacing, pulled out a chair and slumped into it. 'Am I being interviewed now? Should I have a lawyer present?'

McIntyre smiled, took a sip of her coffee. 'That's entirely up to you, Ms Ferris. Meantime we'll just sit here and wait for the teams to finish searching the site, aye?'

A silence fell over the room that McLean was quite happy not to upset. The coffee was good, his chair comfortable. A biscuit or two wouldn't have gone amiss, but you couldn't have everything. Outside the window, no longer obscured by Ferris's pacing, he caught the occasional glimpse of a Health and Safety inspector, accompanied by one or two uniform officers as they criss-crossed the site, poking their noses into anything and everything. He was fairly confident they would find enough to justify the warrant, but every passing minute brought with it an element of uncomfort-able doubt.

'I need to make some phone calls.' Ferris stood up sud-denly, pulling out her mobile phone. 'My boss –'

'Actually, I wouldn't mind a word with your boss myself,' McIntyre interrupted. 'Get him on the line, why don't you? Or her. We never did quite get to the bottom of who owns this place, and the paper trail is extremely complicated.'

'Maybe later.' Ferris sat back down again.

'Might I see your phone?' McLean asked.

'My phone?' A flicker of worry flashed across Ferris's face. 'But it's mine.'

'Is it? Or is it a company phone? The warrant allows us to examine all company records and to search this facility. I rather think your phone is included in that remit, don't you think?'

Ferris paused a moment, biting her lip with uncertainty. Then she seemed to come to a decision, slid the tiny handset over. 'Knock yourself out.'

McLean picked it up. The screen was still on, but he was unfamiliar with the menus. He passed it to Harrison, who set about tapping and swiping like a teenager.

'Here we go, sir. Recent calls. A couple to the US. One to the private line to our station, that's interesting. Oh, and a call to a Mr Alan Lewis. Ring any bells?'

'Well, well, well.' He reached for the phone as Harrison passed it over, saw the name and number. Pieces of the puzzle started to slot into place, and the picture emerging was not a nice one. He opened his mouth to speak, but a knock at the door interrupted them all. It swung open before anyone could answer, and the gnarled face of Sergeant Gatford peered in through that gap.

'Sir, ma'am. Think you might want to come and have a look at this.'

'First I just thought it was because everything here's so new, sir. Only on closer inspection it seems there's rather more to it than that.'

McLean stood in the open doorway to the storage shed at the back of the compound. It wasn't very full, despite young Bobby the Plook's assertion that all the maintenance kit was stored in there. A single off-road buggy, a bit like a pumped up golf cart, had been parked off to one side, and a metal container of the kind normally found being craned onto cargo ships or trundling up and down the motorway at sixty miles per hour had somehow been manoeuvred into one corner. Mostly it was just empty space.

'Floor's very clean.' He stepped inside, following the young Health and Safety inspector, whose shoes squeaked on the spotless and shiny floor. Spotless that was, apart from a curious mark halfway between the entrance and the back wall.

'That's what I thought, sir. It's been painted very recently. And there's this.' The young lad squatted down by the mark, took a penknife out of his pocket and used the blade to carefully scrape at the floor paint. It came away easily, and as he bent to look closer, McLean saw that the concrete below was stained and pitted. A chemical reek wafted up to his nose, a pale reminder of the stench of the truck crash.

'Last time I saw something like this was at the big semi-conductor plant out Dunfermline way. Idiot with a forklift managed to drop an IBC of hydrofluoric acid. They had to shut the place for a week to clean it up. Ring any bells?'

'Not much of it here, though,' McLean said. 'Could just be something they use on site?'

'It's possible. I'll get this analysed anyway. If they're using industrial solvents they'll have paperwork for it. Seems a bit dodgy to me, though.'

McLean didn't say it, but he had to agree. Too many coincidences, and too much evidence of a hurried cover-up. He looked around the empty space, noticing a small fire escape door to the rear. If memory served, this shed was at the back of the compound, where it opened out on to the building site for the greenhouses and tomatoes. He walked over, pushed at the bar that would open the door.

'Don't push that, sir. It's alarmed.' The shout of warning came too late, but no bells set to ringing as the door swung open. McLean looked across a short expanse of neatly trimmed grass and a gravel path to the fence. A narrow gate opened up on to the greenhouse site, far more close to completion than he had imagined.

'Anyone looked in there?' he asked as the young Health and Safety officer trotted up.

'Not sure the warrant covers it, sir.'

'Not sure I care.' McLean stepped out of the storage shed and crossed to the gate. He expected it to be locked, but when he tried the handle it clicked open. Nobody shouted at him, and there didn't seem to be anyone at work. A short distance away, another shed similar to the one he had just left was still under construction, only half its roof on. The small door at the rear was locked, and when he walked around the front, a heavy roller door had been pulled down to the ground, blocking entry. It reminded him horribly of the door over the disused train tunnel where he and Harrison had found the barrels of industrial effluent, but where there had been a personnel door in that one, this was solid.

'I wonder why they're so keen to keep people out of an unfinished shed.' McLean bent down and rattled the padlock. This part of the shed had a roof over it, but further along, where the shed was still open to the elements, another opening had no roller door as yet fitted. Peering inside, he found a partition wall between the two bays. A temporary wooden door had been set into it, held shut with a hasp and padlock.

'You got a set of bolt cutters?' McLean asked of the young Health and Safety inspector, who had followed him from the other site. 'I'd really like to know what's in there.'

'Should be a set in one of the vans, sir. Have you got the authority to open it though?'

McLean shook his head. 'Probably not. But you have, right? I mean you guys can go anywhere if you've reason to believe Health and Safety rules aren't being followed, right?'

The young man's worried frown turned into a wry smile. 'I'll be five minutes,' he said, then scurried off.

McLean wandered the building site while he waited, wondering about the lack of workmen or even security guards. Like Extech Energy, the site was ring-fenced with steel mesh and razor wire, so maybe they felt it wasn't necessary. Or the Extech security guards might have included this place in their rounds anyway, since it was all part of the same outfit.

'Here we go, sir.' The young Health and Safety inspector appeared, rather breathlessly, holding a pair of heavy-duty bolt cutters and followed by a somewhat concerned looking DCI McIntyre.

'What are you up to, Tony?' she asked.

'Following a hunch.' McLean nodded at the young man, who set about the padlock with the cutters. It gave little resistance, and the door swung open on to darkness. The smell that wafted out was enough to confirm his suspicions, though. Bitter and stinging to the eyes, a headache just from one breath.

McLean fished a torch out of his jacket pocket and played the light on the space beyond the door. It reflected off the shiny sides of a stainless-steel tanker trailer, just like the one that had crashed and split, spilling its contents over the Lothian Road and nineteen unfortunate souls. A dozen or more metal barrels, in only slightly better condition than the ones they had found in the disused railway tunnel, had been hastily piled in the far corner.

'Bingo.'

52

News of the find out at Extech Energy must have travelled fast if the flurry of activity at the station was anything to go by. He'd left most of the team out at the site in Livingston, heading back with DC Harrison and DCI McIntyre to break the bad news to the major-incident team. They'd done a great job on the truck crash, but even McLean knew it was time to call in the big guns on this one.

DC Gregg held court among a sea of uniforms, dishing out assignments as if they were rewards for good service. McLean could have just stood in the doorway and watched her efficiency. As a detective, she was thorough but not particularly imaginative, which worked for a certain kind of case. Her true skill, it appeared, was in project management, and here she was a sight to behold. Too soon, she caught sight of him, dismissed her entourage and bustled over.

'Back already, sir? Thought you'd be out there all day.'

'Best to leave it to the professionals. Which reminds me, who's our contact at Gartcosh these days?'

'Not sure. You think we need to get Serious and Organized on to this?'

'Sadly, yes. It goes way beyond Specialist Crime. This is much bigger than either of our pay grades.'

Gregg consulted her notepad, scribbled something at the bottom of the page. 'I'll get right on to it. Be a shame to hand all this over, though.' She looked around the room wistfully. 'I've just got it nicely organized.'

'How are we doing with the other half of the investigation? Any advance on the last body?' McLean looked across the room to the whiteboard. No one had rubbed out the name Reginald Samuel Saunders yet, but someone had scored a line through it.

'Nothing from the DNA people, I'm afraid. We asked the mortuary to send a second sample just in case the first had been cross-contaminated. We've got a fresh sample from your dealer, too, just to confirm whether the problem's analysis or database.' Gregg looked at the floor for a moment, something McLean had noticed she tended to do when bringing bad news.

'Let me guess, it's going to take a few days to get all that done.'

'They promised early next week.'

'OK. Not much we can do about that. The drugs boys come to pick up Sammy yet? That's one case I'll be happy to hand over to another team.'

Gregg consulted her clipboard. 'Don't think so, sir. Last I heard Chief Superintendent Forrester was going to see him.'

'Forrester's here?' McLean's euphoria at the discovery of the industrial solvents at Extech evaporated in an instant. 'Who's with him? When did this happen?'

'Ten, maybe fifteen minutes ago?' Gregg, looked at her watch. 'Why?'

'Sammy's responsible for the death of his son. He shouldn't be allowed anywhere near the man. Fuck.'

McLean left DC Gregg open-mouthed and staring,

hurried out of the incident room and into the corridor. He spotted DC Blane lumbering up the stairs as he hurried down them. 'Lofty. With me. Now!'

He didn't wait to see if he was being followed, but clattered down the next couple of flights, taking two steps, then three at a time. At the bottom, the long corridor to the cells was empty. Even the custody sergeant's desk was unmanned. McLean burst through the doors beyond, wondering how long it would take to locate Sammy's cell.

As it turned out, no time at all.

One cell door stood open, light spilling out into the corridor, and with it a horrible wet, slapping noise. McLean felt a presence behind him, turned to see DC Blane.

'Quickly.' He hurried to the open door, already knowing what he was going to see there.

Pothead Sammy lay sprawled across the narrow cot that hung from one wall of the cell. His face was a mess of blood, lanky hair slicked with it. Chief Superintendent Forrester had a good grip on his T-shirt with one hand and was using the other to repeatedly pummel the drug dealer in the face. With each hit, Sammy's body twitched and spasmed, blood spattering the wall behind him and slicking the floor.

'Stop!' McLean bellowed the command with all the authority of a sergeant-at-arms. He might as well have shouted at the wind. Forrester didn't even seem to hear him, just raised his fist once more and brought it down on Sammy's nose. Before McLean could say anything more, DC Blane pushed past him. Two steps carried him across the room, and in a second he had the chief superintendent in a neck lock, arms pinned. For a moment, Forrester resisted, and then he slumped so completely, Blane almost dropped him.

'Get him out of here.' McLean spoke softly even though he wanted to shout. 'One of the other cells for now, and keep it quiet if you can.'

DC Blane nodded once, hauling the almost comatose chief superintendent up on to unwilling legs and steering him out of the cell. McLean crouched down beside Pothead Sammy, reached a finger in to search for a pulse. 'Thank Christ,' he muttered under his breath as he found one, saw bubbles in the blood around the drug dealer's nose and mouth as he breathed in and out shallowly, unconscious.

'Dear God. I never thought . . .'

McLean looked around to see the custody sergeant standing in the doorway, eyes wide with feigned surprise.

'Aye you did, Jim.' He stood up, pulled a clean white handkerchief from his pocket and wiped Sammy Saunders's blood from his fingers with it. 'Aye you did.'

'Well this is fucking awkward, isn't it?'

It seemed to be McLean's turn to pace up and down in front of the window, this time in Chief Superintendent Forrester's office rather than his own. The man himself had collapsed into the chair behind his desk, staring at the ceiling with eyes that wouldn't have looked out of place on Pothead Sammy after a particularly fine toke.

'He killed my boy.' Forrester's voice cracked as he spoke, weak and on the verge of breaking down completely.

'That's the only reason I didn't arrest you on the spot. Sir.' And the bloody custody sergeant. McLean paused long enough to consider kicking the waste paper bin, then carried on his pacing.

'Is he dead?' Forrester slumped forward, elbows on the desk, and plunged his head into his hands. Blood stained his knuckles and the cuffs of his shirt, flecks of it in his greying hair. It was on his cheeks, too, giving him the appearance of a frenzied axeman.

'Do you really care?' McLean stopped pacing, checked his watch. Half an hour since DC Blane had dragged the chief constable out of the cell. Twenty-five minutes since the paramedics had carted Pothead Sammy off to hospital, alive but only just. Whether the damage inflicted was permanent remained to be seen, but one thing was for sure. Chief Superintendent Tommy Forrester's career in Police Scotland was over.

A light knock at the door, and then it opened before McLean could reach it. Deputy Chief Constable Steve 'Call-Me-Stevie' Robinson slid through a narrow opening like a pantomime thief, closing it swiftly but silently behind him. He paused a moment to look at the two men in the room, eyes settling on Forrester.

'Jesus, Tommy. What the fuck were you thinking?'

McLean was surprised to hear the DCC swear. He couldn't remember him ever being so coarse before. 'I don't think there was much of that going on,' he said.

Robinson turned to face him, eyes narrowed in irritation. 'What a bloody mess. I don't suppose there's much chance nobody else knows what happened?'

'The custody sergeant knew. DC Gregg told me he was going to speak to Saunders.' McLean nodded in Forrester's direction. 'DC Blane helped to stop him. Of the three, I'd trust the constables not to gossip until they'd had a chance to square things up with me, but you know what a police station's like, sir. Chances of keeping a lid on this are zero.'

'Then it's all about the spin.' Robinson stood up straighter now, and in his mind McLean could almost see the DCC clasping the lapels of his jacket. 'Tommy, you need to go home. Get yourself cleaned up. I'll expect a letter of resignation on my desk by tomorrow morning. Tony, as of now you're acting DCI – no, I'll not hear any argument. Jayne will be acting superintendent and I'll take control of the station overall. The drug dealer, he's where right now?'

'Hospital.' McLean pulled out his phone, checked there were no new messages. 'DC Blane went with the ambulance. I'd have heard if his condition had changed by now. For good or bad.'

'Then we must pray it's for good. There's only so much we can do if he dies.' Robinson let out a long breath, sagging a little at the shoulders as he did so. 'You've still work to do, I take it, Tony?'

'More than ever.'

'Then get to it. I'll manage this.'

McLean nodded, walked over to the door and opened it. Before he could go, Robinson spoke again.

'And thank you. I won't forget this.'

McLean nodded again, then left the two senior officers to themselves. As he walked the long corridors back to the major-incident room, he couldn't help wondering whether it wouldn't be better for him if the DCC forgot he even existed.

53

'You still in charge of the investigation into James Barnton, sir?'

McLean stopped in his tracks, turned to see DC Gregg standing half in, half out of the major-incident room. His mind was still full of the chief superintendent's bloody violence and the predicament it had left him in. It took him a while to understand what she was saying. 'The body in the cemetery?'

'Aye, that's the chappie. Only with everything else going on . . .' Gregg glanced up at the ceiling, not exactly where the chief superintendent's office was, but a close enough approximation for him to know what she meant. She stepped fully into the corridor, and McLean saw she was holding a thin sheaf of papers in her hands, looking suspiciously like they were fresh off the printer.

'I really don't want to talk about it, and neither do you. As to Barnton, well, technically Grumpy Bob's in charge. After what we found at Extech, though, I expect it'll get swept up in all that. Barnton worked there, after all. That his post-mortem report?'

Gregg looked at the papers, then back up at McLean. 'These? No. PM came in yesterday. He had a massive seizure that killed off half his brain, apparently. No, these are from the CCTV and traffic boys. Thought you might find them interesting.'

McLean took the papers, turning them over to see slightly fuzzy colour-printed photographs, taken from various CCTV cameras. 'Where's this?' he asked.

'Dalry Road. A couple hundred yards down from the cemetery. Timestamp's around one in the morning.'

McLean shuffled through the images, seeing two men walking arm in arm. Except that it didn't seem quite convincing. He'd seen drunks caught on camera before, even one drunk man being guided home by a more sober friend. This looked different somehow.

'All very interesting, but why am I looking at these? We can't see faces, can we?' He peered closer, holding up the paper until he could almost make out the individual dots of the camera pixels.

'This one's a bit clearer. If you know what you're looking at.' Gregg reached out and flicked through the sheets as McLean still held them, fishing one out after a moment. 'Helps if you've seen the number plate recognition info too.'

McLean stared at the last picture, not enough hands left to shuffle the pages and find the report. 'Why don't you just tell me what it says, Constable?'

Gregg looked a little hurt, as if she'd wanted McLean to see how much work she had put into uncovering what was bound to be a less useful clue than she thought it was.

'See, there's plenty traffic along that road between midnight and two in the morning. Mostly taxis and stuff, but a few private cars, delivery trucks, that kind of thing. Seems young Stringer's got an eye for these things, though, and this one fair pops out when you know what you're looking for.' She pulled out the bottom sheet from the pile and pointed at a number that had been highlighted in yellow. It meant nothing to McLean, but the name of the registered owner alongside it did.

'LindSea Farm Estates?' He followed the line across to the next column. 'Toyota Hilux pickup truck.' Back to the number plate and now he recognized it. 'Gregor Wishaw?'

'That's what I thought, sir.'

McLean studied the photograph more closely now. Certainly it was the right height and build, but it wasn't enough to stand up in a court of law.

'They took him to the Royal Infirmary, didn't they?'

'Aye. He's still there. Broke both his legs and one arm, apparently, so I don't expect he'll be going anywhere soon.'

'You seen Grumpy Bob around?' McLean asked.

'Not sure if he's back from Livingston yet, sir. Could be wrong, mind. Think I saw a couple of the new DCs heading towards the CID room.'

'Ah well. If I can't find him I can always drag Harrison along. Sure she'd love to have a go at questioning the man who tried to kill her yesterday.'

He found DC Harrison in the CID room, arguing with DC Stringer about something on one of their computer screens. McLean managed to get all the way across the room unnoticed, the two of them too deeply engaged in their discussion. On balance, he reckoned Harrison was winning, though.

'Something come up?' McLean couldn't for the life of him remember what he'd set them to work on. Then it popped into his head. 'Jennifer Beasley. You find her next of kin?'

Stringer almost jumped out of his skin, leaping from his chair as if it were on fire. 'Sorry, sir. Didn't see you come in. We were just trying to work something out. I think it's a problem with the database, but Janie here reckons it's deliberate.'

'Back a step, Constable. What's deliberate?'

Harrison had stayed seated, and now she swivelled the computer screen around so that McLean could see it. A couple of open windows showed lines of text that appeared to be some kind of search results. Beyond that he had no idea.

'We can't find Jennifer Beasley at all, sir,' she said.

'What do you mean, you can't find her? She's in the mortuary.'

'Aye, I know that. Her body's there. But she's not in any of our records. She's not got a driving licence or a passport, nothing with social security. I even ran the name through the local libraries and there's nothing.'

'Nothing?'

'It's like she's a ghost, sir.' DC Stringer pointed at the screen. 'Either she's been wiped from the records or we're not getting her name right. I've tried every variation on Jennifer Beasley I can think of though, and that was the name we found in her notebook, right? It was written down. Nobody misspells their own name.'

'What about her hotel room? She must have given them an address when she checked in?'

'I gave them a call, but she'd only put an email address on the form. Don't think Foxton House is the kind of place that cares too much, as long as they get paid.'

'OK. When he gets back from the hospital, you and

Lof—, . . . DC Blane can go round and have another look at her room. We've still got the keycard and nobody else should have been in there. We only had a brief look, so you might find something else. Try speaking to any of the staff, too. You never know, you might get lucky.'

'Hospital? Is Lofty OK?' Harrison asked the question, but McLean could see the worry spread across Stringer's face, too. Hard to believe neither of them had heard. It was a good forty-five minutes since the incident. Time was when that sort of gossip would be halfway to Strathclyde by now.

'He's fine. There was an incident with the drug dealer, Saunders. Lofty . . . helped. I sent him off to the hospital to check everything was OK. He should be back soon enough.'

Harrison frowned, clearly unconvinced, then turned back to the screen. 'There's something we're missing here, sir. With Jennifer Beasley, I mean. What if that's not her real name?'

'Go on.'

Harrison picked up a slim spiral-bound notebook from the desk. McLean recognized it as the one they had taken from the flat. The one with several interesting names in it that he'd not had time to follow up yet. She opened it, folded back the cover and held it up for him to see. It was mostly doodles, scribbles and the dead girl's name, but underneath that were heavy scrawled lines in biro.

'I had a leaf through, really haven't had time to do more than that, but see here? Reckon it says "Maddy's Notebook – Do Not Touch!" Only it's been scribbled over with a ballpoint pen so it's hard to read.'

McLean peered closer. It was clear that something had been scrawled out, but he'd be hard pushed to tell what. On the other hand, Harrison's eyes were maybe twenty years newer than his.

'So you think her real name's Maddy, or Madeleine or something?'

'Aye, but not Beasley. That's not coming up with anything on the system either. Only, if she's really Maddy, then why go by Jennifer? And why can't we find any records for either of them?'

'I take it you've got a theory?' McLean had one himself, but he was interested to see whether Harrison or Stringer might have the same idea.

'It might sound a bit far-fetched, sir. But what if she was in witness protection? Maddy's her real name and Jennifer Beasley's an alias?' Harrison's voice faltered, as if she was unsure, but it was much what McLean had been thinking.

'If that was the case there'd be records still, surely?' Stringer said. 'Witness protection would come up with a whole new identity, and there'd be a DNA record somewhere, wouldn't there? We got no hits at all.'

'We didn't, no.' McLean glanced at the clock above the door, wondering if the DCC was still about or if he was even now spiriting Chief Superintendent Forrester out of the station under cover. 'But that's not to say alarm bells haven't been going off somewhere else.'

'So how do we go about finding something like that out?' Harrison asked. 'It's way above my pay grade.'

'Isn't it fortunate then that someone much more senior owes me a favour.' McLean headed for the door, then

374

finally remembered why he had come into the CID room in the first place.

'Either of you seen Grumpy Bob around?'

'Think he's still out at Livingston, sir.'

'OK. Sort us out a lift to the Royal Infirmary will you, Harrison? I want to have a word with our mutual friend Gregor Wishaw. Meantime I'll go and see if I can't shake loose a few secrets from higher up the tree.'

54

A wilting hot sun burned in a sky so clear it was almost black as McLean stared up at the concrete and glass hulk of the Royal Infirmary. The squad car that had brought him and DC Harrison over had dropped them too far from the entrance to be comfortable, before rushing off on an emergency call. A few hardened souls were braving the heat to sneak a crafty cigarette, but most of the people hurried through the entrance into the air-conditioned comfort inside as quickly as they could.

'Didn't think I'd be back here so quickly, sir,' DC Harrison said as McLean held the door, feeling the welcome draft of cool air on his face. His back and legs felt sticky with sweat; maybe the tweed suit wasn't the best choice for the weather.

'Quickly? Oh, yes. They brought you here yesterday evening. I should have asked how you were feeling this morning. Sorry.'

'No need. I was fine before we got as far as Haddington, but the doctors insisted on giving me a full check-up. Sure I've fried more brain cells out with the lads after we've cracked a case.'

McLean had to smile at that. Time was he'd probably drunk himself senseless, too, with or without the help of his friends. Nowadays, though, the hangover seemed more of a price to pay than the pleasure was worth. Perhaps he was getting old.

A uniform constable sat on guard duty in the corridor outside Gregor Wishaw's room. He looked twice at the two of them approaching, gaze swiftly returning to his fascinating paperback book. Only on the third time did he recognize them and scramble to his feet.

'Inspector, sir. Sorry. They said you were coming. Didn't say when, though.'

'No worries, Jim. Anything good?' McLean inclined his head towards the book, still clutched in the constable's nervous hand.

'I . . . Umm . . . That is . . .'

'It's OK. I won't tell your duty sergeant.' He reached for the door handle. 'How's the patient? Awake?'

'Not sure, sir. Nurse took in some stuff about ten minutes ago. Think she was changing some of his dressings. He's quite a mess.'

McLean nodded his understanding, opened the door and stepped inside.

They entered a surprisingly airy room, lit by a large window on one wall. A frame had been erected around the bed, wires dangling from pulleys and holding up Gregor Wishaw's stookie-clad legs. He had broken one arm as well, his neck in a brace and his face peppered with scabs. But he was awake.

'Wha' the fuck're you doin' here, pig?' His voice slurred with painkillers, eyes narrow as he stared first at McLean, then at Harrison. 'Pigs, aye.'

'It's good to see you, too, Gregor.' McLean drew up a

chair and sat down a few feet away from the bed. 'Thought we'd have a wee chat. Seems you've been keeping secrets from us.'

'Dunno what y'r talkin' 'bout.'

'Ah, but I think you do. See, we know how it all works now. Extech Energy is the collection hub for industrial solvents that really should be being disposed of more carefully. Only that's expensive, isn't it? Far easier just to tanker the stuff out to the middle of nowhere, shove it in some old barrels and hide it away in a disused railway tunnel. How long's that been going on for? How many other sites have you and your friends been polluting? What else are we going to find when we go poking our noses in all of LindSea Farm Estates sheds?'

'It's not . . .' Wishaw tried to shake his head, found that pain and his neck restraint stopped him. ''S'not like that. Waste's just a tiny part'f it. ''S'all about the money. Makin' it clean.'

McLean paused before speaking again. He knew that he'd be in trouble for interviewing a suspect while he was under duress, brain addled by painkillers and quite probably concussion, too. Nothing he got from Wishaw could ever be used in court, and the simple fact of his being here, talking to the man without a lawyer present, could mean he would walk free from any other charges. But, at the end of the day, neither he nor Harrison had been injured, and Wishaw was just a small cog in a bigger machine.

'James Barnton. Why'd you dump his body?'

Wishaw frowned, then winced as the cuts on his face stretched open. 'Who?'

'Barnton. Security guard at Extech. We know you

moved his body from the biodigester site to Dalry Cemetery. Why?'

'Dunno what youse talkin' about.'

'Aye, I think you do. We've got CCTV of you in the Dalry Road the night before he was found. Number plate recognition camera puts your pickup leaving the city not much later that morning. You'd be surprised how easily we can track you, Gregor.'

Wishaw said nothing, but his eyes were filled with fear.

'Here's what I think happened,' McLean continued. 'Barnton died at work. Jury's out on exactly how, but our best bet is he had some kind of seizure. He was leaning back against the garage door when he was found. You know, the garage door behind which they'd hidden all those barrels of corrosive muck? But he'd been there long enough for the blood to settle in his back and start to clot. It left very regular marks on his skin, see?'

Wishaw opened his mouth, but no words came out.

'Couldn't have the police poking their noses into Extech again. Not before you've got the whole operation cleaned up and hidden away on the building site next door. So somebody calls you up, tells you to get rid of the problem. That is what you do in this organization, isn't it, Gregor?'

'Din't do nuthin'.' Wishaw tried to shake his head again.

'You went to his flat, carried him like he was drunk. Maybe thought you'd just leave him there in his bed for someone else to find. Poor soul, died in his sleep. Tragic. But then you got creative. Why'd you do that? Was it the way he looked? Something else?'

Wishaw said nothing, just stared at the ceiling, eyes glistening with tears.

'So you changed his clothes for running gear, grabbed the first pair of shoes you could find. Then you dumped him in the cemetery so it looked like he'd dropped down dead while out exercising. Couldn't do anything about that expression on his face, though, could you?'

Something seemed to break in him, and Wishaw's gaze dropped down to his one free hand, the button close by that would dispense more morphine into his drip. He sniffed, blinked away tears he couldn't bring himself to cry, then looked up at McLean, eyes wide.

'Poor bastard was scared to death.' Wishaw's slur disappeared, his voice barely a whisper. 'Ain't never seen nothin' like it. Sat there, eyes wide, like he'd screamed himself dead. Never was one to believe in ghosts, but if you asked me now I'd say he'd seen the devil himself.'

'What about the cemetery? Why dump him there?'

'Din't look right, lying in his bed there. He was too stiff, and that look on his face.' Wishaw's voice cracked as he spoke. 'First person to see him'd ken he'd been moved. ''Sides. Who ever died in their bed, right?'

'You know interfering with a corpse is a serious crime, aye?' Harrison spoke up from the far side of the room, where she'd been standing quietly, taking notes. 'Especially for someone who's still on licence.'

Wishaw looked over towards her, then back at McLean. 'You think I give a fuck about that? About going back to prison?'

'You should. There'll be no parole this time.'

'Parole?' Wishaw let out a noise that might have been laughter, might have been crying. The tears were back either way. 'It's too late for that. I'm fucked and I know it.'

'How do you mean?' McLean asked.

'Cos I saw him myself. Saw what Jim must've seen. Last night at the tunnel.'

'Last night? When you tried to run us down with your truck?'

A momentary confusion covered Wishaw's features, as if McLean had accused him of something inconceivable.

'Weren't trying to run you down. I was trying to run it down. Thought I could kill it. Aye, that's some joke.' Wishaw tried to laugh, setting off a spasm of coughing.

'What do you mean "it"?' McLean recalled the scene, the impossible image his mind had conjured up. It wasn't possible that Wishaw could have seen it, too. He hadn't breathed deep of the toxic fumes. 'What did you see?'

Wishaw's face had turned red now, his coughing more severe. His eyes grew wide as his free hand thrashed weakly around the covers for the morphine button and oblivion. His breath came in ragged gasps and sooner or later one of the monitors would trigger, bringing a nurse running.

'You. Saw. Him.' His words came out as a hoarse gasp as his hand finally found the button and pressed it hard. The drug stilled his spasm, and as he relaxed his voice trailed away. 'You saw him. The devil. He was . . .'

The roads were mercifully clear as McLean drove back to the station, a pensive DC Harrison in the passenger seat beside him. Gregor Wishaw's last words before the morphine took him off to his happy place had been disturbing on several levels, not the least of which was that McLean had seen something. He'd put it down to the fumes coming out of the tunnel, a trick of the evening light. It certainly hadn't been any kind of devil; he was fairly sure of that. And yet something had made Wishaw react, and stupidly.

'What did you make of his story, then?' he asked as they approached Cameron Toll and finally found the traffic.

'Wishaw?' Harrison thought for a while before continuing. 'I'm inclined to believe him, actually.'

'What? About seeing the devil?'

'Well, maybe not that. But I don't think he was trying to kill us. Not by ramming that shutter door with his truck. I mean, just look at the state of him now. All he really needed to do was block us in the tunnel. We'd be unconscious in minutes, dead in half an hour. If what he told us about Extech and moving Barnton's body is true, then the most sensible thing he could have done was run. No way killing us would have made his problems go away.'

'I agree, and, sure, he's prone to violence, but Gregor Wishaw's never been suicidal. So why did he ram the door?'

Harrison stared out of the windscreen as they moved slowly up Craigmillar Park, heading towards Newington. 'It was just you, me and Wishaw back there yesterday, wasn't it, sir?' she asked finally.

'You mean before the cavalry finally showed up?' McLean risked a glance sideways as he overtook a line of parked buses, but Harrison still wasn't looking at him.

'Only. It's weird. Maybe my head got too messed up by the chemicals in the tunnel. But when I try to think through the sequence of events I keep coming up with their being someone else there all the time. Someone actually in the tunnel with us. I can't put a face to them, though. Can't really describe them at all.'

It was McLean's turn to sit silent for a while, concentrating on the road ahead until a set of red traffic lights brought them to a halt.

'I think we all got rather more fumes from that tunnel than we realized.' Even as he spoke, he knew he didn't really believe what he was saying. But the alternative didn't bear thinking about.

'If you say so, sir.' Harrison sounded like she didn't believe it either. 'What next, then?'

'Time to concentrate on wrapping up all the loose ends. If half of what Gregor told us about their operations is true, the Organised Crime boys will be all over this by the end of the day. Think I'd like to find out who's behind all this before they do. There's still one body to identify, too, and we need to track down the mysterious Jennifer Beasley's next of kin if we can. Draw a line under the crash investigation.'

The lights turned green, the road ahead clear for a moment. McLean took off with perhaps a little more enthusiasm than he'd intended, the car leaping forward as if it too was eager to get things wrapped up. He eased off the throttle, arriving at the next set of lights as they turned red. It was going to be one of those afternoons. They weren't far now from the site of his old tenement flat, and looking out the side window, McLean saw the old café where he and Kirsty used to go for breakfast on those rare mornings when he had the day off. Before that it had been a bank, directly across the road from a branch of a rival bank. That, too, had closed, although it hadn't yet been converted into anything else. No one did their banking in person any more, it seemed. Everything was online these days.

'Did anyone get in touch with Alan Lewis?' he asked as the lights changed once more.

'Alan –? Oh, the finance guy.' Harrison opened up her notebook, flicked through a couple of pages. 'Were we supposed to?'

'His number was on Claire Ferris's phone, remember? And he was the money behind Finlay McGregor, the hauliers. What's the betting he's got an interest in LindSea Farm Estates, too?'

'You think he might be the mastermind of the whole operation?' Harrison looked sceptical. 'Isn't he, like, one of the richest men in Scotland? Why would he get his hands dirty with something like this?'

Down East Preston Street, and McLean craned his neck to look up at the remains of his old tenement. Scaffolding still clung to the facade like metal weeds, but work had begun behind it to replace the burned-out building. He wondered if all the flats were sold now. The city was booming and property prices heading steadily upwards. Lots of places to put dodgy money and shoogle it about until it came out clean.

'I don't know,' he said finally. 'Perhaps we should ask him.'

55

'Apparently Lewis didn't come in to work this morning, sir. PA said she didn't know what his movements were for the next few days.'

McLean looked up from his desk to see DC Harrison standing in the open doorway. He'd asked her to arrange a meeting with the financier while he caught up with developments out at Extech Energy. Mostly that seemed to be the Organised Crime team asking stupid questions as they took over the investigation. It was frustrating, but important they get the handover right, otherwise something would come back to bite him sooner or later. At least he'd left Grumpy Bob in charge.

'Umm . . . Isn't that what a PA's meant to be for?'

'Funny you should say that, sir. She was very put out when I suggested the same thing.'

'Aye, well. Nobody likes a critic. You get a home address for him?'

'Two, actually.' Harrison entered the room and handed him a slip of paper. 'He's got a place in the New Town and a lodge up in Perthshire. According to Hayley the PA he might be at either of them. Or on his way to London, New York, Tokyo, Sydney . . . I get the feeling she was giving me the runaround, but you never know when you're dealing with someone worth billions.'

McLean was about to say, 'How the other half live, eh?',

then remembered his own house across town. Not quite the same league as Lewis, it was true, but he was certainly closer to the 1 per cent than the 99. He scanned the two addresses, trying to work out where they were. The New Town house was just around the corner from the place where they had found Eric Forrester's body, another very desirable part of town favoured by people who spent as much time in other countries as they did in Edinburgh. The second address, if his geography was right, would be of great interest to DI Ritchie. She'd probably spent many hours sitting in a crumbling bothy on Lewis's Perthshire estate, waiting patiently for her gang of gun runners to pass through. It might have been a coincidence, but then he didn't really believe in coincidences.

'Have you tried his mobile?' McLean asked.

'Going straight to message.' Harrison paused a moment, checked her watch. 'I could track it, I suppose, but that takes a mountain of paperwork. Probably an hour or two, and that's only if he's got it switched on right now.'

'Get on it anyway. And while you're at it get someone to speak to Border Control, just in case he tries to leave the country.'

'You want us to stop him at immigration?' Harrison's eyebrows shot up in surprise. 'Do we have sufficient cause to do that?'

'Probably not.' McLean shook his head, handed back the page of addresses to Harrison as he stood up. 'Technically it's not our job even to find him any more. That's Organised Crime's investigation. It'd be nice to know if he's left the country, though. Keep me up to date on that mobile-phone search, won't you?'

'Where are you going, sir?' Harrison asked. 'So I can find you if I get an update?'

'To the canteen, Constable. Breakfast was a very long time ago. I have a date with a mug of tea, some sandwiches and a very large slice of cake.'

The text message came in before he had made it twenty feet, let alone the canteen, his large mug of tea and an even larger slice of cake. McLean fished his phone out of his pocket, thumbed the screen until it revealed the words.

> Got something you might find interesting. Here until seven, maybe eight. Angus.

The clock on his phone told him it was just gone half past two, even if it felt like much later. Halfway down the stairs, he looked around, up the stairwell and then down. There was nobody about and nothing so urgent that it couldn't wait an hour or so. Harrison would be that long getting results from the phone company, even if they were playing nice. If not, it could be tomorrow before they could find out where Alan Lewis was. A walk down to the Cowgate and the city mortuary might even give him a chance to collect his thoughts. He tapped out a quick 'on my way just now' message by way of a reply, then carried on down the stairs and out the back door.

Too short a distance to really get into his stride, but McLean nonetheless relished the freedom that walking gave him. It would have been better had the afternoon not been stifling hot, still air smothering the city with fumes. The heat hit him the moment he stepped on to the tacky tarmac of the car park, and not for the first time he rued the decision that morning to wear a tweed suit. By the time he reached the front door to the city mortuary the sweat had started trickling down his back, pooling in uncomfortable places.

At least it was cooler inside, and quiet as it ever was. McLean nodded to the receptionist, who buzzed him through to the business side of the building without any fuss. He stood awhile in the corridor leading to the examination theatre just enjoying the chill draught from the air conditioning. Maybe walking hadn't been such a good idea after all. It had been too hot to think.

Angus was in the middle of another post-mortem examination, so McLean aimed for the observation gallery and the corner of it where you could sit without seeing what was going on. Obviously not a tricky case: the job was done in just a few swift minutes, the pathologist snapping off his latex gloves as he made his way back to his office.

'Thought I saw you lurking upstairs,' Cadwallader said a minute or two later. He still wore his scrubs, spattered with something McLean didn't want to think too hard about right now.

'You said you had something I might find interesting.'

'Yes, well. Give me a minute.' The pathologist stripped off his dirty scrubs, revealing a surprisingly thin and fit body for a man of his age. McLean maintained eye contact as his old friend fetched a fresh set of overalls and pulled them on. It wasn't the first time he'd seen those grey underpants and black socks.

'Sorry about that. Quite a busy schedule this afternoon

and Tom's off sick. Or more likely overdid it last night. Still, we've all been there. Come.' Cadwallader slid past McLean, motioning with one arm for him to follow. 'Your lad from the crash. The one who we thought was the drug addict but it turned out wasn't.'

'What about him? You've got an ID?'

'Not exactly.' The pathologist led McLean past the cold store to a small room that was inhabited mostly by cardboard boxes. A desk at the far end held a computer screen, keyboard and mouse. Cadwallader pulled out the chair and dropped himself down into it, flexing his fingers before attacking the keys.

'University pinged this over an hour or so ago. They've done the two women, too, but I'm told you've already identified them. It's a bit rough and unfinished but this is what your unidentified dead man probably looked like.'

Cadwallader reached for the mouse as the screen lit up. A couple of clicks revealed an image of a man's head, side on. They hadn't tried to put any hair on it, which was what confused McLean at first. The features looked almost feminine, slim nose and angular cheekbones in a long face with a slightly weak chin. The one eye was blank, too, lifeless. Then the pathologist did something with the mouse and the head turned fully around to face them.

'Maybe this will help, aye?' He clicked again, casting shadows and light over the features, and McLean took a step back in surprise.

'I . . . I've seen this man.' But that was impossible.

'You have?' Cadwallader blinked behind his wire-frame spectacles, peered at the screen as if the fact McLean had seen it before meant that he, too, should know who it was. 'Where?'

'At the crash scene.' McLean studied the image again, his head full of nightmares. 'But he was alive then. I spoke to him.'

56

'Looks like you might have been right sir.'

McLean was so distracted by his thoughts he hardly registered he was being spoken to. He'd walked back from the city mortuary in a daze, oblivious to the heat and the sweat trickling down his back. The computer-generated face haunted him, there was no other way to describe the feeling. Perhaps it was the unnatural colour, the lack of proper eyes or any hair. Or maybe it was the way just thinking of that face brought back the acrid smell and squat, dull headache.

'Sorry?' The words sunk in and he turned to see DC Stringer walking up the corridor towards him. The young constable had a spring in his step and a sheaf of papers in his hand.

'Looks like you were right. About the witness protection thing for Jennifer Beasley. This just came in from the NCA liaison at the Crime Campus. Heavily redacted, but the DNA matches.'

'Do we have a name?' McLean took the pages, leafed through them. It was mostly a waste of printer ink as far as he could see.

'Not yet, sir. DCI McIntyre might know though. There's another DCI just arrived from Gartcosh not half an hour ago. They're both in her office right now.'

'Thanks.' McLean was about to turn and head up to the

senior officers' floor, but then he remembered something. 'Did you and Lofty go and see her hotel room?'

'Aye, sir. Wasn't anything there, mind. Place had been cleaned out. I had a word with the receptionist and she said our lot had already been in and taken everything away.'

'Our lot?'

'Aye, I asked that. She said it was a couple of nice polismen. One had an English accent.'

McLean tried to think back to when the DNA results had come through on the bodies. It would make sense that certain records would be flagged for the NCA if they belonged to people on witness protection.

'Why would they make her disappear?' He voiced the question out loud, not really expecting an answer.

'I don't know. Maybe to protect someone else?' Stringer suggested.

'Aye, that'd make sense. No need for a cover-up otherwise.' McLean handed back the useless report. 'Think I might go and have a wee chat with this DCI.'

McIntyre's office door was closed, which was never a good sign. McLean paused a moment, like a guilty schoolboy sent to report to the headmaster, and listened to the quiet rumble of voices within. Just two people inside, unless there was a third there only to observe. He couldn't make out what they were saying, though, so knocked gently on the wood.

'Yes?' That was McIntyre's voice, he was fairly sure of that. McLean opened the door, popped his head through a small gap as if he had only been needing a quick word and didn't want to disturb anyone. The detective chief inspector sat at her desk, a single chair on the other side occupied by the man McLean had been expecting to see.

'Oh. Tony. Come in.' McIntyre got to her feet, beckoning him into the room with a wave. 'You remember DCI Featherstonehaugh?'

'With a name like that, how could I forget? I take it you're here about Jennifer Beasley?' McLean took a little satisfaction in the brief look of surprise that flitted across Featherstonehaugh's face.

'What do you know about her?' he asked.

'Not as much as you, I'd wager. She's come through some kind of witness protection, that much is pretty obvious given that you're here and her room at the hostel's been cleaned out already.' McLean settled on to the uncomfortable chair. 'Reckon her real name's Maddy, or Madeleine. Not clever of her to keep on using it.'

'Madeleine,' Featherstonehaugh said after the briefest of pauses. 'Yes. She's always been a bit pigheaded about that. Silly, really. If she didn't like being Jennifer we'd have given her something else. After all she went through.'

'And what exactly was that?' McLean asked.

'Ah, yes. Thought you'd probably ask that.' Another pause, longer this time. 'You were the detective who found the little girl up in the attic of that brothel . . . What? Twenty years ago? Twenty-five?'

A cold sensation filled McLean's gut at Featherstonehaugh's question. The image of Heather Marchmont's face, her almost silent 'Thank you' as she died in his arms. Her blood on his hands both physically and metaphorically.

'We had a similar thing down in England about fifteen years ago. Children being kept as . . . Christ, it still hurts every time I say it. Sex slaves. No other way to describe what they were.'

'I never heard about this.' McIntyre spoke, but her words echoed McLean's own thoughts.

'No, you wouldn't have done. There were no prosecutions.'

'None?' McLean remembered the raid on the brothel, the local dignitaries whisked away under covers to hide their identities, the prostitutes paraded in front of the press. There'd not been many prosecutions back then either, and none of them had been against the clients of the establishment. It was always the way with sex. Punish those forced to sell themselves, not those doing the buying. Money always worked that way.

'We'd have liked to, but it would have been difficult. Everyone was dead, except the children.'

'Children? Plural? So there's more than just Maddy – Jennifer, I should say.'

Featherstonehaugh shrugged. 'They tell me you're being made up to DCI, Tony. And I have it on good authority Jayne here's going to be taking over SCD at this station as detective superintendent. I'm pleased to hear it. This city needs good people looking after it.'

'But we're neither of us senior enough to get clearance for what we want to know,' McIntyre said.

'It's out of my hands.' Featherstonehaugh held them up just in case either of them might think he was lying, or not know what hands were. 'But if it makes you feel any better, the DCC doesn't know either. I'm not sure if the chief constable does, come to think of it. His predecessor did. Wasn't too happy.'

'What the fuck are you going on about?' McLean wasn't given to swearing often, but sometimes it was necessary.

'What I'm trying to say is I can't say . . . well, anything really.'

McLean counted to ten in his head. No point getting angry; that was what the man from the NCA wanted. Angry people didn't think straight, couldn't connect up the dots.

'So the fact that Madeleine is dead doesn't matter to you.' McLean allowed one second to let Featherstonehaugh open his mouth to protest. Two people could play this game, after all. 'Or I should say, it does matter to you, but it doesn't change the fact you can't tell me who she really was. Is that right?'

Featherstonehaugh closed his mouth again, eyes wary now.

'She was rescued from a fire that killed all the adults in a place that was probably not what you and I would call a brothel. More a private club where rich people with sick minds went to indulge their perverted fantasies. I'm warm, aren't I?'

Again, Featherstonehaugh said nothing, and now McLean could see the glint of enjoyment in McIntyre's eyes.

'You won't tell me about her, and you mentioned children, plural, which would suggest you've more than one tucked away in your protection scheme. New identity, living as ordinary a life as is possible after their early experiences. You're still keeping an eye out for them, so the threat's still there, isn't it?'

Featherstonehaugh's silence was answer enough. His earlier smirk had gone, replaced by a much colder, more calculating look.

'Do I need to remind you how Maddy came to our attention?' McLean asked. 'That we're also trying to identify one more body? A dead man, much the same age, whose DNA was mysteriously mixed up with that of a petty drug dealer? A petty drug dealer who's alive if not exactly well, by the way.'

'I can't confirm or deny anything, Tony. I'd like to but I can't.' Featherstonehaugh shook his head slightly, and for a moment McLean almost believed him.

'If you want to claim the body, it's in the city mortuary. Tell Angus I said it was OK.' He stood up, made a show of straightening his chair. 'Meantime I've plenty other things to be getting on with.'

57

'Please tell me you've had a response from the phone company.'

McLean had spent a good ten minutes searching for DC Harrison, finally finding her in the CID room, where he should have looked first. She sat in a huddle with DCs Stringer and Blane, the new detectives forming their own little clique of self-protection.

'Nothing yet, sir. But I ran his car through the NMPR system. Nothing seen going over the Forth Bridge, so it's unlikely he's gone north to Perthshire. He's not answering any of his phones, though.'

'What about Border Control?'

'Nope. His passport's not been scanned any time recently. If he's gone abroad he's done it on the sly.'

'Well, if I was doing a runner I'd probably not want to leave too many clues either. Doesn't really seem his style, though.' McLean leaned against one of the many empty desks in the large room. Not much call for them now the whole of CID had been restructured and most of the detectives that were left had been shipped off to Gartcosh.

'What about you two?' McLean turned his attention to Stringer and Blane. 'Get any further with the mysterious Maddy?'

'Hit a bit of a brick wall there, sir. Looks like she's been systematically erased from the records.'

'Perhaps not so surprising.' McLean told them what he had learned from Featherstonehaugh.

'Would they do that? Re-home two victims in the same city?' Harrison asked when he had finished.

'Not on purpose, no. I get the feeling there's a lot more to the story than I'm being told, and they're not happy that Maddy, Jennifer, whatever her real name is, was trying to track down her friend. I think that's what they call a security risk.'

'But why would they care? I mean, if all this happened when they were kids, and they're both adults now?' DC Stringer asked the question. Beside him, DC Blane had begun tapping at his keyboard and clicking his mouse, attention focused on his screen.

'I can only assume the threat is still there. Either that or what they know could cause serious embarrassment to very influential people. Given how cagey my new friend from the NCA is about sharing any information, I'm going to go with the both.'

'Might have something for you here, sir.' Blane clicked his mouse again, then swivelled his screen around to where McLean could see. 'Sixteen years ago. Big old country house burned down. Wee village called Hatfield Broad Oak in north Essex. About an hour out of London. Only survivors were a couple of young children, not related, taken into care.' He scrolled down the lines of text. 'Doesn't give their names, but some fairly important people died in the fire, see?'

McLean scanned the words looking for the story between the lines. The news had completely passed him by sixteen years ago, but he'd been a junior constable back then, struggling to cope with the death of his fiancée. A house fire in the Home Counties that claimed the lives of two judges, an ex-Cabinet minister and a multi-millionaire hedge-fund manager wouldn't have stuck in his memory even if he had seen it at the time.

'Scroll back up to the top, will you?' He flicked his fingers at the screen, then waited while Blane fumbled with the little wheel on the top of his mouse, too small for his enormous fingers. Eventually the line he was looking for came into view. A publication date at the start of the next millennium and the name of the journalist who had filed the piece.

'Robert Simons. See if you can't track him down. Have a word with him about the fire. Maybe drop the name Maddy into the conversation. You never know, it might jog his memory. Chances are he knew exactly who the children were but didn't name them because someone told him not to.'

'On it, sir.' Blane reached for the phone beside his screen and started dialling.

'You want me to help him with that?' Stringer asked. Both he and Harrison were standing now, their eagerness to get stuck into this new investigation clear. It was a distraction, though, not something they should be wasting time and resources on. Jennifer Beasley's true identity wasn't a mystery, after all. There was at least one person in the building right now who knew it. But Stringer and Blane worked well together, and with the Organised Crime division taking over the Extech investigation there wasn't much else left for them to do.

'OK. But don't waste a lot of time on it. I've already told

Featherstonehaugh to claim the body. Chances are he'll be taking the other one, too.

'You want me to keep looking for Lewis, sir?' Harrison asked. It was another piece of a puzzle they no longer had to put back together, but McLean hated leaving a job half done.

'Aye. Keep on that. Needs be, we'll pay his town house a wee visit.' He checked his watch, the afternoon marching on. 'First, though, I'm going to get myself that cup of tea.'

And with any luck there might even be some cake left.

'Might I have a quick word, Tony?'

McLean looked up from his table in an almost empty canteen. The last piece of cake lay on a plate in front of him, a mug of tea beside it. He'd hoped for a moment's calm in what had become an impossibly busy day. A chance to get his thoughts together, puzzle out the mystery of the facial reconstruction he recognized, and think up a way to refuse the promotion foisted on him by the DCC without losing his job. DCI Featherstonehaugh clearly had other plans.

'Sir?'

'Please, call me Tim. Less formal than "sir" and easier to say than Featherstonehaugh.' He pronounced his own name incorrectly, then smiled at a joke he'd surely been telling for years. 'And, besides, we'll be the same rank soon enough.'

'If it's all the same, I'll stick with "sir" for now. Was there something you needed?'

'Rather the other way around, isn't it? Or am I wrong

that you've just set your band of sleuths to finding out all about Maddy?' Featherstonehaugh had a smile on his face that was halfway between friendly and punchable. He pulled out a chair and sat down, eyeing the cake hungrily.

McLean drew the plate closer, setting the mug of tea as a barrier between them. 'How long have you been at Gartcosh?' He hoped the change of subject would throw the detective chief inspector off his stride.

'Six months now. Not sure what I did to piss off my boss, but to be honest Scotland's a lot nicer than London these days. Too much division what with the Brexit non-sense. All those politicians flailing about like they've got a clue what they're doing, making life impossible for us poor civil servants. No, your lot seem a lot better organized. Or at least better disciplined. Much more interesting being up here. And that facility you've built over there is something else. You any idea how many foreign law enforcement agencies have sent teams to see what we're doing? It's mental.'

McLean had interviewed enough witnesses to know a man beating around the bush when he saw one. 'There something I should know?' he asked

Featherstonehaugh paused a moment before answering. McLean was fairly sure it was an act, but he was happy enough to indulge the man. It was always better to be on the right side of the NCA. They could make life difficult or they could be extremely helpful, depending on the phase of the moon. The longer he took deciding what to say, the more time McLean had to eat his cake, too.

'It's about Jennifer. Maddy. You're right. She and the young boy were the only survivors of that house fire your

DC Blane uncovered. She wasn't meant to be here in Edinburgh. The last place we had her was a flat in central Manchester about six months ago. Then she went off the radar. Nobody knew where she was until her DNA match popped up on our screens. Caused quite a bit of consternation, I can tell you.'

'Why are you still keeping them hidden? They're both adults now, should be doing their own thing.'

'Witness protection's for life, Tony. You know that.'

'What about the boy? I take it you set him up here, in Edinburgh.'

'About five years ago. He goes by the name Edward Gosford now. Ed. He's got a place in Gorgie, but he's not answering his phone.' Featherstonehaugh pulled a slim piece of paper out of his jacket pocket and handed it over. Two lines of an address, a mobile number. 'You're not supposed to have that. You certainly didn't get it from me.'

'You were quick enough to move in on Jennifer Beasley,' McLean said. 'Why not round up the lad, too?'

'Beasley was protocol. Clean up. I'd love to go and knock on his door, but you wouldn't believe the trouble we'd be in if we did anything more active than observing Ed right now, and he's nowhere to be seen. If he's got wind of what's happening, chances are he's gone to ground, but I can't risk rocking that boat. Just thinking about the paperwork makes me itch.'

'So you want me to do your dirty work for you.'

'Something like that.' Featherstonehaugh shrugged. 'Look, you're local CID. You can go to his place and nobody'll ask any questions. More importantly, there won't be a paper trail that people we don't want finding Ed can follow.'

'They're still out there, then? Still looking for him?'

'You know the sort of people we're dealing with here, Tony. They never give up, and they're very, very patient. There's only two people in the whole of the NCA who know Edward Gosford's real name, and quite frankly I'd like to keep it that way. Makes my life a whole lot easier.'

'You care about him, don't you.'

'Of course I fucking care about him. He's had a shit life so far and deserves a break.' Something in Featherstone-haugh's features changed, as if the DCI were thinking about his own past and not that of some young man in witness protection. 'Look, he didn't do well coming up through the care system. Hardly surprising given what happened to him before. He was two when his mother sold him to those people. Six when we found him and Jennifer.'

McLean made the paper disappear like a skilled magician. 'Poor bastard. I still don't know why you couldn't tell me this before, though. And I think you're forgetting the main reason why I wanted to track Jennifer down. She's dead already, and if she was here looking for her friend, then there's every chance he's dead, too. Except that if it was him, you'd have matched his DNA like you did Jennifer's, right?'

Featherstonehaugh shook his head sadly. 'Wish it was that easy, Tony. There's another thing you should know about Ed. Well, a couple of things, really. The first is that he's what you might call a driven individual. He's spent most of his short adult life tracking down what he considers to be injustice and exposing it to the world.'

'Sounds like we should be recruiting him.'

'Believe me, I've tried. He's not big on being a team player, though. Likes to do things his own way. Can't say as I blame him, after all that's happened to him.'

'So what's the second thing?' McLean asked.

'He's something of a hacktivist, if you're familiar with that term. Breaks into corporate computer networks and exposes all their dirty secrets to the world. As far as I can tell, he's not in it for the money, just some personal moral crusade, but he's very good at it. When the DNA search pinged Jennifer's record, I double-checked Ed's just to be certain it wasn't him.'

'I assume it isn't, otherwise we wouldn't be having this conversation.'

'I don't know if it's him. His record's been tampered with and the entry on the DNA database is missing entirely. He must have hacked the NCA and we didn't even know. I dread to think what other systems he's been in.'

McLean finished his cake, leaned back in his chair and took a long sip of coffee. Too many coincidences were piling one upon another now, but one in particular niggled away at the back of his mind.

'You set him up here five years ago. That'd be when he left school, right?'

Featherstonehaugh cocked his head to one side as he considered the question, then nodded. 'Before my time, but yes.'

'Where was he before that? Who was looking after him?'

'I can't tell you, Tony. You know that.'

McLean drained the last of his coffee, then stood up to

leave. 'It was Helensburgh, though, wasn't it. And he didn't hack the NCA database, you let him in. He just did a little more than you asked him to, am I right?'

He didn't wait for the DCI's answer. Didn't need to. It was written all over the man's face.

58

He'd never really thought highly of Gorgie when he'd been a beat constable, and twenty years on it wasn't much improved. Like most of Edinburgh there were good bits and bad bits, but the difference between them was not as marked here as in some parts of the city. Judging by the cranes and boarded-off building sites, it wasn't immune to the development frenzy that had gripped most of the capital, though.

It took a long time to find a parking space, and McLean couldn't help thinking that maybe spending about a tenth of the money on something like Emma's old pale-blue and rust-brown Peugeot would have made more sense than his Giulia Quadrifoglio. The shiny new Alfa looked as out of place as a tweed suit at Tynecastle.

'Dad's a Hearts fan.' DC Harrison nodded her head in the direction of the football stadium as she closed the passenger door. 'Used to take me to matches on a Saturday afternoon.'

'Don't tell Grumpy Bob. He's a Hibs man through and through.'

'Can't stand football, sir.' Harrison smiled at a joke only she heard. 'Much happier out with my uncle seeing the touring cars at Knockhill.'

'I can see why you and Manda Parsons get on so well.'

A hint of a blush spread across the detective constable's

face, so faint you might not notice it over her normally florid complexion were you not trained in the skill of observation. McLean filed it away as a nugget of unimportant information, then turned on the spot, trying to find the address he'd been given. They crossed the road to an already open tenement door, stepped into a dark hallway that might have been quite pleasant once. Now the paint on the walls was flaking off in great chunks that littered a flagstone floor untroubled by a broom in many years. It smelled like a public toilet, and the afternoon light struggled to lift the gloom. A broken bulb hung from a short flex in the ceiling.

'What exactly are we hoping to find here, sir?'

McLean stood at the bottom of the stairs, looking up to the skylight high overhead. The question wasn't as easy to answer as he might have liked.

'Jennifer Beasley wasn't her real name, right?'

Harrison nodded. 'Aye, Lofty told me. She was given a new identity. New life far away from the people who might still be looking for her.'

'That's more or less right. But her new life wasn't here in Edinburgh. She was set up in Manchester, had a job there, too. The NCA kept a very loose eye on her, which is probably why they didn't notice she'd gone missing. They only found out she'd tipped up here when we ran her DNA through the database. Pinged some automated warning.'

Harrison followed McLean's gaze up the stairwell. There were two landings above them, four tiny bedsit flats. 'You think she came looking for this place?'

'I think she came looking for the young man who lives here. He was the boy who survived the fire. And if what

DCI Featherstonehaugh told me is right, he's the boy who set the fire in the first place, knowing it would kill everyone in the house, himself and Jennifer Beasley, too.'

'It didn't, though, did it. They both survived, otherwise we'd no' be here.'

'Yes, they survived. If ending up in a place like this can be called survival.'

Harrison looked around the dingy hallway. 'And you think he might be the last victim? Wouldn't his DNA be on the NCA files, too?'

McLean started to climb the stairs. 'Funny you should say that. I suggested it to our new friend DCI Featherstonehaugh and he said the file had become corrupted. He also said that the fellow who lives here is something of a genius with computers and hacking. Left me to join up the dots.'

No one answered a knock at either of the two doors on the first landing. McLean carried on up the stairs regardless. He couldn't have said what drew him, some sixth sense, something deeply ingrained by his years of detective work. Maybe it was just his nose that led him to the furthest door from the top of the stairs. Like all the others, there was nothing as sophisticated as a name plate, not even a torn-off strip of paper with a name scrawled on it in biro and fixed to the rough wooden door with sticky tape. He reached for the handle, then paused, dug a pair of latex gloves out of his pocket and pulled them on. Only then did he reach once more and twist the handle. The latch clicked, and the unlocked door swung open on to darkness.

'Anyone home?'

Silence greeted them, oozing out of the flat like warm

tar. The air was stale, as if no one had breathed it in many a day. McLean stepped through the tiny hall reminiscent of so many Edinburgh tenement flats. Doors led to a tiny kitchen, tinier shower room, bedroom and surprisingly spacious living room. The decor could perhaps best be described as 'previous owner', but at least it was tidy.

'Smells like some of the student flats I used to visit. You know, the ones where there's only boys?'

McLean didn't. He'd bought his place in Newington after one term in halls of residence, lived there on his own until someone had introduced him to Phil. Even with the two of them it was still more than big enough. He knew what Harrison meant though.

'I was thinking more Grumpy Bob's place in Sciennes, but maybe a bit tidier.' He stepped into the narrow galley kitchen, its rotten sash window looking out at a scrubby communal garden to the back of the block. The sink was empty, a single washed mug and plate on the drainer, cutlery in a little metal pot with holes in it. When he ran a finger under the tap, it came back dry. No one had been here in a while.

The bedroom told much the same tale. It was clear a man lived here alone, the pile of dirty clothes heaped in one corner gave that much away. Otherwise it was nondescript, a place for sleeping, and not often at that. The living room was clearly where Edward Gosford spent most of his time.

An ancient television sat in one corner, opposite a sofa that looked like it had been rescued from a skip at least twice, and squat coffee table strewn with books and magazines. Set up at the opposite end of the room to the window, a wide table had been pressed into use as a desk. Two blank screens towered over a jumble of keyboards, trackpads, books and jotter pads. Screwed to the wall beside the desk, a whiteboard bore many layers of scribbled notes, a few receipts and the menus for some local takeaways attached to the bottom of it with colourful magnets.

'Looks like someone had a bit of an accident, sir.'

McLean turned around to see Harrison crouched down beside the sofa. She pointed a finger to where a cafetière lay smashed on the floor. Coffee grounds piled on the carpet, surrounded by a dull brown stain. A mug on the table was empty, its inside clean if a little stained, and when he bent down and rubbed at the floor his glove came away still white.

'Happened long enough ago for it all to dry out. Doesn't look like anyone's been here in a while.'

'A week perhaps?' Harrison didn't have to add what had happened that long ago.

'Maybe.' McLean put the mug back down on the table, glanced at the books. Mostly technical titles for programming languages he'd never heard of. A small stack of computer magazines had been placed to one side, a slim smartphone tucked under the top cover. Not the sort of thing a person would leave behind when heading out, surely?

'Don't suppose this has got any charge in it if it's been sitting here a week.' He pressed the button on the front and was surprised when the phone beeped, lit up. The battery icon was almost completely empty, but what shook him more was the image on the lock screen. Two people standing in front of a brand-new truck, smiling as they held up an industry award of some kind. The phone squawked, then the screen blanked out as it died, but not before McLean recognized one of the people in it.

'This is Mike Finlay's phone.' He held it up for Harrison to see, only then noticing that she had crossed over to the desk. The light from the two screens washed over her face as she tapped at the keyboard with one gloved finger.

'How was it we came by this address, sir?' She swivelled one of the screens around for McLean to see. It took a moment for him to step closer, longer still to start making sense of the multiple windows stacked on top of each other.

'Someone's been busy.'

Harrison leaned forward, tried a couple of the mice lurking in the detritus on the desk top, then found a track-pad. She tapped a couple of times, minimizing some of the windows, bringing up others, eyes flicking this way and that far more swiftly than McLean could keep up with. 'There's stuff here Lofty really needs to see. Financials, contracts, emails. Oh my.'

'What is it?'

Harrison had brought up an email programme, selected one message in particular and maximized it on the screen to make it easier to see. McLean noticed the name in the 'from' header, Jennifer Beasley. The message itself was short.

Dan. It's me, Maddy! Can't believe I've found you. Been searching for years. We need to meet up. Compare notes. Bring it all out into the open. They've hidden us too long. People need to know!

'Is there a reply?' McLean asked.

'Just a moment.' Harrison closed the window, the cursor arrow darting about the screen before she found what she was looking for. 'Here we go.'

McLean read quickly. The email was from an Edward Gosford, the same name that Featherstonehaugh had given him.

> Maddy? For real? Jesus. I've been Ed for so long I'd almost forgotten Dan. Yeah, we should meet up. Lots to talk about. Christ, how long has it been?

'There's a whole conversation. Looks like it's been going on for a couple of weeks. The last one's here.' Harrison tapped again, a final message from Beasley.

> The old Picture House sounds good. Coffee and cake at ten. I'll wear a red scarf so you recognize me. So much to tell you. It's so exciting! Maddy.

'That's the day before the crash. Picture House would be the old Caley Picture House. It's right by that bus stop. Ten o'clock, have them heading there half an hour or so beforehand. Poor bastards.' McLean stared at the screen without really seeing it, the whole tragic story now unfolding in his mind. And then something occurred to him.

'Those other files you had up a moment ago. The research ones. Are they dated?' He held up the mobile phone, clicked the button on the top in the hope of squeezing just a few seconds of life out of it, but the screen stayed blank this time. Harrison tapped at the trackpad, reopening the windows that she had closed.

'Some of it's old stuff, sir. But this file's only been

created in the last day or so. Why do you ask?' She pointed at a document that would be of great interest to the Organised Crime team. Clearly Edward Gosford was very good with computers.

'Because it's after the crash. If this is Finlay's phone, then Ed or Dan or whatever his name is can't be dead. He was there, though, probably saw what happened and decided to find out who was to blame. He's been one step ahead of us all the way.' And now McLean remembered the young man, eyes wide with shock. But that didn't work. That was the face re-created from the skull.

'There was a Daniel Penston in Jennifer's notebook. You think that's him?' Harrison's question distracted McLean from his train of thought.

'Could be. Chances of Featherstonehaugh admitting it are small, though. Why?'

'Because if it is him, I think I know where he might have gone.' Harrison scrolled down the document, pointed at the last few lines. McLean read them swiftly and as he did so the last pieces of the puzzle started to fall uncomfortably into place.

59

The leafy back streets of the New Town were home to much of Edinburgh's old money. Vast terraced town houses, suited more to Victorian living than the needs of modern life, many had in the past been converted into flats or offices. Now that process was being reversed, but some corners had never changed in the first place. Unexpected closes and squares centred on private gardens, the massive trees an indication of how long it had been since this modern city had been planned. Alan Lewis's money wasn't old. He had forged it out of the new financial regime that grew after the deregulation of the banks in the 1980s. Nevertheless, he had found himself an ancient lair in which to hide, taken on the trappings of the gentry despite his humbler roots.

'That's his car there, sir. Thought I recognized the number.' DC Harrison pointed to a shiny black Bentley, its windows almost as dark as its muscled flanks. The number plate wasn't personalized, no awkwardly misspelled version of his name or reference to his company. It merely showed that, like McLean's new Alfa, it was only a few months old.

'Not sure if that's a good sign or bad.' McLean peered in through the windscreen, past the resident's permit, to the black-leather interior. Nothing lay on the passenger seat or in the footwell, but then he'd not really expected anything. Looking up from the car, he saw the four-storey bulk of Lewis's town house looming over them both. If its windows were eyes, then they were sightless and old, the stonework around them blackened by soot from fires last lit half a century ago. Stone steps led up to a shiny black-painted door, and something about the way the light played on it struck McLean as wrong.

'You tried his phone, aye?' He crossed the pavement, climbed the steps, Harrison close behind him.

'Three or four times, sir. Mobile and landline. They both just kept going to voicemail.'

McLean pressed lightly on the glossy wood, and the door swung slowly inwards. Not just unlocked, but unlatched as well. He knew that Edinburgh wasn't a bad city for burglaries, but leaving your front door open wasn't something most people did.

'Get on to Control. I think we might need a squad car over. Maybe more than one. See if you can't get a message to DCI Featherstonehaugh, too.' He dug out a pair of latex gloves and snapped them on. Then pushed the door all the way while Harrison made the call.

It opened on to a small porch, glazed double doors leading to a larger hall beyond. For a moment he wondered whether Lewis was simply in the habit of leaving the front porch accessible for any delivery drivers, but then he noticed the double doors had been left just slightly ajar, too. It was an odd way to leave them, as if whoever had passed through was only paper thin. Or the wind had caught them after they hadn't been closed properly.

'They're on their way, sir. ETA five minutes. We going to wait?'

McLean frowned at her. 'What do you think?' He didn't wait for an answer, but pushed open one of the glass doors and stepped into the hallway. It hadn't been all that noisy outside, just the hum of the city as background, the occasional distant wail of a siren. Now the silence was almost total, underlined by the slow tick tock tick tock of an old grandfather clock standing between two closed doorways. Wide stairs of dark wood climbed towards a halfway landing at the back of the house, light filtering through an impressive stained glass window.

'Hello? Anyone home? Mr Lewis?' McLean walked across the hall, opened the first of the doors on to a well-appointed drawing room. The air had a stale quality to it that suggested people didn't go in there very often, and when he ran his gloved finger over the surface of a nearby occasional table, it came up in a fine smear of dust.

'Phone's over here.' McLean looked back out to the hall and saw Harrison pointing at a modern handset on an antique sideboard. She had pulled on gloves, too, he noticed. 'Looks like there's just the one message. That'll be me, most likely.'

'Leave it for now. Let's just check all the rooms. Touch as little as you can, aye?'

Harrison nodded her understanding, moving off towards the back of the house. McLean checked the opposite side of the hall, an empty dining room as unused as its twin on the other side. He found more signs of life in Lewis's study, but still not the man himself. Bookshelves lining the walls were filled mostly with dry economics and finance texts, a few biographies and a sizeable collection of Mills and Boon romances, all well thumbed. Well, there was no accounting for taste. He was leafing through the third in a row, surprised to find that they had all been signed by the authors, when a distant voice reminded him of why he was there.

'You'll want to see this, sir.'

He replaced the book, went back to the hall, trying to work out where Harrison had gone.

'Up here. The bathroom.'

McLean followed the voice and found the detective constable waiting for him on the first landing. More stairs led to higher floors, but she indicated for him to follow her through an open door. Lewis's bedroom lay beyond, set to the front of the house and overlooking the private gardens shared by the other addresses in the close. Beyond the massive bed, another open door led to an en suite bathroom.

'He's in the bath.'

The flatness of Harrison's tone was a warning, but it still couldn't prepare McLean for what he saw. Alan Lewis lay in the bath, the clear water making his body look bloated and distorted. There was no mistaking the fact that he was dead. One arm covered his modesty, for all that it was worth. The other dangled over the side, pointing to the marble floor. A small puddle of drips had accumulated beneath his fingers. All of these things McLean noticed as he tried hard not to focus on Lewis's face.

The dead man stared at nothing, a point in the middle distance that might have been where the ceiling met the corner of the far walls, or might have been head height to a short man standing over him as he lay in his bath. His lips were curled back to reveal yellowing teeth, a swollen tongue. But it was the terror in his eyes that McLean would find hard to forget. A look all the more horrifying for being almost identical to one he had seen just two days before.

The same sheer terror as that on James Barnton's face.

'I guess that's why he wasn't answering his phone,' Harrison said, her voice a little squeaky. McLean dragged his gaze away from the dead man, looked over to where she was standing in the bathroom doorway. He couldn't remember ever having seen her face so pale.

'Go downstairs. Wait for the squad car to arrive and let them know what we've found.' He reached out, touched her gently on the arm and steered her away from the horrific sight. Contact brought her back to herself, a little colour flushing her cheeks.

'Sorry, sir. Bit of a shock, right enough.'

'That'll be the understatement of the year.' McLean turned back to the corpse in the bath. 'Better get on to Control again. We'll need the duty doctor and the pathologist. All the usual stuff.'

'You think this is suspicious? He didn't just have a heart attack or something?'

'Front door open? And we've been trying to get a hold of him all day?' McLean shook his head. 'No. I'm sure he was under a lot of pressure, but I don't think Mr Lewis died of natural causes. Angus can be the judge of that though, but only once you've spoken to Control.'

Harrison took the hint and hurried away. McLean was tempted to go after her, not wanting to spend any more time with the dead man than was strictly necessary. He'd seen death plenty of times before. Too many times, some would say. After a while, it became easier to deal with the aftermath. A dead body was just an empty vessel, a series of clues that might help determine how the end had come. The sudden, senseless violence visited upon the crash victims had been horrific, but only in a slasher movie, slaughterhouse manner. It was terrible, but all too easy to explain what had happened to them and so he had been able to compartmentalize their deaths, let his subconscious deal with them over the course of a few bad dreams, and move on.

This was different in the same way that James Barnton's death had been different. Both had left bodies largely undamaged, the only clues their expressions of utter, abject terror. To look at Alan Lewis's face was to see raw, primal fear.

'What the hell spooked you?'

McLean spoke the words aloud as much to centre himself as anything. He needed a clear head here, a detective's head. He crouched down, looking around the bathroom for clues that there might have been someone else in here when Lewis had died. The bath was cast iron, with a roll top and one of those wonderful column plugs he remembered from his childhood. Dust bunnies had collected underneath, away from the cleaner's reach, but apart from the puddle of water beneath Lewis's fingers there was nothing untoward in the room. Except there was something that was bothering him. Something he couldn't quite put his finger on.

McLean reached out, turned the back of his hand to the

side of the bath, and that was when it clicked. The water was still warm. Hot, even. Knowing he'd get a ticking off from Angus, McLean reached out and gently turned the dead man's hand. The flesh on the tips of his fingers had barely begun to pucker. He hadn't been in the bath long at all. Had only died very recently.

McLean thought he saw a flicker of movement in the corner of his eye. Turning a little too swiftly, his head reeled as the blood drained out of it. For a moment he saw a shadow on the wall, the silhouette of a person running from the room.

And then DC Harrison screamed.

60

McLean stood up too quickly, catching the side of his head on the roll top lip of the bath. Reeling at the impact, he staggered into the bedroom, unsure how it had suddenly become so dark in there. Sunlight speared through narrow slits in shutters he hadn't noticed were closed before, casting more shadow than light. One ray splayed across the bed, the crumpled form of DC Harrison laid out on the mattress. He stumbled over, vision still starred from the blow to the head.

'Harrison? Janie?' He reached a hand out to shake her shoulder, but she didn't respond. Face down, unmoving, he couldn't see if she was even breathing. Nor could he see any reason why she should be this way.

'Come on, Constable. No time for kipping.' He rolled her over and almost screamed himself at the look on her face. It mirrored that of Alan Lewis in the bath, of James Barnton, propped up against a headstone in Dalry Cemetery. Hardly daring, he reached for the exposed skin of her neck, just below her jaw, trembling fingers feeling for a pulse that wasn't there.

Something clicked in his brain, and the training kicked in. He loosened her collar, checked her airway was clear and started CPR. Backup was on its way, wasn't it? Did he have time to stop and call Control? What the fuck happened to her?

It felt like hours, but was probably less than a minute before the detective constable started to respond. A gentle finger to her neck again revealed an erratic, weak pulse, and her eyes began to flicker beneath closed lids. Sitting upright on the bed, McLean breathed a sigh of relief, only then feeling a tinge of embarrassment burn the tips of his ears as the unusual intimacy of the situation dawned on him.

'Don't try to move. Help's on its way.' He wasn't even sure if she heard him, but at least he could see she was breathing now. He slid off the bed, still a little disoriented himself, reached up to the side of his head and felt the start of a nice, sore lump forming there.

'I didn't mean to hurt her. Honest.'

Startled by the voice, McLean spun round in search of who had spoken. His head throbbed painfully, stars dimming his vision as something moved in the deep shadows. A figure shuffled towards him, vaguely man-shaped but oddly distorted, and as the light played across it, McLean saw a creature from his worst nightmares. Skin bubbled and burned from a face locked in a permanent scream, arms bent at impossible angles, broken white bone poking from gaping wounds. A stench of chemicals and ordure filled the room, choking him and forcing tears from his eyes. He took an involuntary step back as the creature emerged more fully into the light, something that might have been a hand reaching out for him.

'All I did was touch her.'

McLean took another step back, almost overwhelmed by the horror, the stench and the sheer impossibility of what he was seeing. His leg hit the side of the bed, DC

Harrison still sprawled out behind him, forcing him to stop as the apparition came ever closer. He could hear its breathing now, a choking, bubbling sound like a man drowning in a bath of acid effluent.

'What are you?' The words croaked out of McLean's throat, but the act of speaking them cleared his head a little. It also made the apparition pause, cock its head to one side like an inquisitive dog. There were features in that broken, bloody mess, and by some strange trick of the light they began to emerge more clearly with each startled blink.

'Edward?'

The grotesque shook its head, becoming less horrific with each passing moment, more like the face McLean had seen on the computer screen in the city mortuary. More like the young man clutching the red scarf at the crash scene, lost and bewildered.

'Dan?'

The young man stopped completely now, just an arm's reach away. McLean couldn't see anything clearly, his head fuzzy. How hard had he hit it?

'How do you know my name?'

'You were there, at the crash. I saw you, remember?' McLean reached out to touch the apparition, then remembered Harrison's scream, Lewis's face. 'You went to meet Maddy.'

'How could you possibly know that?' The young man spoke with a soft, quiet voice, his accent hard to place beyond English. McLean's head ached with the stench of chemicals and the dull thudding of the lump forming on his skull.

'We've been to your flat, Dan. Seen your computer. You had Mike Finlay's phone, so you must have been there when he died. James Barnton, too.'

'I never meant to hurt them. Sure they deserved it, but I didn't . . . I just . . .' The young man pawed at his face as if trying to claw the skin from his cheeks, and as his agitation rose, so the room darkened and the chemical reek grew ever stronger. McLean could scarcely breathe, let alone think straight. How had he come to be here? How could any of this make sense? Maybe it didn't. Maybe that was the whole point. This was where logic fell apart and Madame Rose's world of waifs and spirits, unnamed ghosts and gathering darkness finally had its place.

'You didn't kill them, Dan. You couldn't have killed them. You died in the crash, with Maddy at your side.'

Silence settled over the room like the haar rolling in off the North Sea. The young man stood as motionless and limp as a hanged corpse, head dropped and arms by his side. Then slowly, he raised his gaze to meet McLean's, a dark fire in his eyes, and screamed like a banshee. A crushing weight fell upon McLean, as if the air had grown too heavy on his shoulders. It gripped him tight, squeezing the breath from his lungs, wrapping his head in a vice. His vision blurred as his eyes began to pop. Slowly, he sank to his knees under the pressure, feeling his ribs crack with the strain.

And then as soon as it came, the weight was gone. McLean looked up, gasping for air, to see the man who had been Daniel Penston fade away to nothing, his scream drifting off into a wail of despair, echoing to the depths of McLean's soul.

*

The mournful wail in his ears drifted away, morphing into the sound of approaching sirens. McLean shook his head, wincing as a stab of pain lanced through his brain. Light oozed back into the room like brackish water, the shadows banished to the far corners. Beside him, DC Harrison let out a low moan as she began to stir, and through the door in the bathroom, Alan Lewis was still dead in his bath. Of Edward Gosford – Daniel Penston – there was no sign, but then why would there be? He'd died in the truck crash on the far side of the city over a week ago. There was no way he could have been here, in this room. No way he could have been anywhere near Extech Energy when James Barnton had died, or in the portable-cabin offices of Finlay McGregor, scaring Mike Finlay so badly he tripped over his own feet and speared himself on a lethal shard of broken glass. No way he could have hacked into the corporate network of Alan Lewis's financial empire and revealed all its nasty secrets.

'Inspector? Constable? Anyone?' A voice drifted up from below, filtering through McLean's thoughts and dragging him back to the present. The situation was almost hopeless. How could they explain Lewis's death, let alone Harrison semi-conscious on the bed. Bad enough the gossip among the junior officers when that little story got out; worse still if someone thought she might be medically unfit for active duty. He'd seen one young detective constable go that way. There was no way he was going to let it happen to a second.

But how to persuade whoever was calling from the hallway downstairs that this wasn't what it looked like? McLean scanned the room, searching for something, anything that might possibly explain what had happened here. Time to improvise.

Checking his latex gloves were still intact, he hurried around the bed, grabbing the bedside light off the stand. Its flex was just about long enough to reach. He tugged hard, easing the wire under the bathroom door. Lewis still lay there dead, head fixed in that rictus grin of horror. Suicide or murder, would anyone care? He lifted up the dead hand, still unpleasantly warm from the bathwater, wrapped it around the base of the lamp. So the prints would be distorted, if they took at all. There wasn't much else he could do.

'Sorry about this. But then again, you brought it on yourself.'

He dropped the lamp into the bathwater, pleased to hear a slight spark as it shorted out. Back in the bedroom, he hurried over to Harrison, who was struggling to sit upright, her head clutched in her hands.

'What the fu—, . . . hell just happened?' She looked up at him, squinting against a pain he could easily imagine.

'You stumbled. Cracked your head on the bedpost, remember?'

'No . . . I . . . There was a young man. I . . . He –'

'You stumbled coming out of the bathroom, cracked your head on the bedpost. Remember.' McLean said it more forcefully now, and something must have sunk in. Harrison nodded, just once, wincing as pain shot through her head again. He put a hand on her shoulder. 'You'll be fine. Just let me do the talking, OK?'

Harrison opened her mouth to say something, but then

426

Detective Constable Stringer burst through the door, closely followed by DCI McIntyre. Her gaze flitted from the bed to McLean, to Harrison and then back to McLean.

'Jesus Christ, Tony. What the fuck happened here?'

61

I'm dead.

You'd think a person would know something like that when it happened, but apparently not.

Things make sense now. Well, sort of sense. The past week going by in a blur, the accident that wasn't really an accident, the people going crazy whenever they saw me. How they screamed and died.

Because I'm dead.

I watch them from the shadows, white-suited forensics technicians like you see on the telly. There's plenty of them, traipsing across the bedroom and into the bathroom where Alan Lewis lies. He's dead, too, nothing more than meat going soggy in the warm water. There's nothing left of him here, so why am I still around?

Everything changed when he said my name, the man in the tweed suit. Nobody was supposed to know that. And yet somehow he did. Was that what kept me here? The fact I was unnamed? But I wasn't the only one without a name.

Maddy. I remember now. She found me, never gave up looking. I'd given up. I'd lost all hope of ever finding her, ever having a life. But she found me.

And then we died. And it was all my fault.

Somehow I'm downstairs now, watching the technicians come and go. The detective's there, looking a bit shaken up. I guess meeting a dead person might have that effect on you. It didn't go well for that security guard, after all. Not for the fat man in the bath either. I'm just glad he was there to save the young constable. She didn't deserve that.

The detective rubs at his face, says something to the older woman standing in front of him, and then looks over in my direction. No one else can see me; I'm dead, after all. And yet somehow he can.

'Dan?'

The voice is distant, quiet. It doesn't come from any of the people milling about this hall. I look around, see the shadows begin to wash away, the walls dissolve into whiteness.

'Dan? Are you there?'

It's an adult voice, laden with years of hardship, but I can hear the child still in it. All around me is nothing, as if I am falling through warm clouds, weightless, not a care in the world.

'Maddy?'

I'm spiralling down into the light, and now she is with me, in front of me, arms held wide. I've not seen her in fifteen years or more, but she's exactly how I imagined she would be. Pale blonde hair wafting in an unfelt breeze, and a long red scarf wrapped around her neck.

She smiles, and nothing else matters any more.

62

His head still hurt, a small lump towards the back of his skull that throbbed in time to his heartbeat. McLean wanted nothing more than to go home, collapse on the sofa and treat his injuries with fine malt whisky. That didn't look like it was going to happen any time soon.

'You say you just found him there, in the bath, dead?' DCI McIntyre stood in the main hall of Alan Lewis's house as an army of forensic technicians trooped through and up the stairs. They wouldn't find anything, but the financier was rich enough and important enough for them to have to look.

'Door was open when we got here. Looks like he killed himself.' McLean winced slightly as he nodded his head in its direction. He was sitting on an elegant antique chaise longue, waiting to be dismissed from the scene.

'Why did you even come here? I thought we'd handed all of this over to the Organised Crime team.'

'So did I, but I don't see them anywhere yet.' McLean tried to stretch the knots out of his neck, but movement just made the ache in his head worse. Keeping still was hard, though. He wanted to get up, get out of this place. Soon enough the paramedics would bring the body down and he'd rather not be here when that happened. Sitting beside him, DC Harrison stared blankly across the room. She should probably have gone to hospital, but McIntyre wasn't letting her go anywhere just yet. At least she was still alive.

'What did you expect? You only raided Extech, what . . .' McIntyre checked her watch, '. . . just over twelve hours ago. They've hardly had time to read the background reports.'

'Lewis was behind it all, Jayne. He financed Finlay McGregor, put up all the money for Extech's biodigester site. He even owns a majority share of LindSea Farm Estates. He's been cleaning money for everyone from Colombian drug cartels to the Russian mafia. Probably a few Tory politicians, too.'

'So what the hell's he doing dead in his bath, then?'

McLean shrugged. 'Everything was about to blow up in his face. He might be rich, but there's no way he was going to buy his way out of jail on this one. Probably thought ending it all was preferable.'

McIntyre looked unconvinced. 'How is it you know all this? And don't try to tell me Lofty Blane uncovered it. He's good, but not that good.'

McLean leaned back until his head rested against the wood panelling of the wall, ignoring the stab of pain from the bruised lump. Daniel Penston's computer, with all its hacked information, was still in his flat in Gorgie, along with Mike Finlay's mobile phone. Hopefully by now DCI Featherstonehaugh was there, too, making sure neither item mysteriously disappeared. But how could anyone explain either of them when the young man who lived there had died in the truck crash?

'It's . . . complicated. Do we have to go into it now?'

A commotion at the top of the stairs interrupted

McIntyre's response, a stumbling and gentle swearing as two paramedics manoeuvred a stretcher with a bodybag strapped to it down the slippery polished wood steps. For a moment, he thought they were going to drop it, and he had visions of the bodybag bursting open, Lewis's wet, naked form sliding out like a newborn infant. The paramedics recovered their balance, though, and soon enough they had placed the stretcher onto a trolley and were wheeling it out the front door.

By the time it had gone, a slower, more measured tread creaked the stairs on its way down. McLean looked around to see his old friend Angus Cadwallader approaching, his assistant, Doctor Sharp, just a couple of paces behind as she struggled with his heavy bag.

'I can think of worse places to die than in a warm bath in my own home.' Cadwallader tried a smile. 'Evening, Jayne.'

'Angus.' McIntyre nodded her hello. Beside him on the couch, McLean could see Harrison fidgeting nervously. It was fair enough; he didn't really want to be here either.

'So you reckon it really was suicide, then?'

Cadwallader inclined his head slightly. 'You never miss a thing, do you, Tony. Aye, suicide looks most likely. We'll know once I've had a closer look at him back at the mortuary, but that won't be until the morning.'

McLean hadn't realized how tense he was, but at the pathologist's words the pent-up tension dropped away. There would still be questions to answer, forms to fill in, decisions to justify. Lewis's financial empire would surely unravel, and there would be revelations to come, but none of that mattered to him. Let the Organised Crime experts deal with that; his job here was done.

A movement in the shadows, right in the corner of his eye, dragged McLean's attention to the dark corner where the stairs turned and crossed the passageway that led to the back of the house. For a single eye-blink he thought he saw Daniel Penston standing there, watching.

Another blink, and he was gone.

The light was fading by the time McLean dropped DC Harrison off at the front door to the tenement flat she shared with Amanda Parsons. They had said very little on the journey across town, each occupied with their thoughts about the events that had unfolded in Lewis's house. Either that or she was just as dog-tired as he was and had no energy left for conversation.

'No need for an early start tomorrow. Sandy Gregg will be co-ordinating the handover to Organised Crime, so you'll not be needed for anything. Get some rest. You've earned it.'

Harrison smiled, nodded her understanding. 'Might want to think about taking your own advice, sir.' She closed the car door on him before he could answer. Cheeky, perhaps, but the truth in her words stung. He checked his mirror, indicated and pulled out into the traffic. Time to go home and face Emma's justified wrath.

It wasn't that he had been consciously avoiding her, but the analytical part of his brain could see the patterns all too well. The conversations that never happened, the bad dreams that left him weary all day, the way he convinced himself that letting her sleep late in the mornings was a good thing, these were all signs. How must she feel, all alone in that great old mansion? What must it be like to go to bed before him, wake to find him already up and gone? He had to try harder, be a better person. It wasn't just him on his own any more. They were a couple, and soon they would be a family.

The kitchen light blazed out on to the gravel driveway as he pressed the annoying little button that operated the handbrake, killed the engine and stepped out into the warm summer evening. The first thing he noticed was the quiet, as if someone had placed a bubble over the house and garden. The second thing he noticed was the eyes, staring out at him from the bushes. The cats were back, and whereas before that had given him a feeling of security, now it hurried him inside in unaccountable fear.

Stepping into the kitchen only made the fear worse. A chair lay on its back on the floor, a spilled mug of tea splayed across the rough wooden surface of the table.

'Emma?'

McLean moved swiftly to the far door, then stopped in horror. A single handprint marked the painted surface in something dark and red. What he had taken to be tea spilled from the mug on the table took on a more sinister tone as he saw drops spreading on the floor, their spatters marking a path from table to doorway and on up the corridor.

'Emma!'

More forceful now, his voice sounded strange in the silence, the pounding blood in his ears the only response. McLean fought the urge to rush forward, years of training overriding the protective instinct. Instead he pulled out his phone, thumbed at the screen as he followed the blood trail towards the hall.

Mrs McCutcheon's cat lay on her side at the bottom of

the stairs, and for a moment McLean thought she might have been attacked, that the blood might have been hers. But she stirred at his movement, sprang to her feet in a surprisingly lithe motion. Then she arched her back, tail straight up and twice as thick as it normally appeared. The hiss wasn't directed at him, he could tell that much, but it was terrifying all the same.

'Detective Inspector McLean. I need a squad car and an ambulance to my location. Now.' McLean gave his address to the surprised man in the control centre as he climbed up the steps. More blood slicked the dark wood, what looked like lumps of flesh speckling the surface here and there. He shoved the phone back in his pocket and took the last few steps two at a time.

'Emma!' It was a shout now, the trail leading him not to their shared bedroom but the nursery. Another bloody handprint smeared the freshly painted door, more blood and gore leading across the room to the bathroom beyond. A mobile phone lay on the carpet beside the cot that had only just recently arrived, smears across its screen and dulling the chrome surround. McLean rushed to the bathroom, pushed the door fully open, his mind whirling with fear and horrible certainty.

Emma sat in the bath, knees up, arms clutching them to her chest. There was blood everywhere, and for a moment he thought she was dead, hacked to pieces by some crazed axeman. But she stirred as he rushed towards her, looked up at him with tear-filled eyes.

'You didn't come home.' Her voice was like a little child's, weak and faint. 'I tried to call, but the pain . . . And then . . .'

McLean knelt down beside the bath, ignoring the wetness that soaked through the knees of his trousers. He reached out and put an arm around her, felt her cold and shivering body. A trail of blood and bits tracked down to the plughole, stained her legs and bare feet.

'It's OK,' he said as she sobbed into his shoulder. 'It's all going to be fine.'

But he knew deep down that it wasn't. It would never be fine again.

63

'I'm so sorry, Mr McLean. Late miscarriage is rare, but not unheard of. Especially in first-time mothers who are . . . older.'

McLean barely heard the words. He stared across the ward to where Emma lay asleep. Surrounded by the white sheets and pillows, her pale features looked somehow deathly, even though he knew that she was alive and not in any serious danger. The same couldn't be said for their daughter, or what might have become their daughter had she been given the chance. The ambulance had arrived swiftly, along with a squad car and two constables, but it had always been too late. Even if he had been home when it had started to happen it would have been too late.

'We'll keep her in overnight for observation, but apart from the shock she'll be fine.'

Something in the nurse's words finally got through to him. He didn't know her, didn't seem to know any of the busy hospital staff, but she had a kind face and a soft voice. From the Western Isles, if he was any judge.

'I should have been there.'

A momentary flicker of confusion ran across the nurse's face. 'But you were there. You called the ambulance.'

'Earlier. When it started.' McLean shook his head, knowing he was being stupid and yet somehow unable to stop himself. 'I just should have been there with her.'

The nurse laid a gentle hand on his arm. 'You can stay as long as you like. I know visiting hours are over, but, well, they tell me you're a policeman. Come here more often than most.'

McLean wondered who 'they' were and what else they said about him. 'It's OK. I'd better head home. I'll be back first thing to pick her up, OK?'

The nurse nodded, then hurried off to deal with some other emergency. McLean had been fully intending to stand up, go out to the car park and drive home, but instead he just sat and stared into the distance. He couldn't process anything at all. Not the events that had unfolded since they had raided Extech Energy that morning, not the revelations about Jennifer Beasley and Edward Gosford, Maddy and Dan as he should probably call them. His mind refused to even go near what he had seen in Alan Lewis's house, and the full enormity of what had happened to Emma hovered over him like a thunderstorm waiting to break.

So wrapped up in not thinking, he hardly noticed as someone sat down next to him. Or perhaps it was his subconscious reassuring him it was a friend, knowing by the bulk and the curious scent of rosewater and mothballs that he had no need to respond.

'I'm so, so sorry, Tony.'

Madame Rose's words finally penetrated his fugue state. McLean blinked dry eyes, then looked around to see the transvestite medium sitting alongside him. Despite the hour she was as well turned out as ever, makeup meticulously applied, hair coiffured to within an inch of its life. Her face betrayed her, though, etched with sadness, eyes shiny.

'It's not your fault. Could have happened to anyone.' The words came out automatically. He wasn't even sure what they meant.

'But it happened to you, and to Emma. How is she?' Madame Rose reached out and enveloped his hand in hers, patted it once then withdrew. The contact brought McLean back to himself.

'Physically, she's fine. Lost a lot of blood, but they've put her on a drip, keeping her in overnight.' McLean ran his other hand through his hair, feeling the grit and sweat of a long day between his fingers. 'Mentally? I really don't know.'

Madame Rose stood up, groaning in that quiet way old people do. She faced him, so close that looking up at her all McLean could see was a halo of fluorescent ceiling light around her head.

'Emma's a survivor. You should know that by now, Tony. My concern is more for the child she carried.'

McLean opened his mouth to reply, but for a while couldn't find the words to say. He was too tired to take it all in, and Madame Rose's strangeness wasn't helping.

'The child is dead, Rose. What did you think happened here? A premature birth? This was a miscarriage, probably brought on by exposure to too many toxic chemicals or something like that. Christ knows, the two of us have been in contact with enough of the stuff this past week.' McLean's voice cracked as he spoke, the full horror flooding into his mind, threatening to overwhelm him. He buried his face in his hands as much to hide the tears as anything, tried to hold back the sobs that wanted to break through. A hand on his shoulder steadied him.

439

'Go home, Tony. There's nothing to be gained from you staying here. Go and get some rest.'

McLean nodded once, although he couldn't meet Madame Rose's gaze. He struggled to his feet with almost as much difficulty as the old medium.

'We'll speak more of this later,' Rose said, and he felt like he was being dismissed from a verbal disciplining by his old housemaster. A little boy, he turned and limped up the corridor towards the hospital entrance. And all the while he couldn't decide whether it was the sadness that was crushing him, or relief.

The tiredness that had disappeared when he had first found Emma in the bath returned now with a vengeance. It was past midnight; he'd been up since before five the morning before and he couldn't quite remember when last he'd eaten anything. Had there been cake? If so, it was long gone. He had followed the ambulance to the hospital in his Alfa, buzzing with adrenaline. Now the thought of driving back across town filled him with weary dread. Leaving it in the hospital car park wasn't exactly an option, though.

How he made it home without crashing, McLean couldn't be sure. He'd get a bollocking if anyone ever found out he'd driven in that state, but he was frankly too tired to care. The crunch of the gravel under his wheels as he turned up the drive woke him from a stupor far too close to actually sleeping at the wheel.

The constables who had arrived at the same time as the ambulance were long gone now, just Mrs McCutcheon's cat waiting for him in the kitchen, her greeting no more than a muted chirrup and a brush of her head against his hand. In the rush to get to the hospital, nobody had bothered to pick up the chair or right the overturned mug. He could see how the events had played out now. Emma in her dressing gown, having a cup of tea while she waited for him to come home. Whatever triggered the miscarriage it must have come on fast. She'd knocked over her mug and the chair, hurried to the bathroom. Why she'd gone to the nursery he didn't know. Perhaps he'd ask her some day. Right now he didn't know how he was ever going to speak to her again.

He wanted to sleep, wanted to sit in the corner and cry, wanted everything to be the way it had been before . . . when? McLean felt the tears blur his vision, felt the lump in his throat. Fought them both back.

In the laundry, he found a bucket and a mop. Filled the one with warm soapy water and carried them both back to the hall. Starting there was as good a place as any. He dunked the mop in the water, squeezed it out until it was almost dry.

Then he set about the task of cleaning the blood from the floor.

Acknowledgements

It's my name on the cover, and my words you've just read, but a whole team of people are involved in getting those words into the best order possible and presenting them to you in book form. If I try to name everyone, I'll undoubtedly forget (and thus insult) someone. I owe a debt of gratitude to everyone who's had anything to do with this book, from my first commissioning editor, all the way through to the legions of booksellers hand-selling my books in shops across the country and on to you readers, without whom I'd have to raise cattle for a living.

I am especially grateful to all the team at Michael Joseph. This is our thirteenth book together and each one has been a joy. A big shout-out to Joel Richardson for his wise editorial input (and breakfast), to Beatrix McIntyre and Mark Handsley for making sure my more idiotic continuity errors and typos never made it to the final product. Thanks too to Laura Nicol, Beth Cockeram and all the other people who have worked to make these books a great success. I'd name you all, but the list is so long.

Huge thanks to Kenneth Stephen. It's been five years since you first got me on the telly, Kenny, and still you manage to interest the media in my antics. Long may that continue!

A special thank you to the crime writing community. I may be a Fantasy hack at heart, but you all welcomed me in with open arms. Those at the scene of the crime are a special bunch. A nicer bunch you'd never want to drink with.

Of course none of this would have happened without my agent, the indefatigable Juliet Mushens, aided by the supremely organised Nathalie Hallam at Caskie Mushens. I am very lucky indeed to have such talented people at my back.

And last but by no means least, my thanks to Barbara, who keeps the ship from crashing into the rocks while I'm gazing off into the distance.

Enjoyed **THE GATHERING DARK**?

Find out where it all began in the first chapter of **NATURAL CAUSES**, the opening instalment in the internationally bestselling **INSPECTOR MCLEAN** series.

I

He shouldn't have stopped. It wasn't his case. He wasn't even on duty. But there was something about the blue flashing lights, the Scene of Crime van and uniforms setting up barriers that Detective Inspector Anthony McLean could never resist.

He'd grown up in this neighbourhood, this rich part of town with its detached houses surrounded by large walled gardens. Old money lived here, and old money knew how to protect its own. You were very unlikely to see a vagrant wandering these streets, never mind a serious crime, but now two patrol cars blocked the entrance to a substantial house and a uniformed officer was busy unwrapping blue and white tape. McLean fished out his warrant card as he approached.

'What's going on?'

'There's been a murder, sir. That's all anyone's told me.' The constable tied off the tape and started on another length. McLean looked up the sweeping gravel drive towards the house. A SOC van had backed halfway up, its doors wide; a line of uniforms inched their way across the lawn, eyes down in search of clues. It wouldn't hurt to have a look, see if there was anything he could do to help. He knew the area, after all. He ducked under the tape and made his way up the drive.

Past the battered white van, a sleek black Bentley glinted in the evening light. Alongside it, a rusty old Mondeo lowered the tone. McLean knew the car, knew its owner all too well. Detective Chief Inspector Charles Duguid was not his favourite superior officer. If this was one of his investigations, then the deceased must have been important. That would explain the large number of uniforms drafted in, too.

'What the fuck are you doing here?'

McLean turned to the familiar voice. Duguid was considerably older than him, mid-fifties at least; his once-red hair now thin and greying, his face florid and lined. White paper overalls pulled down to his waist and tied in a knot beneath his sagging gut, he had about him the air of a man who's just nipped out for a fag.

'I was in the neighbourhood, saw the patrol cars in the lane.'

'And you thought you'd stick your nose in, eh? What're you doing here anyway?'

'I didn't mean to butt in to your investigation, sir. I just thought, well, since I grew up in the area, I might've been able to help.'

Duguid let out an audible sigh, his shoulders sagging theatrically.

'Oh well. You're here. Might as well make yourself useful. Go and talk to that pathologist friend of yours. See what wonderful insights he's come up with this time.'

McLean started towards the front door, but was stopped by Duguid's hand catching him tight around the arm.

'And make sure you report back to me when you're

done. I don't want you sloping off before we've wrapped this up.'

The inside of the house was almost painfully bright after the soft city darkness descending outside. McLean entered a large hall through a smaller, but still substantial, porch. Inside, a chaos of SOC officers bustled about in white paper boilersuits, dusting for fingerprints, photographing everything. Before he could get more than a couple of steps, a harassed young woman handed him a rolled-up white bundle. He didn't recognise her; a new recruit to the team.

'You'll want to put these on if you're going in there, sir.' She motioned behind her with a quick jab of her thumb to an open door on the far side of the hallway. 'It's an awful mess. You'd no' want to ruin your suit.'

'Or contaminate any potential evidence.' McLean thanked her, pulling on the paper overalls and slipping the plastic covers over his shoes before heading for the door, keeping to the raised walkway the SOC team had laid out across the polished wood floor. Voices muttered from inside, so he stepped in.

It was a gentleman's library, leather-bound books lining the walls in their dark mahogany shelves. An antique desk sat between two tall windows, its top clear save for a blotter and a mobile phone. Two high-backed lea-ther armchairs were arranged either side of an ornate fireplace, facing the unlit fire. The one on the left was unoccupied, some items of clothing neatly folded and placed across the arm. McLean crossed the room and stepped around the other chair, his attention immediately drawn to the figure sitting in it, his nose wrinkling at the foul stench.

The man looked almost calm, his hands resting lightly on the arms of the chair, his feet slightly apart on the floor. His face was pale, eyes staring straight ahead with a glazed expression. Black blood spilled from his closed mouth, dribbling down his chin, and at first McLean thought he was wearing some kind of dark velvet coat. Then he saw the guts, blue-grey shiny coils slipping down onto the Persian rug on the floor. Not velvet, not a coat. Two white-clad figures crouched beside them, seemingly unwilling to trust their knees to the blood-soaked carpet.

'Christ on a stick.' McLean covered his mouth and nose against the iron tang of blood and the richer smell of human ordure. One of the figures looked around and he recognised the city pathologist, Angus Cadwallader.

'Ah, Tony. Come to join the party have you?' He stood, handing something slippery to his assistant. 'Take that will you, Tracy.'

'Barnaby Smythe.' McLean stepped closer.

'I didn't realise you knew him,' Cadwallader said.

'Oh, yes. I knew him. Not well, I mean. I've never been in this place before. But sweet Jesus, what happened to him?'

'Didn't Dagwood brief you?'

McLean looked around, expecting to see the chief inspector close behind and wincing at the casual use of Duguid's nickname. But apart from the assistant and the deceased, they were alone in the room.

'He wasn't too pleased to see me, actually. Thinks I want to steal his glory again.'

'And do you?'

'No. I was just off up to my gran's place. Noticed the cars . . .' McLean saw the pathologist's smile and shut up.

'How is Esther, by the way? Any improvement?'

'Not really, no. I'll be seeing her later. If I don't get stuck here, that is.'

'Well, I wonder what she'd have made of this mess.' Cadwallader waved a blood-smeared, gloved hand at the remains of what had once been a man.

'I've no idea. Something gruesome I'm sure. You pathologists are all alike. So tell me what happened, Angus.'

'As far as I can tell, he's not been tied down or restrained in any way, which would suggest he was dead when this was done. But there's too much blood for his heart not to have been beating when he was first cut open, so he was most likely drugged. We'll know when we get the toxicology report back. Actually most of the blood's come from this.' He pointed to a loose red flap of skin circling the dead man's neck. 'And judging by the spray on the legs and the side of the chair, that was done after his entrails were removed. I'm guessing the killer did that to get them out of the way whilst he poked about inside. Major internal organs all seem to be in place except for a chunk of his spleen, which is missing.'

'There's something in his mouth, sir,' the assistant said, standing up with a creak of protest from her knees. Cadwallader shouted for the photographer, then bent forward, forcing his fingers between the dead man's lips and prising his jaw apart. He reached in and pulled a slimy, red, smooth mess out of it. McLean felt the bile rise in his gorge and tried not to retch as the pathologist held the organ up to the light.

'Ah, there it is. Excellent.'

Night had fallen by the time McLean made it back out of the house. It was never truly dark in the city; too many street lights casting the thin haze of pollution with a hellish, orange glow. But at least the stifling August heat had seeped away, leaving a freshness behind it that was a welcome relief from the foul stench inside. His feet crunched on the gravel as he stared up at the sky, hopelessly looking for stars, or any reason why someone would tear out an old man's guts and feed him his own spleen.

'Well?' The tone was unmistakable, and came with a sour odour of stale tobacco smoke. McLean turned to see Chief Inspector Duguid. He'd ditched the overalls and was once more wearing his trademark over-large suit. Even in the semi-darkness McLean could see the shiny patches where the fabric had worn smooth over the years.

'Most probable cause of death was massive blood loss, his neck was cut from ear to ear. Angus . . . Dr Cadwallader reckons time of death was somewhere in the late afternoon, early evening. Between four and seven. The victim wasn't restrained, so must have been drugged. We'll know more once the toxicology screening's done.'

'I know all that, McLean. I've got eyes. Tell me about Barnaby Smythe. Who'd cut him up like that?'

'I didn't really know Mr Smythe all that well, sir. He kept himself to himself. Today's the first time I've ever been in his house.'

'But you used to scrump apples from his garden when you were a boy, I suppose.'

6

McLean bit back the retort he wanted to give. He was used to Duguid's taunting, but he didn't see why he should have to put up with it when he was trying to help.

'So what do you know about the man?' Duguid asked.

'He was a merchant banker, but he must have retired by now. I read somewhere that he donated several million to the new wing of the National Museum.'

Duguid sighed, pinching the bridge of his nose. 'I was hoping for something a bit more useful than that. Don't you know anything about his social life? His friends and enemies?'

'Not really, sir. No. Like I said, he's retired, must be eighty at least. I don't mix much in those circles. My gran would have known him, but she's not exactly in a position to help. She had a stroke, you know.'

Duguid snorted unsympathetically. 'Then you're no bloody use to me, are you. Go on, get out of here. Go back to your rich friends and enjoy your evening off.' He turned away and stalked towards a group of uniforms huddling together smoking. McLean was happy to let him go, then remembered the chief inspector's earlier warning about sloping off.

'Do you want me to prepare a report for you, sir?' he shouted at Duguid's back.

'No I bloody well don't.' Duguid turned on his heel, his face shadowed, eyes glinting in the reflected light of the street lamps. 'This is my investigation, McLean. Now fuck off out of my crime scene.'

Read on in . . .

'Oswald's writing is in a class above'
Daily Express

THE BESTSELLING **INSPECTOR MCLEAN** SERIES

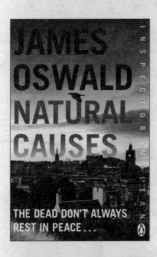

'Creepy, gritty and gruesome'
Sunday Mirror

THE BESTSELLING **INSPECTOR MCLEAN** SERIES

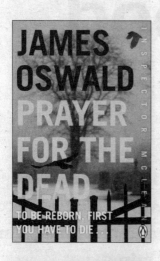

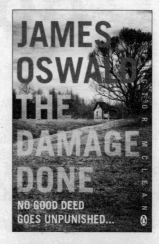

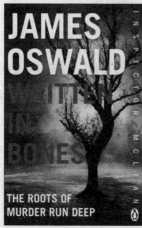

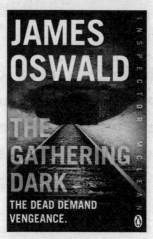

'The new Ian Rankin'
Daily Record

dead
good

dead good is the home of killer crime books, drama and film and we're dedicated to discovering, sharing and recommending thrilling crime.

Whether you visit to find out about your favourite author's new book, to enter an exclusive competition or to find out more about your favourite crime drama, Dead Good is the place for you.

Subscribe to our newsletter at
https://www.deadgoodbooks.co.uk/